The Polka Dot Girl

The Polka Dot Girl

Darragh McManus

Winchester, UK
Washington, USA

First published by Roundfire Books, 2013
Roundfire Books is an imprint of John Hunt Publishing Ltd., Laurel House, Station Approach,
Alresford, Hants, SO24 9JH, UK
office1@jhpbooks.net
www.johnhuntpublishing.com
www.roundfire-books.com

For distributor details and how to order please visit the 'Ordering' section on our website.

Text copyright: Darragh McManus 2012

ISBN: 978 1 78099 181 8

A CIP catalogue record for this book is available from the British Library.

Copyright Acknowledgements

'And death shall have no dominion'
And Death Shall Have No Dominion, Dylan Thomas, lines 1 and 9, from Twenty-Five Poems,
JM Dent & Sons, 1936

'Experience is wine and art the brandy we distil from it'
A Mixture of Frailties, Robertson Davies, Scribner, 1958

Design: Stuart Davies

Printed and bound by CPI Group (UK) Ltd, Croydon, CR0 4YY

We operate a distinctive and ethical publishing philosophy in all
areas of our business, from our global network of authors to
production and worldwide distribution.

CONTENTS

About the Author

Darragh McManus is a writer and journalist. His first crime novel, *Even Flow*, was published by Roundfire in 2012. Other books include the non-fiction *GAA Confidential* and the comic novel *Cold! Steel! Justice!!!* For more than a decade he has written reviews, features and opinion columns for several papers, including The Irish Independent, The Sunday Times and The Guardian. He also writes YA fiction and stage plays. He lives in the west of Ireland.

www.darraghmcmanus.com

For women everywhere

Chapter I

Madeleine

SHE was dead by the time I got there, and by the looks of things she'd been dead for quite a while before they pulled her from the water. Some horrible things in that water had done some horrible things to her face, and it looked like it had been a really pretty face once; say, 30 seconds before whoever it was threw her into that water with those horrible things doing those horrible things to her pretty face...

Jesus. I needed a cigarette and a strong coffee. We were on a half-rotted wooden platform at the far end of the docks with no nothing down there, never mind a coffee machine, so I settled for just the cigarette.

I spat out a scrap of tobacco and took a nice, long, warming drag. I figured it was going to be one of those nights that hang around too long, outstay their welcome, insist on dragging their feet and yours both, hour after hour, until you're just about ready to finally tell them to piss off, take a hike, when bingo, you realize it's morning and they're already gone, and you're the only one left hanging around. How does that happen? I'd had too many of those nights recently, but then I reminded myself: you're the law, this is the job, shut your whining face and do it.

This was going to be one of those nights. My watch read 1.20am by the pale yellow glow of a streetlight and the work was only getting started. Two divers trawling the harbor bottom for any more evidence (hopefully not another body) while a third sat in the boat, looking cold and bored; two forensics officers setting up portable equipment inside a disused steel shipping container; three uniforms sealing off the area for about 50 yards in every direction. Doing all the right things in this very wrong situation.

The call had been made by a prostitute, a middle-aged dame known to most of the dicks who worked the Vice detail. Cops and her fellow working girls called her Poison Rose; someone said her actual name was Manning, but I didn't know yet for sure. She sat on a low plastic stool nearby, taking nips from a bottle of whiskey the color of old brass and staring out at the flat blackness of the water. All the other prostitutes had skedaddled, presumably, by the time we arrived. Her face resembled a mask, under heavy face-paint and the glare of spotlights; she reminded me of a character from Japanese Noh theater. Yeah, that's me—smarter than the average bear…

Poison Rose could wait a little while longer. I left my witness to her burnished whiskey and dazed reflection, and walked 30 yards to where my victim lay. The girl was laid out on some sort of black plastic sheeting, or maybe it was canvas—fabrics were never my specialty. She wore a polka dot dress, white with black spots, hiked midway up one thigh, plastered wet to the other at the knee. I didn't like to see that, a girl exposed that way in death. As if reading my mind, the coroner waddled over and tugged the dress down, patting it smooth on the victim's pale shins like the way you might tuck a child into bed.

The coroner on duty tonight, Farrington, was actually the assistant coroner—the head body-slicer was on holidays in the mountains. Lucky so-and-so, always seemed to be *in absentia* when a really gnarly case rolled in…and I didn't just mean that in the physiological sense, though the sight of the girl's destroyed face made me simultaneously want to throw up, light a second cigarette and pass out. I didn't have much of a stomach for gore.

No, this was going to be a real doozy politically, too. Her features were mangled beyond recognition but I clocked the girl straight away—clocked the tattoo on her upper left breast, a beautiful flower, maybe a rose, twisting on its own thorny stem. I'd seen it, and her, a few times before, at black-tie functions, at the theater, even once or twice at a ball-game with her partner *du jour*. I knew who she was, alright, and Farrington knew but wasn't letting on, and before morning broke everyone in this claustrophobic little burg would know that Madeleine Greenhill had been murdered and thrown in the water for the fishes to feed on.

My stomach rolled again at the thought of it. I took a few steps closer to Farrington to distract my mind. The assistant coroner had the sort of face that you just knew had been adorably cute as a child—a real round-cheeked cherub—but now, pushing 50, had expanded to piggy fatness, in line with the rest of the body. The eyes seemed to almost literally be pushed back into the head by the pressure of roiling waves of blubber, and that anachronistic, medieval hairstyle didn't help. But Farrington was okay, what you might call "real stand-up": decent, stoical and about as sensitive as anyone can be after two decades of exposure to the worst excesses of behavior and the grossest examples of biological breakdown.

"Genie, Genie, Genie. What's the good word?"

Farrington didn't look up from a crouched position, hunched over what used to be Madeleine Greenhill, one hand gingerly poking at the corpse with something long and sharp and shiny, the other steadying that corpulent mass like a flesh tripod set square on the ground. One of the girl's shoes, a black strappy sandal, had shrunk in the water and now cut into her ghostly flesh, squeezing her slim calf into a grotesque shape it never knew in life. The other sandal, presumably, was slowly burrowing down into mud and saltwater.

I nodded hello, even though I knew it couldn't be seen, and said, "Hi, Farr. What's the good word? The word is there isn't any good. Not coming out of this, anyhow. That's, uh, yeah, that's what the word is telling me."

Farrington looked up, glared at me but more as a warning than an act of aggression. Then a quick smile, a return to the work and a strained levity in the voice: "Hey-ho-hey. Let's all keep smiling, shall we? Let's do our job and keep smiling and let others worry about tomorrow, alright?"

I hunkered down beside Farrington and Madeleine—quit it, I told myself, this is not Madeleine, there is no Madeleine Greenhill anymore—I hunkered down and said, "So what can you tell me?"

Farrington spoke and worked together: "Hard to say for sure and definite, but I think she was dead before she hit the water. Her lungs seem relatively clear. And see this here...?" Pointing to a dark bruise on the girl's forehead which bloomed outwards, soft and terrible. "...clearly a blow. Our old pal, 'blunt force trauma.' I think Mad...the *victim* was struck on the head, probably hard enough to kill, then dumped in the harbor. Certainly unconscious going in. So she didn't, you know, uh...suffer. She wouldn't have been aware of what happened after that. It was just...lights out."

I gave silent thanks to whatever god was partly looking out for beautiful young murder victims that night; small comfort is still comfort. I thought, This at least will soften the edges of her mother's pain, if only a little. I knew her mother by name; everybody knew her, either personally or by reputation. Now it was my responsibility as the initial investigating officer to inform Misericordiae Greenhill that her only daughter was dead, and I dreaded it more than I usually dreaded those dreadful, dead-full house calls. Old Misery—incorrect translation, but that's what everyone called her when they were absolutely sure she wasn't listening. She had famously once punched the then-Mayor at a charity ball in an argument over theology, if you can believe it. Then there was that rumor, last year or the year before, about Madeleine and her new flame and the leg-break beating dished out to said flame on mama dearest's orders...

I didn't tend to go for rumors but I bought that one. Old Misery was a hard-nosed bitch with a heart like granite, diamond-eyed and borderline evil; she was capable of anything. And yet I felt sorry for her. No woman should ever have to hear the news I was about to bring her.

Farrington was still talking; I tuned back in on the words "…tests should prove it but if I had to give a hunch, which I don't, I'd say our victim had been intoxicated. Which also makes it easier to throw her in the briny."

"What makes you think that?"

Farrington spoke *sotto voce*: "I'll deny saying this if you quote me, but check this out." There they were, trailing out from Madeleine's sleeve, running into and through and out of the crook of her elbow: the track-marks of a needle. Holy hell. Misericordiae Greenhill's kid was a junkie? No wonder Farrington didn't want to know about it.

"When we have a toxicology report that can't be naysayed, that proves it 1000 per cent, I'll go on the record: the girl was using. 'Till then, I didn't notice these tiny holes in her arm here, and you didn't either. I'm only telling you because."

I said, "Got you. Thanks, Farr." I stood and tried to fill my lungs with good, fresh air, something to scour them clean, rinse out the rank aftertaste of death from my body. Then I remembered I was standing in a shabby harbor at the western end of a ruined old beauty of a town; clean air is in short supply around these parts.

Farrington stood too, gazing almost tenderly at Madeleine, and said, "*Yeeahh*. Yeah, I think you kiddies have got a new little sandcastle to play with."

That's what we sometimes called our investigations: "sandcastle", or "castle" for short. As in, "What castle are you working on now?", or "Damn, I'm bored. Can't wait for a really big castle to get stuck into. Get my hands properly wet, you know?" It's the work we do, it inures you to finer sensitivities. You feel the empathy in your gut, it's safe there, you'll never lose it and become less than human; but in the forebrain it's all bravado and foolery, all crotch and swagger. This helps us not to care too deeply about those many sad, hapless victims; care too much for all of them and you'll never be able to help one of them.

Some cops are naturally soft-hearted, some are just callous shitbirds anyway, but we all put up the same front.

Or maybe it's that we're frustrated idealists, the definition of a cynic. That's where the name comes from: like a real sandcastle, we patiently build something up out of the available material, putting shape and structure on things, but the metaphorical waves just keep coming and wash it all away again, most times. You start out with sunny hope in your heart and end up with the same cold mess you had at the beginning.

Or maybe that's just me. Odette always told me I was too soft to be a cop... Jesus. Odette. She *knew* Madeleine Greenhill— taught her piano for a while, a few years back. Said she was a sweet enough girl, a little wild maybe, but sweet. Mark that as one more name on my list of awkward impending conversations.

I slapped Farrington on that ample back, feeling fat wobble with the impact, and said, "Alright, Farr. Thanks again. And..." I drew a hand across my mouth. "...*zip* about that other thing."

Farrington nodded solemnly, then gestured towards one of the tech team who had a futuristic-looking camera slung about their neck. "Okay, Annie Leibowitz, come on over here. You've got ten minutes and then I'm moving this poor girl to a better resting place, so get snapping." The crime scene photographer jogged over, the camera bouncing from side to side on its neck strap. Farrington hollered to the young uniformed officer standing guard on the perimeter, just inside the main entrance gates: "Hey! Wake up. Where's that transport I ordered? Call them again, and tell them if it's not here within five minutes there is gonna be one *seriously* pissed-off assistant coroner, and I've got the big knives, right?"

I steeled myself, lit another cigarette for good luck and strode towards Poison Rose, still staring, still sitting, still sipping. I crouched on the ground beside her and pulled out a notebook and pen.

"Hello. My name is Detective Auf der Maur. I need to ask you some questions."

Rose looked up at me and smiled suddenly, as though she'd recognized someone she knew. She said, "You're a pretty young thing, aren't you? Well, not so young, but pretty. And *little*. You're like a dark, shiny little princess."

Her eyes misted over, a sort of intoxicated glaze seeping down from whiskey-soaked mind to damp chin. I smiled, a mite embarrassed, and said, "Right. Thanks for the, uh, thanks for the compliment. Listen, I need to ask you some questions. I need your real name for starters, your full name. Are you listening to me?"

Rose's gaze had returned to the water where the divers' boat was turning, coming back to land, spewing out a crescent moon of foam under the crescent moon of heaven. They hadn't found anything else, it seemed. I was about to repeat my question when Rose spoke, sounding faraway; it almost felt like I was hearing a voiceover in a movie even though she was right there.

"I know that girl. The…" She pointed a thumb towards Madeleine Greenhill's corpse. "…the dead girl. I know her. I mean to say, I *knew* her. Back in the day. You know, the old days. She was younger then. *I* was younger. I was pretty, too." She smiled at me again, unhinged and depressing, her face-paint cracking. "Pretty like you."

"Look, I'm sorry. You couldn't have known her. That girl is no more than 21. You must be confused."

She wasn't listening to me; she wasn't there anymore. "I knew her. She looked different, though. Her hair…lighter. Not a brunette like she is now. 'Course, she's not *anything* now. Sad, isn't it?"

I stubbed out my cigarette and sighed heavily. This was going nowhere and I had more than one somewhere to go. Poison Rose, I figured, had a poisoned brain; she was off the planet, floating free, her moorings cut loose by the sharp edge of substance abuse. I turned and spotted a kid in the standard dark green beat-cop uniform, lurking on the periphery, looking more like a rubbernecker than an active participant. I stood up and whistled over.

"Come here, officer. What's your name?"

"Uh, Browne, Detective. I'm Jerry Browne, Silberling Street. I, ah, I caught the squeal from Dispatch. After the initial emergency call from, uh, that lady there. Me and my partner, Officer Mulqueen. That's, ah, that's her over there."

Another grunt stood about 15 feet away from us, a thin, serious-faced young woman with blonde hair tied in a bun, discreetly moving from foot to foot in an effort to ward off the cold. I nodded and said, "Go on."

"Yes, uh, I caught the squeal like I say, reported body find, possible homicide," Browne said. "Gunned it over here as fast as we could. Met Miss, uh...Miss Rose here when we arrived. Seemed pretty *compos mentis*, you know, a bit tipsy but she could talk okay. Brought us over to the, uh, the body, where it was floating out there. We could see it. Officer Mulqueen secured the area while I called you guys. Called Detectives Division, crime scene unit, dive team, snappers, I mean photographers, as per procedure."

"What time did you arrive? As close as you can to the exact time."

"Shortly after half-past 12, Detective. We got the call, like, two minutes after. I remember this because my watch gives a little beep on the half-hour. You know, one of those digital ones? Two beeps on the hour, one on the half. So I heard the beep and then a minute or two later, Dispatch came through with...this."

"Anyone else I should know about?"

"Divers got here fast, marked down the girl's location and pulled her out. What else, what else? ...Just two security guards. They have a shack back towards the main gates but off a ways. Stupid place to put the security office. They say they didn't see or hear a thing. Probably didn't. Probably asleep the whole time.

But I've got their names if you need to question them."

The officer stood there, silent, all talked out for now. I did a quick situation breakdown in my mind: forensics and Farrington would soon have all they needed or could get from the scene. Poison Rose was no use to me drunk and nowhere near sober. And I had to break the news to Misery before someone else did. In a place like Hera City, that was likely to happen sooner than I wanted.

I said, "Okay, Browne, this is what we'll do. Take Poison Rose to Silberling Street lock-up. Put her in a cell for the night, on her own. We're not booking her, we just want to sober her up. She's away with the fairies right now. Give her a cot and a hot meal, some coffee. Let her sleep for a few hours. Tell the night desk you're acting under the orders of Detective Auf der Maur, Homicide. I'll come by myself in the morning, early. And be *gentle* with her, with Rose. Alright? Any questions?"

Browne said, "No, Detective", then paused and smiled shyly. "Well, one. If you don't mind me asking. Are you, uh, Eugenie Auf der Maur?"

"That's right. Why?"

"I think you knew my cousin in the Academy. Marcella Donat? Big, cropped hair, sort of, uh…" Soft laughter. "Like a bull in a china shop. And that was *her* description."

I smiled as well. "I remember Marcella. Big Cella, yeah. Great girl. How's she doing? Haven't heard much of her since we worked Fraud together, and that was a while ago. She still a cop? Hasn't had a nervous breakdown yet, I hope."

I laughed. Browne said, "No, no nervous breakdown but she's not in the force anymore, either. Quit, uh, two years ago I think it was. Bad back, this recurring disk thing. They were scraping off each other or something. Basically couldn't handle the physical stuff anymore, and the life of a desk cop, well…"

"Not Marcella's thing, right?"

"No, Ma'am. Although she still, I mean, she's gone private, so

9

she's still a detective kind of. Does research for people, traces, runs down debt welchers, all that."

"Right. Good for her. Tell her Genie said hi the next time you're talking to her."

"Certainly will, Ma'am."

"And I'll talk to you in the morning probably. Good night, Officer Browne."

I moved off, tipping my finger to Farrington who was packing equipment into a large leather satchel that looked too small for everything being shoved into it. I glanced back at Poison Rose, now wrapped in a rough hemp blanket and being gently led by Browne and Mulqueen, away from that pitch-dark, deathly-still water and towards their patrol cruiser which I could see parked across the street outside. Rose looked baffled and dead beat. I sure felt the second part.

I was almost at the gates, and still looking behind me, when my right heel got caught in a crack in the concrete. I stumbled, my leg going one way and the rest of me going the other. The heel broke off, four inches of hard molded plastic just snapping like that, and I fell, my knee cracking off the ground. *Shit.* Clever girl to wear heels to a crime scene at these disintegrating docks. I righted myself, pushed myself up off the ground, dusted myself off, metaphorically and literally. I took off both shoes, dangling them by the strap, and looked back at all the other women: the techs, the divers, the cops in uniform, Farrington, even Poison Rose, all of whom were struggling to keep a smile off their faces. I was embarrassed as hell, mortified, red-faced.

I mentally shrugged and then made a deep bow to my audience, saying, "Thank you, thank you, thank you." When Farrington started to applaud, I knew it was time to leave. I smiled at her and got out of there as quick as bare feet would get me.

Chapter 2

Misericordiae

MISERICORDIAE Greenhill lived in the biggest, grandest building atop the tallest hill with the finest view in the whole city. You could call the place "magnificent", except even that four-syllable whopper of a word didn't quite match up to the profound, doomed splendor of Caritas Heights. Architecturally it had a Gothic feel, almost ecclesiastical, which I guess was appropriate enough. The place had been built 80 years previously by Frances Ivy Greenhill, Misericordiae's grandmother, on the instructions of God. Well, that's how she'd always told the story. Direct orders from on high, charging her to erect a charitable institute for the fallen and indigent, the mentally damaged, the drug-addled and booze-raddled.

They say Frances heard voices in her head for years, which suggests that maybe she should have checked herself in as the joint's first patient, but the Greenhills operate on a different level to the rest of us: when they get the command from invisible deities, they act on it, without pause or doubt, and you'd better stand the hell out of the way while they're doing it. Hence the construction of this creepy, overpowering, staggeringly beautiful building and surrounds. Hence the name: Caritas Heights, meaning the Latin for "charity." And hence the name bestowed upon Misericordiae's mother and, in turn, herself: the Latin for "mercy." Oh, irony. What's the Latin for "tough old broad you don't wanna fuck with"?

I pulled my rust-bucket of a car to a halt at the electric gates which stood a full 200 yards from the main house, rolled the window down halfway and pressed the intercom. There was silence for about ten seconds—my watch read 2.15, but I figured a place like this had round-the-clock staffing—then an electric crackle announced engagement at the other end. A voice, thin and frosty: "Yes, good evening?"

I tried to keep my tone deferential but authoritative. "Good evening to you. This is Detective Eugenie Auf der Maur, Hera City PD. I need to speak to Madam Greenhill urgently."

"One moment please."

Silence again. I debated whether or not to have a quick smoke before I reached the house—sure, why not? I lit a Dark Nine medium-strength and flicked the match out the window, running through the spiel I was about to give to Misericordiae. It was stupid but I was nervous. I was the law, here on official business, wholly without fault in this affair, and yet I was nervous. I mean, really: how exactly do you tell the most fearsome woman you're ever likely to meet that her only child and heir has been beaten to death, her body left to molder in the harbor, to be discovered by a drink-sodden prostitute who's somehow convinced of the impossibility that she knew the young victim? I decided to leave that part out. Misery would suffer enough pain and humiliation before this hour was done without me adding to it.

The electronic locks snapped open just as the disembodied voice returned and said, "Please pull up in front of the house, Detective." I rumbled the car over clanging steel tubes, crunched across gravel, then eased onto a long asphalt driveway. Jesus, what a place. Breathtaking, majestic, scarcely conceivable until you experienced it up close. I, like everyone else, had seen Caritas Heights many times at a remove, in the media. News reports of sparkling charity balls and political fundraisers. Rare interviews with La Greenhill in the society pages, those almost obsequious tributes to her good taste and better character. All those grainy old documentaries about the history of the institution, how Frances Ivy had passed on the house and gardens and social responsibility to Misericordiae versions I and II, how the current inhabitant had eventually moved the charitable facility to a purpose-built complex on the outskirts of Hera City—her gift to the people—and reclaimed the mansion for herself, as home and hearth.

But not just herself, of course: for her daughter Madeleine also, borne at the age of 45. A late blessing in a blessed life, now taken before her time. The house was all Misericordiae's once more.

I knew the history but hadn't quite appreciated the magnitude of Caritas, how simply awe-inspiring it was, until I was cruising towards it, under the overhanging branches of enormous trees, surrounded by verdant lawns, mazes, stable houses, huge Art Nouveau-styled greenhouses. And then the house itself, rising before me like an ornate monster from the ocean depths as I turned the last corner and slid to a stop in the front courtyard. It looked like a mixture of a late-Middle Ages cathedral, a Tsar's palace and the fever-dream of a precocious child. A crazy confection, over-the-top but weirdly diffident at the same time, and somehow it all worked together. There were even gargoyles, frightening-looking things, their blind stone eyes giving me the hard stare.

Two large spotlights flashed on, triggered by motion detectors. I stubbed out my smoke and took a deep breath, still unsure of what path to take here. Talk around it, be diplomatic, soften the truth, lead up to it gently? Or straight in there, straight to the heart of the thing? Which would anger Misery less? Which would hurt her less? The gigantic front door, heavy and dark like the entrance to a mausoleum, creaked open. A shaft of light blinded me momentarily, then I saw a tall, very thin woman all in black—trousers, bow-tie, penguin tails and slicked-back, cropped hair—step outside. She stood there, presumably waiting for me to do something. So I did something, exiting the car and walking towards her. I held up my ID badge, which hung on a chain around my neck.

"Detective Auf der Maur. I think we've already spoken."

The woman bowed slightly, no expression on her face. "Yes, Detective. Good evening. Please, come inside. Madam Greenhill will be with you shortly."

"Yeah, look, sorry about the lateness of the hour. Obviously I wouldn't call at two in the morning unless it was absolutely..."

She didn't appear to be listening to my ingratiating chatter, and I thought, Why the hell are you ingratiating yourself with this butler you don't even know, anyway? I shut up and followed her into the house, which was almost as breathtaking inside. I felt like I was stepping through a cinema screen and into a fictional world, and stopped just short of pinching myself to wake up. A main hallway large enough to hold a baseball field, with two stone staircases arching away and up on either side. Exquisitely tiled floors, oak-paneled walls, intricately embroidered drapes as big as ship's sails, priceless artwork from around the world on pedestals, in frames, a million-crystal chandelier hanging from the ceiling ten miles above our heads... I could go on but I'd better stop there or I'll tear up my next paycheck out of pure envy.

I spotted a coat of arms—brass on mahogany or teak, I was guessing—fixed to the wall on the mezzanine landing. A griffin or phoenix, some kind of mythical creature anyway, raised up on its back legs, grimacing like a tomcat hissing away a rival. The medieval-style scroll underneath read:

THE FAMILY GREENHILL

"...AND DEATH SHALL HAVE NO DOMINION"

Surprised it wasn't in Latin, what with the names and all. The butler led me to the right, through double doors into a reception room roughly three times the size of my entire apartment block. The décor here followed the overall *motif*: lush, imposing, sophisticated, timeless, with just the right undertone of decadence, there in the deep colors, the rich fabrics. She gestured to a fireplace, unlit, where stood two gorgeous burgundy leather armchairs.

"Please, if you could wait here for one moment," she said. "Would you like me to light the fire?"

I shook my head. "No, no. I'm fine, I'm not cold."

"May I get you something to drink?"

"A coffee might be nice. Help me stay awake."

I gave a lame smile and immediately wished I hadn't. The butler bowed again and exited as soundlessly as I'd imagine it's possible to be without learning how to hover. I flopped into one of the armchairs, totally bushed, my arms hanging down almost to the floor, then thought, No: project a professional air. I took up position standing by the wall, ostensibly examining the adornments. A fabulous collection of artwork, varied but each complementing the other *just* right: here was a Frida Kahlo self-portrait; there was a very rare preparatory sketch by Sofonisba Anguissola for *Madonna Nursing Her Child*; and either that was a remarkably good copy of Tamara de Lempicka's *Irene and Her Sisters*, or else...

"It's the middle of the night, my daughter is not home and the police are at my house. Would you care to confirm that my worst fear has come to pass, Detective?"

I started, surprised, and whirled around. Misericordiae Greenhill stood just inside the door, wrapped in a brown velvet nightgown, her arms folded across her chest, looking at me straight on. She was taller than I imagined, taller than she looked on TV, as if the force of her personality, diminished by the glowing screen, expanded into the boundless spaces of real life. She was also nicer looking than I would have expected; though her face had never been pretty, it had a certain handsome robustness, a sort of pleasing solemnity. She didn't look angry or sad or worried or carefree or ferocious like I'd thought she would, or anything at all, really—she just looked at me, blank-faced, waiting for my reply.

I took two steps forward and reached out my hand. "Detective Auf der Maur. You're correct. I have some...bad news."

She took my hand and shook it firmly, still holding me in

those fierce, crow-gray eyes. "Pleased to meet you, Detective. I think I met your mother once…a long time ago. Well. Let us get to it. Please."

Misericordiae pointed to the two armchairs by the fire. I moved over and gingerly sat into the nearest. She sat opposite me, stiff-backed, her hands folded on her knees. I noticed she wore brown velvet slippers, a match for the nightgown. Misericordiae stared into the cold fireplace, breathing steadily, as though she were waiting for the right moment for someone to speak. I breathed rapidly, trying to work out if I was meant to be the speaker. Then the butler reappeared, carrying a small table which bore a tiny china cup of delicious-smelling coffee, cream and crystallized sugar in silver containers, and a small measure of brandy in a large glass. She placed the table next to me and the brandy into Misericordiae's hand.

The old dame smiled vaguely and said, "Thank you, Ileana." She turned to me: "My one occasional vice. Ragnaud-Sabourin brandy, served just above room temperature. Not a well-known brand, I think, and I'm sure I couldn't tell you if it's of high quality or not. But it suits my palate. I find it…warming. And particularly helpful in times of stress."

I nodded dumbly and made a show of mixing some sugar and cream into my coffee. This whole situation felt even more awkward than I had feared. I tried to formulate my opening sentence, put the words in the proper order. How to make the bitter truth sound palatably sweet? It can't be done, Genie, so just get it said.

I put down my coffee cup and turned to Misericordiae. "Madam Greenhill, your daughter Madeleine is dead. I'm sorry to have to tell you this. Her body was found at Whinlatter Docks this evening. Police arrived on the scene shortly after half-past 12. We're treating Madeleine's death as murder. That's all I can tell you for now. And I truly am sorry for your loss."

She nodded, twice, three times, taking in the confirmation of something she already knew, deep down in the bones, in the womb, in the physical and metaphysical blood-link between every woman and her child. She probably knew it as soon as it had happened.

"My expression may not suggest it, Detective," she eventually said, "but this is the worst moment of my life. I was taught as a child to keep one's emotions to oneself, to suffer in private while at the same time fulfilling one's social obligations. That is a part of my nature, I cannot alter it now. This is why my face hasn't changed, why there are no tears rolling down these dry old cheeks. But I assure you, my heart is breaking." She nodded again. "My heart is breaking."

I hadn't expected this. Quiet acceptance? Talk of tears? A gentle kind of sadness? I'd expected—to be honest, a part of me had even *hoped* for—an explosion of that infamous temper, the volcano eruption of pride and wrath. This was a woman, for instance, who had once solved a labor relations dispute by firing the union organizer from her job, then purchasing the apartment rented by the woman and her young daughters, evicting them and sealing the place up as a vacant, permanent reminder to everyone else: don't cross me. And that was only the start of it, of her, the legend of Old Misery.

Yet here we sat, silent, with Misericordiae Greenhill sighing and taking neat sips from her brandy. I downed the coffee in one slug and, feeling strangely emboldened, pulled a pack of cigarettes from my inside jacket pocket and said, "May I smoke in here?"

She nodded permission. I lit a cigarette and sucked the smoke down deep into my fluttering tummy. *Aah*—never fails to soothe. She stood and moved to the mantelpiece, handing me back a dull-gold ashtray in the shape of a turtle. The thing looked like it was worth more than the department building, equipment included, and I was hesitant to use it until I saw the gritty residue of past cigarettes and cigars, ground into the reptile's patterned belly.

Then Misericordiae spoke again, her voice sounding ancient, resolute, unbreakable, like a statue of antiquity in the middle of a desert. "Tell me everything you know about this matter. Please, do not excise any of the details, even those you may feel you should spare me because they are…unsavory. I presume you know enough about me to know that I would eventually find out what I needed. But I would prefer to hear it from you, Detective."

I swallowed heavily and said, "Alright. Madeleine was killed by person or persons unknown, and her body put in the water. She was wearing a white polka dot dress and strapped sandals. We're not sure yet how she resurfaced, but we should know soon enough. Early coroner examinations strongly suggest that the cause of death was blunt force trauma—a blow to the head. We're certain she didn't drown. Again, we're not yet sure about time of death, but a call was made to emergency services around 12.30 by the woman who discovered the body. A full technical sweep of the area has been carried out, photographic record, et cetera. Madeleine's body has been removed to the morgue at police headquarters for a full autopsy. And that's all I know right now."

"This…woman who found my daughter. Who is she?"

"She's a prostitute. Has been for a number of years. The woman is called…everybody knows her by a nickname. I actually don't know her real name, but I'll know by the morning. We have her in lock-up for the night, sobering her up. She's, ah, she's a drinker. An alcoholic, probably. She's a bit of a fixture in that, uh…scene. Been around a long time."

Misery nodded again, this time like she was formally ending our interview. I finished my cigarette and stubbed it out, thinking, what kind of goddamn shit-heap town has the cops kowtowing to the civilians like we're the ones under investigation? By rights I should have stood up five minutes ago and told her, respectfully but firmly, that this was official police business and she had no right to ask for details. Ask? Excuse me, *demand* details, like she demanded obedience from everyone else who worked for her or cozied up to her or otherwise entered the dense gravitational pull of the great Misericordiae Greenhill. Then I remembered that this *was* a goddamn shit-heap town and I was a junior dick in my second year at Homicide, fifth year in total, who didn't have a thousandth of her power and influence. So I kept my head down and my mouth shut, feeling equally ashamed of doing both.

"Thank you, Detective," she said. "I won't bother you again. But I needed to know the bare facts of the matter. It was imperative, for some reason." She turned and fixed me with that unnerving stare, and I hopped to my feet like a dog pleading for a treat.

Misericordiae continued, "I always knew this moment would come. This, you calling in the middle of the night, or someone like you. Madeleine... Madeleine was a good girl but she careered through her life, powered by a misguided sense of rebellion. She wanted to punish me, I presume, or irritate me, or do whatever it is that defiant daughters generally do to hurt their mothers. Whatever it took." She smiled ruefully and drained her brandy. "Well, my dear, you've succeeded. Good night, Detective. Ileana will show you out."

With that Misery glided past me and swept out the door like a wisp of dark smoke. Ileana, the silent butler with the impassive face, had done that little trick of hers again, moving about so silently that I didn't notice she was there until I heard her cough behind my shoulder. She held a hand towards the open door. A discreet dismissal, but a dismissal nonetheless. I was so relieved to have made it through that ordeal that I didn't care enough to feel insulted. I didn't even mind so much that I'd have to turn around and come right back there in about 12 hours to find out Madeleine's movements earlier that day.

I drove straight home, listening to a jazz station on the car radio. Sure, it's a cliché—the wiped-out cop, in the middle of the night, driving through the dark streets with clarinets and cymbals in her ears, a smoke in her mouth and a fresh murder on her hands. All it was missing was the rain. But hey, I never said I was original. Besides, I'm a sucker for the classic stuff. I drove home and slalomed the car to a halt outside my apartment block, stuck the police parking permit on the dashboard and staggered inside. I was half-asleep by the time the elevator stopped at my floor, and two-thirds of the way there by the time I'd undressed and washed my mouth out with Listerine. Oral hygiene could wait. That call to Odette could wait. Everything in the world could wait until I got some sleep.

I flopped onto the bed and fell into an embrace with Morpheus in record time. Like I said at the beginning, it had been a long night.

Chapter 3

Rose

I READ this line somewhere once, "Patience—hard to keep it, 'cause it comes and goes." Patience: never one of my strong suits, and the next morning I found myself putting a severe strain on what little reserves of the stuff I had. Patience: I could almost physically feel it oozing away, out the soles of my feet and falling in tears from my eyes, seeping into the cracks in the tiled floor of the station interview room. Patience, my ass: *you* try to have some when you're dragging information out of a half-demented old soak like Poison Rose, when you're struggling to force cohesion and sense onto illogical ramblings. I feel sorry for women like her, truly—I wish the world didn't drive them hard into the arms of obliteration. But sympathy doesn't help me in my work, and work I had to do.

Rose had been transported from Silberling Street by Officers Browne and Mulqueen earlier that morning. They looked bright-eyed and wide awake, which was impressive considering they hadn't been to bed all night. Good work by two good young women—I'd keep an eye on them. Rose had sobered up by now, this being half-ten, though I don't know if boozehounds like her ever get truly sober. The alcohol stays in their system, doesn't it? Like mushed-in layers of grime on a window, maybe. One swish of a wet cloth isn't going to help you see clearly. Now she was sober and violently hungover. I had the weirdest sense that she might actually have been more lucid if she was still drunk, but it was too late for that; I wasn't going to throw her a fifth of Wild Turkey at this stage.

I yawned deeply, took another large slug of coffee and said, "One more time, okay? Let's go through it one more time, make some sense out of all this. Then you can go home or do whatever you want to do."

Rose nodded herself, slipped a cigarette out of her purse, a bejeweled thing that looked big enough to hold a small dog but small enough to hold most of the remnants of her broken-down life: smokes, make-up, some cash, maybe a change of underwear, probably a bottle of something as quick as she got out of here. She said, "Okay, little miss. You want to know, so Rose will tell you. I hit the streets about nine, which is a bit earlier than my usual time but I'm behind on my rent so I need the extra money. Nothing doing on Bolo or the Zig-Zag. *Hours* I spent there—nothing doing. Couple of wealthy dames cruising Bolo but none of 'em looked like they'd be interested in a..." Rose smiled sardonically. "...*mature* lady of professional experience like me. Real chicken-hawks, the lot of 'em. Only after the young stuff."

She was referring to Hera City's two main red-light areas: Bolo Street (specifically, the far south end of it), a broad thoroughfare which cut diagonally through the city for four full miles; and the Zig-Zag, a crowded, chaotic, haphazard collection of slummy buildings, spread over about 35 blocks, which housed brothels, strip joints, gambling dens, sweatshops and God knew what else. Supposedly there was even an opium den in the Zig-Zag, though I wasn't sure I believed that. Could have just been urban legend. The unofficial skinny had it run by a Chinese clan, a wizened old crone and her beautiful triplet daughters, but that sounds a little too good to be true...or too bad, depending which side you're coming from.

I said, "Please, if we could get to the point. You discovering the girl's body. I don't want to rush you, just, you know."

Rose sighed and said, "*Anyway*, being in dire straits and needing a trick something awful, old Rose finally shuffled off to the docks. It's dangerous there but what the fuck. A girl's gotta do what a girl's gotta do. You know I got stabbed there once? Years ago. Right under the heart. I'm lucky to be alive. 'Lucky to be alive', she sang. La, la, la, la, lucky to be alive."

Christ on a bike. You see what I mean about patience?

"She was floating on the top. Of the water, you know, out about 20 or 30 feet or something from the wharf. The one where all the real big ships come in? And I'd had a lousy night. Just one trick, this butch bitch who wanted to play rough. I said, 'No damn way, sister, Rose doesn't truck with your kinda trick.' Y'see, I'm a poet, too."

She began laughing but it quickly disintegrated into a hacking cough, a real lung-wrenching, body-lifting spectacular. I let Rose get her breath, bring her system back to her approximation of normal.

Eventually she said, "Met her about a hunnerd yards back the street. Nah, more. Hunnerd an' 50. We fell into one of those old alleyways. She was insistent at first, but sort of nervous, too. Guess it was her first time with a pro, I don't know. Kept pushing up against me, breathing right into my ear. Something hard in her pocket, too. It was really digging into me, ya know? I said, 'Is that a gun in your pocket?' She laughed real hard and got this funny kinda...*tender* kinda look on her face then. She stroked my hair and goes, 'You're funny, buttercup. I like you.' That's what she called me—fuckin' *buttercup*! Can you believe it?"

Lah-dee-dah. I needed another cup of Joe. I excused myself—Rose didn't look like she cared either way—and exited the interview room. It led onto a corridor: to the left, the office of Chief of Detectives Ann Etienne, to the right, the main office in the Detectives Division building, which was where most of the dicks had their desks and which led, in turn, to the muster room, front desk, holding cells and admin offices. I went right. The place was buzzing even though it was still pretty early; I guess crime is a 24-hour gig, so ours is too. A couple of the women looked up and nodded hello, or smiled over as I passed. A few stood around the coffee-maker, shooting the shit, killing time, delaying the start of their working day. These gals were Vice, for sure—I could tell by the hairstyles alone. They each had a trendy 'do: two wore a sort of feather-cut, one a long bob with a severe fringe.

It's funny, but for some reason, the detectives in different sections seem to gravitate towards a specific look, particularly when it comes to hair. Unless someone is working undercover, we all have to wear at least smart casual, if not an actual suit, while we're on the job. So a civilian wouldn't necessarily know a Homicide dick from Narcotics or Vice or Robbery or Lady Godiva herself. But we could usually tell each other apart because of the hairstyles. It was nothing official or premeditated, just the different directions the dames of the Detectives Division had taken. It was the way it was because it was the way it was. Vice, like I say, tended to be up with the fashions of the time; maybe it helped them fit in better in that milieu. Narcotics girls often had longer hair, plaited or woven into a bun, worn high on the head. We used to joke that prolonged exposure to those wicked, wicked drugs had made them apathetic and slatternly, too whacked-out to get a proper haircut. Robbery, almost to a woman, had shoulder-length hair in a neat ponytail. They were that bit more gung-ho than the rest of us. And as for Homicide? Sort of a mix, though many of us liked it short.

I resisted getting a crop for a few years—I'm very small with quite delicate features, and used to worry that it would make me look babyish, too much like a little girl playing make-believe in a big girl's world. I kept it to my shoulders, layered with a long fringe, until one night when a suspected felon, this big bruiser with arms like sides of beef, used my black hair to swing my face around to her waiting fist (which was the size of half a side of beef). When I woke up, I took the scissors to it myself and have kept it cropped ever since.

The patrol officers, of course, get stuck with a hideously unflattering uniform and have to hide their hair under a cap. You can bundle it up with pins or hair-grips if you want, but most of them just get it cropped and to hell with it. We've all been there. It grows back.

I strolled to the coffee machine and the three women moved to allow me access. One of them, Littlestone, I'd been talking to earlier. She'd filled me in on Rose, her real name, her background. Born Rosemary Manning, aged 47 or 49 or 51, nobody seemed to know for sure; lived in one of the shittier apartment blocks in one of the shittier streets in the east side sprawl. I noted down the address though it was likely that Rose would be gone from there, or kicked out, within a few weeks. That's usually how it was at the more wretched end of the prostitution racket in this city. Transient women, directionless, with little to keep them steady or hold them in place. Poison Rose had been a hooker, Littlestone estimated, for over two decades. Before her time on that beat but her predecessors reckoned they knew Rose. Apparently as Rosemary Manning she'd been a teacher, languages or literature, something refined like that. Steady job, steady life, until something came along in her mid-twenties to knock her flat on her ass. Cue going off the rails, cue desperation, cue an abiding, poisoned romance with the bottle and turning tricks to pay for it. There were rumors of a child, probably unsubstantiated. Rumors she'd once killed a trick in self-defence, a little more likely.

I pushed down the lever and hot, bitter coffee belched into my mug, a few drops splashing my hand. The mug was a silly old thing, squat and wide with a picture of a clown on the side. Like most everyone else I had a mortal dread of clowns, but it had been a gift from Odette, one of the last things she gave me. She'd picked it up for chump change in a flea-market on…I forget the street. One of the side-streets off Pasiphaë Prospect, I think. (This formed the main east-west axis of Hera; in other words, the horizontal to Bolo Street's vertical, though not quite at right angles.) Odette told me the street name but I forget it now. I guess she was right about me never paying attention.

Littlestone tapped me out of my reverie by saying, "Y'gettin' anywhere in there?"

"With her? Rose?"

"Yeah. Any joy?"

I shook some sugar into my coffee and replied, "Nah. Not so far. Bits and pieces. She remembers things but it's all messed up in her head, you know? Her memories don't come forward the way ours do. Even memories from last night. I mean, she thinks 20 years ago and yesterday took place 'round about the same time."

Littlestone nodded. "Yeah. Anyway, hope I was of some help. And good luck, Auf der Maur. Anything else you need, you know where I am."

"Yeah, thanks. What you gave me, it helped, for sure."

We both went our separate ways, her to a desk in the furthest corner of the room—Vice had a little enclave over there—and me back to the interview room. I took a deep, calming, resolute breath and opened the door. Rose was staring at the smoke curling from her cigarette, following its fluid, erratic movement like she was gazing at a mysterious belly-dancer, a pale skinny girl, exotic and erotic, her limbs bare and her face forever obscured. I said to myself, Cut that crap out, Genie. Cut out the flights of fancy. Get over there and knock some *facts* out of this old broad.

I sat opposite her and snapped, "You were telling me about your one trick of last night. So go on. You wrapped up business and what then?"

She raised her eyebrows. "*Ooh.* Straight to it. Alright, little miss. What happened then was that she headed back towards town, on foot, and I carried on to the docks. Also on foot. Figured I might find a bit more action down there. Figured my *luck* was in! Ha ha ha!"

"And...?" I said, impatience palpable in my voice.

"And..." Her face dropped; something clouded her eyes. This wasn't booze or madness, though—this was recollected memory. She was seeing Madeleine Greenhill's dead body again. "I snuck in by the side gate. Security light's busted out there, ain't it? And those gals don't give a shit about the likes of me, anyway. Toss 'em a 20 every few weeks and they turn the other way." There was a long pause; I held my breath. "And you know the funniest goddamn thing? My eyesight's shot to hell but I saw her the second I looked over there. That's, what? 60, 70 yards away and she was lying flat in the water and I spotted her. 'S like I was *meant* to see her, don't you think, Detective? I don't believe in fortune or coincidence or any of that stuff, but I was meant to see Misericordiae Greenhill."

"Madeleine. You saw Madeleine Greenhill."

"Yeah... You know who I mean."

So she knew who the victim was. Someone must have blabbed in the lock-up. Provisionally knock off two gold stars from Browne and Mulqueen's accounts.

"Go on, Rose."

"I saw her. Saw that polka dot dress. I shuffled on over there and got up close to the edge. Saw her black hair, her face all mangled. She was floating, sort of bobbing with the waves. Her arms and legs out like that, you know?" She sprawled in her chair, four limbs spread-eagled stiffly. "I knew she was dead. I mean, you *would*, wouldn't you? Didn't matter that her face was gone. You could tell."

"Okay, so wrap it up. Did you see anyone else in the vicinity?"

"The vicinity?"

"The area. The docks. Did you see anyone else?"

"Not down that far. There were people back up in the security shack, near the entrance, and I could hear shouts and noise from across the water, the other side. The pier over there. Women loading a boat or unloading it or something. But where I was, nah."

"What did you do when you saw the body?"

"Walked back to the street, found a phone, called Josie Law, told 'em where to find me, walked back to where the girl was still floating and waited for Josie. I had nearly a whole bottle for company."

She cackled, an awful, depressing sound. I said, "You didn't inform the on-site security guards?"

Rose snorted with derision. "Those clowns? They're so dumb, they got trouble figuring out which shoe to fit which foot every morning. Listen, sister, I might pay those miserable cows their backhander when required, but I wouldn't trust 'em to investigate a cereal packet."

I smiled. "So you don't think much of them, then?"

"*Now* you get me, little miss."

"And what made you make that call? I mean, you could have just left her. A woman in your...position. You don't necessarily want to attract our attention."

There was a flash in those bloodshot, watery eyes; an angry spark from the core of Rosemary Manning. "I'm a human being, ain't I, godammit! Just 'cause I work as a whore. That's all it is, *work*. Not the real *me*. I'm a human being and I got empathy like anyone else and when I saw that poor little girl floating there, dead..."

I hushed her with my hands and said, "Alright. Alright. I apologize for that question. It was unnecessary."

"Fuckin'-A unnecessary."

That was about it for now, about all I was going to get, and I had things to do, calls to make, domineering old matriarchs to brace for information. I said, "Okay, Rose. You did great. You're free to go."

She looked almost surprised. "*Go*? Go where?"

"Home, I guess. Don't you have an apartment somewhere? Someone told me you had. East side sprawl."

Rose smiled, a funny mixture of sarcastic and indulgent. "Exactly. You answered my question, sweetheart."

I directed her to the front desk and instructed the duty

sergeant to have Rose sign out. No personal possessions to be returned; we hadn't taken them off her in the first place, and in the second place, there weren't many of them to take. She looked terrible: exhausted, scraped-out, old beyond her years. I felt sorry for her but what was I supposed to do?

I did the lamest thing possible in the circumstances—I asked her, "Do you need a ride anywhere?"

Rose walked past me, out the door, out into the early-morning crispness, calling back over her shoulder: "No thanks, little miss. Think I'll take a walk. Stop and smell the flowers and all that. The old town ain't so bad this time of the morning."

I looked out at the sun shining. For a second, I almost agreed with her.

Chapter 4

Farrington

STRAIGHT back to my desk, at the rear of the main office, to take care of some business, the drudgery, the shit-work. First: I called Odette. I knew the number off by heart, of course; you don't share your life with someone for more than three years and not know their telephone number better than your own birthday. It went straight to her message service. My heart jumped—just a little— when her voice came on, soft and measured like I remembered it: "You've reached the home of Odette Crawford. I can't take your call at the moment. Please leave a brief message with your name, number and reason for calling, and I'll..." I hung up. I didn't want her to hear about Madeleine Greenhill from a disembodied message, that wouldn't be too sensitive on my part...and also, subconsciously, I was probably angling for an excuse to call 'round to her in person.

Second: I called Farrington. Her office was in the forensic section of HQ but I didn't dial that extension, gambling that she might still be in the morgue. She was.

"Genie, Genie. We meet again. Or not, as the case may be."

"Hey, Farr. Who was that kid answered the phone?"

"That's Bella. She's a Med student. Doing an internship here. Which I have to say suits me fine. We're short a few hands here anyway."

I laughed. "She hasn't been grossed out yet?"

"What, by me or the stiffs? Nah, she's okay. Strong stomach for a young girl. Nice stomach, too. She wears those little crop tops, you know those? Mmm..."

"Cool it, Farr, you might suffer an embolism. And you know what that'd mean, don't you? You wouldn't be able to help your favorite Homicide dick solve her case."

"And that's why you're ringing me, I know. Hold on a

second." Her voice receded into the distance momentarily. "Hey! Keep the noise down, would ya? I've got the freakin' Chief herself on the line. Sorry 'bout that, Genie."

"Not a problem. So what have you got?"

"What have I got? Well, we finished the full autopsy about an hour ago. Your victim was definitely killed by a blow to the skull. Sorry, *blows*. She was struck no less than three times, probably more, in the same general area. Bottom-left of the os frontale, if you wanna get technical."

"Which I don't."

"Approximately one-and-a-half inches above the left eye-socket. The frontal bone was cracked just over that eye, in two places. Obviously there's bruising, but what's kinda weirding me out is that it isn't bigger. Damage like this, her forehead should have been a dark-purple mess. But this, it's...small. Like someone was *poking* her."

"Poking extremely forcefully."

Farrington said, "Yeah, I mean, it's just a figure of speech. Nobody poked nothin'. This girl was *hammered*. The front and back of her brain were badly bruised—what us medical types call coup and contrecoup injuries. Anyway, there's your cause of death. Cranial trauma causing subdural hemorrhage. In simple language, severe and fatal brain injury."

"Anything else?"

"Well, you saw her last night—there isn't much of a face left for anything else. Although I don't think it would have made much difference, but she got pretty chewed up down there."

"Oh, *Jesus*! Farrington! Do you have to talk like that?"

"Just trying to toughen you up, kid. You're a police officer, you gotta act like one. Anything else, you say. Hardly any water in the lungs, therefore dead when she went in, like I hypothesized last night. How easily genius comes to me. We've examined the contents of her stomach—very little, as it happens. Madeleine was a picky eater, though not such a picky drinker.

We found the remains of a chicken sandwich, some mints and a *lot* of booze. Her blood-alcohol levels are high. Not crazy high, but high. And, ah…there's also that other thing we talked about. Remember?"

I nodded discreetly, then remembered she couldn't see it and said, "Mm-hm. I remember. You have proof?"

She did that drawly thing she does. "Yeeahh. I think I do. Talk to Chief Etienne about it this afternoon. I'm sending the results directly to her. She can make the call."

"Gotcha. Alright, Farr, I'll talk to you later. Maybe meet for a beer some night next week?"

"Beers are on you, Genie. Stay frosty, girl."

We hung up simultaneously. What now? Now third: gather my resolve and call Misericordiae Greenhill and get the dope on Madeleine's last known movements, as far as she knew them. I was about to call information for the number when one of the girls from admin swung by the desk, and I mean *swung*, her hips lifting from side to side like a sail boat lilting on the ocean swell. She was a plump girl but cute with it.

She snapped her heels together and thrust a buff-colored envelope towards me, saying, "Detective Auf der Maur, you're back. I wanted to wait until I met you before delivering this. The lady who handed it in was insistent that I give it personally to you."

I raised an eyebrow. Most mysterious. I said, "This lady. What did she look like?"

"Uh, she was tall, pretty skinny. Short hair. Sort of a serious expression. Not exactly the cheerful type, you know?"

Ileana the butler, I presume. I thanked the girl and took the envelope and she turned on her spike heel and swung right back to her post. I looked around to see if anyone was watching, not quite understanding why I did that, and scanned the envelope: it was marked on the front in careful handwriting, "Detective Eugenie Auf der Maur, Homicide Division. STRICTLY PRIVATE."

Okay. I slit the top and pulled out a card, large and rectangular, and pure white except for a tiny embossed cross in the top-left corner, glowing a sort of pearl color. On the inside it read:

"Detective—

I would like to thank you for your discretion and tact last night. I realize that being the bearer of bad tidings is an onerous cross for any woman to bear. I wish you the very best of luck in pursuing this case. I use the word 'luck' though I do not doubt your capabilities as a police officer in any way. But all of us need fortune's good graces from time to time. Regardless, I have full faith that you will resolve this matter expeditiously and find my daughter's killer.

I entreat you once more, Detective: find Madeleine's killer.

Yours, etc,

Misericordiae Greenhill."

Well, how about that—a message from Misery herself. What's the word, synchronicity? "An apparently meaningful coincidence in time of two or more similar or identical events that are causally unrelated." Did it fit this situation? Odette would be able to tell me. Hell, Poison Rose would probably know, if she could reach back far enough into her past and her memories. But linguistics was never really my forte. And the Jungians never delved into the Byzantine subconscious of a woman like Misericordiae Greenhill.

What a strange way of phrasing things: "pursuing this case", "resolve this matter expeditiously." More appropriate to a business letter than an impassioned communiqué with the person investigating her daughter's brutal murder. And then the final line: "I entreat you once more, Detective: find Madeleine's killer." What was that: a threat? An encouragement? Or just the desperate appeal of a grieving mother, the last hope, her cry against the dying of the light?

Enough, Genie. Quit philosophizing, keep digging. I got the number from information that I meant to get five minutes before and called Caritas Heights. A soft purr on the other end, going on for more than half a minute, then a click and a voice—not one I recognized, therefore not Ileana, which I must confess didn't upset me unduly. There was something unnerving about that woman.

The voice I didn't know said, "Caritas Heights, how may I help you?"

"Madam Greenhill, please. Tell her it's Eugenie." No need for the staff to know the boss lady's business, I figured.

"Yes, Ma'am."

I attached a portable recording device to the connecting fixture on my phone's receiver, sparked up my first Dark Nine of the day and took two or three deep drags, blowing the smoke of the first out my nose while I was sucking in the second and third through my mouth. It's an impressive trick, I grant you. Then Misericordiae was talking to me, that calcified, ageless voice carrying across electric wires and electronic signals and losing none of its potency.

"Detective Auf der Maur. Your discretion is appreciated."

"Sure. And thanks for the note. I'll, ah…I'll do my very best."

"I'm certain you will."

"Um, I need to know some things about Madeleine. Her movements yesterday, and the days leading up to it. Where she went, who she hung out with, that sort of thing. Anything you can give me. Is now a good time?"

"You mean, am I in a fit state to talk about her? Will I have an emotional breakdown halfway through?"

"I guess that's exactly what I mean."

"I am in a fit state. Carry on."

"Over the phone okay? I can call to you in person but this suits me fine if it's alright with you."

"It is."

"Okay, then." I pressed "RECORD" and said, "When did you last see Madeleine?"

"Yesterday morning. Just before ten. I was leaving for Mass, which is a two-minute drive. I usually walk, but it had been raining all morning so I had my driver bring me to the church. We left the house at roughly ten minutes to ten. On my way out I met Madeleine in the main entrance hallway. Am I going too quickly for you?"

"Whu-? Uh, no, no. It's fine. Yesterday was a Tuesday. Do you often go to Mass on weekdays?"

"I go every day, Detective. There are few Catholics in Hera City, but we are quite devout. Service yesterday was by Mother Torres. The homily was concerned with the spiritually healing power of charitable works."

"Right. Did you speak to Madeleine when you met her?"

"Our customary and perfunctory few words. She was rushing out the door, the way she always did. Madeleine gave the impression that she couldn't stand to be in our home for more than five minutes, yet when I proposed buying her an apartment she declined. You don't have children, do you, Detective?"

"Me? No."

"Some young women are a law unto themselves. Not all, but certainly Madeleine was one. Impossible to fathom. Totally self-contradictory. She demands what you don't have and when you offer that, she wants the complete opposite, and so on. She claims to hate me but refuses to leave."

She was speaking of Madeleine in the present tense. Death makes a nonsense out of time, I guess.

"Anything else you remember?" I asked.

"There was a friend of hers. Dreary sort of creature, always dressed in dark clothes. She pulled up to the front of the house in a Porsche coupé. I can't say I approved of her driving. A little careless. Madeleine ran out the door to her. They looked happy to see each other."

"Do you have a name?"

"Of course I have a name. I know about everyone connected

to my family, tangentially or directly. She is a close acquaintance of my daughter. Her name is Virginia Newman. Her mother Margaret is an architect. She actually designed one of our corporate buildings, though I don't know her personally. The girl is…flighty, I believe. Dropped out of school where she was doing a degree in Anthropology. The same school Madeleine attended, incidentally. She currently runs a trinket shop in the Old Village. Ethnic jewelry, incense, books on divination, that sort of thing. Nonsense and beads and worthless junk."

Jesus. She really *does* find out what she needs to know. I made a mental note to steer clear of Misericordiae Greenhill's personal orbit.

She went on, with a contemptuous tone, "An *artistic* type. The only daughter. Almost certainly a little spoiled but seems good-natured enough. More misguided than wicked, I would imagine. Rumors of promiscuity, probably true. Rumors of drug abuse also, but those are probably nothing more than rumors."

I actually blushed at the words and was happy we'd done this interview over the phone. "Rumors of drug abuse": rumors about Madeleine's own predilections, rumors about needle-tracks and pin-hole black-bruise eyes, rumors and more than rumors, verifiable truths that could explode into a hell of a godawful mess. I wouldn't be surprised if Chief Etienne buried the whole thing, and a part of me wouldn't blame her, either.

"Detective? Is that all?"

I started a little, bumping an elbow off my coffee mug and spilling some onto the desk. I scrambled for a napkin and slapped it down in the middle of the spreading mess. I said, "Sorry, no. Just a few… So this was the last time you saw Madeleine alive. Were you concerned when she didn't come home yesterday evening?"

"No, because she did come home. I was out, at a social engagement, but Ileana—you met her last night—told me that Madeleine had returned shortly after six o'clock. 'Picking up a few things,' she told Ileana, whatever that means. A change of clothes, I suppose. She wasn't wearing that polka dot dress when she left that morning, certainly. She was dressed in trousers, which I cannot *abide* as casual wear. For someone in your position, of course, they are presumably a necessity."

"Yes, Ma'am. Sometimes."

"In any event I would not have been concerned about Madeleine staying out all night, because that is what she did. She was known to go missing for days at a time. Sometimes for more than a week. I tried to reason with her, I tried to discipline her, I tried everything I could. But that girl just would not listen. And now, you see where it's got her."

"Um...yes, Ma'am." I gulped. "I, uh, I presume I don't need to verify with your butler that this conversation took place?"

"You may if you see fit. It happened as I've told you, but by all means be thorough. Please, be thorough."

"No, that's... That should be fine. So, uh, Madeleine, she was in the habit of staying out, maybe staying with friends, whatever?"

Misericordiae laughed quickly and bitterly. "Friends! Yes, I suppose you could call them friends. Spongers and wastrels, sycophants, leeches...Madeleine chose an odd sort of friend. The late-night bar and strange bedroom were her natural habitat, Detective. But... I assumed she would grow out of it. Get it all out of her system, that stupid, childish need to rebel. I assumed she'd walk close to the edge for a few years, perhaps even stepping the wrong side of it once or twice, then come to her senses and return to her rightful place. To her home. As we both know, I assumed wrongly."

I sighed loudly and for once didn't care what Misery thought of it. Suddenly, I felt tired, and it wasn't only the short night's sleep. This was spiritual tiredness, existential tiredness, a sort of exhaustion of the self. I had, to use that weary cliché, a bad feeling about this one. A feeling that it had started ill, as they always did, and would end even worse.

Finally I dragged myself back to the task at hand: "Did Madeleine have any enemies? Anyone capable of...doing something like this?"

Misery considered the question. I gave her time and space both. Then she said, "No one individual comes to mind immediately. But you must understand, Detective, Madeleine was *surrounded* by potential enemies. That world she inhabited. Dive bars and strip clubs, gambling dens, these disreputable places filled with dangerous people... Please don't presume I'm merely being judgmental here. I have my faith, yes, and my moral code, and I admit my disgust at those women and their base, contemptible lives. My own daughter disgusted me by her actions. But that's by-the-by. My disdain for Madeleine's life and the swamp in which she wallowed are irrelevant. What I'm saying is that any one of those women is potentially my daughter's killer. Would *you* be surprised to discover a bookmaker or pimp, some sleazy dancer, had done this awful thing?"

"No, Ma'am. I guess I wouldn't."

"Look there, Detective. Go down into that underworld. I am certain you'll find your killer within."

"Alright. Thank you, Madam Greenhill. That can't have been easy."

"It wasn't, but it had to be done. I'm sending you another envelope, with a list of Madeleine's known acquaintances, her most common haunts, her movements as much as we knew them. Her life, really, such as it was. If anything else comes to mind, I will inform you as soon as possible."

"That's great. Thanks. And if there's anything else *I* think of, I'll let you know."

"Of course." She paused; I could almost hear the pause, like it was a sound instead of a silence. "I love you, Mother."

"I beg your pardon?"

"Those were her final words to me. Isn't that peculiar? She told me she loved me."

"And you say this was...peculiar?"

"Certainly. Madeleine has never once said that to me before."

Chapter 5

Odette

THE rest of the day was a washout, literally and metaphorically. It started to rain about four seconds after I hung up the phone on Misery and kept coming down until after I hit the pillow that night. I spent ten minutes wondering why La Greenhill had gone into so much detail about her daughter, with me, a nobody, a civil servant, an insignificant speck in the tapestry of Hera City—her city. Almost like she was confiding in me. I figured, a woman like that protects her privacy, her secrets, to the death...and that's only partly a figure of speech.

Then I figured again: Misericordiae is *so* powerful, so dismissive of other people and where they stand in relation to her, that she doesn't care what I know. She told me exactly what she wanted to tell me, no less and certainly no more. Then I figured again and again: all of this only applies up to a certain point. She doesn't mind me knowing Madeleine was a wild child because anyone with eyes and ears already knows this; but woe betide the person who stumbles onto something *really* juicy, like for instance the fact that said wild child had graduated from partying and sleeping around to a hard line in poppy-derived narcotics...

Forget it, Genie. Like Farrington said, it's not your call. Which reminded me: I dialed the Chief's number and got no answer, so I strolled over to her office where her secretary told me Etienne was out for the rest of the day. Some sort of Departmental heads pow-wow, policy formulation or what-have-you. And that left me swinging in the breeze for now. Forensics, in all likelihood, would still be processing the physical evidence from the crime scene. I had already shaken down Poison Rose for whatever could be shook. The autopsy results I knew. All that remained was to hit the streets, hit the docks, start snooping around, and I couldn't do it. Too miserable outside, too tired in my body and mind. I set my phone to message, grabbed my jacket and headed to Odette's house.

She lived in what could almost be described as an upper-middle-class cliché. The top apartment in one of a row of brown-stones—what a contrast to my concrete bunker across town—on a street where dogs were walked, trees were mature and abundant, little girls played hopscotch and nobody owned a car that was either new or cheap. Classic models and styles, gorgeous machines with crucifying price-tags and, in some cases, smartly tailored chauffeurs to boot. Some of the women who lived here were relatively cash-poor—and I stress relatively—but all were asset-rich. Odette came from old money, one of the founding families of Hera City. The kind of people who talk about how "old" their line is, like all the rest of us just sprang into existence three or four generations back, out of the rocks or the mud or something. I always hated that snobbery— that stupid illogicality—but Odette wasn't like that. She carried a little of the Crawford sense of entitlement in her genes, and it surfaced the odd time, but she'd always paid her own way and made her own way…except for the brownstone, of course. It's not easy to afford a joint like this on a music teacher's salary.

Odette was cool. She was cool, she was mine, and now she wasn't.

I rang her bell and lit a Dark Nine, stepping away from the door and back onto the pavement so she could see me. The intercom two-way hadn't worked since before we broke up, and I knew she wouldn't have fixed it. Odette was incapable of anything even approaching manual labor. She couldn't change a tire if her life depended on it, which was why she didn't have a car. I took the car when we split; I'd been its only driver, anyway.

A shadow moved past the curtain, I counted out a minute and, bing, right on the point of 60, the door opened. Odette looked a bit harried, flustered, though not unhappy to see me.

She even managed a smile, the first I'd gotten from her in a long time.

"Genie. Hi. How are you?"

"I'm okay. You know, just tipping along…"

"Listen, I've got a pupil. I'm sorry, she's preparing for grading exams, I only have a few minutes."

"It's alright. Don't…put yourself out. I just need a moment."

She blurted out, "I really do have someone with me. I'm not trying to avoid talking to you."

I smiled wryly. "Odette, I *told* you—it's alright. I'm here on work business, anyway."

She frowned in perplexed curiosity, then pointed to the sky. The rain was still pelting down, hammering off the pavements, spritzing off the trees, pasting my hair flat to my crown. "Would you like to step into the hallway at least? You're soaked."

"Sure."

She backed into the main lobby of her building and stepped aside to allow me enter, then closed the door. The place was quite dark with the door shut, the evening lights not yet on. Odette crossed her arms over her breasts and leaned her weight on one hip. I could read her body language instantly, instinctively. And this meant, you've got my full attention.

I shook myself off like a dog coming out of the ocean and took a deep breath. Then I looked at her and said, "I'm here to tell you that one of your former students has been murdered. I didn't want you to read about it or hear it from someone else. This only happened last night so it hasn't made the papers yet."

She put her hand to her mouth. A long, slim hand, a musician's hand. "Oh my God. What happened? Who was she?"

"Madeleine Greenhill."

"Madeleine… You don't mean *the* Madeleine Greenhill?"

I nodded.

"Madeleine." She drifted off into reverie and reminiscence. "Yes, I had her as a student two or three years ago. You remember, don't you? I used to take classes in the Conservatory of Music at Hera U. We had, we were getting something done with the study here, redecoration. I rented out that room in the university. ...Madeleine. Quite talented, as I recall, though she didn't keep it up. A nice girl, I thought. Pretty. Good-natured. Something very...honest about her. You know? A kind of openness. Like she'd find it hard to lie."

I shrugged. What did I know? Carry on, Odette.

"Her mother...they didn't get on, I don't think. Oh, Madeleine was a handful, I'm sure. I'm not saying... I didn't think there was any *bad* in her, though." She snapped back to the unpleasant present but kept gazing at the floor. "How did it happen, Genie?"

"Beaten to death. Her body was found last night at Whinlatter Docks. We're treating it as murder. It *is* murder, there's no question about it. And it's my case, which is why I'm here. Anyway, sorry to have to tell you all this."

Sorry, sorry, sorry. I'd found myself saying that a lot lately, even though I hadn't done anything. I said sorry, I felt sorry, every goddamn thing was sorry. And now I'll say it again: sorry, I made a mistake just then, when I said I hadn't done anything— I had. I'd treated Odette shabbily, taken our relationship for granted. She was passionate and deadly earnest; once she committed to something, she *committed*. I was sort of a drifter, an observer, one of those folks who, for whatever reason, remain on the periphery of their own lives. I loved her, no doubt about it, but I hadn't given myself over to *us*, wholeheartedly, with every last drop of my essence. She was very important to me but I was the most important thing to her. A subtle difference, but a fatal one.

Eventually, six months ago, she realized this and called it a day. She had moral courage and a desire for happiness in her life, two qualities I wasn't entirely sure I possessed, and she did the needful, the mercy killing, the emotional euthanasia. I was upset, of course, but also relieved. At least, I think I was relieved. It's ironic but in some sense I've gone on loving Odette as much as I always did; whereas I'm positive that she, once the decision was made, systematically erased me from her heart, scrubbed away the last traces of Genie. And I don't blame her for that. It's just ironic, like I say.

Anyway, fuck it, I'd said sorry to her enough times—neither of us had the stomach to hear it again. So I limited myself to saying, as I moved to the front door, "Hey, I'll get out of your hair. I hope everything's okay with you. You look like it is, though. You look good."

She did look good. Tall and broad-shouldered, fair-skinned, brown-haired, like a duchess in a very old painting, the lady waiting on the turret stairs. What is it about a shrimp like me and tall women? Little make-up as always, her hair un-tinted and barely styled. Odette was dressed in a brightly colored skirt and blouse, really smart duds, which looked sort of incongruous in the gloom of a dark room on a rainy afternoon. She also wore a beautiful diamond necklace, which looked even more incongruous to me, but what I know about fashion could be stamped on the necklace's clasp. I wondered if she had kept any of the jewelry I'd bought her during our time together. Considering my taste, or lack of it, I probably wouldn't hold it against her if she'd dumped the lot.

Odette smiled and said, "Thanks, Genie. You look tired. Are you sure you're okay?"

"Yeah. I am tired, we had a late one last night. But I'm fine, thanks."

She opened the door—the rain was positively Biblical out there by now. Odette said, "If you're certain…"

I was outside when I thought I heard her say, "Listen, why don't…"

I turned back to her and waited. She stared into space. I waited a few more seconds. Odette didn't say anything. She smiled goodbye and went back inside.

I said, "I'd like that, O" and walked away. I didn't get too far, though. It was raining so hard when I stepped off the pavement that I couldn't hear myself think, let alone much in the way of atmospheric noise. I sure as hell didn't hear the low-slung black car as it slalomed towards me from behind my left ear as I crossed the street. So thank God for all the other senses, or I'd be pasted onto the tarmac by now.

I clocked the vehicle in my peripheral vision on my first step off Odette's stoop and onto the sidewalk. I didn't really know I'd seen it but I knew I'd seen it, sliding by about 20 yards away and doing a slow turn on the street. By my fourth step I was at the edge of the road itself and my instincts were telling me something was off. Something about that car, it didn't fit: the area, the brownstones, the well-tended trees, the elegantly dressed old lady strutting past, her long raincoat and large umbrella. The way it hung low to the ground, the blacked-out windows, the growl of an obviously retooled engine, a souped-up engine... Again, I didn't know I was thinking all of this but I was thinking it. By my eighth step I was on the street and the rain was louder than a military tattoo and I remember that I'd noticed that the car's number plates had been covered up and then I knew for sure. And I knew it was barreling towards me, skidding through the water, aquaplaning in a vicious, whipping curved motion, aiming at me like a heat-seeking missile.

Thank God for my sixth sense, and thank God for appropriate footwear. Because of the torrential downpour I had swapped my heels for a pair of walking boots, those high-tech things with a watertight sealant and grooved rubber soles for extra grip. Otherwise me and my chichi shoes would be looking forward to a nice eternity getting to know one another better. Hey, at least I might finally have got used to the way they pinch my toes.

The death car was right on me and I yelled and lunged forward, took two giant steps, the boots grinding down onto the asphalt and pushing me away, just far enough. I rolled to the ground with the momentum and felt the car swoosh past, slapping my coat tail. I splashed into a puddle and swallowed rainwater and then my training kicked in, automatic reactions taking over: by the time I had continued the roll and raised myself onto one knee, a few seconds later, my gun was in my hands, held steady at arm's length and pointed at the black car as it screeched to a halt 25 yards away.

I don't even remember reaching for the holster on my trousers belt and flicking up the clasp and yanking the gun out and releasing the safety, but I must have done all that because now I was pumping two bullets into the back of the car, ka-*thunk* ka-*thunk*, one embedding itself in the rear windshield, one going wonky and twanging off the trunk. The car squealed like a skewered Harpy as the driver reversed back from the curb, wrenched the wheel to the right and drove off. Shock and adrenaline fought for control of my system and adrenaline won out. I sprung up from the ground and started running. The vehicle couldn't get proper traction, it was sliding more than driving on the treacherous surface, and I got to within 20 feet, firing off another two shots. The first went wild, hit I don't know what, and the second busted out the back left window.

Now I could see my quarry, sort of, as shards of glass fell to the ground and rain danced on the rooftop. A big woman, thick-necked, with short, spiky hair, wearing a dark jacket, leather if I had to guess, and what looked like the ends of a tattoo snaking up from within it to caress her neck. I still couldn't see her face properly, needed to get closer, and I kept running but the distance between us was getting wider now as she got accustomed to the conditions, working within them instead of angrily butting up against them. She stopped forcing the car and started *driving* it. I saw her manipulate the gearstick, manual transmission, presumably down-shifting, and then she finally had purchase and was peeling away from me.

I tried to remember the layout of these streets—I used to live here, I walked here, I knew this place—and something in my memory shouted *go left* so I went left, running up a narrow street with ornately designed apartments, hanging baskets, bicycles propped up against front doors. That's the sort of area this was: you could leave your bike outside without fear of robbery, and I was dashing through it with a loaded gun in my hand and a murderous driver in my sights. I stumbled, skidded, fell and hit my knee, ignored the sharp jab of pain and got my ass up off the ground and *ran*. I turned the corner and there she was, in my sights for real: she'd had to stop, the lights were against her and the traffic was too heavy to chance breaking them. I kept running, thought about taking a shot, knew I would never risk it because she was too close to the other cars and who knew what way the bullet might ricochet? I had to get up close, make sure, make safe, and then the goddamn lights changed and she was scorching through the gap in traffic, clouds of spray rising around the car. It looked like a Turner seascape on wheels.

I stopped, put my hands over my head, drew in desperate gasps of air, swore under my breath. I started shaking as all that adrenaline realized it had nowhere to go so decided to organize a Grand Prix around my bloodstream. No point running anymore. Whatever had just happened, whoever she was, she was gone. But I was still alive.

Chapter 6

Etienne

"SOMEONE tried to run me off the road, I've told you. Correction—someone tried to run me *into* the road."

"Alright, Auf der Maur. Don't lose your temper with me. Run through it again. Indulge me."

Chief Anne Etienne was nothing if not thorough. I'd already told her, about 1500 times, what had happened to me the day before, and here she was asking me to "run through it again." Run it through, run me through, run me into the tarmac. I had felt great when I woke up, mainly because of an ironically excellent night's sleep. Normally after getting shook up like that I'd be a bundle of nerves, an insomniac livewire with a pinball machine for a head. That night, though, for some reason, I slept like the proverbial baby.

After losing the perp I'd gone back to Odette's street to pick up my own car. She wasn't anywhere to be seen. I figured she either hadn't heard the ruckus outside—a distinct possibility, given the almost orchestral sounds of rainfall—or else had thought she heard the gunshots but figured them for a car backfiring. They just didn't do gunshots in a swanky place like that. Though now that I thought about it, they didn't do backfiring cars either. I decided not to ring her bell—no point in worrying her, and my pal in the low-slung motor was a thousand miles away by now. Instead I coaxed my own Dumpster-on-wheels into life, drove home and took a long, soothing bath. Lots of essential oils and even more essential wine. I slid into a pleasant drunkenness and got out of the bath before I slid into an unpleasant drowning. I ate a sandwich, watched a little TV and hit the sack to sleep the sleep of the just.

Now I didn't feel quite so great and Etienne was the cause of it. In point of fact, she was annoying the crap out of me. I only mentioned the incident to her in passing—I couldn't even remember how it had wormed its way into the conversation— and now she was pressing me for details, more details, endless details.

I sighed as discreetly as I could and said, "Okay. I was on Datlow Street. Number 57, to be exact. This was about three. I was calling to an old friend who knew Madeleine Greenhill. She used to teach her music. This is a few years back. Anyway, I wanted to tell her first-hand about the kid. You know, because... Then I had planned to swing by the docks, see if I could get some kind of different angle on the thing."

Etienne nodded, her fingers steepled under her chin. I continued, "I met my friend and did the needful. I was only there, like, five minutes tops. I came back outside, stepped onto the street and pow, this car charges at me. I dived out of the way, I just made it really, pulled my gun and fired a number of shots. Then I..."

"Hold on, hold on. Back up. Did you get a license plate?"

"Nah. Smudged or...I don't know, obscured in some way, anyway. Black four-seater, low-rise, tinted glass. Looked like a piece of shit but sounded like a monster. She'd done some serious work to that engine. I didn't get the make."

"Mm-hm."

"I hit the car at least three times, though I don't reckon I hit her. Gave chase on foot down Datlow, then left onto...Kingship or Gentry or whichever one of those I was on, and came out on Arboretum Avenue. I could see her, up ahead of me, stalled at the lights."

"And you didn't manage to reach her. Well, obviously you didn't, or she'd be in our custody by now. Alright." She straightened her tie—a tic she had, something she did while thinking. "What's your take on it, Auf der Maur? Give me your gut instinct. Ten seconds after this woman had driven off, what did you think had just happened?"

"I dunno, Chief. I thought I'd just had a lucky escape, probably... I mean, there are three possibilities here. One, a standard hit-and-run. A drunk or junkie or some other fuck-up, pardon my language. A reckless driver. Either didn't see me or saw me and was too fried to care. Whichever. I don't think that was the case."

"Two?"

"Two, a hit. Someone wanted me dead. This smelled like a professional job, Chief. She was one tough bitch. Even after I'd fired at her, shot out her back window, blown a chunk out of the ass of her car? She didn't blink. She did her job. She kept her cool and got away."

"I thought her job was to kill you."

"Which brings me to three. It wasn't me they were after. What I mean is, they didn't expect the target to pull a Beretta 950 and hit back. I think maybe this woman thought I was someone else — not a cop, I don't know what but someone else. Someone unarmed, an easy mark. She made a mistake, went gunning for me, then realized I was gunning for her and got clear. Which, again, suggests a professional. Once she clicked I wasn't her woman, she adapted to the situation, the altered circumstances, and changed the plan."

Etienne shifted her position on the swivel chair, her big bony frame laboring through a strange sort of choreography. She said, "I'm with you. There's no reason why someone would want to kill a member of the Hera City Police Department."

Don't you just love the nebbish propriety of officialdom? I respected Etienne, even liked her up to a point with her sober sincerity and bad haircut, but the way she gave the full title of the HCPD made me want to laugh for some reason.

She said, "You clearly weren't the target, but obviously we don't have a clue who was. It may or may not be connected to your current investigation. I suppose my advice is, keep it in mind. Store it away for easy access in the future."

"Yes, Ma'am."

"So what now for you?"

"Now I'm going to talk to forensics about the crime scene, then take a trip down there myself. Maybe question those security guards, though I'm not over-confident they'll have anything to offer."

"Alright." There was an extended, loaded pause, one of those pauses that are clearing the throat of an awkward impending conversation. "I've spoken with Joanne Farrington. I take it she has already briefed you on the Madeleine Greenhill toxicology report?"

I said warily, "She mentioned it."

"She mentioned it. Well, the examination shows that the girl was a heroin user. Farrington estimates for about four months or so: needle marks, bruising, topical infection, the early stages of kidney damage, you know the list." Another pregnant pause. "I'm…unsure what to do with this information, Auf der Maur. I don't fully understand why I'm telling you about it. …You know, I presume, who the girl's mother is?"

"I spoke to her yesterday and the night of the murder."

"Misericordiae Greenhill is… I've known her a long time. I wouldn't say we're friends as such, but… I know her. I know what she's capable of, for good and bad. I would prefer to talk to her about this in private before making any decisions."

I nodded and didn't say diddley. This was *way* above my pay-grade.

Etienne said, "I'm not talking about burying evidence or any illegal activity. But politics is politics, and if we can make this case without the world and her mother knowing that Greenhill's daughter was a drug abuser, so much the better. *We* need to know, but not everybody does. Agreed?"

I nodded again and said less than diddley. Etienne said, "So we understand each other. Good." She rose from her chair and slid her long arms into a jacket that looked like it had been marinated in starch. "Sorry, I've a meeting with the city prose-cutor in ten minutes. You remember that serial killer case from last winter? The woman's lawyer is pressing the insanity button like her life depends on it."

"Which it does."

She gave the kind of smile which suggested that she found what I'd said funny but wasn't allowed to formally admit that. "Yes, well... You know my attitude to the death penalty. To me it's barbaric but it's not up to me. I put my own opinions aside and do my job, as do you. So go on, get out of here and do your job."

"Yes, Ma'am."

I was at the door when she spoke again.

"Auf der Maur?"

I turned back to Etienne. She smiled once more and said, "I'm glad you weren't hurt yesterday. I'd hate to lose a good detective like you."

I smiled too. "Thank you, Ma'am."

Forensics is a funny thing, isn't it? The whole endeavor seems so inimical to our traditional concepts of police work, and yet how vital and central it is to a successful resolution. Not all the time, but often enough to have earned the lab ladies our esteem and, in those instances when we're at the end of our tether, when we haven't got a goddamn clue, our boundless gratitude.

I joined the Hera City police mainly because I wanted control over my life and my environment; in other words, I wanted to learn how to protect myself and others. That's what comes with growing up the smallest girl in your class—you're never allowed to forget that just about everyone can push you around, and at some stage in my teenage years I decided: nobody is pushing me around anymore. I also joined out of a youthful, well-meaning sense of moral righteousness; you know, simply because it was a good thing to do. To dedicate one's life to the cause of justice, to balancing the horrible imbalances of greed and anger, lust and pettiness.

It all sounded swell at the time and I still believed in a lot of it, at my core, though idealism and optimism had been worn to a duller sheen by a dozen years of disappointment, ugliness and, especially, repetition. It's like the thing about sandcastles: you build something up, painstakingly construct a slightly better, nicer, more decent corner of the world, and then whoomp! The waves crash in and wash it away, and the worst thing was, we saw the same waves over and over. People didn't change, they didn't act any differently to their forebears; they did the same stupid, selfish, vindictive things as they always did. There were slight variations in the details, that's all. To paraphrase the tee-shirt slogan, same shit, different case file. But we carry on regardless, building our castles, pitting blind hope against grinding experience, holding on tight to those odd moments of triumph and vindication, those rare bright spots in the blackness where, yeah, good *does* win out. It happens. Not often, but often enough, just about. I mean, what else are we supposed to do?

Of course, I also joined the police because I figured it for a life of excitement, variety, camaraderie, maybe even a little danger. Nothing like facing down your demons first thing in the morning. And, not coincidentally, the cops also had the coolest stuff. I'm such a baby, I know. Firearms, powerful cars, body armor, night-vision, bugging devices, all the latest technology, et cetera et cetera… I'm being a little facetious here, but I'd be lying if I said there wasn't a certain edgy, scary thrill in having a license to carry a weapon. A license to use it.

All of which brings me back to forensics, who are, to a woman, the antithesis of the gung-ho, thrill-seeking patrol cop, the obsessed detective, the visionary (or delusionary) section chief. The women who work in forensics are methodical, patient and modest. They don't have grand notions about themselves like many of us dicks do. They don't feel they have something to prove. They don't crave excitement or peril. They don't want a more glamorous existence. They don't do ego, aggression, ambition or politics. What they *do* do is a fine job, always professionally and courteously and meticulously. The forensics gals are pure scientists who happen to work in a police department, and we love them.

I took a sip of coffee and dialed through to the lab complex, which was based in HCPD headquarters uptown—a new, purpose-built construction, bomb-proofed after a demented anarchist with a working knowledge of nitroglycerin went kaboom in the old lobby a few years back. Three cops were killed, two admin staff and a lady surprising her daughter by bringing a packed lunch to her workplace. I knew one of the cops; we'd trained together. What a weird experience it was to attend her funeral: the shining coffin, the forlorn bugle call, the rifle volley in salute to a fallen comrade. She had a daughter, too, an angelic little blonde who thankfully was too young to fully understand.

Besides forensics, HQ also housed most of the HCPD brass, records and accounting, press center, technological research, weapons training and the emergency response command center, among other things. It was a truly dynamic place, bustling, sparkling with energy, although I didn't especially yearn to work there. I liked to visit but I liked where I was more. Besides, Detectives Division was housed in one of Hera's oldest and most beautiful buildings, a six-story Art Deco masterpiece which had once been the personal palace of an industrialist who dedicated the first half of her life to accumulating a fortune and the second half to blowing it on booze and gambling. The city purchased the building 20 years ago, moving the dipsomaniac ludomaniac out and moving the dicks in.

"Forensics."

"This is Auf der Maur, Homicide. Is that you, Leigh?"

"Hi, Genie. Good to hear from you. It's been a while."

"It has that. Listen, I'm calling about the Madeleine Greenhill crime scene. Case number one-one-four-three-dash-six-two-forward-slash-D-for-Doris."

"Sure. Just lemme pull that up here on screen... Okaaay... We did a full sweep of the area two nights ago, as you know. Found very little, unfortunately. Obviously nothing on the victim, or nothing we can use. The water would've washed off any hair, skin flakes, fibers, you know. Our dredge of the riverbed provided zip. It's like a sewer down there anyway. One of the divers actually got a skin rash from the water. Anyway, I can tell I don't have your sympathy so we'll move swiftly along."

I laughed and said, "Please do."

Leigh continued, "We did find a few potentially interesting little bits and pieces on dry land. First: slivers of steel about ten yards from the pier nearest to where the body was floating. That's...yeah, Pier 22. I say slivers, they were more like flakes. Very small but we spotted 'em. 'Cause that's what we do, she said proudly."

"And what's the significance? I mean, it's a docks. Place has to be full of metal containers and whatever."

"These were different. We analyzed them—tempered steel. Not your average everyday iron, which is what you're thinking of. May be nothing, may be something, but they didn't come from the immediate vicinity. Also: prints, a few feet from the metal flakes. Dug into a thin layer of mud so we know they're fresh. Don't match the victim's sandals or the prostitute's shoes. We reckon boots. Heavy, industrial. Maybe work boots, like for a building site or something? Deep ridges on the sole, probably made from some form of plastic or hardened synthetic rubber."

I had a feeling that this was about the sum total of it. "Anything else?"

"The girl's second sandal. We found that washed up on the *other* side of the harbor, the pier directly opposite. Figure she went in wearing both and that one came loose, floated back up. It was slapping against the struts, you know, the wooden pylons? Just floating there so we grabbed it."

Just floating there. I pictured Madeleine's corpse bobbing on the water, her ungodly-pale complexion, her dress billowing, her hair wafting about her face like plant tendrils, and actually shuddered, an unholy chill running up and down my spine. Death is a creepy thing and murder is creepier still.

Something struck me then. I said, "Hey, do you guys have any thoughts on how Madeleine's body came back to the surface? I mean, I assume she was weighted down."

"She sure was. The damage to her face, you don't get that near the surface. That's the beasts of the murky deep you're talking about. To be honest, we don't know for certain how the killer weighted the body. Trisha—you know Trisha, right? Anyway, she reckons it was your standard rope-and-concrete-block deal. Which would bring the girl down to the bottom, but there's always the possibility that the knots will come loose. Didn't seem to be any definite rope marks, but I guess that's more the coroner's field of expertise than ours, huh?"

"Yeah... Okay, that should do it. Thanks, Leigh. A font of knowledge, as always."

"You're welcome. How are you, anyway?"

"I'm alright. Never mind how am I, how are *you*? Still with the lovely Elenora?"

Leigh laughed. "Yeah, still driving each other crazy. Hey, how's Odette? Give her a *big* hello from me, okay?"

I didn't bother telling her about Odette. She was just making small talk, being nice. My problems weren't Leigh's problem. I said, "Will do, Leigh. Adios, chica", and hung up the phone.

Chapter 7

Madeleine

I WENT to the canteen and bought coffee and a bagel, warm and smothered in cream cheese, found a large table under a window and spread out each one of Hera's newspapers before me. The murder dominated the front pages of all the morning dailies. Some of the previous evening's papers had run the story, without many of the details, as the fourth estate played run-around with chronology and our department's deliberate obfuscation. We were playing this one nice and close, what with the characters involved; but things leak, information wriggles out of our control, people say stuff they shouldn't to people they shouldn't, and by this morning the basic facts of the case were known by anyone with the money to purchase a copy or the good graces of a friend to loan theirs.

The upmarket broadsheets told the story in a stately, dignified way: "Police to investigate murder of Greenhill heir", "Body of Madeleine Greenhill discovered", "Scion of city's most famous family found dead." The tabloids took their customary robust and insensitive tack, reducing the complexities of a tragic situation to blunt slogans-for-morons in huge letters: "Misery for Misery after brutal slaying"; "Mad bashed to death in sleazy docks." One even went with the pithy, but surprisingly lyrical, "Murder most foul!" You had to love them. The only folks in the whole of Hera not cowed by and frightened of Misericordiae were also among the most disreputable. They were amoral, atavistic, vulgar, even borderline criminals sometimes, but goddamn it if they didn't have guts.

There were a few quotes from the Mayor, prominent city councilors, Chief of Police Irene Ealing—media interaction in this case stopped with her. I was under orders not to even breathe in the general direction of a reporter. Anything the press needed to know came through Ealing's office, and she would decide exactly what it was that they needed to know. In short, very little.

Some cream cheese oozed from the bagel, onto page three of the *Hera Investigator*—that really is its name—which had a picture of Madeleine, taken at some social function or other, next to an op-ed piece which screamed at readers, "Hera going to hell in a handcart: if a Greenhill can be murdered, who is next!?" The cheese had landed right on Madeleine's face and was congealing there, ugly and clotted, turning the color of death. Ugh. Too much like the real thing, that poor girl destroyed, first her life and then her beauty.

I pulled the page free and crumpled it up, then changed my mind and decided to have a proper look at the picture. I wiped it sort of clean with a tissue and studied it. Madeleine was wearing a stunning sequined dress. She looked so young; she *was* so young. Behind her stood five or six other women, some in cocktail dresses, some in long-tailed tuxedos matched with stovepipe hats and pointed boots. At the rear of the group stood a tall girl, a little older than Madeleine, slightly stoop-shouldered as if she was self-conscious about her height. The photograph was blown up too big, almost pixelated, the finer details blurred into oblivion, but even so, there was something about that girl, something in that sly smile: a kind of intrigue, an ambiguity, a whispered mystery...

I mentally slapped myself in the face and said, Get a grip, for Christ's sake. You're not profound, you're just lonely and probably horny. I could feel my cheeks redden in private embarrassment. I did what I'd intended to do originally, scrunching up the page and tossing it in a wastebasket as I returned to my desk. And there, waiting on that desk, was another of those buff-colored envelopes, again with the neat handwriting: "Detective Eugenie Auf der Maur, Homicide Division." This time, though, there was no directive about strict privacy. I guess Misery figured, how private can a high-profile murder case really be, anyway?

The dockside security guards could wait. I spread the three thin, stapled documents out in front of me. Document one: Madeleine's KAs for the two years before her death. Document two: Madeleine's favorite bars, clubs, restaurants, theaters, all that. Document three: Madeleine's life in *précis*. Jesus, her mother was a meticulous woman. And thank goodness for that.

I started with the last one and read backwards for an hour and a half. Almost immediately I was feeling sorry for her, sorry enough to send up a promise to heaven: I'll get the fucker for you, Madeleine. It's the least you deserve. I felt sorry for her because she never really had a chance of being a normal girl, and I had a hunch that, underneath the wildness and kinky glamour and tang of scandal, that's exactly what she was. She was the kid who had everything but nothing she wanted or needed. She grew up under the intolerable pressure of being Misericordiae Greenhill's daughter, a position neither volunteered for nor desired. How could you *not* go nuts with a childhood like that, staggering under the massive weight of dead generations and ridiculous wealth and old stone and always, always the expectations of your mother and your city and yourself? Being a Greenhill meant you *were* someone, but maybe Madeleine didn't want to be someone; maybe she just wanted to be herself.

Of course, none of this was spelled out in Misery's synopsis. She gave me facts and I surmised, I inferred, I probably projected a little, if I'm being honest. But it felt *true*, my analysis of Madeleine's life and who she was, like I had cut through to the heart of her. It felt like I knew her, and I knew I liked her.

Madeleine was born exactly 20 years and ten months before the day she died. Educated at home between the ages of six and ten, by private tutors and no doubt Old Misery herself, then St Severa's Boarding School until 17. Showed an early aptitude for sports—hockey, volleyball, archery—and also science and literature, but never really followed through with any of them. Briefly suffered from an eating disorder in her mid-teens, like many girls of that age. Was considered quite religious by her school, though never any suggestion of taking orders. Studied piano aged 17: enter Odette to the drama, stage left. Graduated St Severa's with honors aged 18 and enrolled in an exclusive third-level college, the LaVey Institute, to study Comparative Religion. Dropped out after less than six months and returned home, I'm guessing to a welcome about as warm as a polar bear's ass.

The rest was hearsay, assumption and muddled intelligence. Madeleine dived headfirst into a life of drink, sex and partying, of fast cars and faster women, running through money in the reckless manner beloved of those with too much of it, and Misericordiae kept a close watch the whole time. I assume she had detectives following Madeleine almost round-the-clock, but even those consummate chameleons can't gain access every-where, so there were bound to be gaps in the narrative. It must have chewed Misery up to see this disintegration in her only daughter's life, but Madeleine was discreet enough, so the grand name of Greenhill was somewhat protected. As the old girl had already told me, she figured the rebellious typhoon would blow itself out eventually. And in the end it did, but not in the manner either of them would have hoped for.

File number two: the atlas of Madeleine Greenhill's life for the last 24 months or so. Places she went to, places she stayed over, places she blew money, trips she took and escapades she enjoyed. I knew virtually all of the names on the list, either as a patron myself or as part of my work. A *lot* of bars: some respectable, some quite sleazy, none particularly dangerous in my estimation. Jazz clubs, supper clubs, discotheques, burlesque houses, theaters, cinemas, casinos... This young lady's appetite for destructive adventure was only surpassed by her energy. Most of these joints were alright, as in they weren't the sort of estab-lishment a pillar of society likes associated with their family, but they were safe, upfront, legit...or semi-legit, anyway. Not the sort of dump where an argument about spilled drinks spills over into a knife fight or worse. (Unfortunately, I know quite a few of those, too.)

I had a gut feeling that Madeleine's murder wasn't directly connected to this list, on which only one name stood out as unfamiliar: That Island, identified by Misery's PIs as "a private club", with an address way out in the 'burbs, nestled quietly in the bosom of a prosperous residential area. Strange sort of location for a club. I filed it away in the back-brain and moved onto the remaining file.

This detailed Madeleine's known associates during her adult life. Given her ubiquity across Hera's night-life underworld, the girl must have known a hell of a lot more people than would fit onto a few A4 pages. I figured Misery and her staff had evaluated and then discarded the temporaries, the transients, the one-night stands and fleeting friendships, the roulette wheel buddies and drink-sodden hook-ups. Thanks for making my job easier, Madam Greenhill. I scanned the names quickly to begin, then reread each entry more carefully, searching for a clue, a sign, a direction to take, trying to open my mind to suggestion.

After 40 minutes I was satisfied with my own evaluation and had prioritized ten women to track down and interview. If I struck out there, I'd work my way down to the next ten and the ten after that, though I hoped and expected that this wouldn't be necessary. Normally a case resolves itself one way or another within a few weeks, either with or without the investigating officer's contribution. If experience was anything to go by, one of these ten would help me find Madeleine's killer, and if they didn't the forensic evidence would, and if that didn't we'd catch a lucky break or a confession or a helpful snitch, and if *that* didn't do it something else would. And if none of that came to pass, I wouldn't catch her at all and Madeleine's murder would go un-avenged by the woman investigating it. So it goes for us, and for all the dead girls.

This was my top ten:

Bethany Gilbert. Former classmate in the LaVey Institute, kept in touch since Madeleine dropped out. Drinking partner and general all-round moocher. From a working-class background, got into LaVey on a scholarship and far from affluent. Treated Madeleine like a flesh-and-blood cash machine. In her final year at college.

Mary-Jane Tussing. Likewise to Gilbert, though her mother was in a higher income bracket. Therefore presumably not a scholarship candidate...? Anyway, she sponged off Madeleine plenty. Also in her final year.

Azura LaVey. Founder and sole owner of the eponymous "institute." Strange, exotic sort of creature. Murky background, the biographical details constantly changing; a relentless self-mythologizer. Dangerously charismatic, said to exert an almost messianic influence over some of her students. I'd never met LaVey but anyone I knew who'd had the privilege summed the woman up in three words: don't trust her.

Camilla Castelmagno. Casino and nightclub queen of Hera City. Tough cookie, though I'd always found her to be straight-talking and free of bullshit. Suspicions of criminal activity—smuggling, bootlegging, money-laundering—never quite proven by the HCPD. The kind of broad whose sins are more venial than mortal. I was guessing Madeleine had dropped enough money over the years to pay off several of Camilla's mortgages.

Virginia Newman. The "dreary" girl Misericordiae mentioned. Mother the architect, daughter the New Age flake. One of the last people known to see Madeleine alive. Bump Virginia up near the top of my to-do list.

Winona (Noni) Ashbery. A psychologist and guidance counselor Madeleine visited during her bulimia/anorexia phase and stayed in contact with. Lived alone, had a private practice. Not much about her, maybe because there wasn't much to know.

Seemed like a solid citizen.

Orianne Queneau. Professor of Metaphysics at Hera University. Elegant woman, famously looked much younger than her years. Said to be a brilliant mind, though I couldn't say: I was about as *au fait* with metaphysics as I was with moonbeams, medieval militarism or macaque monkeys. Sometime guest lecturer, I noted, at LaVey. Probably didn't mean anything, maybe meant something. I'd find out.

Sasha Hiscock. Here was an interesting one: television presenter and socialite, as familiar with the paparazzi flashbulb as with her own kitchen. A strikingly good-looking woman, tall, almost fearsome in her angular beauty. Too-perfect women like that always made me nervous. Knew Madeleine from the whirl of Hera's high society. Currently dating the Deputy Mayor, a complete asshole with ambitions for higher office. Yeah, I've tangled with her once or twice.

Anneka Klosterman. Champion athlete in an impressive range of disciplines: fencing, skiing, diving, shooting, distance running. God, what sort of freak of physiology was this? Often seen accompanying Madeleine to the fights; not thought to have ever been a romantic couple.

And the last shall be first: Odette Crawford. I had been a little surprised to see Odette's name on the original document; I didn't realize her and Madeleine remained acquaintances after the music classes fizzled out. I wondered why she didn't mention it to me the other day, figured it was nothing, but decided to put it to her anyway. I was following a lead, sure, but I was also being nosy. I wanted to know things about Odette's life, things that she didn't want me to know. Of course Odette had nothing to do with any of this—she didn't really need to be on this list—but I wanted to sneak into her life anyway, wanted to indulge my voyeurism and poke around in the underwear drawer of her private business. And no, it doesn't make me feel any better to admit that.

Now I had a list of names and addresses, a bunch of questions needing answering, a half-packet of cigarettes and a newfound sense of get-up-and-go. So I got-up-and-went, heading for the underground parking lot where I gut-punched my car into life, got stuck into that half-pack and hit the trail. First stop: Winlatter docks. As luck would have it, the same two bozos who were there the night Madeleine was killed were on duty this afternoon. By the dull, empty expressions on their faces, the fact that their feet were propped up on the CCTV desk in their crappy little shack, and the air of slack-jawed indolence about the place, I figured them for typical on-site security goons. Dumb broads with just about enough brain-cells to do what was required: check locks, keep an eye on the cameras, have a stroll around every few hours, roust the winos and hookers if they were beginning to clutter up the place…shit-work like that.

The docks, as an unwritten rule, operated under their own steam and their own jurisdiction; things generally got taken care of, nobody fucked around with the dockers or the merchandise, and if they did, a knuckle-duster to the mouth three or four times tended to ensure that they wouldn't do it again. We hardly ever got brought down here, certainly not for thefts and suchlike; the women of the docks handled that by themselves. The cops were only called upon when something really bad went down: sexual assault, serious drugs felonies, murder.

And murder there had been so here I was. I rapped on the glass door of the security shack—you were right, Officer Browne, it *was* a stupid place to locate them—and stepped inside without waiting for an answer. I flashed my badge and said, "Auf der Maur, HCPD, Homicide. You guys have been expecting me, I presume?"

They nodded like mentally deficient cattle and looked at each other. I said, "Names, please?"

The fat one pointed to the fatter one. "She's Minsky. I'm Brite."

I smiled and said, "I'm sure you are", pulling up a stool and whipping out my notebook. "Alright, ladies, I can see you're busy so I won't take up too much of your time. You were both working on the night of the 15th, correct?"

They nodded simultaneously.

"How comes it that you've moved from nights to days?"

Brite said, in a rural-sounding drawl, "Shift change, Detective. You work four nights, two days off, then a week of days, then three days off. No, four days off. Which is it, Skee?"

"It doesn't matter," I said. "One of you tell me what happened that night. How you heard about the girl."

Minsky took up the story. If anything, she spoke even more slowly than her partner. "We were here playing cards. Playing gin rummy. I had a run of good hands. To be honest we didn't know nothing was wrong until that patrol officer come in here and told us a body'd been found."

Brite said, "In the water."

"Yeah, in the water. Officer Browne told us the full story. A dead girl, floating out by Pier 22. We just done what we were told, Detective. We didn't know nothing was wrong until right that very moment."

"Don't know why that old whore didn't come to us first," Brite said, screwing up her eyes like she was concentrating really hard.

I said, "But that's it? You didn't see or hear anything suspicious, anything out of the ordinary? Think back to that night. Did you notice anything unusual? Maybe someone you hadn't seen around here before?"

Minsky—no, actually it was Brite—said, "Mmmm...no. Can't say we did. The usual couple of pros working it. Four or five of 'em. 'Bout a dozen tricks over the course of the night. The weather was kinda shitty, so business was bad, I guess."

"We're not in trouble for letting that type of thing go on, are we, Detective?" Minsky interjected. "The bosses, they just say, 'Turn a blind eye, ladies.' Ain't our business, they tell us."

"No, you're not in trouble. How many other prostitutes were here when Officer Browne came in to you?"

"I don't think there was any. Figure they must have gotten their asses out of here when they heard sirens. Only old Rose stayed put. Which, you gotta hand it to her for that."

A dead-end like I'd expected. I said goodbye to the two geniuses and had a stroll around the docks, beginning in the main entrance yard and working my way slowly to where Madeleine had been discovered. I didn't really know what I was looking for or hoping to find, if anything—the tech team had already scrubbed the place clean for physical evidence. Maybe something less tangible, a hint, or a hint of a hint. I stood at Pier 22 for five minutes, smoking and not thinking about the case, hoping to trick the universe into letting its guard down and letting me in. I finished my cigarette and flicked it into the water, hearing that soft fizz as it quenched, and turned to go. There was nothing down here, nothing but rusting metal and crying birds and sad little girl ghosts whispering of vengeance.

Chapter 8

Azura

BY that evening I had an empty tank, all my cigarettes smoked and a tiredness headache the size of a hungover horse. Unfortunately, what I didn't have was much more skinny than I'd had when I started. Literally pulling out the list and ticking the names off one by one with my trusty green pen, I had begun to track down as many of my top ten as I could find. First stop, purely because it was geographically closest to Dicks HQ, the LaVey Institute: two students, one sometime teacher, one curious, enigmatic founder.

Let's deal with her first. My grandmother, a traditional kind of lady with a wealth of homely expressions, used to say of someone she instantly disliked on meeting, "I took a set against her." That was her only explanation and that explained everything: she took a set against the person, meaning she unconsciously made a snap decision that she didn't care for them, or didn't trust them, or didn't want anything to do with them. There was no logic to her thinking but it made sense. And I took a set against Azura LaVey when I shook her bejeweled hand across a ridiculously over-large desk in her ridiculously over-decorated office situated in the main building complex.

Actually, I went further than Nana: I didn't like LaVey before meeting her, carrying a sort of prejudicial premonition with me as I drove through the manicured gardens of the Institute to which she gave a name and an ideology. I didn't like the fact that she made me wait in the anteroom to her office for 20 minutes, despite the fact that I had phoned ahead and what the hell was more important than assisting the police in a murder investigation? I didn't like the atmosphere of pretentious weightiness, the ethnic doodads and trinkets dotted inside and out across the small campus, the cod-philosophical slogans rendered in oh-so-tasteful tapestries and chiseled into artfully asymmetrical sculptures. 'The end is the beginning is the end'? Oh, *please*. What does that even mean? And I didn't like the cold-eyed stares of her receptionist, almost literally suffocating under the orange foundation make-up plastered across her borderline-hideous face. I consoled myself with the spiteful thought that I'd probably be unpleasant to others, too, if I looked like that.

And a set was irrevocably taken by the time we'd said our hellos, I'd sat back into an annoyingly low armchair and LaVey had retreated in a cloud of organic perfume to the far side of the desk. And when I say far, I mean *far*. I felt like asking for a bullhorn just to conduct the interview properly. Her office was sun-drenched and warm, suffused with the color of melting gold, furnished with soft throws and tiny works of pottery and outlandish-looking plants that would have been at home on the set of a sci-fi horror movie.

She shifted her bottom on her chair and assumed an air of almost cosmic placidity, like it was a pretty humdrum occurrence to be answering the questions of a Homicide dick. I figured, either she really is as Zen as all that, or she's too cool to be wholesome and has prepared herself for this well in advance. She really looked the part, I had to admit, of a visionary pedagogue, a preacher of esoterica: her features an intriguing mélange of races and cultures, of unknown histories; her clothes soft and flowing, all wispy materials and discreet adornments; her dark hair with its defiant white streak, bundled loosely like a water nymph. Or maybe a doyenne of Olympia, nonchalant and imperious, floating through the enchanted bubble of her own little paradise. Chalk all that down as more black marks against Madam LaVey. I hate people who are so much more poised than me.

She didn't say anything, didn't even offer me a token cup of Joe, so I shrugged and thought, Fine, let's get to it. "You know why I'm here?"

LaVey sighed, an embellishment in the sigh, and looked towards the ceiling. "Yes. Poor Madeleine. That poor, sweet girl."

"She was a student of your college until less than two years ago and remained friends with some of your girls."

"Correct. You've done your homework, Detective."

She gave me the most patronizing smile imaginable and I wanted to smack it off her face. Instead I said, "We don't call it homework, Ms LaVey. We call it gathering information as part of a homicide investigation. Do I have your full co-operation now?"

That took a bit of the edge off her attitude; the smile disappeared like a magic trick. I continued, "What can you tell me about Madeleine? What you knew of her during her time here."

"I never knew Madeleine particularly well. She was a quiet girl. Kept to herself. Obviously she had friends, many friends, we encourage the girls to be sociable, to get to know others... The LaVey Institute believes in educating the whole person, not just in the academic sense but as a fully rounded spiritual entity."

"Very admirable. May I ask: what exactly is this place, anyway? What's your, ah, your philosophy?"

"Our philosophy—I say ours, I mean mine. As I'm sure you know, I founded the Institute 15 years ago as an alternative to the existing third-level educational establishments in Hera. Though those are all commendable in their own way. This is a haven of learning outside the mainstream, you might say. We focus on those subjects which, in my judgment, can help make this city a more enlightened, evolved place. The humanities, art, architecture, music, drama...an appreciation of aesthetics and ethics, culture and spirituality. The investigation of beauty and truth."

She smiled again, supercilious; she'd found her footing once more. The spiel simultaneously felt rehearsed and wholly genuine. I said, "And Madeleine took Comparative Religion, correct? Seems a heavy sort of subject for a girl of 18."

"Oh, no, Detective. Heavy? Not at all. Madeleine was a highly intelligent young woman, highly gifted, a deep thinker, thoughtful, almost profound... Comparative Religion is one of our more intellectually rigorous courses and it suited Madeleine. She liked to apply herself to something, to test her intellect. And of course, she was also a seeker. She *yearned* for something more, something deeper. Such a pity she didn't find it here."

"I thought you didn't know her very well."

"Did I say that? Yes, well, my staff and I talk about the girls, as one might expect. It is my business to know about each and every one of my students. And, I may add, my pleasure."

I nodded. I had a feeling—it was more than a feeling, it was a full-on certainty—that LaVey was keeping things back from me. She knew more about Madeleine than she let on, and that pissed me off almost as much as the fact that I was gazing up at her from my sunken seat. Time to take an aggressive tack. Time to stand up, metaphorically and literally.

I pushed myself out of the armchair and said, "You realize that withholding information from me is as serious an offense as lying outright. You do know that, right?"

She didn't even bother to pretend to look shocked. "Withhold? Detective, please. What possible reason could *I* have to withhold anything? I am a mere educator. Madeleine was one of my students, albeit briefly. Our stars were aligned momentarily and then we floated apart once more."

Was this woman for real? I fought the urge to violently puke across the whole length of the desk as she said, "That's all I can tell you, because that's all I know. But I'm sure her former class-mates will have their own perspective on the child."

I gathered my things and said, "I'm sure you're sure. If anything else comes to mind, be sure to let me know. And I'm sure I'll be seeing you again real soon, Ms LaVey."

Having left my new best friend something small to chew over, I turned on my heel and exited. Next stop: the dormitories. It probably seems a bit odd for third year students like Bethany Gilbert and Mary-Jane Tussing to still use on-campus accommodation, but apparently that was the way they did things in this freaky-deaky little institution. Azura exhorted "her girls" to fully immerse themselves in the LaVey way, to live the life as well as study the prescribed material, to actually "experience" their education and not just soak it up from books and the words of lecturers. Ugh, creepy. Sounded like a cult or something.

Outside in the afternoon sunshine I stopped a student, a chubby, pretty thing with a disarming smile, and asked for directions to Minerva House. She pointed me towards an ivy-encrusted building across a quadrangle. As I crossed the campus to the senior dorms, I remembered my own educational adventures as part of my HCPD training. The Department encouraged all the girls to continue their academic pursuits, though it wasn't mandatory. So I took a diploma in, believe this if you will, Philosophy and Modern Art. I couldn't wait to leave the recruit dorms after the compulsory first 12 months for my own pad — even a tiny coldwater fleapit with a shared bathroom meant so much to me at 19. I love my mother, we always got on just fine; I had a nice, uneventful childhood. And yet I never countenanced moving back in with her when I had the choice: I plumped for independence, the edgy challenge of taking care of yourself. Maybe it's because I was so small and thus felt the urge to make my own mark, to step confidently and assertively into the world.

And maybe it's because, while I'm sociable enough, I also like my own space, both material and psychological. Since I passed the first year I've always lived alone, except for those three-and-a-half years with Odette. Was it really so long? That time has become compressed in my memory, a blur of an eye-blink in the narrative of all our histories. And, I suppose, that's all it ever was.

I had contacted the college administration from my office, telling them to find the two girls and have them wait for me in their rooms. I thought about pumping each individually first, see how we got on, then maybe bringing them together and trying to engineer an interesting chemical reaction. And talk about a reaction: as I peeked my head inside Bethany Gilbert's room, the first I met along the corner, I was greeted with this: "'Bout fucking time. What do you cops use for clocks, a fucking sundial?"

I raised my eyebrows in a passable approximation of an affronted authority figure. Gilbert was sitting cross-legged on her bed. She had a strong working-class accent which she'd striven to soften but clearly came to the surface during times of stress. The girl was plump and sulky, her body swathed in layers of dark fabrics, her eyes smudged in kohl. She looked and acted like an overgrown toddler who's just had her dummy taken away.

I said, "The benefits of a LaVey education obviously don't extend to vocabulary or manners. Swear at me one more time and I'll haul your ass downtown."

I wouldn't have thought it possible, but her face got even sulkier. I half-expected Gilbert to start squalling and throwing her things about the room…though in this mess, it'd be pretty difficult to tell any difference. She reached for a coke, snapped it open and chugged down half in one smooth movement. At least she didn't finish with a belch.

"My name is Detective Auf der Maur," I said. "I'm investigating the murder of Madeleine Greenhill. You were her friend, correct? Look at me while I'm talking to you, Bethany."

She grudgingly graced me with a glance and said nothing.

I said, "Okay, now answer my question."

"Yes, alright, alright. We were friends, sort of. I mean, I don't know, we weren't bosom buddies or anything. I knew her when she was here, that's all."

"I have information that you two remained good pals. You hung out together, went drinking, whatever. Come on Bethany, she only died a few days ago. Surely you haven't forgotten Madeleine already?"

She sighed, deflated, like she knew she'd lost—which she had.

Ego and youthful boldness are no match for the power of the badge.

Gilbert said, "Yeah, we hung out. Sure. Madeleine always had lots of money and she didn't mind spreading it around."

"And you didn't mind taking it."

She flashed me an angry look. "Well, what the hell would *you* have done? My mom isn't rich, okay? I got here on a scholarship. Ain't I entitled to a few nights out? Don't I get to have fun? ...Yeah, I used Madeleine for money. And she used me right back."

"How so?"

"Company. Someone to get liquored up with. Go places with her. You know, clubs and shit like that. She didn't have many friends. *Real* friends, I mean."

I felt she was giving it to me straight, and I felt that pang of empathy for Madeleine once more. The poor little rich girl. What an awful cliché, but that didn't make it any less real for her, or any less painful and pathetic. And weirdly, I also felt sad for Misery at that moment. The ogre of Hera City, the woman with an iron fist and a heart of cold stone, the dangerous dictator you dared not cross...and the mother who loved her child as fiercely as every other woman and now was bereft, amputated, an actual part of her body and spirit, the most vital part, torn out and destroyed. Right then I didn't give a damn what kind of woman Misericordiae Greenhill had been and probably still was; I just wanted to find her daughter's killer, for her sake and the girl's and mine and everybody's.

"Did she have any?" I asked.

"What? Real friends?"

"Mm-hm."

"I don't know... Maybe. There was one girl she seemed real sweet on. I don't mean sweet like that, you know, sexually. Madeleine was just fond of her, I think. She used to talk about her a lot. Like they were soul-mates, that kinda nonsense, but

Madeleine was naïve like that. She believed in all that sugary crap. In happy endings."

Poor you, Madeleine. Poor hopeful child. I said, "Did you know this other girl?"

"Sure. Virginia something. I met her a few times. She was alright. But a fucking flake, too, like Madeleine. Sorry, I didn't mean to swear."

Hello, stranger. I mentally moved Virginia Newman up another notch or two on my list and continued: "Where did you two like to go? You and Madeleine. Where did you go partying?"

"I dunno. Different places. Clubs. Bars. What, are you looking for names?"

"*Yes*, Bethany, I'm looking for names."

She sighed again, like this was the most difficult thing anyone had ever been asked to do in the history of the world. "Uh…let's see. Uh, Xanadu. That's a club off Pasiphaë. The western end of it. Reaper's. Bush Babies. Hasta la Vista. That… Uh, shit, where else? Musique Drum. That's a really cool place. I don't know, lots of places. Madeleine liked anywhere, really. She didn't care. So long as there was booze and someone to drink it with."

"Drugs?"

"Categorically no, and that's totally sincere. Not in front of me, anyway. I can't stand drugs, never did 'em. My aunt died of that crap. Madeleine, I don't know what she did, but definitely not when I was there. She liked to gamble, though. And she slept around some. Not, like, a total slut? But she had her fair share of good times in the sack. *Not* with me, ever, in case you're thinking."

"When did you last see Madeleine alive?"

"Not for a while. Two months, maybe. We drifted apart, you know? Like, uh, we were like two stars crossing in the night sky and then, uh, we drifted apart."

I nodded. "Funny. That's almost exactly the same way as your Azura LaVey phrased it."

Gilbert shrugged. "Is it? I wouldn't... I don't know about what she said."

I moved towards the door. Gilbert called out to me: "Listen, Detective. You won't say anything to Madam LaVey about all this, will you? I don't mean Madeleine, I mean the drinking and nightclubs and stuff. We're not... She doesn't encourage us to abuse alcohol or, uh, hang out in seedy places. Not that, you know, we can do whatever we like, it's not a prison here. I just... I don't wanna get her annoyed about nothing, yeah?"

I tilted my chin at her in a non-committal way and strolled down the hallway to Mary-Jane Tussing's quarters. She was sitting at the desk in a cheery, neatly kept room, reading a book which looked very old, very expensive and very difficult. On first instinct it seemed a pose to me: the dutiful student ready and willing to help the authorities with their enquiries. First instinct was reinforced by the too-bright smile and over-eager way she leaped from her chair and crossed the room to shake my hand, saying, "Detective Auf der Maur, isn't it? Mary-Jane Tussing, but call me May-Jay, everybody does. Please, come in."

Whereas Gilbert was blunt and crude but easy enough to read, Tussing did a subtle, clever impersonation of a polite and helpful person, but was actually a slippery character. There was something fake about her, and I picked up on it almost instantly. She was too slick in her manner, too mature and confident, like an advertising executive crafting the persona of a 20-year-old college kid: all the research had been carried out, objectives identified, strategy formulated. Now all that remained was a willing sucker to buy the product, and I was damned if I'd be that sucker.

I made a point of not using that cutesy nickname May-Jay like "everybody does", but said instead, "Ms Tussing, when did you last see Madeleine Greenhill alive?"

"Ooh...let's see. Four—no, three weeks ago. I met her at the Players Play On Theater uptown. I was attending a production of

Lady Gregory. Do you know the place?"

Smarmy little shit. Yes, Mary-Jane, us pigs manage to drag ourselves away from the trough once in a while to experience some culture. In fact, I had meant to catch that play myself. Anyway, on we go. I ignored her provocative question and said, "And? How did she seem to you?"

"Oh, the usual." She smirked, then assumed an expression of pained regret. "Madeleine. Poor Madeleine. Wasn't it awful? How could somebody do that to another woman?"

"That's what I'm trying to find out. What do you mean 'the usual?'"

"Well, I don't like to tell tales out of school... She was a little, you know—a little drunk. And she was with a girl, I'm sure she was perfectly nice, but she *looked*..."

There was a flat pause. I said impatiently, "Looked what?"

"Well..." Tussing lowered her eyes and voice simultaneously. "Like a *hooker*. Not a streetwalker—that's the correct term, isn't it? Not one of those. More 'high-class', I suppose you'd say."

"Describe her to me. This so-called looked like a hooker."

"Tall, good figure, wavy blonde hair. Very beautiful. That's why I don't believe she was a street girl. I mean, she was a knockout. I bet she could charge just about anything she wanted. I'm sorry, where are my manners? Would you like some tea? Coffee?"

I waved my hand "no." Tussing wasn't exactly a "knockout" herself, but she was a pretty attractive girl. She had a nice figure, slim but shapely, and the curve of her upper thigh made the fabric of her trousers kick out in a way that would be pleasing to many, though probably not to Tussing herself.

I pressed on: "You hung out with Madeleine a lot. Is there anything you can think of, anyone you remember, maybe someone you guys met in a bar some night, someone who sticks out?"

"Oh...I don't know. I didn't actually know Madeleine all that well, really. We hadn't met in a long time."

"Except for the Lady Gregory play."

"Yes, right. Except for that. We used to… I mean, this is going back a while, Detective." She laughed prettily. I knew she was holding out on me but held back myself on calling her on it. "Yes, we used to be friends, a while back. But really, I haven't partied with Madeleine in a long time. I don't actually drink at all anymore, as it happens."

"Good for you. Mens sana in corpore sano." Then I took a flier: "But I have it on good authority that you and Madeleine were close friends right up until the end."

"I don't know who told you that but I'm afraid it simply isn't true. We were acquaintances once, no more than that. Madeleine Greenhill and I were never friends."

Another one renounces you, Madeleine. They were happy to suck up to you for booze and gambling money, happy to ride your coattails for nihilistic kicks and some of that reflected matrician glamour. And now that you're cold and dead they're equally happy to claim they barely knew you. In fact, if it wasn't for the inconvenience of a nosy cop asking them all these unwelcome, uncomfortable questions, Madeleine, they'd have forgotten you already.

I felt physically ill listening to this shit. I could feel my temper and temperature rising, and was about to really lay into Tussing, excoriate her, go totally off-beam, hang professionalism and screw objectivity, when she did me a favor: she said, "Bethany Gilbert. She was more of a friend than I was. If you want to know about Madeleine, talk to Bethany."

I eyeballed her. "But you three hung out in the one gang, right? So you'd know what she knows."

"No. I don't know Bethany very well. We live in the same building and share some of the same classes. I don't believe I ever met her with Madeleine."

Hold on a second. Something wasn't right here. I said, "Let

me get this straight: you live three doors down from this girl and both of you were in Madeleine's social group, and you say you don't know her very well. How is that possible, Ms Tussing?"

Tussing chewed on her lower lip and didn't look pleased. I think she was regretting ever mentioning Gilbert. She said, "I didn't say I don't *know* Bethany, of course I know her. I just…don't know her very well. We're not particularly close. And I don't think I ever met her with Madeleine. I'm giving you the truth, Detective."

"I have to tell you, I don't believe that."

She flushed and looked like she wanted the ground to swallow her up. But fair dues, she held my gaze. The girl had nerve, I'll give her that. I didn't speak; I let the silence expand and fill the room, raising the pressure, heating the air molecules, quickening our pulses and giving us a hum in our ears.

Eventually she cracked and began to speak, her composure regained somewhat: "Will that be all, Detective? I'm awfully sorry but I have a paper due tomorrow. Comparative Religion is a tough subject. I'm not the cleverest girl in the world. I need to put in the hours."

"That was Madeleine's course too, right?"

"That's right. Poor Madeleine." Here came the so-sincere-it-was-plastic expression again. "Anything I can do to help you find her killer, I will. *Anything*. Oh, Madeleine." Cue the extended, "contemplative" pause. "She was a seeker, you know? She was looking for something more in life, something…deeper."

Give me a break. These were almost exactly the same words as LaVey had used half an hour before. I smiled sardonically and said, "How weird. That's the second time that a student has almost directly quoted Azura LaVey back at me. First Gilbert, who of course you don't know, and now you. It's almost like you girls have been coached."

Tussing said, "Coached? I'm sure I don't know what you mean."

"Yeah. Do me a favor, May-Jay: tell Madam LaVey not to be so sloppy the next time she's giving you a line to feed the cops. It's better to alter it a little, you know? We're more likely to buy your bullshit then."

I left before her jaw actually hit the floor, but it was certainly en route.

Chapter 9

Cassandra

I GOT some dinner at a dingy little joint in the heart of the Zig-Zag, a noodle shack so fogged up with cooking steam that the staff provided you with a flashlight and directions map to help you find your food. I had left the LaVey Institute shortly after five and spent the next hour cruising Hera City, listening to the radio, smoking, thinking. By now I'd spoken to several people who knew Madeleine Greenhill reasonably or very well, and I still didn't feel like I was any closer to an understanding or a resolution. I didn't feel like I *knew* anything, beyond the clouded, poignant personal history of my victim and the technical details of her demise. She was born, she lived, she died to violent hands, the end. Or rather, let me add an ellipsis and a question mark: the end…?

Hell, no—I was only getting started, and so was the media circus surrounding Madeleine's murder. Well, what else did we expect? This was *big*—the most shocking story to hit newsstands since a mayor-in-office and the daughter of a convicted drug trafficker were photographed *in flagrante* by a reckless paparazzo who'd been tipped off to their whereabouts by a money-hungry hotel maid. Hera isn't the kind of place where just any old somebody gets killed: we generally reserve that singular honor for the low-life, the scumbags, the flotsam and jetsam of our thriving underworld. And who cares if some callous pusher or loser hooker gets offed, right? One less for us to worry about. Except, of course, it's actually one more for someone like me to worry about.

The fact that a Greenhill had died in violent circumstances was taken by the more histrionic radio commentators as proof, if it were even needed, that Hera was a city in terminal moral decline. The lives of Madeleine, and people like her, were considered intrinsically more valuable than the life of Jane Q Dirtball, recently deceased dealer/assassin/loan-shark enforcer/whatever. Which, you know, maybe they were. I don't know, and in one sense I don't care. Moral judgments aren't my bailiwick. I investigate what happened, regardless of who it happened to, as fairly and dispassionately as I can manage.

But shock-jocks and attention-seeking columnists aren't bound by such tedious restraints, which is why I switched off the radio when the pitch passed beyond "melodramatic" and moved somewhere to the north of "collective hysteria", pulled the car to a halt and trotted into Old Ma's Noodle House. I wondered, as I was slurping down my warm, soupy sustenance, what Old Ma actually looked like. I didn't think I'd ever seen her. Did she still run the place, or had she handed on the reins to Young Ma, her daughter? (The girl's real name was Bao but everyone called her by the nickname. She took it in the spirit of affection with which it was said.) Or maybe there was an Even Older Ma, say a sister with whom she fell out 40 years ago, who had now returned to claim her rightful share of the family business. Such is how I amuse myself sometimes. I'm a fun girl to be around, aren't I?

I paid the waitress and stepped out into the warm night, darker along this street than the more salubrious parts of town. It was always darker in the Zig-Zag. I swear, sometimes I think the power company sends less juice through to the streetlights here, and there are less streetlights to begin with. The Zig-Zag is our dirty attic, our jumble-filled basement, that room filled with junk and crap and the dust of neglect that you seal off from visitors, locking the door and pretending it doesn't exist. Anything can happen in the Zig-Zag because nobody who matters is watching. But someone was watching me as I began walking the three blocks to my parked car.

I could lie and say my sixth sense told me something was off from the second I hit the cracked pavement, but like I say, that would be a lie. The Zig-Zag is a mess of colors and noise, a sensory riot, a fucked-up cacophonous kaleidoscope. You'd hardly notice an atom bomb going off down here until you swallowed the mushroom cloud. So I hadn't a clue that the bulky woman in the knit-cap and bomber jacket was on my trail. I pieced it together retrospectively, but at the time she was just another dumb punk doing the Zig-Zag hustle. She wasn't even that, she was nothing, she didn't exist for me. I lit a Dark Nine and continued on my merry way, thinking about nothing really by this point, just dragging my tired ass home to a cool drink and a cozy bed. I'd made my way through only three members of my top ten list, and already I felt like I'd been questioning people about Madeleine for months. Tomorrow, as they say, was another day…more's the pity, considering how laborious all of this was.

I took a last hit from my cigarette and flicked it into a drain. I stopped and squinted up at a street-sign—was this where I'd parked, or was I the next block up? Turning to get my bearings, I saw Young Ma come running towards me, waving her arms like a maniac dashing through a swarm of wasps. Her mouth moved, soundlessly at this distance, and she held up something dark and cubic: my wallet. Silly girl, you left it behind you. I smiled at Young Ma and nodded my thanks. As I began walking back in her direction, she smiled too and gave a little bow, waiting for me in a weak pool of sodium-oxide light. And then her expression changed, lightning-fast, from courteous friendliness to agitation as she spotted something to my right, and then changed again, bang, to jumpy fear, and she looked back at me and pointed in that other direction, and by then I was close enough to hear her: "Lady, look out! She's behind you, look out!"

I spun around on my heels and was propelled backwards with tremendous force by a sort of "pointed" punch. It felt like the world's smallest but most powerful fist had caught me just right on the breastbone. I flew off the pavement and crashed into a pile of refuse sacks and half-crushed cardboard boxes. Then I saw my assailant pounding towards me, powerful, muscular, built like the proverbial brick shithouse. She walked with an inelegant stomp and had a face like hard plastic. No emotions, no little tics, no sign that she was even breathing. This asshole was inhuman, robotic, pure menace in motion. I was breathing hard through the pain, each inhalation making me hurt, each exhalation making me hurt worse. She was holding something in her right hand and it flashed in the neon light of a nearby strip club: a thin baton of tempered steel, about an inch in diameter I guessed, with a sort of trigger at the base. The woman snapped the top 18 inches, an extendable section, back into the main tube with terrifying strength and placed her thumb over the release button. She was coming for me now, coming for the kill.

Then it hit me with all the force of that first blow: Jesus Christ. That's the weapon which killed Madeleine. And this is the woman who murdered her.

I think I would have died there and then, stupefied and in shock, if Young Ma hadn't grabbed a pot of boiling water from a street-side food vendor and hurled it at my attacker, screaming, "Crazy bitch! You leave her alone!" The water splashed the woman's thick-set legs—she looked like pain was nothing more than an abstract concept to her, but it distracted her long enough, it gave me life-saving time. I sprang to my feet as the killer took two large steps towards me and pressed the release button. A foot-and-a-half of hard steel lunged forward like a snake's tongue but I was gone, diving to the side. The baton hit the wall and gouged out a chunk of plaster. I stumbled onto the road, cars swerving and honking at me, probably figuring me for a drunk. The killer turned to me, anger in her face now, and charged without warning. I pushed back my jacket and pulled my piece and got off one shot before that metal lance scored its second hit, though thankfully this time just a glancing strike against my left hip, whirling me off-balance and to the ground.

My gun clattered away and I knew I was a goner for sure. I closed my eyes and could feel tears welling up in them, and then some kind of stubborn pride kicked in, a "screw you" to mortality, and more, a need to know who and why and what-the-fuck, and underneath all that, a renascent desire to go down fighting. I opened my eyes again and she was standing over me, snapping the weapon back to its "ready" position. I noticed that blood was gurgling out of a wound in her shoulder, though she didn't seem to pay it too much mind. My aim had been true, but maybe not true enough to keep me alive. The light caught her face, or two-thirds of it, and I realized I knew her. This was the same woman who'd tried to run me down outside Odette's house. Had I been the intended target all along, then? Something told me no, it wasn't that straightforward.

But who cared about any of that? I was about a fifth of a second away from meeting my maker. The crazy fucker looming over me smiled down and said, "Night-night, buttercup. Say hi to Madeleine for me, huh?"

She poised with the baton, about to place it to my head, thumb at the release catch, and then I heard the sweetest thing in my entire life: sirens, coming closer, coming close, swinging through the night, sounding like angel-song. The woman cursed silently, shoved the baton into her jacket pocket, realized she was bleeding, put a hand to the wound and ran off, escaping into the frenzied jungle of the Zig-Zag. Just like that, and just like before, she was gone and I was still alive.

Physically I figured I was okay, bruised and hurting but not seriously damaged. I didn't have the stomach or patience to go through it with the patrol officers, to relive the thing in tiresome detail; tomorrow would be time enough for that. So I hot-footed it out of there after retrieving my gun and giving Young Ma a hug so strong I half-feared it might crush the two of us. And after all that, I forgot to take my wallet.

I didn't want to talk to my fellow cops, but I wanted to talk. Two blocks away, across the street from my car, I found a payphone and called Odette. The same soft tone, the same measured speech pattern...and the same answering machine message. "You've reached the home of Odette Crawford. I can't take your call..." Fuck it, I thought, and fuck you, Odette. Why aren't you at home? Why aren't you there when I need you? I know there are no obligations anymore, there is no "us" anymore, but goddamn it, I *need* someone right now.

And now I was really pissed off, almost physically weighed down by stress, unrelieved adrenaline, and more than that, some indefinable ennui. Loneliness, I guess. I admitted it to myself: right at that moment, I was lonely. I wanted company. I wanted to touch someone, in some way beyond the banalities of professional interaction or the maniacal extremities of lethal combat. I wanted fun, I wanted sex, I wanted conversation or a connection, and if I couldn't get any of those, I wanted temporary oblivion.

As the old saying goes, be careful what you wish for.

I hit for a bar nearby, a familiar old haunt with a familiar old tab, and was onto my sixth or seventh brandy, that floaty, slippery feeling of inebriation now soaking through my head, when someone came and stood next to me. I smelled her first: a distinctive perfume, something almost traditional about it but at the same time untried and newborn, for want of a better word. And more savory than sweet, if you follow me. Notes of orange blossom and oakwood, a hint of patchouli, and something else, something hiding in the background, reluctant to reveal itself... Her perfume made me think of joss sticks and Middle Eastern food, of a woman clad in black on a murderously hot day, kohl lining her amber eyes.

Then I heard her, a gentle voice, precise, with a pleasingly sardonic undertone. She said, "Experience is wine and art the brandy we distil from it", and it took me about two days to clock that she was speaking to me and not someone else.

I turned to face her and what a face it was. I almost knocked over my drink. This girl was smokin' hot. Beauty to launch a thousand ships of desire, a body built for both comfort *and* speed. She was in her early twenties, tall and voluptuous, with fiery red hair in soft waves, large green eyes, plump red lips, alabaster skin...and a figure to make a sculptor cry or lose their nerve or just give up on the whole damn thing. No, she was like a sculpture made flesh, the idealized rendition of the womanly form come to life. And she was talking to me.

Naturally I responded with all the wit and charm of the average barfly: "Brandy is dandy but winer could be finer", laughing and lifting my glass in salute. "Though clearly it isn't, or I wouldn't be drinking this stuff." I tipped a finger to the bartender: "Same again, please." Then I turned to my Venus de Milo in her fitted suit, waist nipped in impossibly tightly by the belt, and said, "You want a drink?"

She smiled warmly and slid onto the stool beside me, her skirt rising slowly along her perfectly turned thighs. I swallowed heavily and stared into my glass. She said to the girl behind the counter, "I'll have what she's having", then to me, "Actually, what *are* you having? Just out of curiosity, you understand."

"Curiosity killed the cat. Pronounced dead on arrival at morgue. Police open full investigation. Curiosity called in for questioning but released due to lack of hard evidence. ...Shut up, Genie. You're not funny." I lit a cigarette and offered her the pack. "Ragnaud-Sabourin. Never heard of it myself until a couple of days ago and never drank it until tonight, but fuck me if it doesn't go down easy. Actually surprised a dump like this sells it. Classy goddamn stuff."

I laughed and the bartender frowned, then tried unsuccessfully to hide the frown. I said, "Kidding, kidding. I love this place."

The red-haired beauty accepted a cigarette and said, "So where exactly does one find out about obscure brandies these days?"

"Crazy old coots, mainly. You need a light?"

"Please."

She plumped up her plump lips and placed the cigarette between them, looking at me expectantly. My eyes were wet and my mouth was as dry as sand. I flicked the lighter and she puffed a smoky cloud around her head. She looked like she'd just stepped out of an impossibly glamorous old black and white photograph.

"And why is a young woman like you hanging around with crazy old coots?"

I bowed ironically. "I thank you for the compliment, but I'm not so young. Not compared to you, at any rate."

"How old are you? If you don't mind me asking." She smiled, brilliant and overwhelming. "You can refuse to answer if you like."

Refuse *you*? Yeah, right. "I'm 31. Just gone. You?"

She took a sip of her drink. "Oh…a little younger, but not too much. Mm. That *is* nice."

"These mad old broads know their brandy. What's your name?"

"You can call me…Cassandra."

I smiled to try and hide my disappointment. "Right. A pro. I should have known. A looker like you…"

"A pro? You mean a *prostitute*?" Her laugh was like sparkling wine being poured down a tower of crystal glasses. "No. I'm not a pro."

"So what's with the name thing?"

"I'm not a prostitute, but I don't necessarily always like to use my real name. Girls have secrets, don't we?"

I shrugged—sure, we have secrets. Whatever you say. Jesus, she was distractingly attractive. It was hard to just sit here and concentrate on having a simple conversation. Her beauty kept interrupting, getting in the way, distorting things, like it had its own gravity. I wanted her so badly I almost literally ached, and I was annoyed at myself for that. I felt uncontrolled, bereft of volition. I was naked, incapacitated by sex and sensuality, made stupid by it.

"So what sorrows are *you* drowning tonight?" I asked, purely to distract my thoughts.

"I sort of figured you weren't having a party. Got a lot of sorrows to drown, honey?"

"Ah...I don't know. Yeah, I suppose so. Sorrows to drown, memories to kill—stuff to forget. Drink is a fine companion on your journey towards obliteration."

"That's good. Who said that?"

I squinted at her, mildly confused. "Actually, I think I did."

She smiled again and blew a smoke ring which sailed out before us, then paused before ascending, floating up towards the lights above the bar, glasses hanging from hooks, shimmer and reflections. It looked like a cheap version of paradise up there. Angel, devil, sin and desire, that heavenly body.

I said, "So why do you call yourself Cassandra, Cassandra?"

"I told you why."

"I mean, why that name? What, you foretell disaster and nobody will believe you? I know that feeling, kiddo."

"Actually, I'm more of an anti-Cassandra. I'll tell you that something wonderful awaits in your future, but you still won't believe me."

I turned to face her straight on. "Yeah? Like what?"

"Like you and I will be in bed together by midnight and we won't leave it until midday tomorrow."

Whoa. The world went tipsy on me then, or maybe I went tipsy on the world. The bar spun around my head and I thought, This is all going *way* too fast. These fantastical situations simply didn't happen to me, to Genie, solid little Genie with her solid cropped hair and solid wardrobe, a regular kinda gal. I felt like I was being led, hand-held, into an entranced spiral, pitch-black, silent and velvet-lined, a vortex of mania and delight going down, down, down into the belly of the world...

"Are you alright?"

She touched me on the shoulder and I realized my head was on the counter. The bartender gave a concerned look; I snapped back to attention, affronted, and shouted, "I'm fine! Everything is fine. Two more here. You'll have another, won't you, Cassandra the anti-Cassandra?"

She said, "Whatever the lady desires" and slugged back her brandy.

The bartender hesitated, looking around for her supervisor. I raised my hands, composed a "serious" sort of face and said, "I'm *fine*. You know me, right? I'm often in here. You know me. I don't cause trouble. So." I clicked my fingers. "Two more of your finest Sabnaud-Blabourin. Pssschh! Did you hear what I just said? I fucked up the pronunciation."

Cassandra and me giggled together, conspiratorial and giddy. The bar girl slung out two brandies and we floored them, then two more, before moving onto shots of Jagermeister. Fiery, choking, almost medicinal. Bang, bang, bang, and another for good luck. No more conversation at this stage—she'd said what she wanted and we both knew exactly what I wanted and why talk when you can gaze in open-mouthed lust and admiration instead?

I told the bartender to put it all on my tab and then we were stumbling out the door, sloppily throwing ourselves and each other into overcoats and hats, and then we were stumbling into a cab which had miraculously pulled up to the curb right where we needed it, and then Cassandra was kissing me in the back of the cab, the spicy after-smell of the shots on her breath, as the driver sighed in a bored kind of way and drove us to my apartment building, and then we were stumbling in my front door and tumbling to the floor together in a swirl of clothes and limbs and mussed hair and perfume clouds and her mouth on mine and my fingers entwined with hers and our bodies entwined and our selves entwined and then all was blackness and silence and rest.

Chapter 10

Anneka

THE following morning, the whole case exploded.

Cassandra the wonder woman hadn't quite stayed until midday, but she hadn't blown without saying goodbye, either. When I woke up I felt hungover but sort of ecstatic, too. I fell out of bed and reeled across the room in a pleasant state of mild post-coital delirium. I was still sore from the baton attack—a small, nasty-looking bruise was darkening on my chest—but I didn't care about that, I didn't care about anything. For the first time in a long while, I felt happiness: unadorned, empty-headed, bright-white happiness. I felt good about things.

The rich, warm smell of brewing coffee wafted into my orbit. So she fixes breakfast, too, I thought to myself, smiling. I threw on a big old tee-shirt which came down to my knees—someone must have left that here—and padded along the carpeted hallway from bedroom to living-room. Cassandra stood by the cooker in the kitchenette alcove, watching my two-cup cafeteria as it hissed and spluttered over a gas flame. She was wearing pale-colored trousers, silk or something fluid and liquid like that, and a burgundy blouse. Those were her clothes—mine definitely wouldn't fit—and I half-tried to remember if she'd carried a bag the evening before. Her hair was gathered on top of her head in a loose bun, a witch's nest of red and gold. She looked at ease, chilled out, the picture of a goddess in domestic contentment, but still a goddess. I smiled and shook my head in cheerful astonishment for about the hundredth time since she'd slid onto that bar stool beside me.

Then she spoke without turning around: "Hey, you. I found some coffee, which I have to presume is yours. You want a cup?"

I said, "Please" and walked towards her. My feet were cold on the wooden floor of the sitting-room and colder on the kitchenette tiles. My rented apartment was a bit of a dump and I'd promised myself for ages that I'd do it up. I just never got around to it, or never had the time, or didn't care enough in the first place. Small, dim and messy, a typical singleton crash-pad. I didn't spend a whole lot of time here, I wasn't really into interior decorating and all that jive, I didn't share the place with someone else. So why bother spending my precious time accessorizing and prettifying and putting my stamp on it?

Although I felt a little more bothered now that another human being was seeing the place with fresh eyes. I wondered what sort of home Cassandra lived in. I wondered if she was rich, if she had a sprawling house and servants and a regal driveway like that at Caritas Heights. I wondered if I should feel embarrassed at bringing her into my roughshod wreck of a two-roomer, its scruffiness and dinginess crying out for her attention under the unforgiving glare of natural light. I could actually *see* columns of dust motes in the light-beams streaking in through the window. My question answered itself: yes, Genie, you should feel embarrassed.

Cassandra didn't seem to mind one way or the other. She spun around with two steaming cups of Joe and handed one to me, along with a smile that made my heart leap into my mouth and my loins leap into the spot my heart had just vacated. I smiled back and said, "Thanks", taking a sip and adding, "Mm. That hits the spot."

"How's your head? A little sore?"

"Just a little. I'll live. Anyway, I'm used to this sort of thing."

She tilted her head and raised an eyebrow. "Yeah? So I'm not the first chick you've picked up and brought back here, huh?"

I reddened in self-consciousness. "I meant the alcohol."

"I know. I'm teasing."

"I know you're teasing."

We smiled at each other again, standing close together, holding our cups under our chins, not saying anything for a long moment. Then Cassandra drained her coffee and said, "I have to go. I'm late already. But I didn't want to leave until you got up and I didn't want to wake you so, you know, what's a girl to do?"

"Thanks. You're a doll."

"Thanks back. I *am* a doll. Pull my string and watch me walk."

She mimed tugging at a cord in the center of her back and started walking back and forth, stiff-limbed like a child's wind-up toy. I laughed and jolted my coffee cup, spilling a few drops onto my chest.

I blurted out, "You're more like one of those porcelain dolls. Like something Victorian. Perfect and beautiful."

She stopped lumbering and walked normally to the sink. "That's sweet."

"I mean it."

"*You're* sweet."

"Stop saying 'sweet' so much. We'll get diabetes of the ears."

We both laughed a little. Cassandra rinsed out her cup and grabbed a dark-brown shoulder-bag from the armchair underneath the breakfast counter. She said, "I really do have to go, Genie. Sorry, it's such a cliché in a situation like this, but…pfff." She shrugged and threw her arms in the air.

"You know my name." I laughed. "Sorry, that sounded weird. I just, I don't remember telling you my name."

"You didn't. You said it while we are at the bar. You told yourself to be quiet. 'Shut up, Genie.' Those were the exact words. Apparently, you're not funny." She walked to me and kissed me on the forehead. "I don't mind if you're not funny. All the other stuff makes up for it."

"Like how I'm so sweet?"

She kissed me again, this time on the mouth. "Exactly. Can I see you again?"

The question sort of took me by surprise. I hadn't really thought about what happened next, or perhaps I had but didn't consciously admit it because that would mean admitting that what I wanted to happen next involved me and her and another tryst and maybe more than one more, and that mightn't be what she wanted, and I didn't especially want to hear it spoken out loud. All those wants, all this want inside me.

But now the question was out there and it would be rude not to reply. I said, "Yeah. I'd like that." Then I grabbed her by the wrist and said, "Fuck it, that's not it. I'd *love* to see you again."

"Okay. How's about we meet in two nights' time, same bar? About nine."

I nodded eagerly. To hell with a cool façade. I thought maybe she was going to give me a phone number, or take mine, but hey, whatever she wanted—I was just happy and relieved and, I belatedly realized, dog-tired and late myself. We embraced and kissed on both cheeks, French-style, and then Cassandra opened the door and floated out the door in a vapor trail of poise and perfume and the bitter sweetness of separation.

I showered quickly, finishing my coffee while I dried off, and rummaged through my underwear drawer. I wanted something pretty but functional for today—white cotton pants, comfortable and snug-fitting. There's nothing like putting on a fresh pair of underpants. The satisfaction of snapping the waistband against your tummy, running your finger around the legs until they fit just perfectly, until you don't even notice them, like they've become an outer skin... It's your armor against the world. You feel you can take on the whole shooting shebang when your underwear is right. This morning my underwear was right and I was queen of the universe.

Half an hour later I was at the Detectives Division building and the universe had been turned inside-out and upside-down. I was greeted on arrival by the duty sergeant, a stout woman named Stearns. I literally stepped one foot inside the building and she, evidently waiting for me, caught me by the elbow and guided me to a quiet corner. I smiled quizzically. I figured it was someone's birthday or retirement and Stearns wanted me to discreetly sign the card and toss a ten into the envelope. No such luck.

She said, "Detective Auf der Maur. You're handling the Greenhill murder, right? You need to see something."

I nodded slowly, then raised my eyebrows in a gesture of "Okay, sure." Stearns directed me, still holding my elbow, left and left again and then down two corridors until we reached a line of holding cells: small, plain, unpainted and not too comfortable, but basically clean, semi-decent rooms where perps and alleged perps could sweat it out, mull it over, get annoyed or start to worry. There in the first cell, sitting in a line on a bench facing the bars and facing us, were five women, none of whom looked sweaty, thoughtful, annoyed or worried. On the contrary, they looked composed, almost indifferent. None of them spoke or looked around; they kept their eyes on the middle-distance and their thoughts to themselves.

Finally I turned to the duty sergeant: "Okay, Stearns, you got me. I give up. What exactly is going on here? Come on, don't keep me in suspense."

She sucked on the inside of her cheek before answering. "Detective, these women claim to have killed Madeleine Greenhill."

"What do you—? *All* of them?"

"All of them. They presented themselves to the front desk early this morning, individually but within about two hours from first to last. We took statements, formally charged them. They're waiting on lawyers to get here, but that feels like routine to me. Each one has waived her right to silence. They've all sung like Maria Callas. And they all say, 'It was me.'"

"They say... Hmm." I moved us away from the holding cell, about 15 feet further down the corridor. Now our only audience was a hobo, passed out in a pool of her own urine. Now we could talk more freely.

"What do you mean, 'me?' You mean 'us.'"

She shook her head. "Nuh-uh. They're saying 'me', as in each one claims to have done the deed *on her own*. We haven't questioned them in detail yet—I was waiting for you. I was about to call when you came in the door. Anyway, basically each one of those five women insists that she murdered Madeleine Greenhill, by herself, and she doesn't know any of the others. Never seen them before. Can't account for the fact that these other women are claiming responsibility for the crime she committed. Blah, blah, blah. Clearly, this is all bullshit, but that's the story so far. And that's all I got for you."

I nodded. "Okay. Okay, thanks, Stearns. Good work. And thanks, as well, for…you know. Keeping it quiet."

"No problem. I kinda figured something like this, I mean a case like this and then all these whack-jobs showing up… Fuck it, the press'd have a field day. I said I'd let you sort out the wheat from the chaff before anyone else needs to know."

"I appreciate that. Listen, organize me an interview room. Start sending them in ten minutes from now. Knock on the door with the next one every ten minutes after that. Let's keep this snappy. Keep 'em on their toes."

She handed me a bundle of papers: typewritten statements of confession in an oddly comforting old-fashioned font. "You got it, Detective. Ten minutes, interview room four."

I walked past the holding cell and looked inside once more and what do you know, there was number nine on my Misery/Madeleine list: Anneka Klosterman. She didn't see me. I whistled to Stearns and hissed over: "Leave the tall one 'till last. The huge blonde in there."

Stearns gave the thumbs-up and I stepped outside for a smoke and a blast of fresh air—the smoke to keep me steady, the air to get me wide awake. I speed-read the women's statements and fully agreed with Stearns that something was off-kilter here. It *was* bullshit. No way do five supposedly unconnected people simultaneously get the urge to confess to a crime that they couldn't possibly all have committed. No way do they all somehow know which police building to present themselves at. No way can they be *au fait* with certain details of the case before they'd been made public knowledge: for example, the fact that Madeleine was killed by blows to the head but, because of the peculiarity of the weapon, there was little bruising.

No way, no day. There was obviously a leak somewhere within the Department, someone breaking the law and slipping classified information through a gap in the fence. The whole thing smelled like a stalling tactic, a ruse, somebody constructing a Trojan horse to distract me from the real villains hiding inside, weapons at the ready, brave, fanatical, poised to strike. And it was working. I was obliged to interview each one, go through their statements, drag out the whole charade—and in the process, waste my precious time.

Exactly one hour after my smoke/fresh air double-whammy, I had spoken to the five and had them transferred to the mid-town lock-up to await an arraignment hearing. Four of them stuck fairly rigidly to the same story, told it in the same dispassionate way. Four of them avoided eye contact and, when asked various questions to throw them off, blankly refused to talk. Not even an "I refuse to answer"—they stared at the table and one or two shook their heads "no." They'd obviously been drilled in what to say and how to say it (or not say it), but the fucking thing of it was, I couldn't really prove that. Officially, I had to take their nonsense at face value, process the charges, sleepwalk through the convoluted series of maneuvers that was our justice system.

And here's what they had to say, in summation and give or take a few minor variations in detail: "I, insert name here, murdered Madeleine Greenhill at Whinlatter Docks on the evening of the 15th, sometime between 11.30 and 12.15, using a pointed weapon of some sort but I don't remember what. I struck her on the head several times until she was dead. Then I tied her legs to a concrete block and threw her in the water. I left the area. I am coming forward now because of my guilt at having committed this awful crime. I have no explanation or reason for doing it. I have never seen any of those other four women before. I acted alone in this matter."

Yahda yahda. I ladled out the questions, scribbled the replies, made sure the interviews were caught on tape, and from beginning to end I had to stop myself from asking aloud, "What's the point of all this?" I knew for a fact they hadn't done it because I knew who had; I'd danced with her the evening before. Almost certainly she hadn't acted on her own initiative—that one was a professional for sure, and they normally only kill for money and per instruction—but none of these women was involved, at least not in a significant way. I didn't yet know what their game was, but murder wasn't it.

Those four seemed fairly normal—though clearly that's relative, given the bizarre circumstances—in stark contrast to Klosterman, who resembled a drawing from a comic-book more than an actual person. A pneumatic colossus of a superhero, formidable and indestructible, her fist raised in triumph as she soared through the brightly colored pages, smashing her way off the paper and out of this world. The others were rather less imposing. Nora Hofton, 49 years old, a mother of two who illustrated kids' books part-time. Alejandra Villegas, 24, who ran a crèche exclusively catering to executives in Hera's banking district. Dinah Spaulding, 35, an unemployed actor and "creative consultant", whatever that meant. Liz Arendt, 39, a numbers cruncher at one of the city's main insurance brokers.

None of them looked particularly special, except for Villegas who had the type of youthful prettiness that won't last beyond 30. None had any priors except for Spaulding, busted twice for weed possession and once for causing a public disturbance. None were currently in a steady relationship, or so they said. None seemed capable of murder, and definitely not the kind of grisly, visceral, up-close-and-personal brutalism that did for Madeleine. None were destined to be players when we reached the endgame, of that I was sure.

Klosterman was different. She came last. The officer who brought her in to me called the suspect "Clusterfuck" as an insult, and watching this Amazon step into the room, I had to admire the cop's sheer guts. Klosterman was an inch or more beyond six foot, rangy and lean but incredibly powerful-looking, with a build like a javelin-thrower who used other javelin-throwers in place of javelins. I stayed sitting so the disparity in our heights would be less noticeable, pointing to the chair opposite me. The duty cop shackled Klosterman by the leg to her seat. She was handsome in a severe, Nordic kind of way; a permanent expression of detachment with hints of potential cruelty.

Klosterman sat and stared at me. I took a deep breath and braced myself for a difficult interview. She looked up at the fluorescent light above our heads for a moment, then back to me, saying, "I have nothing to say to you. Everything is in my statement."

"I thought you waived your right to silence."

"I did. I spoke freely to that other officer. It's all in my statement. I have nothing to add."

"Yeah, well. We'll see. How did Madeleine die?"

"I told you I have nothing more to add. Are you stupid? Why does she not understand me?" This was addressed to the air, to the room, an invisible audience.

"Watch the attitude, alright? I'm not the person in cuffs facing a murder charge."

Klosterman sighed impatiently. "Then *charge* me. That's how it goes, isn't it? I tell you I did it, you charge me in a court of law. So do it."

"Don't tell me my job."

"You don't seem to know your job. Who are you, anyway?

Where is the Chief of Police?"

I laughed. "You want to see Chief Ealing? What for? So you can abuse her, too?"

"Tssch. I am not talking to you."

"Fine. *Fine*. Whatever. We'll just sit here in companionable silence." I lit a cigarette and blew the smoke straight into her face. She blinked at it angrily, then shot me a look so fierce, so focused, that I was glad of the fact she was chained to a chair welded to the ground.

Klosterman said, "I will ask you politely not to do that again. Cigarette smoke contains over 3000 carcinogenic chemicals. It is extremely bad for one's health."

"Right, you're the athlete. Sorry, I forgot about that. What with the confession and the murdered girl and all. So how's that going for you? There isn't going to be much fencing and skiing where you're off to, sweetheart. Just a lot of long, confined days and nights."

No response. I said, "I hear you're a crack shot. So why not use a gun on Madeleine?"

Still no response. I pushed on: "What, you wanted to see her eyes before she died, is that it? You goddamn evil bitch. She was your *friend*. How can someone do that to a friend? Or were you just using her, too? Like all the rest of you assholes."

She didn't like that. She shouted, "Madeleine *was* my friend! I cared for her! Don't you dare say I used her!"

I let her words hang in the air, let them assume an importance, a solidity and heft. Then I said quietly, "So why did you kill her?"

"Madeleine died becau…" Klosterman stopped herself just in time. She smiled at me, as if to say, "Ah-ah-*ah*. Almost got me there. Almost, but not quite." What she actually said was, "I have nothing more to add to my statement."

We were done here, but at least I knew one thing: Anneka the superhero didn't do it but she was involved in the murder, in some shape or form. My heart sank a little: this was starting to assume the shape, or rather the sour odor, of a conspiracy. A labyrinthine tangle, a road that twists and rebounds and turns back on itself, with the crazy baton woman at one point and Klosterman at a different point and unknown others dotted along the route. And someone at the top. There was always someone at the top, giving directions.

I buzzed the officer outside the interview room. When she came in I pointed at Klosterman and said, "Get her out of my sight." The cop unshackled her from the chair and said, "C'mon, Clusterfuck, let's march. One foot in front of the other." The door banged shut behind them so loudly I almost jumped with the noise.

Chapter 11

Kildare

TEN minutes after talking to Klosterman, I'd put in a call to the Department head-shrinkers to have the five women psyche-assessed for compulsive confession syndrome. I didn't expect any of them genuinely suffered from it—my nose was still tingling with the scent of conspiracy and my brain was screaming, This is a fix, Genie, it's a con, it's smoke and goddamn mirrors. But you have to go through the proper steps, right? So step I did, like a diligent marching band keeping time to someone else's drumbeat.

And an hour after that, I was being bawled out by Chief Etienne for leaving the scene of last night's little *pas de deux*. Someone talked to someone who knew someone who'd seen me. Etienne wasn't happy; she breathed heavily through her nose like a horse with sinusitis; she rubbed her temples, first the left, then the right. She looked on the verge of an explosion of temper, though oddly, there was something almost sad in her eyes, too, like a parent brought low by too much love and not enough influence. Like Misery. But I didn't want to push that—I was caught, dead bang. I was in the wrong, and we both knew it.

Etienne said, "Where did you go after this incident occurred? And *why*, in God's name, did you not stay on the scene and report it?"

I chewed on my lower lip and bit hard on my confession. "I'm sorry, Chief. Truly, I'm sorry. I, you know, I screwed up. No question, I made a big mistake. I shouldn't have legged it like that. I was just, I don't know, I thought I was okay, I mean physically I was fine, and..."

"*Fine?*" She snapped a three-page stapled report onto the table for effect. "This says you were struck at least once by a steel weapon of some kind. You tell me you're fine?"

"Honestly, I am. Yes, I was attacked. I took a shot, but there's no damage. Look… I was going to tell you everything this morning, then I got sidetracked by the five songbirds down in mid-town. You know about those, obviously."

Etienne nodded and said nothing.

"Yeah, so… Chief, I swear to God I was going to make a full report this morning. I mean, I'm here now. It's just that… Last night, uh, after the thing happened, I don't know, I had to leave, I needed to get some space. I was, Christ, I was probably in shock. I don't know, it's not an excuse. But it's a reason. I wasn't thinking right, and I needed to get out of there."

I held my breath. The moment became sort of heavy, heavy but empty, the silence punctuated by the ticking of Etienne's ostentatious-looking hanging clock and the distant clatter of keyboards, telephones and conversation down the hall. A siren swung from somewhere beneath us, in the bowels of the building, and onto the street outside. I idly thought about how they didn't normally spark up the sirens until the car was outside; what a weird sonic effect it produced. I thought about sirens and girls in uniform and car tires squashing on asphalt as they rode over a bump in the road—anything to distract from this moment I was stuck in.

Then Etienne nodded slowly and I breathed out as quietly as I could; it was going to be fine. She was still pissed, for sure, and this was a black mark in my copybook, but no more than that. I could swear I even saw the hint of a smile cross her lips before she spoke again.

"I worry about you, Auf der Maur. About all of you. This can be a dangerous profession of ours. And this is, as I recall, the second attempt on your life in less than a week."

"Yes, Ma'am. And it was the same woman both times."

She raised an intrigued eyebrow—the shape of it was surprisingly delicate, it didn't seem to suit this stiff-limbed hulk of a woman. "So you *were* the target, then, that first time? On…where was it?" Etienne raised a finger in the air and held it there like an orchestra conductor delivering a dramatic pause to the music. "Yes. Datlow Street."

"Actually, I don't think I was. I know how it seems, but I don't... It just doesn't *feel* right. Last night, yes, absolutely—I was the mark. But the first one... No. Something isn't fitting right in my head."

"Alright. Well, I trust that head of yours, Auf der Maur. So go on."

"The woman last night, that crazy bitch—she's the one who did Madeleine. Uh, Greenhill. Madeleine Greenhill, that psycho killed her. I know it, Chief. Because, okay, first she said something about the girl. She mentioned Madeleine to me. 'Tell Madeleine I said hello', something like that. And the weapon, it was this pointed baton thing: steel, with a retractable inner section. Comes flying out when she releases a catch—wham! I felt it, here..." I tapped my chest for emphasis. "It had to be her. The physics matches up. She had the stuff for it, too. She is absolutely without empathy, feeling, any kind of human... She's a stone-cold killer, that one. Which is why we're gonna catch her. A pro like this, with this much of an idiosyncratic MO—no *way* she hasn't left her footprint somewhere in our system."

"I agree. Go through the mug-shot library—it's tedious, I know, but it's the only way for now. Collar one of the desk jockeys down there if you need help. But I still don't understand why she tried to kill you last night. And why you think it was different on Datlow."

I hummed in my throat for a moment, squinting at the bare fluorescent light running across the ceiling. The Chief never was much for decoration. I said, "Last night, if I had to guess..."

"You do."

"Last night was unfinished business. Because she messed up a few days ago, because I got away. So now she's got a witness, someone who can identify her, that someone being me. She needs to shut me up, permanently. Datlow...? That, I still think, was mistaken identity. She got the wrong gal, which wouldn't exactly bother this asshole's conscience, but howsoever. She missed, I got a look at her, she tracked me to the Zig-Zag and tried to tidy up her loose ends."

This time Etienne really did smile, not just in my imagination. "And you got away again."

"Yeah. My guardian angel is on overtime. And actually, to give credit where it's due? The patrol cops, they were on the scene remarkably quickly. Those kids deserve a raise. Their siren scared her off, I think."

A shudder passed through me then, unanticipated, gut-deep, a bodily recognition of dread, of how close I'd come to dying the night before. It really had been that close—another second, two seconds, and lights out for Genie, for good. But fuck it, I couldn't brood on it. I was scared but I had to ignore it; my survival might depend on that.

"That's all well and good," Etienne said, "but we have a problem. From what you say, our woman with the steel stick won't stop until she's done."

"No. She won't." I smiled cheekily; for some strange reason, I felt self-assured all of a sudden, almost bulletproof. "But it's okay, Chief, 'cause I'm gonna nail the fucker first. Pardon my, uh, rough language."

"Okay. Go and do it. And stay on edge, Auf der Maur. Until this situation is resolved."

"Yes, Ma'am."

I rose to leave, gathered my bag and keys and notepad.

Then Etienne said, "You never told me where you went from the Zig-Zag. Last night, after that incident." She shook her head with a trace of weariness. "Do I even want to know?"

I smiled reflexively at the memory of Cassandra my wonder woman; I fancied I could still smell her perfumed hair, taste the vague fruitiness of her lipstick, feel tiny hairs pricking awake along her upper arm. I said, "No, Ma'am, probably not", and left the room.

Back at my desk, back to the shit-work. I sighed heavily as my padded chair sighed beneath me. First I had to file a report on the attack last night, make it official—Etienne, bless her, was sorely in love with finicky officialdom, she was hooked for life, joined at the hip. I often wondered if she was swaddled in red tape as a baby. But I didn't mind too much; the Chief genuinely cared about her girls, so I'd make myself care for a little while, too.

I kept the report short and fairly imprecise, something like this: "I had a meal in the Zig-Zag, I left the restaurant at whatever time, returning to my car I was attacked and struck twice by an unknown assailant, I fired once and may have wounded her, patrol cars arrived, the assailant fled, I was physically and psychologically fine, I left the scene and went..." Well. I couldn't include the wondrous Cassandra, for obvious reasons. My fingers danced out a light tattoo as I typed, "I left the scene and returned to my apartment where I gave myself a thorough medical check to confirm I had not suffered serious injury."

That last bit was partly true: we're all trained in first aid and emergency medical response, how to spot when something is seriously wrong. In my underwear the following morning I had swiftly gone through the basic check-list for the sort of blows I'd received: I twisted my spine, I pressed hard with both fists on my chest and upper back, I rolled my head and touched my nose and maybe walked on my hands in a straight line. I was okay, still in one piece.

I printed off two copies of the report, one for Etienne and one for admin, and stuck both into my in-house mail-out slot. Then I grabbed a coffee and hit for the catacombs.

This was what Hera City dicks playfully called the vast, dank, labyrinthine reference center located two floors beneath the HQ building uptown. The brass *hated* the name because it reminded them that their shiny new edifice, this glittering testament to power and order, wasn't all perfect geometry and tasteful design flourishes. That bomb a few years back had reduced the old place more-or-less to rubble, but only above-ground: the foundations were solid and ran deep. Three subterranean stories of reinforced concrete, the middle layer of which still contained almost all of HCPD's paper records—including the mug-shot library.

I balanced the plastic cup of coffee on my knees and slid into a parking space three blocks from headquarters. You can never get street-side parking near that place, and the staff parking lot—also underground—is always full, so why bother with the hassle? I killed the drink while walking to the building, tossed it in a Dumpster with a conveniently open lid and decided to postpone the pleasure of a smoke until I was trawling through the photo gallery of Hera's most wanted. HQ looked undeniably impressive as I approached—even amidst the surrounding multi-story buildings, it dominated, it was broad and forceful, its glass-front sparkling in the early afternoon sunshine, the bronze HCPD banner grave and engraved above the entrance.

I showed my badge at reception and signed in for use of the library, then strolled through the main concourse—it was spectacular, light falling through the glass ceiling like heavenly drizzle, ivies and creepers bringing the supporting pillars to life—and on to the amusingly archaic basement elevator, at the back of the building. The thing clanked into life and moaned rustily as we descended, then shuddered to a halt. No sign of the doors opening. I smiled to myself and lightly touched my weapon: "Whaddya reckon? Think we should blow the lock out?"

Then the doors were heaved open by a panting administrative officer, a smallish woman with an incongruously large head and short legs, in that dark green rank-and-file uniform. She held up a finger to bid me allow her a moment to get her breath back, then gasped, "Sorry. Freakin' doors. Older than I am. Need a little persuasion sometimes, don'tcha?"

She patted the elevator affectionately—I stifled a smile. The woman stuck out a hand and grinned, saying, "Hiya. Officer Kildare. It's Detective Auf der Maur, right? Your office rang ahead. Said give you any and all assistance. I said, that's what I'm here for." She beckoned me to follow her, still chattering: "Auf der Maur. What a great name. I mean, I like my name, sure, but Auf der Maur? Now *that's* a cool name. What's it mean, anyway?"

"Um...I'm not sure. Sorry. I think it's the name of a river."

"A river, huh? Well, whatever, it's fantastic. I love the sound of it, you know? *Auf der Maur*. Real, I dunno, exotic. Anyway, shut up me, says you. Don't wanna be listening to this old flake rambling on all day."

I laughed. I liked this woman. "You're not old."

She continued to lead me through the twilight gloom of the enormous basement. Row upon countless row of shelving, stretching back to unseen boundaries, filled with corrugated-cardboard boxes, numbered and catalogued and filled with files—the scrolls and annals of this city's criminal history.

Kildare said, "Nah, maybe not on the birth-cert but sister, I feel it. Down here every day for 20 years, like a, hell, I'm like a mole in the dark!" She laughed too, a sort of honk through the nose. "Snuffling around for crumbs in the dark. And you know what?" She gave a lovely smile of pure professional pride. "Wouldn't change it for the world. Besides, my kid's in college now, you know what those college girls are like. They ain't cheap to keep, I'll tell you that much. Studying medicine. *Says* she'll look after me when I'm old and infirm, but I'm not so sure about that. Nah, I'm kidding, she's a great girl. Okay, here we go."

We entered a large room at the rear of the catacombs, cooler than the muggy main area, and brighter, with three powerful halogen lamps on the ceiling and small spotlights over a row of desks. Kildare said, "This is the reading room. You get your files or whatnot out there, bring 'em in here for a good old squint. Now you, I understand, are looking for pictures, okay? So, I mean, could we narrow it down a bit? The mug-shots are catalogued by date and category of crime."

I shook my head. "Nope. She's almost certainly got a record but I couldn't give you specifics. I've an awful feeling I'm going to have to go through the whole collection and hope for a break."

"Well, hold on now. Let's see if we can't... I've got a pretty good memory, Detective—good at puzzles, you know, those ones where you gotta recall what you put down earlier? And I've seen pretty much all these birds at some point. So whyn't you tell me what this lady looks like, your target?"

I lit a cigarette and blew out heavily. "Hm. Big. As in, tall *and* bulky. Big build. Cropped hair, sort of spiky. Tough-looking; a tough face. Uh, let's see... A mean kind of cast to her, you know?" Something blinked on in my mind. I said, "Actually, she looks a bit like that pro wrestler, what's her name? She's on TV a lot, she's a big star I think."

Kildare's eyes lit up. She said, "Sure. You mean Dolores de los Lobos? 'Course that's just a stage name. She's actually called Anne-Marie. Anyway, that who you mean? Dolores, she's the current HCWF champion, five years running. Beat that clown Shakira Underworld in her last bout. Gee, I hate that Underworld. She's such a *clown*."

I smiled. "I...guess so, yeah."

"Alright. Gimme five. No, ten."

Kildare rifled through a series of mug-shot books with impressive alacrity as I metaphorically put my feet up and literally finished my smoke. A little while later she slammed several books onto the desk, each marked with cardboard tags at the relevant page. We went through them, slowly and methodically. What a depressing set of images; a hell's anthology of ignorance, stupidity and pure badness. Even as an experienced cop, it still hit me sometimes. Most of the women had hard, dull faces, staring blearily at the police camera, belligerent and brainless, blunted of feeling, an animalistic sort of non-life. A minority looked out-of-place and plain scared. One or two leaped up at me for a moment, maybe that's her, it could be her, she could have been younger then, skinnier, longer hair, but only for a moment. None of these were the woman I wanted. The baton lady had a low profile.

Eventually I shook my head and said to Kildare, "Nah. I don't see her. Thanks for your help, but… Looks like I'm gonna have to take the long way 'round."

She gave a sweet sort of sympathetic look and said, "Anytime at all, Detective Auf der Maur. You need to come back here and recheck anything, whenever you want, you know where I am. Where I *always* am, ha ha!"

Kildare erupted into that honking laugh again. I smiled and shook her hand. "I might just do that."

I gathered my few things and we walked in easy silence back through the dungeon of records. She called the elevator and wrenched open the doors when it arrived. I made to step in, then turned and said, "What's her name, anyway? Your daughter."

Kildare blushed and stared at the ground. She said quietly— really it was hardly above a whisper—"Dolores. She's called Dolores."

"Yeah? After the wrestler?"

She nodded. After a long moment she looked at me, grinning. "Most moms would prefer their daughters did a good college degree instead of getting involved with some silliness like pro wrestling. Can you believe it? I'm the opposite way around!"

Chapter 12

Misericordiae

BY the time I returned to Dicks Division something rather unexpected had happened: Marcella Donat had left a message, asking me to call her as soon as possible. Big Cella? Why would she want to speak to me? We hadn't talked in a few years, though I'd always liked her well enough. She was brusque and uncomplicated, smart in a convergent sort of way, generous and guileless. What you saw was what you got, and with Cella, all 14 stone of her, you saw a lot and she gave a lot. But she was a civilian now, out of the game; what was it Officer Browne had said about her cousin? Private detection, tracing missing people, running down debtors, something like that...

Alright, time to end the mystery: I dialed the number she'd left and heard the receiver being lifted, then a grunt of salutation. Yeah, I had the right person.

I said, "Cella? It's Genie Auf der Maur. You left a message for me?"

She sounded pleased to hear me speak but there was a thin strip of tension running through her voice, like an iron filament in a block of stone, as she replied, "Genie. Holy shit, girl, it's been how long? So weird to hear your voice. How are ya, anyway? Hey, thanks for calling. I know this all must seem a bit..."

"Out of the blue?"

"Yeah, out of the blue." She chuckled quietly. "Holy *shit*. Little Genie on my phone. But how have you *been*? You're okay? You made Homicide, huh. That's, uh, that's good, that's really fucking impressive, Genie."

"Thanks, Cella. Yeah, I'm fine, I'm okay. Everything's okay. Homicide is pretty cool, it's interesting. How are you getting on? I met your cousin, uh, Jerry Browne. Met her a few nights ago at a crime scene. She's a good kid."

I could hear Cella lighting a cigarette at the other end, the whoosh of combustion like an electric whisper along the line, then her wheezing breath; heavy ladies probably shouldn't smoke so much. "Yeah, Jerry's cool, she'll go a long way I think. She's got the stuff for police work, you know? No fear, that one. She's young and strong and, just, no fear." There was a pause. "Genie, I need to speak with you. I mean, in person. We need to meet. It's important."

The filament of tension had thickened. She continued, "Not on the phone. I don't, I wanna meet in the flesh. As soon as you can. How are you fixed?"

I frowned, intrigued, then grabbed a pen and writing pad and said in a calm tone, "Okay, Cella. That's fine. We'll meet up, sure. You just say where and when."

"This afternoon. At Madeleine Greenhill's funeral."

It didn't want to, it resisted like a perp struggles against the cuffs, but I forced the old rustbucket to keep going and keep carrying me east, almost in a straight line across Hera from the Detectives Division building towards the Church of the Redemption in Bradshaw, a swanky area nestling under the tall hills that bordered the city on that side. The church was less than a mile from Caritas Heights, which explained how an old dame like Misery managed to walk there for mass every morning.

As I drove I wondered: why was Cella Donat going to Madeleine's funeral? She wouldn't say over the telephone. Then I realized, with a thoroughly unprofessional touch of guilt, I hadn't even known the girl was being buried this morning. But of course, they had to do it sometime — real life (and real death) carry on, measured and relentless, indifferent to my investigative progress. Cella had quickly filled me in: all the post-mortem work being done and done, Misericordiae had reclaimed her daughter's body and arranged the funeral quick-sharp. For a woman with her power, presumably, organizing something at short notice is never much of a problem. Which still didn't explain why Cella was attending, or why I felt a little guilty.

I pulled to a stop at a discreet distance from the church. There was a slight conflict of interests here—I was the investigating officer—but to hell with it, I was also a woman with a brain and a heart, I felt love and anger, as uncomplicated and inexorable as that. More than that: I felt almost responsible for Madeleine now, like I was deeply, personally involved. That had only happened me once before on a case, this one involving a child sold into sex-slavery. The only time I'd pulled my weapon with the express intention of killing someone; not arresting or restraining or self-defense, but blowing the sick bitch out of her little cotton socks. That someone could warp the concept of motherhood so badly out of plumb, that she could sell out her biological and existential birthright for a few bucks... It enraged me, it turned me into someone new. Someone worse.

I hadn't fired. I stood with my gun pressed to her forehead for what seemed like hours, trembling and screaming at her to justify her existence, to give me one good reason not to end it... My partner at the time had eased the piece from my hand, whispering reassurances and pacifications, then cuffed the mother and bundled her off to justice and safety. I didn't move for 40 minutes. Right at that moment I was hollowed-out, just a faint reflection of myself. And the woman, I realized afterwards, hadn't managed to come up with that one good reason.

Now, by whatever strange dynamic of mind and emotion, I felt involved with Madeleine. I felt *for* Madeleine. I didn't know why; there was no particular reason for it. I'd worked on far more depressing cases than this, violent, grim fantasias that would turn your hair white, but somehow had managed to float above it all. Like I said before, you feel the empathy in your gut, you'll always feel that, but you don't care too deeply. You *can't*. And yet, and yet... Here I was, walking towards the Church of the Redemption for the funeral of this pampered little brat, and shit yeah, I cared. I stood just outside and looked right up the building's façade as it erupted into the heavens, sheer and dizzying, and I felt sad for her—for her life and, especially, her awful death. Just this massive wash of sadness, useless, bitter-sweet, I was filled with it, overflowing. I let the wave pass over me and through me. I shook my head and grit my teeth and went inside.

The place was smallish, dark and ornate, that very Catholic ostentation: sculptures and stained-glass, highly wrought metals, lush fabrics, wooden pews so old and worn that they were virtually black. The church's impenetrable walls and murky corners seemed to absorb and muffle everything, so that each sound was earned, wrenched from the surroundings. An absolutely beautiful speaking rostrum stood to the front and left of the altar, carved balsa wood, a thin golden staircase winding up and around it like a seductive serpent. A small, unimposing-looking woman was up there, giving the homily—Mother Torres, I presumed, as mentioned by Misery during our interview.

Her soft old hands fluttered like doves as she said, "'…we like sheep have gone astray.' Let us listen to that verse once more: 'All *we* like sheep have gone astray.'" She paused for emphasis and gave a melancholy sigh. "Madeleine Greenhill was one of us; she was of our people. And we know her people. Her mother and grandmother are among the finest women ever to grace this city. And despite all that's been said of Madeleine—despite the mistakes she may have made, the wrong turns this young girl took in her life… Madeleine, too, was a fine person. She was beautiful, inside and out. She was filled with light and grace and hope. And yes, let us never forget, please, she was one of us…"

I tuned out her voice and scoped out the crowd—small, surprisingly small, considering the enormity of this whole thing. Barely three dozen in the congregation: a few loyal friends, Church members, individual representatives of Hera's various interest groups showing exactly the right balance of compassion and sobriety. At first I was surprised at the tiny turn-out but then I figured, no, this is correct, this is Misericordiae. Discretion and gravity, that fiercely held sense of privacy. And I admired her, just a little: it seemed to show a certain respect for death, an appreciation that nothing is more intimate and yet more immense.

My gaze drifted a little more. I caught what I took to be a nervous/brave paparazzo lurking by the door, hiding her camera, getting the bad eye from an ever-watchful Ileana, who sat up front in the angled pew behind Misery. The old girl, true to form, was on her own, hands crossed over her lap and holding rosary beads, her expression timeless and inscrutable. She seemed to be looking past the casket, which was closed—no surprise, considering what had happened Madeleine's face post-mortem. Then a weird thing happened: a shaft of light broke through the gargantuan stained-glass window behind the altar and brushed past Misery's face, caressing it like a gentle breeze, and she softened, she looked 30 years younger. She looked like one of us.

I blinked hard and cursed my propensity for flights of fancy. It was this place, with its seductive air of doom and magnificence—it played tricks on your mind. Quit it, Genie. Quit it, quit it, quit it. Get out of here.

As I slowly backed towards the entrance I cast my eye around one more time. Nobody I recognized straight up; no Odette, who knew Madeleine so maybe might have turned up, though she'd always said she was squeamish. Funerals and cold dead bodies weren't for the likes of her. And I still had to talk to her. My hand was reaching for a pack of Dark Nine, hidden within the womblike confines of my pocket, when I thought I saw the girl from the picture: the society photograph, printed in a newspaper, of Madeleine with a group at some party a few years back. The tall girl from the back, stoop-shouldered and intriguing, the way she'd fixed my eye, something about her projecting out into three-dimensional space from the flatness of the page…

She, or someone like her, was standing across the way, her head bowed but turned towards me. Then someone jostled me and I stumbled slightly and sunlight blinded me for a moment. I squinted back into the sepulchral murk of the church and couldn't see the girl, couldn't really see anything. Now I was outside the building anyway, so I lit my cigarette and smiled and thought, Another flight of fancy, Genie. You're losing it, girl.

I hung around for 20 minutes at the periphery of the church grounds, smoking too much and trying not to think about anything. I think I failed. Eventually the funeral attendance filed out and then the coffin, pristine and awful, carried by six strong women and led by Mother Torres. I stayed where I was and watched from a distance as they rolled slowly to the graveyard behind the building, an oddly unkempt patch of garden, crooked headstones and weeds run amok. It wasn't my place; I didn't need or want to witness Madeleine being interred.

More smokes, more trying to have blank thoughts. The priest's words carrying ever so faintly on the still air. Suggestions of incense, collective murmurs. After a while the crowd returned in my direction, mostly silent, heads down, elbows squeezed here and there, brief words muttered up close. None of them greeted me as they passed, en route to waiting drivers; they didn't even seem to notice me. I was fine with that. Finally came Misericordiae, walking with a cane which I took to be more decorative than practical, Ileana to her left, Mother Torres to her right. Misery smiled at the priest more affectionately than I would have thought her capable of, and kissed her cheek. They pressed hands and Mother Torres went back inside the church. I still hadn't seen Cella and was about to give it up for a wasted afternoon when Misery saw me, nodding over—the sort of nod that's less a greeting, more a directive. I threw my cigarette aside and walked up to her.

She kept those crow-gray eyes on me as she said, "Ileana, start the car, please." The butler ghosted away, leaving us alone. I smiled dumbly, out of social embarrassment.

"Detective Auf der Maur. I appreciate your attendance here today."

I shrugged noncommittally and there was that stupid goddamn twinge of guilt again.

"How are things going?"

At first I thought she meant for me personally, then realized, of course, she meant the case. I mentally slapped my forehead and stammered, "Um, pretty good. We're, uh, we're getting places. I'm sorry, there's a lot I can't tell you. It's, uh, regulation. Until, you know, the case is closed. They're very strict on that, I'm sorry."

She nodded in understanding. "That's alright. You have your professional obligations. May I ask: do you know yet who killed my daughter? I don't want a name, or some kind of guarantee that this person will be brought to justice. Just a yes or no." She paused. "I suppose what I want, Detective, is a little hope."

I held my breath, looked up to the sky past her shoulder. Then I breathed out slowly and said, "Yes. I think I do. I'm almost 100 per cent sure."

"Good." Misery nodded again, this time in satisfaction; I felt like a school-kid getting an A on her assignment. "Good."

Silence hung in the air, low and heavy like foreboding. I wanted to leave; Misery stopped me by saying, "A small crowd. That's as it should be, I feel, for a funeral. Though Madeleine may not have approved."

She gave a sly little smile, out of the corner of her mouth. I smiled too, probably more out of astonishment than anything else. Who would have thought it? Old Misery had a sense of humor, and such a black one at that.

"None of her *friends* showed up, needless to say. I wasn't surprised. Madeleine meant nothing to them. She was useful for a while, and now she's dead. Nothing more to be squeezed from her."

I said, "Yeah, that's… It's shit. Forgive the language, but that's a shit state of affairs. It's not right."

"No, it is not." She paused once more. "Virginia Newman was here. The only one of Madeleine's acquaintances to bother attending her last moments on this earth. I don't have much time for the girl, but to give credit where it's due. She clearly cared for my daughter. I won't forget that."

Something clicked, some seemingly random spark leaped a bridging gap in my mind. I said, "Virginia Newman. Could you describe her for me?"

"Tall. Good build. Long curly hair, dark brown. A mopey sort. Slouches a lot. Pretty enough, I suppose."

"What was she wearing today? Did you notice?"

"I did. She wore a two-piece skirt suit, dark green, almost black. Carried a small bag of similar color. A silver brooch on her breast. Her hair was pinned on each temple."

I smiled. "You could have been a cop with those powers of observation."

"Oh yes, Detective. I notice things."

I thought, I'll bet you do. Then I said, "I think I might have seen her earlier. In the chapel. I think maybe it was her."

"She was here, as I said. I presume she's left by now. They've almost all left. Just Ileana and me remaining. And you, of course."

"Yeah. I'm still here."

There didn't seem a whole lot to say after that, and Misery looked tired. It was kind of strange, how she seemed more tired than sad or bereft or upset. She was all of those things, of course—I knew she was scalded, burned out inside, by the pain. But right then, there was an old, tired woman standing, slumped, in front of me.

She said to the gravel-covered ground, "You didn't come to the graveside."

"No. I didn't feel it was… I had no place being there, really."

"Do you believe, Detective? In God, or some higher power?"

I considered the question as I lit a Dark Nine. "I don't know. Sometimes I think maybe, other times..." I raised my hands and shrugged. "Probably not, if I'm being honest with myself. But sometimes I'm more scared than honest, you know?"

Misery began walking slowly towards the street and her car, and I fell into step. After half a minute she said, "I believe. I am Catholic, as you know, and I have always had faith in God. My God, not someone else's. And certainly not this vague, modernist interpretation of 'God is everything' or 'God is in us.' This mystical mumbo-jumbo." She coughed, a harsh, unpleasant sound, suggestive of some murky future. "It gives me strength. There, today, as my daughter's remains were being covered with earth, as the earth fell... I drew strength from my faith. Solace. Mother Torres's homily, the words on rebirth and resurrection, how none of us are beyond redemption... I sincerely hope my Madeleine was redeemed before she departed. I wish it more than anything."

"You know, um, for what it's worth? I think she was. I think wherever Heaven is, Madeleine is there. She's okay."

The old lady nodded again, a sort of unclear gesture, hard to decipher. I wondered if I'd overstepped the mark and amazed myself with the realization that I didn't really care.

We'd reached the gates when she spoke again, without looking at me: "Isn't it strange how some myths of the afterlife offer such little comfort, or hope of a happier time to come? In Ancient Egypt only the royalty expected paradise to be just that. They expected a 'happy ever after.' Everyone else assumed they would carry on as before—enslaved and bowed down for all eternity." Misery turned back and offered me her hand, saying as we shook, "I prefer our way. I prefer hope. I am a realist, but...I am also a mother. Goodbye, Detective."

I didn't reply. I had no reply, really—I'm not wise or experienced or quick-witted enough. Instead I watched Ileana gently usher her mistress into the luxurious gloom of an enormous Rolls-Royce. As they drove away, almost silently, I reflected on the terrible irony of her situation: if anyone could be considered royalty in Hera City it was Misericordiae Greenhill, but I was absolutely convinced that there couldn't be a happy ever after for her.

Chapter 13

Cella

VIRGINIA Newman, I decided, whether or not that was her I saw, could grieve for today—my questions would hold. She deserved that, and Madeleine deserved it, too: one day for two friends, together, cloistered, left alone. I was crossing the street, returning to my car, when Marcella Donat slipped in beside me and scared me half to death. For a big girl, she was surprisingly good at staying out of sight and moving without being noticed. Maybe her and Ileana could have a race one of these days, the ghost-glide derby.

I actually yelped when Cella grabbed my arm, and fell into embarrassed laughter. "Jesus! Cella. My heart! You nearly…"

Then I stopped talking and took a good look at her. She hadn't changed at all from our days together in Vice. Cella hadn't changed since she hit puberty. A big lump of a woman, not far shy of six feet tall and built like a tank. She was quite pretty in the face, with dimpled cheeks and hair that shone soft and golden, like warm melted caramel. But she had the mass of a bruiser, a back-alley bouncer, and I noticed she still wore the most unflattering, shapeless clothes it was possible to buy—baggy trousers, a jacket that looked far too big even for Cella, her shirt collar askew and a tie desultorily pulled around her neck. A coal sack would have been more complimentary, no joke.

She hadn't changed, and I was glad of that. My life had taken so many weird lurches and spikes over the last few days, it was soothing to wallow in the familiar. It made me feel safe.

Cella smiled and said, "Genie. How the hell are you? Still keeping it short, huh?", flicking the feathered edge of my cropped hair.

"Well, hey, after that time our friend gave me a knuckle sandwich, remember? By pulling my hair…?"

She nodded in remembrance and smiled again. Then she said, "C'mere, you little shrimp" and engulfed me in a bear-hug, a real lung-buster.

I laughed and said, muffled, "Cella, you'll smother me. You forget how small I am."

We separated and I said, "Were you there? In the church?"

"Yup. Hangin' near the back. You didn't see me. I saw you, though."

It was really good to meet her again, but this wasn't a social event. I raised my eyebrows: "So. You want to talk about something—important?"

Cella looked around as casually as she could manage and nodded. She put a finger to her lips and beckoned me follow to her car, parked two blocks away. We didn't speak again until we were sitting in it, windows cracked an inch to allow us to smoke without suffocating ourselves, radio playing at low volume. Cella rooted out a flask of coffee from underneath the passenger seat and poured a cup for each of us. Its steam fogged the windows a little in oddly defined patterns, these liquid streaks and ellipses.

Then she began, in her deep, rounded voice: "I always liked you in the Academy, Genie. And afterwards, too, you know, working Vice together. We're not best buddies or anything, but yeah. The point is I knew even back then when we were kids that I liked you. I knew you were straightforward and honest and decent, and I felt—I *feel*—like I can trust you." She turned to face me. "Can I trust you? I mean, really fucking trust you."

"Yes. Absolutely, yes, you can trust me. Cella, what's this all about?"

"No, I mean I know that. I can trust you, I know. But I'm a nervous type of a woman, Genie. Body of an elephant but the nerves of a mouse. And right now I'm very nervous."

"Alright, well... Talk to me. Just, you know...give it to me straight."

She gave it to me straight: "Misericordiae Greenhill has employed me to find her daughter's killer. In my, uh, capacity as a private investigator. I don't know who put her onto me. She phoned me—direct, herself—the day after the body was found. Asked me to find out who done it, as they say. All *strictly* on the QT, which is why all the cloak and dagger stuff. She warned me not to tell anyone about this job. She actually *warned* me, like a threat."

I laughed and said, "Wow. Way to have faith in the police, Misery."

"Nah, I don't think it's that. This—me—I'm like an insurance policy. She's covering all the bases. If the cops can catch the killer, fine, if not she'll take care of it herself. Which is where I come in."

I tossed my cigarette out the window—apologies to the street sweepers—and said, "So what's wrong? I won't pretend I'm over the moon about this, but it's her right to employ a private dick. It's your right to take the job. So long as no laws are broken…"

Cella laughed queasily. "Yeah. Well, there's the… Genie, I am really worried here. Because what will Misery do with this information when she gets it? I've heard of… Okay, so I've heard these rumors on the grapevine. About a bounty being offered on the killer being brought to Misery—*alive*. So I mean, what's she gonna do when she has her? I mean, is she gonna kill the woman or what? Torture her? I can't be a part of that, Jesus…"

"Shh. Hold on. Let's begin at the begin. You heard these rumors from who?"

"From the sort of sources you don't want to know where I heard it. I'm scared, Genie. Shit, I only took the job because Misery terrifies me. I didn't feel I could say no. And now this, these rumors that she wants to kill the killer herself. In revenge, right? Revenge for the girl. I can understand it, sure, who wouldn't want some payback for something like that? But God, I can't get mixed up in this. I mean, it could all just be urban legend, but anything is possible with that woman…"

I lit another Dark Nine and sipped my coffee and ruminated. Cella was right—the old lady was capable of almost anything. The history of Hera City had a secret, unwritten sub-plot: the alleged deeds and misdeeds of Misericordiae Greenhill. Never proven, barely mentioned in polite society, but an enduring narrative thread all the same, whispers and side-of-mouth suggestions, the quiet babble of insinuation. I was sure I'd only heard of a fraction of it, but what I had heard made me feel wary. Powerless.

They said she'd employed violent thugs to break up a construction workers strike at one of her building projects. She'd used blackmail and intimidation on city zoning officials. She was the biggest polluter in Hera and paid off the environmental watchdogs to turn a blind eye. She engineered a cover-up after six people burned to death in a fire-trap slum building she owned in the east side sprawl. There was more, much more. There were also more outlandish, and frankly not believable, indictments: she was the biggest moneylender in the city. She ran drugs in and out of the Zig-Zag. She had a personal army of assassins who struck at the click of her fingers. (Misery didn't need to do any of that stuff. There was more than enough profit in bending and breaking the rules for her legitimate businesses.)

On and on the river of accusation trickled. But murder? Actual, personal murder? That had never been suggested by any reliable source; that would take Misery across the line separating (relatively) venial sin from mortal. There was no turning back from murder.

I shook my head and said, "I don't see it. A revenge killing? Even for Misery that is just, that's *beyond*... Nah. I don't see it."

Cella shrugged her big meaty shoulders—she moved like a bag of wet cement being worked by a system of pulleys—and didn't reply. She opened a bar of chocolate and went to take a bite, then looked at it and put it aside with a sickly expression. Now I *knew* she was nervous: Cella had a famously unquenchable appetite for unhealthy foodstuffs. We sat in silence for almost five minutes, her smoking and glancing nervously in her rearview mirror, me digesting what she'd said. Okay, so where now? I worked it through: Misery was using Cella and using me to some extent, so why not use the Cella/Misery connection myself? Why not use Misery's time and dollar for my own ends? All I cared about, really, was settling the score for Madeleine—the rest of it was just politics, melodrama and bullshit.

I said, "Let's pool our information. And by that I mean, let's you tell me what you have. On the hush-huh, naturally. If you're worried about the Misery situation, well, here's your out. You help me, get me that bit closer to cracking this thing, good old HCPD takes care of matters, you're in the clear with the old dame. Sound good?"

Cella nodded eagerly, like she'd been just waiting for someone, anyone to suggest something along these lines. She smiled at me, grateful and still a little antsy. I gave her a few moments as she rummaged around under the seat for a crumpled sheaf of notes, eight or ten pages filled with tiny block handwriting. Cella had been extremely busy over the last few days—that's what you call a motivated employee. I was sure Misery would have approved.

She took a deep breath and began: "Okay. I've been running down the names on this dossier Misericordiae gave me. Her right-hand woman, that oddball Ileana, she dropped it off. It's a list of places the kid hung out, people she knew, stuff she did. Very detailed. *Scarily* detailed."

I nodded. The Misery Top Ten, though presumably Cella hadn't actually narrowed hers down to ten like I did. As I remembered, she took more of a blunt, straight-line approach to work: you sat down and spread out the information and began toiling through it, line after line after line. Tedious but ultimately pretty effective. She tossed out several names that I vaguely remembered from my first reading of the Madeleine docs. I'd felt at the time they were only tangential connections and Cella backed up my hunch: nothing to see here. Sometime drinking buddies, the odd former classmate, a woman she'd bought a classic car from, someone else she brought to a social event.

Then we got to the good stuff; my ears perked up and my sixth sense went on full alert. Cella said, "Uh, Odette Crawford. I decided not to hit her until, uh, you and me had, you know, spoken... Out of respect for you, I mean. You and her. I mean, with the personal history and all..." Her words stumbled away into quiet embarrassment.

I smiled and gently patted her hand. "That's cool, Cella. I appreciate it. I'll take care of that myself."

Cella sighed in relief. "Okay. Uh, shit, where was I? Right, next up: Mary-Jane Tussing and Bethany Gilbert. Two ex-class-mates of Madeleine Greenhill. Students of that creep Azura LaVey. Both say they hadn't met Madeleine for a while. So, Tussing: calls herself 'May-Jay', if you can fucking believe that. I didn't like her. Smarmy. I mean, Gilbert was a complete idiot, and obnoxious with it, but I kind of felt she was on the level. Like she wouldn't have the smarts to fool me anyway, you know? But Tussing... Nope. Didn't like her. Didn't trust her. Too composed. For a college student talking to a private investigator about the murder of her friend? And she just breezed through it like it was a goddamn chat with her course tutor."

"Agreed. Tussing is not to be trusted. Next, please."

"Virginia Newman. Nice girl, a bit dull. Nothing much worth talking about here. She met Madeleine the day she died—picked her up from Caritas Heights that morning. Says they hung out for a little while, didn't see her again from, like, early afternoon."

"Anything else?"

"Not in terms of information. She seemed genuinely sad, though. You know? That the Greenhill kid was dead? Like she properly cared for her. Wasn't just using her like the other two.

But I think this Newman chick might be from money anyway, so…no need to sponge off a poor little rich girl."

"Yeah, Misery said the same thing. Said Virginia genuinely cared about her daughter. I think she appreciated the girl coming today."

"She was here, huh? Didn't see her. Anyway, yeah, she was alright. Like I say, nothing special. …You know Tussing's old dear blew all their money?"

I said, intrigued, "No, I did *not* know that."

"Sure. Inherited a fortune from *her* mother—May-Jay's grandma—she'd made it in logging or transport or some shit. Anyway, Mary-Jane senior blew the whole megillah. Bad investments, stupid choices. So Junior's been reduced to the grubby status of scholarship student. *Such* a fall from grace, ha."

"She must be clever, then? To get a scholarship?"

"Dunno. Suppose so."

"Which is funny, because she told me she wasn't the brightest, academically speaking."

"Mm. Dunno. She's LaVey's little pet, anyway. Coupla other girls clued me in while I was loitering with bad intent on campus the other day. Tussing is not a popular girly with the other students. One of 'em said… Nah, I can't. It's too rude."

I smiled. "Go on. I'm a big girl for such a little girl."

Cella smiled too. "She said if Tussing had her head any further up Madam LaVey's ass she could brush her teeth with it."

"Unoriginal, but effective."

"Yeah. Charming image. You want another drop of coffee?"

I nodded yes and she poured out the last of the flask. It had cooled quite a bit but I blew on it anyway as I thought: Virginia Newman clearly had a deep relationship with Madeleine. There probably wasn't a whole lot else the girl could tell me, but I wanted to talk to her anyway. She was one of the few people who I knew for sure met the victim on the day of her death. But more than that, being honest, I wanted to know Madeleine a little better, through Virginia, through their friendship, their intimate history. I wanted to see if she could help explain why I was starting to care this much.

Then I belatedly noticed that Cella had started speaking again: "...anne Queneau. Sorry, *Professor* Orianne Queneau. Teaches Metaphysics at Hera U. Very well-regarded philosophy course. I mean, she's brilliant, there's no doubt about it. But I didn't like her, either. Smooth, intellectual; full of fancy talk, and I don't mean metaphysics."

"What, then?"

"Queneau is like a politician. You're never sure that what she's saying is what she's saying, ya know what I mean? I checked her out, too, her background: highly respectable, cultured, honorary degrees up the yin-yang, patron of this art, founder of that appreciation society. All that education and achievement makes a dumb broad like me suspicious."

I smiled to myself—Cella was a real meat-and-two-veg kind of lady. Not exactly anti-intellectual, but instinctively wary of it. I wasn't wired up that way myself, but knew the type and didn't mind too much: my mom had been just like that. When I told her I intended to study philosophy for a short while she had one comment to make: "But sweetheart, don't you agree you already think about things too much as it is?" One of the many, many reasons I loved that woman to bits.

Cella continued, "Queneau's into a whole bunch of other stuff in her spare time, way-out stuff: all that airy-fairy esoteric crap. You know the sort of thing I mean."

"Mm-hm. And Madeleine?"

"Says she hasn't seen her in over a year. I don't know."

"You think she was holding back on you?"

"Maybe not specifically on that—I mean, for all I know she hasn't seen the girl that long. But something nagged at me... Anyway, seems clean for the night in question. She was hosting a gala dinner at the city museum. Some new exhibition of…whatever. Thing went on 'till the wee hours and Queneau claims she was there all night, except not *there* exactly but in a smaller private room in the building. Wouldn't tell me who with, cited right to privacy and so on. But the old wagon assures me they were 'respectable and well-regarded members of Hera society.' The usual."

The sky was darkening even though it couldn't have been that late, like someone drawing an opaque veil over the city, fuzzing the edges. I felt like a movie character in a scene that's about to fade out. Time to step it up: "Alright. Who else?"

"Sasha Hiscock, the TV presenter," Cella said. "Complete airhead. I mean, smart in some ways, but ultimately a bubblehead. One I *definitely* don't figure for any connection."

"No?"

"Genie, are you kidding me? The woman is terrified of the public finding out she even moved in some of the same circles as Madeleine Greenhill. Hiscock is too self-obsessed and career-obsessed to be a murderer. Christ, can you imagine it! She'd be worried about the blood spattering her new three-grand shoes. Took me two days to get an interview, and even then she had her lawyer present. 'Course, I couldn't tell her who I was working for. Old Misery's name woulda opened up a few doors."

"And she had an alibi for the night of the murder, I'm presuming?"

"You're presuming right, my little friend. Spent the whole evening with our beloved Deputy Mayor." She smiled slyly. "You remember Henrietta, don't you?"

Henrietta Villa. That moron. Sorry, let me rephrase: that back-stabbing, avaricious, greasy-pole-climbing, megalomaniac moron. Villa, in a previous life as the civilian head of Internal Affairs in HCPD, had tried to pin a corruption beef on me and another patrol cop with absolutely no evidence. Claimed we were taking bribes to turn a blind eye to a gambling racket. It was all BS, a clumsy attempt to make a case and make a name for herself.

When I heard about it first, I laughed. Then I got really worried. Then I got angry and threatened to sue her for defamation if she didn't issue a formal retraction and apology to both me and the other girl. It was only later, when I'd cooled off a bit and Villa had scuttled back under her rock, that I realized how close I'd come to getting canned. And realized that I had more guts than I'd known.

I drawled, "My pal Henrietta. How's she doing? You know, I miss her sometimes."

Cella chuckled and said, "I think we all miss Henrietta in our own way. Okay, I got one more for you: Noni Ashbery. Her full name's Winona but everyone calls her Noni. A psychologist and therapist, private practice. Madeleine was referred to her aged—lemme just check this—aged 16. Bulimia and suspected anorexia. Classic signs of a damaged teenager. Anyway, she saw this Noni Ashbery for about six months. Seems to have helped her a lot. I mean, she never went back, so… Sorry, no, that's not the full story. She never went back for the eating disorder thing, but they kept in contact. A loose sort of arrangement. Madeleine would drop in for a chat every now and again. Nothing too structured or formal, but it *was* counseling. So says Ashbery herself. She was very forthcoming. For a medical person, I mean. No problem talking about Madeleine, within certain parameters of course."

"How did you find her?"

"Ashbery? Nice, yeah. Genuine. Straight-up. I mean, she looks exactly like a therapist should look, you know? Soft features, warm smile, even her voice…it was pitched just so. Just right. Really relaxing, being in her company. Yeah, she was very nice."

I took it all in, creating the mental file, cataloguing and ordering, like a sub-program running under the surface, sifting through the data, structuring and assembling.

Then Cella said, "Really, that's as far as I've got. So is it any help to you or what?"

I stretched my back out, twisting and scrunching up my face

with muscular relief. "Yeah, it all helps. Okay, so that's it, that's who you've talked to?"

"Uh-huh."

"Right, well I've met with LaVey myself. Who else, who else? ...Camilla C—might swing by her tonight. Anneka Klosterman's obviously out of circulation."

"Yeah, I hear you guys have her downtown. Heard she confessed to the whole thing. What a lucky break for you, huh?!"

I raised a sardonic eyebrow. "Her and about five others. Ah, it's all a wash, Cella. Someone's playing games. Playing us for saps."

"Any ideas who? Sorry, I shouldn't have asked that."

"No, it's alright. You can ask. I probably won't answer, though." I chewed over her question. If we were going to swap information, well, a swap worked two ways. But I wanted to hold back on my own theories for now. Etienne knowing about it was one thing, but Cella was out of the club; she wasn't one of us anymore. I knew I could trust her, but something told me, no, hold back. I felt I'd be ceding some measure of control over the situation if she knew as much as I did. Maybe it was the Misery connection, and that thought made me feel almost as edgy as Cella still looked. I had decided a long time back in the conversation that I was going to work this Cella angle, but considering it now, becoming fully cognizant of my decision, made me nervous as all hell. You just didn't play games with La Greenhill, but I was about to do exactly that.

"What now, Cella?" I said quietly. "Where do we go from here?"

She lit yet another cigarette and said, "I don't know. Any suggestions?"

Prodding the conversation, nudging it to somewhere she wanted it to go but didn't have the courage to say out loud.

I said the words for her: "I want you to work for me as well as Misery. Only us two will know. Whatever you find out, report to her as agreed between you, but also to me. She won't know about it, I guarantee it."

She nodded slowly, almost like a drugged motion, someone under heavy water. When she spoke her words sounded accelerated by comparison: "Uh-huh. Uh-huh. Okay. I think I can, ah…"

"I need your help, big mama. I admit it straight up. I'm gonna tell you something nobody knows: we've a leak inside the HCPD. Don't have a clue who or how or what's going on, but my five songbirds in lock-up know certain stuff they shouldn't know and couldn't know. I have a leak, and I need someone on the outside, someone I can trust. I need you." I let that sink in then said, "And you get from it what I said already: you're uneasy about Misery and the situation you've found yourself in. Help me out and it's all over all the quicker. I get my woman, you get paid, we all get to fuck off home for a good night's sleep."

Cella smiled and cleared her throat. "Yeah. Okay, Genie, I'll do it. 'Cause I *am* nervous about it, that's correct. I just want this goddamn thing over and done with. So, uh, yeah. We have a— what? An arrangement?"

She smiled. I patted her hand again and said, "An understanding. Cool. It's settled. Look, I'll go now and we'll talk tomorrow maybe."

"Here." She pressed a business card into my hand; phone number and address. I didn't recognize either. Cella said, "I check in like clockwork. If I'm not there leave a message and I'll call you within the hour."

"Okay."

I went to open the car door and she frowned, clicked her fingers, remembering. "Ooh. There was something else. Ashbery, she told me something, I don't know if it's relevant but you're still gathering information, right?"

I nodded. Cella said, "The dress. That polka dot dress the Greenhill kid was found in? Noni said she had an infatuation with the pattern. 'Black spots on pure white.' That's a quote. Madeleine used to talk about it a lot—monochrome polka dot. I don't know what it meant for her, the shrink wasn't sure, but it meant something. Used to draw it, you know, doodling on a notepad, she drew it everywhere. On her hand, even. Black dots against white skin. She thought, this is Ashbery, she thought maybe it was some hangover from childhood, something Madeleine had held onto. Like, uh...what's that term? Like a mental comfort blanket. I dunno, it made her feel safe. Calmed her down, or when she was stressed or upset. Anyway, Ashbery said the girl didn't tell this to anyone else, not even her mother. So, uh, there you have it. That's all I got."

We shook hands, wordlessly parting company, small smiles and barely perceptible nods. We locked eyes and held the gaze and were committed to each other. I strolled back to my car as Cella gunned her engine and drove away at speed, as the clouds of evening rolled in across the day, filling it, obscuring the light. And I thought about Madeleine and her obsession with polka dot. Black on white, bright and dark, empty and filled, space and enclosure. A crossword looked like that, too, didn't it? An accumulation of clues, of hints and teases, obscure allusions, structured in clean black and white.

Reaching my car I stood with the key in the door, not turning it, not doing anything, still thinking about Madeleine and the polka dot dress in which she died. I pictured her returning to Caritas Heights that fateful last night, the images scrolling across my mind like a slideshow; pictured her wearing the trousers Misery had mentioned, going upstairs to her dressing-room, stripping to her underwear and opening the door of a huge standalone wardrobe, something ancient and impossibly grand in polished mahogany or iroko; I pictured Madeleine sifting through clothes on hangers, considering one thing, discarding something else, this skirt, that scarf, taking her time over what to wear; then I pictured her eye falling on the polka dot dress as it struck her, of course, what else could I put on tonight, especially tonight, but this, my talisman, my comfort and succor, my familiar pattern, my monochrome polka dot.

Sure. What else could you have worn, Madeleine, en route to your violent end? I opened the car door and remembered her last words to Misericordiae, spoken that morning: "I love you, Mother." I finally knew then, in my blood, in black and white, that the girl had realized she was going to meet her death.

Chapter 14

Camilla

"I TOLD you once already, small fry—I can't help you. Now ya gonna buy a drink or piss off? 'Cause you're making my customers nervous."

Camilla Castelmagno had a smile on her face that was about as warm as a frozen-over Hell in January. She was leaning against the bar in Coochie Coo's—one of many drinking emporia she owned/controlled in Hera City, and the one she spent most time in herself. Dark, minimalist design, alien-blue strobe lights making our skin glow like it was radioactive. A fantastic acid-jazz tune snaked its way out of spaced-out speakers, it hissed through the room like mist. I couldn't think of the name but I loved this piece of music. Who knew Camilla had such good taste?

She wore a tailored pin-striped suit, three-piece, sharp as a razor blade. She also sported a fedora—yes, indoors—tilted at just the right menacing angle, and a pair of black and white spats booties, buttoned up to the ankle. Classic gangster chic. It was beyond classic, it was almost a parody, an homage. She looked like the villain from an old *noir* movie, or somebody done up as one for Halloween. She couldn't have known I would drop by without warning this evening, but a part of me still believed she'd dressed like that just to antagonize me.

This was the second time Camilla had called me "small fry" and now I had to call her on it. Once you can let slide, maybe nothing was meant by it, maybe she was being playful. Twice is an affront to your authority, the authority of the badge you wear. Camilla scared me a little, I admit it—she was a tough broad, fortysomething and hitting fast for 50, hard-headed and quick with her hands, too ruthless and too smart for us to have ever managed to nail her on anything more than minor beefs: license violations, tardiness in settling her tax bill. She was the queen bee of Hera's underworld and, off the record, didn't deny it. The other crims usually steered a wide berth; the cops harassed and disrupted her business, up to a point. But nobody screwed around with Camilla. You treated her with respect.

Well, fine, I played the game as I was told to play it. But goddamn, I was into something serious here, I hadn't time to dance around the ring in a blur of shadows and feints. I'd come here almost straight from my Cella meet, allowing myself a quick hour for a shower and a sandwich. Now I needed to know what Camilla needed to tell me. And fuck it, she needed to show me respect, too; me and the badge, the job I did, the cause I represented. The fact that Madeleine was dead and someone had to pay for it.

I lit a cigarette, blew smoke in her face and said, "Call me that one more time and I *will* bust your ass, Camilla."

She snorted dismissively. A tough-looking, wiry woman down the bar—also wearing a hat and trouser suit, though not nearly as well-cut—dipped her shoulders and took two steps towards me. Her fingers flexed, her eyes darting from me to her boss. The woman looked scarred and reckless, capable of incredible bravery. Camilla's muscle/bodyguard: what was her name again? Something funny…

My senses pricked fully awake, tickled the skin across my shoulder-blades and up along my neck. I visualized where my guns were, which one I'd reach first if I needed to. I could almost feel my pupils dilate, the moment reduced to a hard black circle. I swallowed and blew smoke in this chick's face, saying, "Yeah? And what the fuck do you want? Police business, sister. Whyn't you go mind your own for five minutes?"

The woman looked at Camilla once more, then me again, licking her dry lips, a strange look of regret and anticipation on her chipped, leathery face. The moment got minutely harder, noticeably harder. I braced myself.

Then Camilla said, "Alright, Merrylegs. It's alright." She

laughed. "Stand down, soldier. Detective Auf der Maur here is an old friend. Just dropped by for a little chat. Ain't that right, sm... Ain't that right, Genie?"

I nodded and smiled. "That's right, Camilla. Old friends."

We both knew where we stood now; and Camilla knew I wasn't in the mood for fun and games.

"You heard her, Merrylegs," she said, while still looking at me. "Go find something to occupy yourself. I think I'm safe enough in the company of Hera's Finest?"

She raised her eyebrows, all *faux*-innocence, and chuckled. I laughed too, despite myself. Merrylegs sloped off to a table in the far corner, pretending to read the *Hera Investigator*, keeping an eye and an ear on us. Merrylegs—that was it. I couldn't quite recall how she got that name. The music had shifted in tone, moving from the liquid-silver intro, that wash of high-hat cymbals and two-note bass, easing down, getting groovy. A looped horn motif came in, off the beat slightly, getting *very* groovy. The spoken refrain repeated at odd intervals. I'd have to ask Camilla what the song was called before I left.

For now I asked her this: "You know why I'm here?"

"Sure. You're checking into the Greenhill kid's murder, and you know she used to hang out in some of my places. So now you wanna pump me. Drink?"

I shook my head. "Working."

"Don't worry, Genie, I won't tell. No? Suit yourself. You'll allow me fix something for myself?"

I fluttered my hand extravagantly in the direction of the bottles behind the counter. Camilla bowed and walked around to them. So: we were still parrying, still shadowboxing. Okay. Be patient, Genie. Be cool.

She snapped her fingers twice and told the bartender, "Take off. Have a smoke for ten minutes." The girl left and Camilla mixed a shot of something clear and a shot of something dark and a third shot into a tall glass, threw in some ice, put her hand over the top and shook it vigorously. Then she grabbed a straw and took a deep sip.

"You know what I call this? The Hoochie Coochie. Makes the girls drop their drawers quicker'n the hookers down Whinlatter."

"Cute, Camilla. Now finish your drink, sit the fuck down and start talking."

I stubbed out my Dark Nine under my toe and popped onto a barstool. She slugged back her drink and glared at me for a few seconds, but there was something half-hearted about it. Like this was a little role she felt obliged to play, out of respect for the whole cop-crook dynamic, but she wasn't feeling it in her gut. Finally Camilla dropped the glare, dropped the glass, came back around the counter and sat next to me.

She said quietly, "Okay, Genie. You've always played fair with me, so this one time you'll get it easy. But next time bring a warrant for my arrest or bring your dancing shoes, one or other."

"Fine. What can you tell me about Madeleine?"

"Madeleine. Madeleine was a wash-out, a space cadet. A total fucked-in-the-head far-gone baby. Poor kid. Shit to hear about that. I mean, she was alright, you know? Nice girl. Always real polite, said please and thank you every time. And there were a lot of times. She started, uh, frequenting my drinking establishments about two years ago. Nah, more. Two-and-a-half, maybe. Though she was legal age, in case you're wondering."

I smiled wryly. "Right. Because you'd never serve to under-age girls, huh?"

"Actually, I don't. Believe it if you want. There's no need in this town. More than enough full-grown dames needin' their fix of alcohol. Don't worry, Genie, I ain't gone all moralistic on you in my old age."

I waved a hand and felt tired—tired in the head, tiredness washing through my mind. "Oh look, I don't care. Right now I don't give a shit about the drinking laws. I just wanna find out what happened to Madeleine."

Camilla nodded. I said, "Go on. Space cadet—how so?"

"Just a flake, you dig? Her head was on fucking Mars or someplace. She spoke like a whacked-out drunk even before she'd started drinking. Crazy stuff, all over the place. I could never understand her."

"Spoke about what?"

"That's what I'm telling you, little genius. I don't know. It was unintelligible, gibberish. Bits of songs. Why she didn't like French fries, or such-and-such the movie star. Whatever had come into her head that minute, random thoughts. Childhood memories, little things she remembered from when she was small. There was a lot of that. The color of a favorite overcoat she had as a kid, what she used to call her toys. And plans for the future, stupid shit that didn't make a lick of sense. Said she was gonna, someday she said she'd 'step through a magic door and become someone else.' Here I quote. And I don't think she meant metaphorically. I mean, I think she believed it. She was going to be transformed, or resurrected, or something."

Now another horn, maybe a sax, was worming its way around the tune, deep and warm, basso profundo, those high-hats still ditzing and spritzing behind it all. Budda-*bum*, tsh-tsh-tsh-tshhh… I let the music play on my senses for a few moments then said to myself, "Guess that's not going to happen now, Madeleine."

"Guess not." Camilla lit a cigarette. "Anything else?"

"When did you last see her in one of your places?"

She shrugged. It's remarkable how certain people can bring so much of their personality and reputation to the most innocuous of actions. Camilla shrugged, and that tiny, uncomplicated movement of the shoulders contained within it insouciance, menace and a bored, amused sort of half-interest. I repeated the question and sensed Merrylegs tensing, just a bit, behind me. I tensed too and asked it a third time.

Camilla sighed and blew out smoke and said, "Dunno. Coupla weeks ago. Not that recent but not that long. I know you're too smart to buy some bullshit about 'Oh but I haven't seen her in months, Detective', so I won't feed you any. It was a few weeks back. The recent past, you could say. Drinking on her own for once."

"So she usually had company."

"Oh yeah. Almost always."

"Who? Did you know any of them?"

"Not by name. I'd maybe recognize some faces if you lined 'em up for me. ...Actually, there was one. Merrylegs. Who was that chick used to hang with Madeleine Greenhill? You know, the one with the brown curly hair. Stacked. Quiet. Sorta shuffled around. What was her name?"

Merrylegs screwed her face into a comical contortion as she thought. She looked like a weasel with an itch. I smiled and covered it by pretending to cough into my hand. Then the muscle said, "Ginny. That's what the Greenhill girl used to call her. Ginny, uh...Ginny Newman."

Bing. Hello once more, Virginia.

Merrylegs added, "Sorry, Camilla, I don't know nothing else about her. But I can find out if you want."

I raised my eyebrows and said, half-laughing, half-affronted, "If *she* wants?"

Camilla laughed as well. Merrylegs said, doleful and sincere, "I'm not trying to be funny but I don't work for you, Detective."

Fair enough. I turned back to Camilla who dismissed her bodyguard with a flick of her hand. I said, "Which of your bars and clubs did Madeleine go to most often? Do you know?"

She chewed it over. "This one, maybe. Saw her in here a lot, but then again, I'm here a lot myself. Uh, lemme think... Xanadu. She liked that. Youngish crowd. Loud music, you know, louder than here." A pause. "Shit. I don't know, Genie. I'm trying to help you here but I just don't know. Some of them, all of them.

Madeleine Greenhill got around, know what I'm saying? Probably wasn't a dive in Hera City where the bartenders didn't know her by name and reputation."

I held back for a moment then jumped straight into it: "Know anything about a drug habit?"

"Whose? Mine? Yours? Or someone else's?"

"So we're back to being cute. Someone else's, yes."

"This someone else being someone we may have just been talking about?"

I nodded. "Mm-hm. Officially I'll deny it, but yeah. She was a user. We found track-marks. Four months, they reckon."

Camilla shook her head, a very definitive motion. "Nah. Nothin'. I ain't heard nothin', and you know that's legit. You know I don't truck with that shit, Genie. I got, ah... Well. Let's just say I got my fingers in enough pies. I don't need the heat from Narco. Again, please believe me, I ain't gone all moralistic on you. It's simple business smarts."

"Methinks the lady doth protest too much."

"You thinks that? Ha. Think all you like, Detective. Just don't fuckin' think I've gone soft."

The last notes were dying away, moving from speaker to speaker, little sonic gasps around the room. The voice instructing us to get together, to put our hands together. The cymbals had almost faded beyond audible range; now there was just an insistent four- or five-note motif, maybe a keyboard, maybe strings. It was hard to tell, it was so quiet, almost gentle, those final breaths, repeating, weakening, dying. I hopped off my stool and said, "What's that piece of music called again? The one that was playing just there."

Camilla regarded me with a look of self-satisfaction—I assumed her artistic taste was being vindicated by me asking. "That? It's called *Rose Rouge*. Sort of acid-jazz. You like?"

"I like. *Rose Rouge*. Red rose. Makes sense, I suppose." We began walking to the door and I said, "Never took you for a music-lover, Camilla."

"Nah. Most don't. To them the arts and my, uh...*business* are incompatible."

"You don't agree, obviously."

"What I do and who I am ain't the same thing, Genie. It's more complex than that. But I think you knew that already."

We had reached the door and Camilla actually had her hand on my back, guiding me outside onto the street, away, away, far away with my intrusive questions and annoying authority to ask them. I didn't care. Like I said, I was tired. It had been a long and extremely busy day, a bizarre day, chaotic, almost fevered. I wanted—I *needed*—a long bath, a few drinks and sleep. To sleep, perchance to dream of Cassandra the wonder woman. I stood on the pavement and lit a Dark Nine, about to turn back and say cheerio to Camilla, when I remembered something I'd meant to ask; not connected to her directly, but she might know something.

"Hey. One more question."

She said impatiently, "What?"

"You ever heard of a place called That Island? Some sort of club, like a private nightclub? I know it's not yours but I thought maybe you might have..."

She had grabbed me above the elbow and whisked me back inside the door before I knew what was what. She bundled me along the corridor, into a quiet corner, still clamping my arm in her powerful grip.

I laughed nervously. "What?"

"What do you know about that place?"

"Not much. That's why I'm asking you. Camilla, what is it?"

"Don't mess with that place, Genie. Even the mobsters don't go there. I'm telling you now. I'm warning you, if you wanna look at it like that. Don't go near it."

She towered over me with a weird look in her eyes, boring into mine but distant, agitated. Not the cool-as-all-hell Camilla I knew, the totally-in-control Camilla. She still held my arm. I gave it a little jiggle to let her know; she looked down at where she had me in her grasp and let go. Camilla breathed out heavily. She looked as tired as I felt. I didn't say anything, just let the moment get its breath back.

Then she looked around the corridor and back at me and said quietly, "Genie, you asked me about That Island so I'm telling you: steer clear. I wasn't joking—you don't mess with that joint. Even the likes of me don't."

"But *why*? I'm sorry, I have to ask. It's my duty as a cop."

Camilla smiled and nodded. "Why? Because it's too goddamn weird. They ain't doing it for the money. You dig me? These broads are into something creepy. I've heard tell of orgies, real bizarre shit, organized for the full fucking moon, or the new moon, whatever, or timed to coincide with the head lady's period. How's that? Weird enough for you?"

"Right. Orgies."

"Sure. Only it's not so much a sexual thing—shit, I can arrange something like that for a client no problem."

We both smiled again. Amazing how that simple lift of the corners of your mouth can release tension, like the face is opening sluice gates of the mind, clearing a blockage.

Camilla went on, "This ain't like that. It ain't...*normal*. Sex and drugs and rock 'n' roll I can comprehend, but this... It's like some kinda cult or something. Channeling spirits, goddesses...chants and incantations, candles, fucking incense, stars and pentagrams drawn in chalk on the floor... This is all what I heard. I haven't been there. I *won't* be going there. These religious cult things, they creep me out. I like my religion straight-up and mainstream. I was brought up Catholic, I don't know if you knew this. But That Island is bad voodoo, kiddo. And I'm telling you this 'cause I like you. Like I said, you always played fair with me. So here's some friendly advice from your Aunt Camilla: *steer clear*."

She lit two cigarettes and gave one to me. I took a puff—*ouch*, that's strong stuff—coughed my way back to equilibrium and said, "But what is it? Is it a nightclub, a brothel, what?"

"Neither. It's a private club. A place where likeminded people gather. No business side to it, no profit. Which always makes me nervous. It exists for its own sake. Basically a very large house, nice gardens, looks pretty from the outside. But the thing is, again, it's *private*. You don't just show up there. You get invited."

"Who owns it? Who's behind it?"

Camilla shook her head. "I don't know. Nobody seems to know." There was a pause. "Why are you asking about it? Was the Greenhill kid mixed up with them? Tell me no, please."

I looked at her for a full five seconds and decided, no, she's not fishing for information or playing the game, she's not being the gangster right now: she's just a woman called Camilla who's concerned and curious. She had the right to know some of it. I said, "I got information—which I believe to be solid—that linked Madeleine to this place, That Island. I'm not sure how closely. Maybe she went there once, maybe she went there often, maybe she knew someone who knew someone who knew the girl who works the coat-check. I don't know. It may not even lead anywhere but I gotta cover all the bases until this thing is cleared, one way or the other."

Camilla nodded once more. Then a thought struck me and I voiced it aloud: "Funny Misericordiae didn't call a halt to her daughter's bad behavior right there. If That Island's as suspicious as it seems, as strange... Just, boomph, 'That's the end of it, Madeleine—no more drinking and carousing, no more carrying on. You've gone too far and now you're coming home.' I mean, it's one thing indulging her rebelliousness, hoping she'll grow out of it. But this sounds way beyond the normal misbehavior of boozing and sleeping around."

"How would she have known? The kid was wild. Misery didn't know the half of it."

"She must have. That's my source: a team of PIs she had

tailing the girl. They referenced the place in a report made to her, but they were discreet about it. Just described it as a 'club' of some sort. No mention of orgies or goddesses or anything close to it."

"D'nno. Maybe the dicks were wary of telling her. I mean, nobody likes being the bearer of bad news, right? Not this bad. Not to someone like Misery. Maybe they got scared, put it in the report, real casual like, so's she couldn't catch 'em on it later, but vague enough that they'd hope the old bird wouldn't notice much." Camilla shrugged. "Hell, maybe she *did* know. Maybe Misery knew all about it and couldn't admit it to herself. It's gotta be a hell of a thing, for a woman like her, facing up to something like that."

That made some sense. Both angles made some sense. If *I* was the paid detective and I came across something this weird, this out-of-bounds, cults and orgies and moon-worship and whatever-the-fuck-else, would I have the guts to give it to her straight? A woman like Misery, that old dragon with the blood-curdling reputation, and more, a famously devout religious traditionalist... Probably not. And then there was the flipside: the possibility that one of her sleuths did give her the full skinny and she couldn't take it. That one was less likely—Misery seemed to me possessed of one of those unbreakable spirits, like a sheer rock wall rising up inside her, strengthening her, straightening her, implacable and impenetrable. But...who knows? Only one person did, and I sure as shit wasn't going to ask her.

"Hey. Snap out of it."

Camilla had one hand towards the door. Merrylegs stood behind her, a little extra encouragement for me to leave. The nightclub queen said, "You got all you're gonna get from me. Now beat it, please. Having the bulls around ain't good for my reputation."

I nodded and smiled. I was doing that a lot lately. "You know, Camilla, for such a rough old dog, you're surprisingly perceptive of human nature. Anyone ever tell you that?"

"Sure. Just before I set her legs in concrete and chucked her in the river. That's a joke, by the way, so don't waste your time checking through the unsolveds."

The three of us ambled to the door. Merrylegs went out onto the street first and stood there, hands behind her back, sad-faced and resolute. I stepped out and said to her, "Hey, why do they call you Merrylegs, anyway?"

She looked at her boss as though seeking permission, then smiled at me. "It's 'cause I'm such a good dancer."

I must have looked skeptical because then I heard Camilla say, "Go ahead, Merrylegs. Show her what you got. Give our little detective some of that soft-shoe shuffle."

The hood lifted the hat off her head and started humming, something jazzy, old school and big band, a nice swing to it. Then she began waggling the hat gently and tap-tap-tapping her way along the pavement, feet crossed, bent low, an easy sway to her, quick-slow, quick-quick-slow. People stopped to watch as she hummed and shuffled and held our attention locked down.

Well, I'll be damned. Merrylegs *could* dance. I left her to it, moving like a professional, like someone in an old-fashioned film, under the cheap yellow spotlights of a Hera City backstreet.

Chapter 15

Arlene

I SLEPT late the next morning. I slept long and deep the night before. For the first time in an age, I dreamed.

Someone cleverer than me once said that dreams were meaningless; they were just the sense information of the previous day being ordered and discarded, the subconscious cleaning house, jettisoning the mental junk, ensuring fresh clarity for another day in the real world. I don't know about that. I slept for ten solid hours and it felt like I was dreaming for every endless minute. It felt realer than real.

I dreamed of Madeleine Greenhill underwater but it couldn't have been Madeleine because her dress was different and she had Misery's face. I dreamed of Poison Rose and she had Madeleine's face. I dreamed of Virginia Newman even though I didn't know what she looked like. I dreamed of ancient-looking crows sitting on Madeleine's tombstone or keeping guard from the high trees above, their horrible discordant cackle like a warning to stay away. I dreamed of murky water lapping against the rotting old piers at Whinlatter, water like an oil spill, tired and viscous, coating all surfaces, sucking Madeleine-who-couldn't-have-been-Madeleine further into the darkness. I even dreamed of goddamn Merrylegs doing her strange little shuffle in the twilight glow of the streetlamps.

I dreamed of Cassandra the wonder woman, who was lying on a fur rug on the floor of a round room I'd never seen before, naked and covering her nakedness with crossed arms and legs. A slice of incredibly bright light streamed in, accentuating her every curve, illuminating her, making her golden. Even in sleep I ached for her, I wanted to possess her absolutely. But as I moved forward and reached out to touch Cassandra she smiled and playfully waved a finger in a "tut-tut" motion and said, "Ah-*ah*—

that's as far as you get, Detective."

I woke up sticking to sweat-soaked sheets and with a dryness in my mouth like I'd been mainlining straight whiskey for four days. And my desire for Cassandra lingered on.

I took a long hot shower to clear my head and heart, got dressed and headed for the Dicks building without breakfast. It was nearing 11 by the time I arrived, hoping my tardiness wouldn't be noticed. I needn't have bothered hoping. Etienne was actually sitting at my desk when I got there, skimming through reports, her reading glasses perched on her nose. They made her look like a bird, for some reason.

She said without looking up, "Jamie Sobel has come forward to represent the five women. Where have you been?"

I spluttered something, a muttered apology, keep it vague, keep the conversation moving forward. Etienne finally looked up. I was relieved to see her expression was more concern than disappointment.

She said, "You're late for work, Auf der Maur. That's not like you. Is everything alright?"

"Uh, yeah. I'm just, I'm tired, Chief. Sorry, I slept in. That's literally it."

"Is this case too much for you? Should I rotate you off it? I can bring over someone from Narco. It's been quiet for them recently. Maybe Guardiola."

"No, I'm fine. I'm on top of it, honestly. I'm just... I'll be okay. Just tired. I had a good night's sleep last night."

"You left a crime scene without reporting, there were two attempts on your life, and now this. You should have been at the arraignment hearing this morning. It's not a requirement but as the investigating officer... Tell me again that everything is fine, Auf der Maur. Because it doesn't seem that way from where I'm sitting. Wherever I happen to be sitting."

She gave a tiny smile. I said, "I swear to God, Chief—everything really is okay. I was just, yesterday was hectic, I was all over the place, I mean literally. I was...exhausted by the end of it. But I'm okay now. It won't happen again."

Etienne nodded, semi-satisfied. "I told you before that I trust your mind, how you think. You're smart and you've got your head screwed on right. I know that. So I'm going to trust you again—for now. But any more odd stuff, anything else happens outside *exact* procedure: I'll pull you off the case."

"Yes, Ma'am."

She gestured to a chair at the near side of the desk. "Sit."

I sat. She straightened her bunch of documents on the desk, lined them up straight with the edge, placed them flat with her spectacles on top. She looked at me again and said, "You heard what I said about Jamie Sobel?"

"Yeah, sorry, she's...what exactly?"

"She is now representing the five women who 'confessed', quote-unquote, to the murder of Madeleine Greenhill. Hofton, Spaulding, Klosterman, Villegas and Arendt. Stood for them this morning at the hearing. During which, I might add, they all pleaded not guilty."

"But we've got confessions. I mean, I know they're bullshit confessions, but they're still confessions."

"Such is the wonder of our legal system, Detective. You can be caught doing the deed on live television and sign a confession in the victim's blood—doesn't matter. You have the right to a trial and the right to plead whatever way you see fit."

"It's such a set-up. Time-wasting tactics. Someone is totally pulling our chain here, Chief."

"Agreed. But there's nothing we can do about it right now. Let's just keep on as we are; as if those women didn't exist. Let's you keep on it."

"Sobel... How the hell does someone like her get mixed up in this?"

"She's a defense lawyer. She works for whoever will pay her. *C'est tout.* Nothing more to it than that, I would think."

Only 35, Jamie Sobel was the most successful, in-demand and well-remunerated attorney in Hera City. A brilliant, incandescent mind coupled with a personality that could dominate a courtroom while somehow never coming across as bullying or overly forceful. Sobel made juries warm to her as a woman and simultaneously believe she was omnipotent, she could not be wrong. I don't remember the last case she lost. As a cop I say this reluctantly, but she was a fucking legal genius. Which is why she charged what she liked and worked whatever cases took her fancy. Which made me figure that whoever was behind the five in lock-up had serious funds behind her, or them. Klosterman was probably solvent enough—public appearances, endorsements of athletic gear, though all that was now dead in the water. But Hofton only had a part-time job, Spaulding had none. Villegas, I supposed, did well out of her crèche. And Arendt would have been pulling down six figures probably, but rich enough to hire Jamie Sobel? Not a chance. CONSPIRACY, with a capital C and capital everything else.

I said, "Who's behind her? Who's paying the piper here?"

Etienne shrugged. "We don't know. And we've no way of finding out. 'Client-attorney privilege.' Extends to financial matters."

"And what happened? In court today."

"All five remanded in custody for trial. The prosecutor is hoping for a month from now, six weeks at most. No bail. Actually, Sobel didn't apply for bail, which I found… They all just filed in, stood there without a peep and filed out again. Like—like sheep. Like drugged women."

"They weren't, I presume? Drugged?"

"Tox reports all negative. They're clean. It's so strange. I was in the building for a meeting. Popped my head into court. Klosterman was the only who showed any sort of…life. Any fire. She's a scary one, that one. But the others? It's like they weren't even there. Their bodies stood before the judge but their minds..."

Etienne shrugged again. She lifted her glasses and the pile of documents and stood up, stretching her back in obvious discomfort. Small detectives' chairs weren't designed with tall bosses in mind. I stood too. She said, off-hand, "Anything else to report?"

I thought of Cella, thought of my two-way information feed. Etienne didn't need to know that right now, if ever. I scrunched up my face, pretending to be thinking, and said, "From yesterday? Um, not too much. Made a few calls on a few people. Got some useful stuff. I mean, nothing I can use right away, but you know. I'm, uh, we're getting there."

Etienne left without saying anything more. I needed a coffee. I'd lied to the Big Kahuna—that hadn't been a good night's sleep at all. It was too deep, too sensual, too many ghosts babbling for attention. I was starting to get a headache from tiredness, that dull throb behind the bridge of the nose.

I sauntered over to the main office, heading in the general direction of the coffee machine. An unusually large group of dicks was clustered around it, chattering excitedly, some making extravagant hand gestures, some with eyes open wide, one or two laughing in a way that suggested they felt they shouldn't be. I slipped between the knots of people and filled my mug with hot brown something—possibly coffee of some sort. Then I turned and recognized one of the group, by face if not by name.

"Hey," I said. "What's all the commotion? One of you win the lottery or something?"

"Hey yourself. Genie, isn't it?"

"That's right."

"I knew I knew you. Met you at...uuh...yeah, Leigh Knowles' party. A couple of months back."

"Leigh's party. Okay."

"Arlene Galanis." We shook hands. "You're Homicide, right? I seem to remember you saying you were Homicide."

"Yeah. Good memory. You?"

"Narco. Two years, three almost. Used to be Homicide myself. Think we might have just missed each other there."

"Cool. So, uh, are you guys celebrating a big bust or something?"

Arlene smiled. "No. Nothing like that. This is bizarre. It's just this weird fucking story. Came in, like, an hour ago. Chick got killed down in the Zig-Zag this morning. They've arrested the shooter. Anyway here's the interesting part: the dead woman? She was a pro herself."

"No way."

She nodded and said, "Yes way. A bad-ass for-real assassin. And you know what she was called? Slaymaker."

I burst out laughing, spluttering coffee onto my chin. "No *way*! Really, this time, no way. You've gotta be kidding me. A professional killer called Slaymaker?"

Arlene laughed as well. "Yes-yes-yes way. And it gets even better: the one who killed her is called Tammy Gun."

"Aw, bullshit."

"No bullshit, Genie. 'Course, that's a fake name. Tammy's proper surname ain't Gun, that's just her handle on the street. But Slaymaker, sure. It's real. I remember all these fucking idiots from my stint in Homicide. Did some time on an organized crime task-force, you know, that kind of thing."

I took another sip of coffee. "What happened anyway? They get into a little tiff over who's supposed to be whacking who?"

Arlene pointed a thumb towards the holding cells. "Girls back there're saying that old Tammy is saying they just got into a fight and ended up in a quick-draw. Like the fucking Wild West, right?! Two gunslingers, facing each other in the dusty streets of the Zig-Zag. Draw, bang! Down goes Slaymaker. Tammy more or less turned herself in. Think a patrol car was passing or something. Anyway that's all she'll say. It was a personal thing, like a fight that got out of control. Says Slaymaker pulled her piece first and she shot in self-defense. What a wonderful fucking world, huh?"

She laughed and thumped me playfully on the shoulder, then moved off, back to her colleagues, back to work. I thought about what Cella had said, the rumors of Misericordiae putting a bounty on the head of whoever killed her daughter. A few days later two shooters get into a "personal thing" and it ends up with one of them dead, and this is all a coincidence, just unhappy happenstance? I don't think so. Misery might want the murderer alive but these dames, the likes of Tammy Gun and Slaymaker, they're too stupid and too greedy to read the fine print on the unwritten contracts of their industry. I figure one of them thought to bring down the other one and bring her to Misery—dead, yes, but half a bounty's better than none at all. And dead women can't defend themselves by saying, "It wasn't me who killed your girl."

But all this was just speculation on my part. I topped up my coffee and returned to my desk, dialing the number Cella gave me. A fairly young voice answered, late teens, maybe early twenties: "Hello?"

"Hi there. Genie Auf der Maur. I'm calling for Marcella?"

"Just a second."

The sound of a phone being put down on a desk. Distant, muffled noises. Then a heavy wheezing, a chair creaking, Cella clearing her throat. She said, "Genie. So soon?"

I chuckled and said, "Hey, Cell. Listen, two quick questions for you. You heard anything about a shoot-out in the Zig-Zag this morning? Two pros slugging it out? One of 'em's dead now."

"Yeah, someone said something…" She lit a cigarette, the flare of a match followed by the wind-tunnel sound of her exhaling smoke. "Tammy Gun and that other broad, right? I got the basic gist. Great fucking loss to society, I'm sure. What about it? Connected to your thing?"

"I don't know. Maybe. Maybe something to do with that contract you mentioned."

Cella paused, remembering. "Oooh. Right. *That* contract. Yeah. I mean, yeah, maybe. Anything's possible in this crazy world we got going here."

"You really think so?"

Her voice dropped the patina of sarky playfulness. She said quietly, "Genie, you know what I think. *Anything* is possible with her. Whether this Tammy thing is or isn't connected, I don't know. But it could be, sure."

"Okay."

"And the second question?"

"Yeah. Uh, you ever heard of a place called That Island? Some sort of private club out in the 'burbs?"

"No, I don't think... What's the name again? The Island?"

I could hear her scribbling in a notepad. I said, "*That* Island. A private club, like a members only thing."

"That Island. No...can't say I ever heard of it. Should I have?"

"Probably not. It's not the sort of joint that advertises in the *Hera Investigator*."

"Mm. And this *is* connected?"

"Think so."

"Alright. Well, I'll check it out. See if I can't dig up something more."

"You're a sweetheart. Talk soon."

"Anytime, kiddo."

The connection terminated. I held the receiver for a second, listening to the distant pips escaping from its plastic mouth. I hadn't spoken to Odette since the day the baton lady ramped her car at me, which made my former paramour the only woman on Misery's Top Ten list yet to be officially questioned. "Officially questioned"—ugh. It sounded all wrong for her. Odette and me, well, we had that history... We'd played our individual roles in our collective drama, running nightly for three years. We knew where we stood there, who we were; we were familiar with the scenery, the dynamics, the characters' motivation, our entries and exits. Now circumstances had arrived at the theater back-door with a fresh script, a radical reworking, and expected us to slip into these new parts with the ease of a versatile veteran.

The role of interrogator to Odette didn't suit me, I realized. I was never good at acting. I was Genie, straightforward, easy to read, honest in all senses. I knew my duty and knew my place. I knew where to stand on the stage. Now I had to stand somewhere else. It made me feel muddled, put out of joint.

I pressed the disconnect button twice and opened a fresh line. Odette's phone rang for ten, maybe 12 seconds, then the sicken-ingly familiar disembodied tones of the message machine. "You've reached the home of Odette Crawford. I can't..." Strike three. Either Odette had given up entirely on answering her telephone or she was currently bound and gagged by a wild-eyed maniac who was ransacking her collection of valuable musical artifacts. Part of the original score for Lili Boulanger's *La Princess Maleine*, handwritten and time-beaten. A violin bow said to have once belonged to Jacqueline du Pré. A beautiful, ornate fan used during *Madama Butterfly* by the incomparable La Divina.

Where had she got all that stuff again? I couldn't remember. And how had she paid for it? I couldn't remember that, either. Her rich parents, I guess.

I'd have to call 'round to our old home. Goddamn. That wouldn't make it any easier. I ordered myself to stop whining, grabbed my car keys and hit for the door.

She wasn't there. Or at least, she didn't answer when I rang the bell at Number 57 Datlow Street six or eight times. I stepped back onto the street and squinted up—no shadowy movement, no twitching curtains, nothing. I pushed the bell again, twice, three times. Counted down the long minute it would take for her to descend the several flights of stairs from her apartment. She didn't appear when I reached 60 and didn't appear as I lit a Dark Nine and thought about what to do next. I was pretty certain

Odette was tangential to this investigation, at most, so I could keep moving forward without talking to her. I supposed I wanted to talk to her, though. I *should* have wanted to, anyway. But I wasn't sure that I did.

I looked up to the window again. Those familiar, heavy-lace curtains. And what lay behind them... I hadn't stepped inside my old apartment door since the night I split, half a year ago. I say "split", but it wasn't really like that. There were no tearful entreaties from Odette, no pleading with me to stay. And on the other hand, no angry demands that I get the fuck out of her life this minute. (Odette never swore, anyway. Far too well brought up for that.) It was all perfectly civilized and rational. It was calm and shivery-cold. An hour beforehand she'd said out loud what both of us were thinking: "It's over between us. You should leave." Such finality in those few quiet words; no appeals, no returns. So why wait, why delay the necessary amputation? I immediately packed my belongings—not many—and walked away without another word passing between us. Literally not one; not even "Goodbye, take care, hope to see you again." Neither of us had anything left to say.

That felt like a long time ago now. We'd gradually re-established communication after a few months, after enough time had passed for wounds to close and emotional equilibrium to be restored. Enough time for us to start forgetting.

The end of my cigarette burned my fingers and I realized I'd been standing here for several minutes, spaced-out, glazed-eyed in reverie. Then sensory instinct kicked in again and I realized someone was watching me watching my old place. Tall, skinny, maybe dark-haired; my peripheral vision scrabbled for scraps of information. She was standing behind me, at about five o'clock as I faced forward, on the other side of the street. I knew, but couldn't exactly see, that she was leaning against a lamp-post, trying to look inconspicuous, to blend in, twisting a newspaper in her hands. I chanced a little turn of the head and saw that she had spotted this and was now staring into the distance intently, like someone pretending to be on the look-out for a rendezvous, a friend running late.

It wasn't the baton killer. This woman's face was obscured but I could tell from the body shape, the absence of that brutal heft, the way my wannabe assassin's shoulders had seemed to roll even when she wasn't moving.

What the hell, I thought, let's provoke something. Let's push things forward.

I stepped off the curb and started walking briskly towards her, one arm in the air. "Hey," I called. "Hey, I need to talk to you…"

She moved faster than I thought she would, dropping the paper and scuttling off, back towards the city center. I stepped up my speed and she broke into a trot and I broke into a jog and she broke into a run. Then she made a quick turn right, onto one of the tiny residential streets off Datlow, and I stopped dead. No point following her down that labyrinth, and anyway, on what grounds was I chasing her? A person had the legal right to stand on a street and the legal right to run in public.

I looked down at the woman's discarded paper, now wrapped around the lamp post like a soft car smash. The headline on the front read "MADDY LAID TO REST", with a very blurry paparazzi shot of yesterday's burial, so murky and out-of-focus it was actually pointless to print it. That could have been a picture of almost anything. It irritated me that they'd called her "Maddy." They didn't know the girl, what made them think they could use that stupid pet name? Her name was Madeleine.

Back at HQ an hour later and I got a break. A definitive, unmistakable, this-could-be-it moment. I found out who had tried to kill me.

The duty officer from my trip to the catacombs, the cheery Kildare, had left an urgent message. I urgently returned her call. And she urgently told me: "Detective Auf der Maur, how are ya?

Listen, don't say anything for a minute, just hear me out, okay? Now I'm real sorry about this but I screwed up the other day, the day you were here? Looking for the big bulky lady who looks like Dolores de los Lobos. We couldn't find her and it's all my fault. See, there was *another* book of mug-shots we didn't go through—they were in another room, we had some problems with damp a while back and had to dry-line the whole place. Anyway some of the stuff got moved around a bit and obviously *some* of it didn't get moved back, ha ha!"

She gave that endearing honk-laugh I remembered from the other day and continued, "Well I found this book, squeezed in under a radiator, so I says to myself, 'Why drag Detective Auf der Maur all the way back up here if it's just going to be a big waste of her time, her time's more precious than yours, you got nothing else to do down here anyway.' You know, am I right?"

I wanted to tell Officer Kildare to please, *please* get to the point—if, indeed, there was one—but I couldn't. I was smiling too much.

She said, "I had your description of the bird in question so I went right on ahead and looked through the mug-shots myself. Gave 'em a good, real *thorough* examination. And, well, that's why I called you."

I laughed out loud, from amusement and exhaustion and strange affection for this sweet, scatty woman I didn't know. "Uh-huh. And...?"

"And I think we got her. I think I'm looking at your Jane Doe right now. And I tell ya, she is one ornery-looking cove. You had her description right, alright."

I was already out of my seat. "I'll be over to you in ten minutes. Hold on."

"No need. I'm sending a facsimile of the page by courier. Full color. Should be at your building by now. Marked for your attention."

"Great work, Officer Kildare. Excellent work. Thank you."

"Just doing my job, Detective," she said proudly. "That's all. Doing my job."

She was called Erika Baton. That wasn't her proper name, I soon found out, and that wasn't the name printed underneath the mug-shot. Here she was plain old Mary Ann Murphy—so obviously a fake, I'm amazed the processing officers bought it. She'd been arrested on a drink-driving rap; the information panel didn't elaborate, didn't tell me if the woman had been charged or convicted or what. But then again, I guess someone like Erika Baton doing time for a DUI is a bit like locking up a serial arsonist for littering violations.

"One ornery-looking cove": Kildare had that right. Erika was younger in this picture—I estimated by about eight years—her hair was even shorter, cropped almost to the bone, and the tattoo was absent. But some faces don't change; some people don't. She had the same hardness about her, the same indifferent, insolent glare; that exact same horrifying blankness of the eyes that I remembered from the other night. Hard to forget a thing like that when someone is leaning over your prone body, whispering obscenities, half a second from ending your life. I thought I felt myself shiver but maybe that was just a cold breeze squeaking in the window behind me.

I found Arlene Galanis at her station, poring over surveillance shots of pimps strutting and strolling along the Bolo red-light drag. Talk about people not changing: they all looked identical, if not in specific features then in aspect—cynical, brutish, suffused with a weird sort of anxiety, a drug-rush jitter. I dropped the picture onto her desk, without comment. Arlene looked up at me, smiled quizzically and examined the photograph.

Then I said, "Do you know this one?"

She nodded slowly. "Sure. Sure I do. Erika Baton. Again, not her real name."

"A pseudonym?"

"Mm. More like a *nom de guerre*. Sounds French, doesn't it? You know, like 'baah-tohn?' But it's nothing to do with that. She's called that because it's her trademark weapon—this retractable steel baton she uses on her victims. Fucking terrifying thing. Never proved, of course. Officially Erika's clean as a whistle, relatively speaking."

"I can prove it. She tried to kill me with it two nights ago."

"Well. That *is* interesting. I mean, this psycho bitch is a psycho bitch, no question, but I never heard of her gunning for cops before. Did she know you were one of us?"

"I don't know. I think so. I think it was a contract for someone else."

Arlene smiled wearily. "Oh yeah. That'd be Erika. She kills for money, not for fun—the fun's in the killing itself, right? An added fucking bonus of her work. ...I think her real name's Erika Schmidt, but none of us are 100 per cent on that. She was suspected of at least a dozen murders during my time in Homicide—again, nothing ever proven. Obviously, or we'd have her in here and not out there."

"How come I've never heard of her?"

"Dunno. She's been keeping a low profile, I guess. I remember rumors, my last month before transfer, something going really bad on a hit; like, the wrong person took it, or maybe a kid got killed. Something awful. I guess fuck-wad here hit the floor for a while, let the heat cool off. From both sides. But I'm just guessing really, Genie."

"Right...that could have been how it played out."

"Yeah, I mean she's an idiot, you know? Good at her job but she's got a fucking rock for a brain. Probably hung out in some crappy apartment watching TV for two years and didn't once get bored."

I swallowed hard and said it: "So how worried should I be?"

Arlene thought about this. She twirled a beautiful pen in her slim fingers as she said, "Well...you're obviously trained and can handle yourself, so I figure you should be okay. But watch your back. Erika's fucking demented. Strong as an ox, relentless, ruthless—and thorough. She's a maniac but she knows how to cover her tracks. Some low-life instinct, I guess. The rat knowing how to escape the sewer. All our witnesses in those other cases had a nasty habit of turning up with their skulls crushed, you know? No witness, no conviction."

"Alright. Thanks, Arlene."

She nodded okay, and I turned to go. Then she called after me: "Hey, Genie. Get the asshole for us, would you, honey? Bring that crazy bitch down."

I nodded back, unsure but determined, and left. The evening was drawing in and I had a date to prepare for.

Chapter 16

Cassandra

NEW romance makes everyone revert to being a teenager. You know that almost-permanent state of adolescence, where everything is heightened, everything's exaggerated, all your emotions are more colorful and more spectacular, and your senses are aflame? A new romance brings you back to that place whatever your age. I sat opposite Cassandra as she blew on a spoonful of steaming minestrone and felt 16 again.

I'm pretty sure the dumb smile pasted across my face hadn't weakened in the hour-and-a-half we'd been together. Remind me again how *I* managed to find myself at dinner with this beauty who was beyond beautiful? Please, don't take me for shallow or over-sexed or anything like that—I'm not. What first attracted me to Odette, for instance, wasn't her looks but different things, indefinable things: her gently sarcastic sense of humor, her love of art and music, the way she used to touch my upper arm while we spoke and leave it there a half-second longer than necessary.

But Jesus Christ, Cassandra… I believe there is such a thing as undeniable physical loveliness, just pure Beauty with a capital B: a face or figure that goes far beyond personal predilections and enters the realm of the universal. A Helen of Troy face, a Cleopatra or Greta Garbo face; the sort of face that could sink a battleship, bring down an empire, turn best friends into enemies and make ordinary women do insane things. Certain faces and physiques are so exquisitely perfect (and I mean that in its purest sense, not that they conform to some pre-ordained notion of plasticky flawlessness) that they almost transcend mere desire and become an art-form—an aesthetic, physiological representation of the divine and the absolute.

This woman really was fabulous, and then some. Hers was an imperial, grave beauty, grand and enduring, almost as intimidating as it was enticing, and I could have gazed on that face to infinity. Cassandra was divine, and amazingly, for this moment at least, she was mine.

We had met in the same bar I first encountered her; thankfully the same bartender wasn't on duty, so I was spared that awful post-binge social embarrassment. We had one drink—beer for me, wine for her; no more Ragnoud-Sabourin—then left for a lovely little bistro-style restaurant on the edge of the Zig-Zag. It was close enough to feel exotic and "authentic", whatever that means, but near enough to civilization so as not to scare away the post-theater crowd and dining paramours. Actually there seemed to be a lot of romance in the air tonight, in this place. An old couple across the way held hands so tenderly I almost cried, it was so sweet; two arty-looking gals in deliberately ugly clothes who stared intently into each other's eyes were, I guessed, on a reconciliatory date; another pair in their forties, sitting near the kitchen, smiled shyly and didn't say anything because it didn't need to be said.

Cassandra was wearing appropriately beautiful clothes: a midnight blue dress, thin-strapped and glittering, which fitted her figure like an angel's touch. She had an unadorned emerald on a dark chain around her neck, her hair piled high in a complicated, messy sculpture of pins and grips and falling locks of red flame. Blue eye-shadow complemented the dress and she had powdered her décolletage with some sort of gold-dust. It sparkled in the soft lights; she sparkled, her skin was glowing. I wore a sharp-cut trouser suit, the pants high-waisted with a fantastic flared kick, the jacket embroidered with a rose motif in red and green thread. My shirt collars were high and stiff and made me feel like someone very cool: proprietor of a fashionable art gallery, insouciant bass player in an alternative rock band. I looked nice, I think. I felt nice.

She pushed her bowl aside and lit a cigarette from the candle burning low between us. I breathed in that distinctive perfume—

it still made me think of the woman fully robed in black, only her kohl-lined amber eyes visible—and accepted the smoke as Cassandra passed it across to me. I took a drag and she smiled wryly, shaking her head.

I smiled too. "What? What's funny?"

"I still can't see you as a cop. I mean, a detective! It's... You, a fully-fledged, bona fide crime fighter. You're so..."

"Small? Unimposing? Immature? Feel free to stop me at any point here."

She laughed. "I was going to say gentle. And sweet. And pretty. Not what I presumed a cop would look like. That was my ignorant preconception."

"Ugh. 'Pretty.' The adjective of choice when you can't think of anything better."

"No, I don't mean it like that. You know I don't. You're more than pretty."

"Well, thank you. I have my moments, I suppose. I pale by comparison with you, though."

Cassandra blushed slightly and smiled down at the table without speaking.

I said, "Sorry. I didn't mean to make you feel uncomfortable. I'm just... Like, it's undeniable, you know? You are—amazing looking. It's just, it's a simple fact. You know it, everyone who's got eyes knows it."

She took my hand and squeezed it. "It's okay. Honestly. It's cool, I appreciate it. ...It's funny, I usually hate when people comment on how I look. And they're always doing it. 'You're too tall, you're too pale, you're beautiful, you're ugly, you're this and this and this.' God! Cringe. I'm there thinking, 'Please, *please* stop talking.' But you—I don't mind really when you say something."

"Now that *is* a real compliment."

"Yeah... It's true. I feel like there's nothing you could say that I wouldn't want to listen to."

"Aw, stop it. Now you're making *me* embarrassed."

She squeezed my hand with greater force. "I mean that, Genie. I didn't think I'd be saying that when we first met, but I do. I mean it."

We lapsed into silence as the waitress cleared our dishes and set down fresh cutlery for the next course. I finished the cigarette and took a break—from her, from the look and smell of her, that exotic perfume dazing my senses, the way her breast sloped down in an elegant curve, the way it rose and fell with her breathing. I needed that break. It had been a hectic afternoon.

I'd gone directly from Arlene to Chief Etienne who, fortunately, was at her desk—I was running on short time by that point. I told her about the mug-shot of Erika Baton. She asked if I could prove it was her who attacked me. I said there were no cameras in that part of the Zig-Zag so it was basically my word against hers; possibly enough for a conviction, depending on the circumstances. Etienne suggested we put out an all-points bulletin on Erika but I nixed it: that would only drive the killer underground because clearly we had a mole in the department. Etienne pooh-poohed the notion at first—her pride, I guess, wouldn't allow her to see it—but I pushed and insisted, referred back to our five songbirds and the specific Madeleine details they couldn't have known but somehow knew. We had to have a mole. Etienne finally agreed with me. She gave me the usual "keep on it, soldier" pep-talk. I thanked her and made two quick calls, putting the word out with Cella, and also Camilla and her army of scumbags and snitches. I told the gangster that I wanted this Erika fucking Baton but to be discreet about it—softly softly catchy monkey. Camilla said she was the soul of discretion itself and she'd maybe see what she maybe could do, *if* she felt well-disposed towards me. I told her to cut the shit. She said, "Maybe, small fry, maybe" and hung up. I tore home and showered and changed and made the rendezvous with seconds to spare.

The rendezvous, the assignation. I was a character in a historical novel, a Gothic romance, melodramatic and intoxicating, the meeting by the lake, the secret *billet-doux* urgently passed to the loyal and valiant messenger.

It was weird—there was a connection here. No, let me reword that: I *felt* a connection. I'm not a girly-girl, I don't believe in love at first sight or chocolate-box fantasies or any of that stuff. And yet, and yet… I felt a connection. We talked as the food arrived and talked more as we ate, about nothing really, trivialities and anecdotes, the instinctive channeling of conversation. We laughed at the same things and reached forward to touch fingers in the same moment. It felt easy and unforced and *right*, like waking up next to someone you care about and looking over at them through sleep-blurred eyes and smiling together and rolling as one into a more comfortable position. But nothing too heavy, not right away.

Two bitter, creamy coffees and a clean ashtray had been placed on our table by the time we got heavy.

"Tell me about yourself. Not Cassandra. The real you."

She deflected my entreaty: "Did you always have your hair short like that? I'm just curious. It suits you."

I let it slide for the moment and said, "No. Got it cropped a few years back when I realized that your own hair could be used as a weapon against you. And me, well—you can see how little I am. I don't need to give the villains any more of an advantage."

Cassandra nodded. "Mm-hm. And has it given you problems? In the job, I mean. Being small."

I considered the question. "Hmmm. Has it given me a problem…? I would probably say, yes and no. As in, it has advantages and disadvantages, you know? On the good side people tend to open up more to me than my colleagues. I think they think I'm not intimidating or threatening; they see me as this cute little kid who for some reason is going around asking questions and flashing a detective's badge. They feel more comfortable around me. But it's not so good if you're trying to shackle a 15-stone meth-head who's just buried a hatchet into the brains of her lover because of an argument over a game of poker. True story, by the way."

She grimaced, her skin actually paling. "Oh my God. That's horrible."

"Sorry, that wasn't nice. I take that back. You don't need to know about stuff like that. What I'm very clumsily trying to say is, being small is obviously a hindrance when it comes to physical tussles with people twice your size." I smiled. "And yet..."

"You tussle anyway."

"Yeah. I guess I like to tussle."

"Good. I guess I like to tussle, too."

Silence again. I lit a cigarette for both of us. Her hands lingered on mine as she took it, and I liked that very much.

Then Cassandra said, "So what's it like? Being a cop."

"It's okay. It's pretty good, I suppose."

"You must like it, though? You've been in the police for—how long?"

"Since I was a kid; since I left school. Went straight into the academy. So that's...what? About a dozen years. More—13. Lucky 13."

"And why did you join up?" she asked. "You don't have to tell me if you don't want. I'm just trying to...I don't know, get the back-story, I suppose."

"'The back-story': I love that phrase. One of those new phrases... Why did I join the police? Um...for a few different reasons. To do some good, you know? To do my part. To be involved in something bigger and more important than just me. There were—a lot of reasons, really. Yeah, I think that was maybe the main one: just to do something good. To contribute to society, right? That moral imperative. But, I mean, there was a personal impetus, too. Small girl in a big world. I wanted to be able to defend myself, physically. To kick ass if necessary."

I laughed and shrugged playfully. Cassandra laughed too. I continued, "This is weird but I'm only remembering this now, something that happened a long time ago. About a month before I joined up. I'd left school and had been, like, toying with the idea of a career in the police. So I was kicking around for the summer, waiting on exam results, whatever. Figuring out my options. Killing time. I was seeing this girl back then, a girl called Maggie, so we hung out a lot too."

"Well, that's a nice way to kill time."

"Yeah. It was. Uh, anyway, about mid-August I was walking home late from...somewhere. I don't remember exactly. Probably Maggie's place but it doesn't matter. And I was crossing Pasiphaë Prospect, there around the junction with, uh, Shoard to one side and Crown to the other? There was a lot of traffic on Pasiphaë that night—I think there might have been a big boxing match on or something. Lot of traffic, lot of noise, this big blustering wind screaming down the Prospect..."

I stopped, my inner eye snapping into focus—I was seeing it all again, lucidly, in full, terrible color. "And...I thought I heard a scream. From an alleyway a ways back, maybe a block or two. I stood on the pavement and listened and there it was, I thought I heard it a second time. But I couldn't be sure, it was too noisy. I mean, that could have been an alarm going off or an ambulance siren or a stray cat howling at the moon. I looked down towards where this—sound, if it even existed, was coming from."

I lit another cigarette and drew hard. "It was black as fucking pitch down there. Like, I mean, like the inside of night, you know? Dark, totally dark, and scary. I took a few steps towards the alley and then I heard the sound again. Definitely, a woman screaming. In pain, scared, *terrified*. But was it? Because I couldn't be sure, you know? I couldn't... Anyway: I couldn't go down there. I was too afraid. And my mind was telling me, you're imagining it, there's nobody there, just go home. Because those alleys, you're too young to remember this but back then? Those alleys off the Prospect were pretty dangerous. Lot of muggings, a few murders, sexual assaults. And I was afraid."

Cassandra placed her hand on top of mine again, its soft warmth permeating down through my skin like water through soil. I said, "I wondered afterwards: if I definitely knew, I mean *knew*, that what I'd heard was real, would I have still walked away? I like to think I wouldn't. I like to imagine swallowing my fear and marching in there and saving the day. I'll never know. All I know is, I walked away because I was scared. I told myself I was hearing things but really I was scared. And the next day I read about a woman being raped and murdered by a gang of vicious bitches. In a dark alleyway. Two blocks from Pasiphaë Prospect. Near the junction with Shoard and Crown."

I looked up at her and she was blurred in my vision and I realized I had tears in my eyes. I also realized I hadn't really thought about that night since I joined the force two days after reading about Helena Khan. That was her name. She was 28, a physiotherapist, single, on her way home from a yoga class. She was buried by her mother and two sisters. They planted a tree in her memory in the back garden of the oldest sister. Her mother died of cancer nine months later. I now remember all of this.

"Oh, Genie." Cassandra stood and leaned across the table, kissing me tenderly on the mouth. She placed a hand behind my head and kissed my eyes. "Genie, Genie. Let me kiss those tears away."

She sat back down, still holding my hand. I smiled and sniffled, saying, "I'm alright. Really, I'm fine. ...Wow. That was strange. I haven't... It's a long time since I thought about that woman."

"So that's really why you became a police officer? To avenge her?"

"No. Not avenge, I don't think. Make right, maybe. ...I swore I'd never again be afraid to walk down a dark alleyway if I thought I heard a scream. You understand? That I would *always* walk into that darkness, fearless and determined, no matter what the circumstances. But I had to train, I had to get tough. No point a midget like me dying along with her. So I did. I got tough."

Cassandra said warmly, "Yeah? How tough?"

"Tough enough, sweetheart. Tough enough."

We smiled at each other, *ping*, right to the nearest millisecond. We even broke the smile at the same time. I drained my coffee and said, "So what do you do? I never asked."

"Oh...this and that. Different things. I run a small—business, a shop sort of. It won't make me a millionaire but it's enough to live on. Anyway my mother is quite rich. She doesn't mind funding my...ha! Life of leisure. Thank you, Mommy."

She raised her glass—I wasn't sure if the toast was mocking or sincere. Then she said, "So are you working on anything interesting at the moment?"

"Yeah, it's... Actually, interesting isn't the word I'd use. It's terrible. Just, uh, really depressing. And you don't need to hear about that, either."

"No, I want to. I mean, if you want to tell me. What do you cover? Murder? Robbery? Everything?"

"Homicide. Murder, yeah. This...case, it's a girl, a young girl, we fished her out of the water at Whinlatter Docks a few nights ago. An only child. It's a fucking shame. Very sad. But, hey— that's my job."

"And have you got a suspect? Or however the professionals phrase it."

"'Suspect' is fine."

"Alright. So do you know yet? Who's behind it?"

I spied the waitress passing out of my peripheral vision and turned to her, catching her attention, mouthing the word "check." I turned back to Cassandra. Time to get heavy again. "Really, that's enough about me. Let's talk about you. Like, ooh, I don't know...your real name?"

She gave that heavenly laugh, perfect teeth and deep-red lips. "My real name. Hmm. I'll give you a clue: it's not Cassandra."

"Seriously."

"I am being serious."

"Cassand... Shit. Okay, I'm gonna stop calling you that. You, there, lady in the blue dress: I want to know about *you*. Okay? You know things about me, I've told you things. Now I want to know about you. Who you are, what you like, where you've come from, where you're going. You know, *things*."

She sighed heavily, running her finger around the top of her wine glass. Finally she said, "I'll do you a deal. If we're still seeing each other in two weeks, I'll tell you everything. My full name, date of birth, what size underwear I take, whatever you want."

"Why two weeks?"

"Just...shh. Be patient. I'll tell all in two weeks."

"Well, to be honest it's a shitty sort of a deal from my perspective. But I don't suppose I have a choice, do I?"

Cassandra smiled and shook her head. The motion loosened a thick strand of hair; it fell past her right eye, swinging slowly like a festival streamer in the breeze.

"Until then I'll give you this: I'm 21 years old. I like reading and sleeping late. I don't like butch women who swear a lot or push others around. I like science-fiction movies, classic and new. I paint for pleasure, very badly. Sometimes I have the most horrendous migraines, it feels like my head is coming apart at the bone. I lost my virginity when I was 18. I like drinking hot chocolate and cool wine. I don't like trying to find parking in the center of Hera on a Saturday afternoon. I'm a Capricorn. My underwear size is 36C at the bust, medium for the pants. I like the feeling of rain on my face, but not too cold. I like making love with sweet, gentle, pretty homicide detectives. Is that enough for now? Will I go on?"

I said, "No. I suppose that'll do for a while. Shall we go?"

She nodded. I excused myself and went to the bathroom. By the time I returned she'd paid the check and was standing by the door with my coat over her arm, a stole over her shoulders.

I said, "You shouldn't have got that. I wanted to pay."

She held my coat out for me to back into. "You can get it next time."

I looked at her, face-on. "So there'll be a next time?"

"I'm sure of it."

"Okay. I mean, good."

We waved goodbye to the proprietor. Stepping outside I saw we were the last customers there. It was cold in the street but the air was still; your skin only noticed the temperature when you moved. I lit a Dark Nine, watched it fog up that still, cold night.

I said, "Where to now?"

"I thought maybe home. You know, to tussle."

I laughed up at her. Who am I to refuse a beautiful young lady her one desire? "Home you or home me?"

"Yours. Definitely yours."

"Okay. If that's what…"

"Sorry, there might be people there I don't want to meet."

I said teasingly, "You mean you don't want me to meet. You're ashamed of me."

The sense of something, some displeasure or impatience, ghosted across her face as she said, "I don't want *anyone* to meet." Then she smiled brightly and took my hand, and began walking towards a cab rank across the street. "Come on. It's just you and me tonight, baby. Let's forget about everyone else. Let's just wrap ourselves up in ourselves. How does that sound?"

"Magical."

We laughed at the same time and then started running for home.

Later, in the wee small hours, I stared at the ceiling of my bedroom, trying to ignore the asthmatic wheeze of my crapped-out air conditioning, trying to concentrate instead on the sound of Cassandra breathing, a deep nasal hum. Trying not to concentrate. What was happening here? I didn't know. I didn't know

that I wanted to know. Most of all I didn't want to over-inves-
tigate it, think too deeply about it, analyze and thus paralyze. It
was good so far—it was better than good—so why stress it?
Leave it alone, I told myself; enjoy yourself for once. Be in the
moment. Be with Cassandra. Be happy. Just be.

But that's not possible, is it? Maybe a Buddhist can "just be",
or a dog or a lump of stone. Normal people like me can't help
being conscious and self-conscious. We can't help thinking the
shit out of everything. Well, I can't, anyway. I lit a cigarette as
quietly as I could and blew the smoke towards the window, open
a few inches at the top, and wondered: was this the start of
something special? Me, her, us—was there an "us" yet? Or maybe
the possibility of one? Or were we just two lonely women thrown
together by circumstance and desire and the most random of
chance, entangled in one another's lives for a while, until the
knots loosened and we fell apart?

Arrgh—shut *up*, brain. Cassandra shifted in the bed beside
me, warmth lifting from her body like off the naked bars of an
electric fire. The movement made me think of Odette for some
reason. Odette: the longest relationship I'd ever had, the one that
still nagged at the edges of my consciousness and conscience like
a judgmental elder relative. I thought about her less and less as
the months went by, but not enough months had yet gone by. I'd
always sort of assumed that she and I would hang around
together forever, and perhaps that was the problem: she saw it as
an affair of passion and vigor and hard work, an active thing; I
saw it as a kind of semi-formal arrangement in which I had
passively, though not unhappily, become involved. Hanging
around. Christ. That *was* it, wasn't it? I hung around in our
relationship, she got involved. Odette lived it and I watched her
living it.

Forget all that, Genie. Fuck the past, bury it, say a prayer for it
if you want, so long as you accept: it's gone, it's dead. There's
nothing more you can do. No crime to investigate here, nobody

worth blaming. I stubbed out the cigarette, put the ashtray on the floor and snuggled into Cassandra's warm flank. She was here and I was here and we were naked together and we liked one another and talked like friends and laughed at the same things and the same time. That was good enough for the moment. Just being was good enough.

I put my arm across her breast and shut my eyes. As I slid into half-sleep I vaguely realized that I had never actually told Cassandra I was a cop. But by that stage I was too tired and sluggish to care or remember, I was gone.

Chapter 17

Bethany

I SAT in court the next morning as our five singing beauties upped and walked. Yep, just like that. Anneka Klosterman, Nora Hofton, Alejandra Villegas, Dinah Spaulding and Liz Arendt withdrew their murder confessions simultaneously. Since there was no concrete evidence against any of them, and each one contradicted the other, they couldn't be held. The judge frowned and harrumphed and vowed to bring charges of wasting court and police time against them, but she had to sign the release forms anyway. So they walked. Jamie Sobel had the good grace not to give the usual insincere defense speech about miscarriages of justice and her clients' good names being returned to them and how she's *this close* to making a false arrest claim against the HCPD. She had the good grace to look a teensy bit embarrassed. Sobel crossed the necessary legal Ts and dotted the Is, ushered her charges out the door and released them back into the world. Oddly, nobody was around for them—nobody came to meet them or drive them away, not their families, no one. The women simply walked off into the crowds.

Etienne had been right: apart from Klosterman, they all acted like zombies. (She acted like she was calculating exactly how much she should display of the profound contempt she felt for the court.) Arendt actually looked like a zombie, with those dark panda eyes set deep in a thin pale face. I was there in person because Sobel had told us first thing that morning what was going to happen, as per procedural requirement in a capital case; the Chief sent me down as the dick involved. I was glad to go, anyway; I wanted to see them in the flesh again, to verify my first impressions. And they were verified: these broads were no more acting under their own volition than a deck of cards. Like four automatons they filed out, blank-eyed, sticking to the preordained script. But it was more than that, more than the women merely playing a part and parroting someone else's words. It was like their brains had been wiped clean. They could still function, they knew where they were and what their names were, but those four just...weren't there. Their minds and personalities, whatever is that holy spark inside us which creates the person, which makes you "you"—it was absent. They weren't even the same as serial killers: there was no malice, no unfettered sadism or fucked-up sexual compulsion. There wasn't really anything. They were like dolls. Four dolls and then Klosterman, the cruel, arrogant child striding at the head of the line.

I met Sobel outside, on the courthouse steps—she lit my cigarette with a platinum-plated Zippo lighter. It looked almost as expensive as her watch which looked almost as expensive as her suit, which looked pretty goddamn expensive. The rewards of brilliance...and knowing how to not be bothered by what she did. I asked her once, you know, the usual line: "How do you sleep at night?" or whatever.

She had replied, "I don't think about work unless I'm working. Do you?"

When I surprised her by admitting, yes, sometimes I did, she said: "Genie, I'm going to say but one thing to you. And you know this isn't an excuse or justification, because you know I don't care what you think of me. We barely know each other, you're not my family, so. And that one thing is: yes, I make a lot of money defending these scumbags. But someone has to represent them in court; otherwise this is nothing but a fascist society. Would you agree with that?"

I reluctantly nodded.

"That someone is often me. And I do my job to the best of my ability—as is my obligation. I don't break the law. I don't even bend it. I use it, I work with it, I play it, I spin it. All within the rules. I do my job. So yeah, I sleep fine at night. And believe it or not, I hope you do, too. I've a lot of respect for the police."

"Whatever, Jamie. Keep telling yourself that."

"I will."

I'd smiled bitterly and shook my head and walked off. The most annoying thing about it was that, as usual, she was correct to a large extent. I didn't like it but the system needed people like her.

Ah, Sobel was actually alright. I'd spoken to her quite a lot, both professionally and socially; she was one of the most straight-talking people I'd ever met. She wasn't needlessly harsh—she had some tact—but Jamie told it like she saw it. I liked that in her, even though I didn't in everyone. I don't know, it was weird; it seemed to suit her, like those expensive threads.

Now she slipped the lighter into the jacket pocket of her black trouser suit and we stood together in silence and a cloud of smoke. After half a minute I said, "Thanks for the light, Jamie. Wanna do me another favor?"

Sobel smiled. "No, I won't tell you who's employing me. You know the rules, Genie. You know I don't have to."

"Hey. Nobody's saying anything about 'have to.' But what about 'want to?'"

"I don't think so. Not without their instruction."

"Ah. So it's more than one person, then?"

She smiled again. "'Their' being used flexibly in this instance. May be a 'they', may be a 'her.' You won't find out from me."

"Thanks, Jamie. Appreciated as always."

"No problem. You take care, Genie."

She stubbed out her cigarette under the pointy toe of an exquisitely crafted leather boot and walked back inside the court-house. I lit another one and felt a familiar tension in my mind, opposing urges pulling inside me, stretching me thin.

Here's irony: not one hour later I returned to the office and there on my desk, in a gray-brown cardboard file-holder, was the psyche assessment of the five women. I'd asked our behavioral brainiacs to look for compulsive confession syndrome—total strike-out. As I expected, really. None of our robots suffered from that strange, rare condition, and I had figured they wouldn't; these confessions were clearly driven by a more controlled, venal imperative.

Indeed, the reports showed that all five were perfectly rational, integrated, functioning women...in theory. And in theory Misery might be inviting me 'round for tea and crumpets next Christmas. Certainly, within the parameters of their field of study, our shrinks had made the correct evaluation: Hofton, Arendt, Villegas and Spaulding weren't psychotic or sociopathic; they weren't afflicted with dissociative identity disorder or delusional schizophrenia or megalomaniac paranoia. In that sense, they were technically "normal." They had been subjected to the tests and questionnaires and interviews, their data rated and collated, and their personality types fell somewhere in the middle, somewhere within the huge fuzzy mass of womanhood.

But I'd witnessed how they acted and moved, seen in their eyes how the flame of life and self seemed snuffed out within them. These broads were not normal on any planet I inhabited. And Klosterman, she had "danger" coming out of her pores. That woman scared the bejeesus out of me.

I decided to forget about the odd five and muse instead on my own interviews so far. I floated upstairs to the staff canteen and sat in a corner with a steaming mug of coffee and mulled things over. I zoned out the ambient noise of conversation and metal clinking on ceramic and the milk foamer squealing angrily, and thought hard: about the Madeleine Top Ten list, about Poison Rose, about Misery and the genius twin security guards. About Cassandra and Erika Baton.

I had got, I felt, a fairly full portrait of what Madeleine was like as a person, but not much else. Gilbert and Tussing said they knew her but denied really knowing her; Camilla had seen her around some, but not lately; Noni Ashbery colored in some psychological background; Sasha Hiscock was tangential at best; Odette and Virginia Newman I still hadn't managed to pin down; Klosterman knew something but getting it out of her looked nigh-on impossible. Misery had told me plenty about her daughter but knew little about her demise. Then there was LaVey and her *aide de camp* Queneau. Those two were somewhere near the heart of it; that's what my own heart was telling me. If there was a conspiracy—forget about "if", there was—LaVey was involved, and probably Queneau. Most of the women in their extended circle seemed to know more than they were letting on; they seemed to be covering up. I made an assumption: LaVey told them to talk freely enough about Madeleine and their relationship with her—up to a point. After that mark, they were ordered to deny, confuse, cover up.

LaVey, you bitch. Nana was always right and I had a set against that fake, that cod-intellectual poseur. She was the one, my gut screamed it at me. But...to prove it. To even know it for sure, myself. There was the almighty rub. I still had no evidence and nobody willing to provide it.

Odette and Virginia, Virginia and Odette... Did they hold the key to the mystery? Hope said yes, realism said probably not. I had to brace them, anyway, but for some reason I didn't feel like doing it today. I'm not sure why. Odette, I just didn't want to talk to right then. I felt resentful towards her, a lingering sort of bitterness, something spiteful and small. Who knows why? But I didn't know how I'd react when I finally spoke to her again. I wasn't certain how professional I'd be. Virginia Newman, though, was different; in that case I wanted to postpone it a little. Like I was savoring the anticipation and wanted to enjoy it a tiny bit longer. This true friend of Madeleine, the girl who showed up at her funeral, the fast-driving flake who stood by her pal even unto death: I was really looking forward to meeting her. But not just yet.

I can't explain any of this. It baffled me and threatened to paralyze me completely, here with my coffee and my corner chair. So I made a snap decision: get out of the building and hit for the bars Madeleine used to know. A shot and a long shot in each, but what the hell, it's how she would have spent her day. At least I'd get to walk in the dead girl's shoes, and maybe that way get a few steps closer to the person who killed her.

Ten o'clock that night and I sat in a busted armchair in my apartment, my stomach reeling but my head straight and sober. I'd done what I promised, had a drink in every bar that I knew Madeleine knew, and it hadn't made me the slightest bit drunk. How odd. My belly was curdling with acid and sourness, but my mind was sharp. Like the booze had decided to only venture downwards. And this was a lot of booze. I have a normal tolerance for alcohol which is why this post-binge sobriety was weirding me out so much. Maybe it was the long walks between bars, the smokes and chats with bouncers in the night air, the bowl of peanuts here and quick sandwich there. Maybe it was that I didn't want to be drunk. I needed to drink but I also needed to think, and tonight I'd done both.

Either way I was sober enough to reflect on my odyssey around Hera City's drinking establishments. There are hundreds of these places but I stuck strictly to those mentioned in the Misery dossier or by others: Gilbert, Camilla. Which made 14 or 15 in total: a few decent joints, some dive bars, a strip club, even a disco called Funky Clown which runs all day, every day, without a break in the thumping techno music or the pervasive air of desperation and horribly enforced jollity. By the end of it I was smoked-out, depressed and had a ringing in my ear. The city itself could be depressing, I realized—or maybe remembered. And then night time gives a different aura to a place: it bleaches all the colors and a lot of the warmth. Everything looks starker, colder; things get murky in the wee hours. I thought about my own wasted nights staring down a bottle or a glass; nothing out of the ordinary, indeed quite moderate for a HCPD cop, but still wasted. Hundreds and thousands of hours literally and metaphorically pissed away. I thought about Cassandra and our potential future, and didn't see us wasting much time together.

Back to the matter at hand. Again, I had got very little useable information. A few little chicks in Reaper's hid their booze when they saw me flash my badge at the bartender but eventually opened up when I assured them I wasn't on the trawl for license violations. They knew Madeleine by sight, hadn't seen her in several weeks. A bit better in Bush Babies: the woman doing security had spoken to Madeleine maybe eight or nine days previously. She was drunk, as she usually was. She stayed late and left with a girl she'd just met, as she often did. She was trouble-free, as she always was. In Musique Drum I had an extremely loud conversation with a 19-stone tattoo artist who thought she knew the girl who'd done the rose on Madeleine's breast. Hadn't seen her in fuckin' ages and ages, quote-unquote, but she'd been doing a lot of solvents lately so her head was all scrambled. In fact she was whacked on paint-thinner and Bushmill's right now. The owner of Kars 'n' Stars reckoned she'd served Madeleine only a few nights before her death, which set my senses a-tingle, but then realized no, she was thinking of someone else entirely and couldn't place the Greenhill girl at all. Hasta La Vista was almost empty for some reason so there wasn't really anyone to talk to. In Swing Kids I met identical sisters, two-thirds of a set of triplets, who claimed to know Madeleine quite well, liked her even better and were shocked to hear that she was dead. They asked me if I wanted to join them in mourning, then called two more double gins from the bartender and set about dealing with their grief.

On and on I went. And here was my conclusion, as I later sat in that armchair and nursed a half-warm cup of coffee and a cigarette: a good number of people remembered Madeleine, some had known her and more had seen her, a few had scammed drinks off her and one or two Good Samaritans had helped her to a taxi when her own legs were too shot to carry her. But nobody could recall seeing her on the last night of her young life; or if they did, they weren't 'fessing up to me. The job has that effect sometimes: people clam up to the woman who most needs them to talk. Ironic, irritating and very unhelpful.

Fuck. *Goddamn.* I let my head drop down over the back of the chair and emitted a slow, pained groan. I was starting to lose hope. I wasn't even fully conscious of it yet—at that moment I didn't stop and say to myself, "I am starting to lose hope"—but the thought was there, wheedling and insistent, a seductive presence on the outer edges of my mental universe, a dust cloud, a phantasm, something black and dense collapsing into itself. My hope was beginning to die.

At times like this I wish I had a cat, warm and soft and pliant, nice to cuddle. Then I realize I can't even keep a houseplant alive for more than a week. Poor little critter wouldn't stand a chance. But I still wished I had a cat.

The phone's ring-tone seemed so loud in the virtually total silence of my apartment that I leaped in my skin a little. I stood and went towards it but it stopped ringing before I got there. Then I noticed the blinking red light next to the handset: that had been an automated alert, telling me I had a message. I dialed into my mailbox and heard: "Uh...yeah. Uh, hi. Hello. This is, uh, Bethany Gilbert calling for that detective, Auf der Maur. Got your number from the cops. Uh, I mean from your colleagues. Yeah, could you, like, call me tonight? Not here. Not at the college. In a bar. The number is zero-four-four-four, 11-18, one-two-one. I'm gonna be there 'till about half-past 11. Yeah, so please call me there, Detective. I need to, uh... It's about Madeleine. I gotta go."

Beep. End of message. What time had she said? Half-past 11. I glanced at the clock: 11.20. I replayed the message to get the number, dialed the joint and the barkeep called Gilbert back just as she was walking out the door. I said, "Bethany. This is Detective Auf der Maur. You wanted to talk to me."

"Yeah, hi. You took your time calling."

I corralled my temper. "I'm calling now, Bethany. We can talk now."

"Yeah, okay. Alright."

"Can you speak freely? Where you are?"

"Uh-huh. There's nobody here but me. Hey, Jenny. Give us a few minutes, would you? Thanks, babe." A long pause. "Okay, she's gone. Jenny's cool but this is seriously fucking private business, you know?"

"Sure. So…whenever you're ready."

Gilbert blew out heavily. I could picture her chubby face, her childish pout, that vaguely ludicrous look of cross-eyed concentration. She blew out again. I waited.

Then she said, "I'm telling you this because I want to help Madeleine. I want you to catch her killer. I know you think I didn't care about her, you think I'm shit and I just used Madeleine for money. But that's not true. I liked her, okay we may not have been best buddies, but shit. She's dead now and that sucks. I didn't want Madeleine to die. I just… She was alright. But now she's dead."

"Are you saying you blame yourself, Bethany?"

"Yeah. I mean no. Why would I blame myself? Stop putting words into my mouth or I'll hang the fuck up right now."

I said softly, "Okay. That's okay. Just go on."

Another long pause. "I can't say much. Alright? All I can tell you is you're on the right track. Yeah. Just, like, keep looking where you're looking. …Listen, Madeleine was involved in some creepy shit, alright? I don't know all the details."

I chanced raising the pressure: "I think you know some of them, Bethany. I think you want to tell me about it."

"Hey, it's my ass on the line here, got it? Not yours, *mine*." She sighed heavily once more. "I'm, uh, I'm a bit scared. I'm not scared, I'm just kinda fucking nervous, you know? There's a lot of... She got dragged into something bad. I don't mean the usual shit, the drinking and all that crap. Who cares about that? This was—*bad*, okay? This was big. A bunch of weirdoes, they meet up and have ceremonies and all kinds of crazy shit. Madeleine told me some stuff about it. Worshipping the high priestess, uh, the goddess, what did she say? The moon goddess, or the sun, or some fucking thing. I don't know, I couldn't understand it. They sucked her into their fucking spider's web and she couldn't get out."

She stopped talking. I held my breath, silently running a name through my head: That Island. The suburban club tagged by Misery's PIs. The spooky place Camilla had warned me about. Then Gilbert spoke it aloud: "That Island. It's a club. Check it out. Not a club like a nightclub, it's a private joint. That's where... Check that place out, Detective. You'll find some answers there."

"You've been there. With Madeleine."

"Wha-? I... No, I've never seen that place. I don't know what..."

"You have, Bethany. You've been there. You almost let it slip when I first spoke to you. It's alright. I can protect you. Just tell me the truth."

"Hey fuck you, okay, Auf der Maur?! You can't protect me. Nobody can protect *nobody*. ...I've said too much, I'm gonna hang up now."

I said urgently, "No! Don't. Bethany, listen to me very carefully. You want to tell me. You feel bad about Madeleine and you want to help me. So help me."

"No, I... Look, the address is 44 Rue de Claudel, in Shrewsbury. You know, that posh area north of the canal? They're so pretentious. With their French names for streets. Yeah, sure you know it, you're a cop. You guys know everything."

I scribbled the address on the back of an unpaid electricity bill. Gilbert continued, "Alright, that's all I can say. Check out that place, Detective. Big mansion, huge place. Big beautiful gardens, all that. And *don't* tell them I mentioned it. I'll deny it. I'll lie my fucking ass off if I have to."

"Okay. Your secret's safe with me. Just, meet me. Five minutes, anywhere you like. Please, Bethany. It's important."

"No, no. Oh shit. I *can't*, okay? No. I just can't. It's not worth…"

"For Madeleine. If not for me or the police or the justice system, forget about all that civic duty stuff. Just think of Madeleine. Meet me, tonight. You name the time and place and I'll be there."

"I don't want to get involved."

"You won't be. This is just you and me. Give me a time and place."

More silence. I debated whether or not to reach for a cigarette. Then I felt it: a change in the atmosphere, a loosening, a drop in pressure. I don't know how I knew but I knew—she'd come around.

Gilbert said quietly, "Half an hour from now, on campus. Exactly half an hour. That's midnight. I gotta go back to the college now. Meet me… There's a secluded area, lot of trees and shit, about 50 yards inside the main gate, off to the right. Do you know the LaVey Institute?"

"I know it. I'll find it."

"There. I'll be hiding—I mean waiting in there. Exactly at 12, got it?"

"I got it. Thanks, Bethany. You're doing the right thing."

She sounded deflated, defeated. She grunted, "Right. Sure. I gotta go" and hung up the phone. I did likewise, grabbed my car keys and gunned it for the door.

You know that mildly queasy feeling you get in your insides from déjà vu? It's like you know something is ever-so-slightly off, not quite as it should be, but because your brain can't actually pinpoint what that is, your guts react instead. Your body is giving you a message: something's wrong. I hardly ever experience déjà vu but I get that feeling on the job sometimes, as a kind of forewarning. When I'm entering a building, say, and the person I'm expecting to be there isn't breathing anymore, and the person who stopped them breathing is now waiting for me, behind a door, with an expression of unhinged bloodlust and a fire-fighter's axe held above their head... My stomach sometimes starts to wobble and roll. Something is wrong.

I knew as soon as I got out of my car that the girl was dead. It was like the stench of it was floating across to me, carried on the night breeze like invisible demons, whispers of the baddest of bad news. My viscera did a somersault and I knew, and then I really did feel sick, properly sick. I shuddered and breathed deeply until I was sure I wouldn't vomit, fitted the standard-issue torch into the belt loop at my back, unholstered my gun, gripped it in both hands and padded quietly towards the small copse which lay in a hollow some 30 yards away. When I was right on the edge of it I pulled the torch and swung the strong beam of light across the tree-line: if the killer was still there, better she be blinded than I go in blind. Nothing. Nobody. Just some thin, anemic-looking trees, like frozen ghosts in the glare of the torch, wasted, almost ephemeral. As if they only came into being by the magic of my light shining on them. I clicked off the torch and listened. No sound except the wind creaking branches, a far-distant hum of traffic. The area was empty, hushed, devoid of human life. I turned the light back on and moved forward.

Bethany Gilbert lay on her back about 30 yards in; far enough to virtually guarantee that nobody would hear her die. And it had been an awful death: her head was twisted in a grotesque position, eyes open in horror, a parody of anatomy. Arms and hands pulled up and in like they were attached to a puppeteer's strings. Leaves and dirt were scattered and disturbed all around her; evidence, if more were needed, of a violent struggle and a violent end. I crouched beside her and shone the light down her body. The first sweep told me I didn't need to bother with the torso—all the damage was done to her head and face. Blood poured from tiny wounds, dozens of them, from chin to forehead, across the skull, one or two on the neck. Dark, horrible blood, still leaking away, still warm, wisps of steam rising from it in the cold air. What the hell kind of weapon could have made wounds like these? A stiletto blade, a small screwdriver? Not a nail-gun, there were no nails in her or on the ground.

I walked back to the car and called it in. No point running around after a perp I knew had fled by now. All I could do was hold my ground, preserve the scene. Dispatch briskly informed me that a crime scene unit and ambulance were on the way; I smiled sourly and thought a hearse would have been more useful. This case had moved from one death to more than one; we now had what is informally referred to as a body-count. Two girls, two murders. And I couldn't help feeling, as I waited for the sirens to swing towards where I stood, that I was partly to blame for one of those.

Chapter 18

Orianne

WHAT was I saying about déjà vu? One more time with feeling: I needed a cigarette and a strong coffee. No coffee machine so I had just the cigarette. One of those nights that hang around too long. Too many recently. Reminding myself again: this is the job, shut up and do it. Except this time I bitterly replied: Oh, go screw yourself, Genie.

Déjà vu: it was like the Madeleine crime scene all over again. Gone past one o'clock in the morning. A dead girl of about 20. Forensics doing what they do. Cop snappers taking pictures of the wooded area, the grotesque corpse, the scattered leaves. Uniforms standing guard on a cordon, keeping rubberneckers and shocked students back. All that was missing was Farrington—delayed by some minor personal crisis, but on her way—and a drunken hooker staring past the dreadful present towards her own dreadful past. Amazingly, Officers Mulqueen and Browne were present as well. They stood just inside the main gates of the LaVey campus, hands lightly touching their batons. The grim-faced Mulqueen was even hopping on her toes again to warm them. She must feel the cold really badly. I thought, She should put on some weight.

I went over to them and smiled wryly. "We really have to stop meeting under these circumstances. Officer Browne, Officer Mulqueen. How are you?"

Jerry Browne stifled a giggle and said, "Fine, Detective Auf der Maur. Great." Mulqueen nodded and didn't come close to an approximation of a smile. That girl was as serious as death. But she didn't realize that I was, too. I joked because I was so fucking serious about all of this, I was afraid my head would break apart with the weight of it. I lit a cigarette and offered them the pack. They refused, as per proper procedure—I wouldn't have cared if they wanted a smoke, but brass said that rookies must show dicks "due respect and deference while in the course of carrying out their duties." Something like that. Some bureaucratic junk.

I nodded and began walking away, saying, "Alright. Stay on your toes, girls."

Things had moved quickly by that stage. As soon as the cavalry arrived, at about quarter-past midnight, I gave them their orders—sit tight, wait for the techies, *no* civilian comes on- or goes off-campus—and stomped towards Azura LaVey's office. I knew she'd be there, even at this late hour. And not just because of my suspicions about her: the woman came across like the sort of devoted egomaniac whose identity is so inextricably bound up in her work that work forms a large part of her day. And night. LaVey was the Institute and the Institute was her—that's probably how she'd have phrased it, in that particular blend of aspirational waffle and aggressive New Ageism.

She was there, but this time not alone. Her right-hand woman Orianne Queneau stood glaring at LaVey as I opened the door without asking for permission or clearing my throat. Her arm was raised as if she was making a point in a heated debate...either that or she was about to strike down LaVey. Chance would be a fine thing, et cetera. LaVey smirked and dragged slowly on a thin, black cigarette in a gold-plated holder. She looked less regal now, more like a spiteful brat. Queneau was a handsome woman, with good posture and sparkling light-blue eyes; she reminded me of an actress, Charlotte somebody, another woman who'd maintained her good looks past 50. She was saying something and hadn't heard me; I stood inside the door and let her say it: "...purity of our intentions. Do you hear me, Azura? You're forgetting that. And I will not have our—*my*—work, my life's devoted effort, reduced to something as grubby, as *venal*, as, as..."

"As...money? Power? Stop me if I'm getting close." I smiled as they looked at me, open-mouthed, shocked, then glanced at each other, an infinitesimal moment of communication. Like two little girls swearing each other to secrecy over that prank they'd pulled. Queneau lowered her hand and pulled at her blouse, straightening it, anything to distract from the awkwardness of the present. She looked flustered, sweatily uncomfortable, but was doing a decent job at hiding it. LaVey didn't look flustered at all, and returned to her smirking and smoking, her back almost to me. She was a cool one, alright.

"Detective Auf der Maur, wasn't it?" she said. "I didn't hear you come in."

I stepped into the room and said, "Grubby and venal. You? Surely not, Madam LaVey."

"Do you usually eavesdrop on conversations? Is that normal procedure for the Hera City Police Department?"

She spat out the last four words like they were all four-letter ones. I said, "Just yours. You fascinate me."

She whirled around to face me. *Faux*-naïve tone of voice, those amber-brown eyes open wide like a startled child. "I? A mere pedagogue, a teacher? What could possibly be fascinating to you about *me*?"

"The fact that two of your students have been brutally murdered within the past week. That's fascinating to me, for starters. You don't mind if I join you in a smoke, do you?"

I lit a Dark Nine and studied their reactions. Queneau actually blanched, her skin blotching in angry red and ghastly white. She put a hand to her throat and gasped, while staring at LaVey, "Two? Who? Who is it this time?"

I said nothing. I watched LaVey: she hadn't reacted at all. The smirk had returned, that fucking smirk I wanted to punch into the back of her head. She casually took a final drag on her cigarette and mashed it into a gravel-filled pot plant near her hand—another of those freaky-weird plants that were artfully placed around the office.

Still no reply. She was taunting me, I realized, playing with me, the languorous cat and her little prey. Finally LaVey lost the smirk and spoke, and God, the insincerity was palpable: "Oh my word. Another murder? No. Detective, tell us."

I smirked myself, oozing contempt, and she caught it but held onto her composure. I got the impression that faking sentiment came as naturally to her as breathing.

"Bethany Gilbert," I said. "Beaten to death not half an hour ago. On *your* campus, Ms LaVey. Fascinating isn't the word for it."

Queneau looked fit to pass out. She lowered herself unsteadily into a chair and swallowed heavily. She began what I presumed were learned breathing exercises, a way to control stress and anxiety: drawn in through flared nostrils, held, eased out through pursed lips. LaVey did no such thing. She placed a bejeweled finger to her lips, feigning concentration and concern.

"Bethany. My God," she said softly. "I only... She was in this office just this morning. And now... Oh, what a dreadful thing to have happened."

I said drily, "I can feel your pain. What was Gilbert doing here today? What did you talk about?"

"Oh...nothing. That is to say, nothing important. Just college matters, some little problems she was having with her courses. I encourage all my girls to come directly to me if they have a problem, Detective."

"Did Bethany have a big problem?"

"No. As I said, it was nothing. Nothing that couldn't be ironed out. But now, alas..."

Jesus Christ. I half-expected her to flutter her hand across her brow, make a deep bow and exeunt the stage. As an actor LaVey wasn't bad, but it leaned more towards artifice than realism.

She said, "Have you caught the person responsible? Have you caught that monstrous woman?"

"You sound like you know her."

"I'll ask you once to withdraw that question, Detective

whoever-you-are. Or face charges of slander."

I turned to Queneau, who obviously had regained her balance, her composure and her confidence. She came and stood by LaVey's side with the stance of a personal bodyguard. Then she said it again: "I insist that you withdraw that question or face the consequences."

What the fuck? Talk about a shift in gears. A minute ago she was virtually reaching for the smelling salts, now she's fronting up to a homicide detective who quite clearly thinks her pal is rotten.

I got on the front foot myself, got up in her face: "Excuse me? Who are you, exactly? Her lawyer?"

"A friend and colleague. And witness to that slanderous remark."

LaVey smirked once more, up at her protector and back at me, raising her eyebrows as if to ask, Well? Whatcha gonna do now, hot-shot?

I took another step closer and said angrily, "I withdraw *nothing*. Report me if you want, I don't care. I don't give a shit about anything except that dead girl lying in dirt and leaves and her own blood out there."

Queneau muttered, "Well, of course we all regret this terrible event. Nobody is attempting to prevent you carrying out your..."

"Neither one of you has asked me any details yet. Does that strike you as odd?"

They remained silent. I went on, "I tell you a student was murdered 20 minutes ago within a hundred fucking yards of this building, and I don't get one question. Like, where exactly? How did it happen? Who called you? You know, the normal things people say in these situations."

LaVey said airily, "Is there a *normal* way to react to something like this, Detective? I would have thought the situation itself was absolutely abnormal."

I shrugged and half-agreed with her. "I guess not. Murder's

never normal. Or shouldn't be, anyway."

Queneau picked up a leather clutch-bag and said, "May I go? I've had a long day and my daughter is expecting me home hours ago."

"No, you may *not* goddamn go. Sit your ass down, Ms Queneau. I have questions for the pair of you."

She began to splutter her objections, all manufactured outrage, but I cut across her by karate-chopping the air and yelling, "Sit down *now*. Before I put the fucking cuffs on you."

She sat next to LaVey on a low couch, an autumnal color, russet-brown, tastefully distressed at the edges. I stood over them, tried to make myself bigger, more imposing, more authoritative. "Did either of you see or hear anything this evening? Any unusual noises, see anyone hanging around?"

They shook their heads simultaneously.

"Where is the campus security guard based?"

LaVey said, "Oh, we don't have full-time security, Detective. This is a respectable establishment. We don't need goons with night-sticks prowling around, creating a bad atmosphere. This is a place of love, not fear or worry. That's a fundamental tenet of our educational philosophy. And like attracts like. Bring in heavy security and quite soon you'll *need* heavy security."

"You could have used one tonight, though."

"One what?"

"A goon with a night-stick."

"Oh. Yes, I see."

"So what are you telling me—the LaVey Institute has no on-site security guards?"

"We have them, certainly. But only a few nights a week. A few hours, two or three nights a week. Just to cover our insurance requirements. There's really no need…"

"Okay, fine. Shut up now."

For the first time the mask dropped—LaVey was annoyed at my rudeness. She ground her perfect little teeth in tiny movements, then remembered where she was and who she was supposed to be, and the relaxed expression snapped back into place.

I stubbed out my cigarette in an ashtray on the huge desk and said, "Would I be right in supposing this was security's night off?"

LaVey said, "As it happens, yes."

"As it happens."

Of course. As it happens. It so happens. Shit happens. Yeah, Azura LaVey was a real happening kind of gal. I decided to change tack, decided to lie, just a little, just enough to raise the temperature: "We're close to a resolution of the Madeleine Greenhill case."

LaVey didn't blink. Queneau blinked a few times, rapidly.

I said, "Figured you'd want to know that. What with your concern for former and present students and all."

Queneau half-stood and exclaimed, "I've had enough of this. Who do you think you're-"

Filibustering. Delaying tactics. Blinding me with bluster and bullshit.

"I told you to sit," I said. "So you will fucking sit."

She sat. I went on, "Five people have already confessed to the crime. What a lucky break for us, huh? 'Course, they've since withdrawn their confessions, but that's how it goes sometimes."

Still no reaction from LaVey. No smirk, no reaction.

"We know who did the deed itself. We're about half-a-minute from arresting her. And when we get her, we'll get the woman behind her. The evil old bitch who paid for murder."

Cool as a cucumber. Cool as ice. Cold as the grave.

"Is there anything you want to tell me, Ms LaVey?"

LaVey looked away, looked unperturbed.

"You could save yourself a world of shit down the line by being honest now."

"This is outrageous!" Queneau stood to her full height this

time and put her hand on LaVey's shoulder. "Don't say one word, Azura. Not one word. And as for you, Detective, I *will* have your badge for this disgusting behavior. This bullying of a wholly innocent woman who has just suffered the worst kind of loss..."

So: Queneau was the attack dog, the metaphorical muscle, the bad cop. LaVey was the serene, blissed-out good cop, floating over it all, impervious and imperious. And I was the only actual cop in that room.

I said, "You act like her lawyer and yet you're just a friend. It's, you know, I find that interesting."

"If you keep harassing her you *will* be dealing with a lawyer next time."

There wasn't really anything more to be said. I waved a tired hand and said, "Class dismissed." They didn't move, didn't do anything. I added, "That means we're done here" and hit for the door.

Queneau was sitting back down, exhaling heavily, as I exited the room. LaVey took her hand and massaged it with her thumbs. The original odd couple.

I had returned to my crime scene then. I stood about 15 yards from Bethany Gilbert's body and smoked and thought for a long time. LaVey and Queneau: what was their relationship, exactly? Old friends? Confidantes? Lovers? No—I didn't pick up any sort of sexual spark. This was something different, maybe deeper... Comrades, confreres, a clique, a cabal, a cohort...co-conspirators. That's what they seemed like, goddamn it.

LaVey was the key. She was the key and the lock, the door, the crocodile-filled moat and drawbridge, the whole freaking castle. So: how to penetrate her defenses? Who was left on my hit-list? Answer: Virginia Newman. LaVey Institute drop-out, Madeleine's closest friend. Way past time for us to have that little chat. So: hello at last, Virginia.

I was tidying up the ends of my thread of thought when Chief Etienne arrived, sometime after 12.30. She explained she'd been working late, catching up on admin. The call came through; she felt she should be there in person. I was glad—Etienne offered to break the news to Gilbert's mother. She told me to go home, get some sleep. She said I looked like "death warmed up." I gave her a brief rundown of my contretemps with LaVey and Queneau. She nodded and hummed and took it all in without comment. Then I told her about Queneau's threat to have me fired and Etienne surprised me by saying, "Don't worry about them, Auf der Maur. Don't worry, you're doing a good job. I've got you covered. Now go home, for God's sake."

I thanked her; I felt oddly touched. Etienne left. I stayed where I was for a little while longer. I'm not sure why: there was nothing I could add, no value I could bring to this situation. And I couldn't look upon Bethany Gilbert again. That expression of fright and horror, her eyes open wide in the most absolute and terrible realization... This is the face of death, I thought. It's not pretty. It's not pleasant. There is little consolation or meaning to be found.

Time dragged on and speeded up and slowed to a crawl and speeded up again. I smoked more, thought less, looked up absentmindedly at fat clouds puffing across the night sky like sailing boats on a cartoon sea. Until there I was, after one, dog-tired now, cold in the night air, smoked out, coffee-deprived, walking away from Browne and Mulqueen. Should I stay or should I go? Too late to hit the Newman home; too late for house-calls. I strode out the main gates of the LaVey Institute, nodding to Farrington as she drove in. She nodded back and scooted to her workplace. My own car was parked across the street. I sat in, radioed through to Dispatch and had them source the home address of a Margaret Newman. Five minutes later they returned with three. One in the sprawl and one right in the town center, which left one in a suburb so exclusive it didn't even have a name. But I knew where it was, and I knew this was my girl.

I pointed the car towards home and a little sleep, hoping I

wouldn't dream. Hoping I'd forget for a few hours.

By 6am I was awake: restless, jittery, my mind racing. By seven I was up and showered, had some food thrown down my neck, against my stomach's protestations. Coffee and a chocolate chinois pastry—the breakfast of little champions. By eight I was at the Newman homestead, a large, well-kept house in a large, well-tended garden. I could see why Madeleine and this "Ginnie" were pals: they came from the same place.

I didn't. I was just about solvent, a working schmuck, with another 30 years of that to look forward to. I drove an old jalopy, wore relatively cheap clothes and did my own hair-dying and bikini-line. I slung the car through the curve of its momentum and slid to a slow halt in front of the house. Red and green ivy crawled up along the walls—magical, more than alive, as though it possessed a mind. It looked like a giant, intricate tattoo on the skin of the building. I rang the bell and after about two minutes a woman answered: deferential, quietly spoken, kept looking at the ground. A live-in maid, I assumed.

"Hello. My name is Detective Auf der Maur, HCPD. I need to speak with Virginia, please. Tell her it's about Madeleine Greenhill."

The girl whispered, "Just a minute, miss."

She went back inside. I enjoyed the view of that ivy while I waited. I remembered reading a magazine article that warned about how ivy ultimately destroyed buildings. It snuck in those little sticky roots and wormed further and further inside, until the plaster and stone cracked and fell apart. "Beautiful but deadly": that was the headline. I didn't care how many walls it broke—it *was* beautiful.

The girl returned and beckoned me follow her; there may have been verbal communication too, I didn't hear it. She led me into a drawing-room and pulled the door ajar on her way out. It was stately, spacious, decorated with just the right number of antique furniture pieces, covered in antimacassars: not too few that the room would feel cold and empty, not too many as to be vulgar.

And something else in that room.

No. No, no, no.

That perfume was unmistakable. It was different to any other I knew and I'd only smelled it twice before: in a drunken haze in a nameless bar, and sitting at a small table in a romantic restaurant. For a moment it seemed so obvious but that was a lie, that was me kidding myself—it wasn't obvious at all. I would never have put the two together. Not until I came to this house and this room and this perfume. Not until this moment. Jesus Christ.

The door creaked open again and I turned around to face her. Cassandra smiled wryly and said, "Hello again, Genie. Please, sit down. We have a lot to talk about."

Chapter 19

Virginia

"FUCK you and your goddamn 'sit down.' I'm *fine*, thanks. I'll stand."

Cassandra/Virginia shrugged and nodded, her hair shaking with the motion. It wasn't softly waved now, it was curlier. And brown, medium to dark. She was wearing loose clothes—linen trousers, a top of indistinct shape, wooden beads on string around her neck and waist—almost hippie clothes. She also wore spectacles but I could see behind them that her eyes were brown. She looked like a different person. I suppose she was one.

I said bitterly, "So. Not green eyes. Not red hair. Not a snappy dresser. Tell me, Cassandra—how much of you actually *is* real?"

She said quietly, "Please don't tell my mother you know me. She's coming in here in a moment. And please don't call me that. My name is Virginia."

"Here," I said in a vicious whisper. "Your name's Virginia *here*. Not everywhere."

"If you want to see it like that."

She caught my eye and held it: not pleading but asking. There was concern but no panic in her expression. Eventually I nodded and looked away, looked into the grand fireplace, at the ashes crumpled there, cold now, bleached and powdered. A clock ticked somewhere in the room. I sensed Virginia—might as well use her real name now—take a few steps away from me, felt a breeze which presaged the door opening again and someone else entering. I turned back: Virginia was guiding her mother towards me by the elbow, saying, "Mother, this is Detective...Auf der Maur, I think you said?"

I didn't respond. She continued, "She wants to talk to me about Madeleine. Madeleine Greenhill, and her murder. Detective, this is my mother Margaret."

Newman senior was smaller than her daughter, slimmer, nowhere near as beautiful. But who was, right? Even dressed down like this, Virginia was beautiful. Oh God, Genie, forget it. Don't think about it. Just stare at the ceiling. Stare at your shoes. Take a mental cold shower. Scour out your mind of all memories.

I shook the woman's outstretched hand and said, "Pleased to meet you."

She said anxiously, "Is everything alright? I get, you know… A police officer comes to your door early in the morning and… Well. Mothers worry, don't they?"

"It's fine, Mother," Virginia said. "It's just a few questions, right?" This was directed to me.

I gave the older lady my most reassuring smile and said, "Please, madam, there's no need to be alarmed. Just routine questioning. Your daughter knew the dead girl. We have to talk to everyone. I apologize for the earliness of the hour. I was passing through. And *Virginia* was on my list."

Margaret didn't notice the edge I'd put into speaking her daughter's name. Virginia picked up on it but didn't outwardly react. Cool as LaVey on a winter's day, I thought. And what else did they have in common?

The girl's mother looked somewhat pacified. She smiled at Virginia, then me. "Alright. Well, I'll leave you to it, then. You don't need me for anything?"

I shook my head.

"Would you like some tea brought in? Coffee?"

"No thanks."

She smiled again, gave Virginia a supportive squeeze on the elbow and left. We were alone again.

Virginia sat on the edge of the settee which faced the fireplace, her knees together, feet splayed, hands joined. She looked larger, slightly cumbersome, like maybe she suffered from some physical awkwardness, a mild dyspraxia. She also looked much younger as herself, without the glamorous clothes and impeccably styled hair; but paradoxically at the same time she seemed older, or more tired, or numbed, or something.

Virginia gathered her thoughts; I let her do it because I was gathering my own. I only really had two: a ferocious anger and a sense of betrayal. Yeah, I realize how melodramatic it sounds, but there you have it—I felt betrayed. I felt stupid, embarrassed, let-down and fucked-over.

She said, "Genie, listen. I need to tell you someth…"

I cut across her. "You didn't answer my question. How much of you is really real? Or… No. Maybe that *was* the real you. The redhead with the green eyes. The fitted dresses and expensive jewelry. And this is the fake, here in front of me."

"Genie, please."

"Don't call me that name. You don't have the right to use that name. You did, but you don't anymore."

"Okay. What would you like me to call you?"

"Anything you fucking want! Like I care."

Virginia sighed heavily. After a long pause she said, "You asked so I'll tell you. The red hair is me—sometimes. The stylish clothes, they're me too. Sometimes. The eye color…" She smiled. "I'm afraid I've been brown since babyhood. Can't change that."

"Contact lenses. I should have known. That green was too green. Nobody has eyes like that."

"I suppose not."

"But they were green both times. So, what? You must have a good memory. Is it hard, having to remember all that? Who you're supposed to be at any one time?"

"Gen… Detective. Please. This isn't helping."

"Yeah? Well, I'm real sorry about that, Cassand… And what the hell am I supposed to call you now? Cassandra? Virginia? Cassinia? 'You fucking asshole'? What!?"

I realized I was shouting and shut my mouth. Virginia looked upset. Not like she was about to cry, but genuinely upset. It wasn't an act. I remembered how she'd felt in bed two nights before: so soft and warm, wreathed in a dream-cloud of sleep and scent. I thought about our conversation in the restaurant earlier that evening, the things I'd told her, how much of myself I'd given up. And to somebody who didn't even exist, for Christ's sake. The bitterness was a taste in my mouth, it threatened to choke me.

Bitterness is like acid, that's what my mom used to say; bitterness and anger and resentment, they burn away your insides. They make you sick. And they're so pointless anyway, because the only person getting hurt is you.

I didn't want to feel like this anymore. I sat on the settee next to Virginia, shucked off my overcoat and said dryly, "You're up early. I didn't think you got out of bed before noon."

She laughed a little and I felt a little better. I still wanted to hurt her, part of me wanted to tear her beautiful fucking head off and throw it in the fireplace. But I felt better for deciding to feel better. Simple as that. Fuck her, Genie. Forget her. Just don't do damage to yourself. She won't appreciate it. She won't even notice it.

"Genie—can I call you Genie?"

I nodded.

"I'm sorry. You can't know how… I realize this doesn't change anything. I'm probably just saying it to make myself feel like less of an absolute shit. But it's true anyway: I'm very sorry."

"Mm-hm. Well, I'm sorry, too. Sorry I ever met you. How *stupid* do I feel now."

"Don't say that."

"Jesus Christ. I almost wish you *were* a pro. Least that way I'd know where I stood. But I should have known, right? Someone who looks like you doesn't hit on chicks like me. Just, boom, no way. Not in a million years. Doesn't happen."

Virginia kneeled and reached for a pack of cigarettes and an ashtray resting on the marble front piece of the fireplace. She lit two and handed one back to me. I took it without speaking. She placed the ashtray on the floor between us and stayed kneeling, an appropriately penitential stance.

"I didn't expect to see you at that funeral," she said without turning around.

"Madeleine's?"

"Yeah. I didn't think you'd be there. I didn't think you'd...care."

"Maybe it was just professional courtesy. Or curiosity. I'm not sure that I do care. Not the way you do, anyway. Misericordiae told me she saw you there. She appreciated it, for what it's worth."

"Old Misery. We've had our—disagreements. She never liked me as Madeleine's friend. But... I didn't give a damn. I wasn't going to miss it. I owed that to Maddy."

Silence, periodically punctured by the metronomic clicks of that clock. Bile rising within me again. I needed to get out of here: my Zen-like appropriation of calm would only last so long. But first I needed to know some things for sure.

"So are you going to tell me or do I have to beat it out of you?"

Virginia turned to me, alarmed. "What?"

"I'm kidding. I don't do beating. But are you going to tell me now?"

"Tell you..."

"That you slept with me on Azura LaVey's orders."

Ka-*pow*. That cut to the bone. Virginia's cheeks colored in shame and embarrassment—even her blushing was aesthetically divine, I noticed sourly—then she looked at the ground for a long moment. I said nothing, let the silence fill the room, let the clock fill the silence. Tick, tick. We're all waiting.

Finally she said, "It's true. I... The first night we met? I'd followed you. I did that and... Yes, I slept with you because she asked me to. But that was only the *first* time, Genie. After that, when I got to know..."

"Save the slushy fiction for a romance novel, sweetheart. I just want the facts. The truth."

She bit her lip. Another long silence. "I'd been tailing you for most of the evening, trying to engineer an opening. Just to—you know, so we could talk, maybe. Just to see what... Anyway, I saw what happened in the Zig-Zag. I saw that woman stalking you, that burly woman with the cropped hair."

"Her name's Erika. Old friend of mine."

Virginia took a moment to click that I was being sarcastic. Then she said, "I was—too scared to do anything, except call the cops. I called anonymously and reported that crazy woman and then ran after you again. ...I'm so sorry, I saw her attack you but I couldn't... Look at me. I'm not a fighter."

"Well. You saved my ass, anyway. Patrol car's siren scared her away."

"Really? You're not just saying that."

"I'm not just saying that."

And more silence. So much silence I felt like I could drink from it, just open my mouth and lean into the atmosphere and swallow a large draught. I broke the silence by saying: "So then you followed me to that bar."

"Yes."

"And did what you were told to do. For fuck's sake. Don't you have a conscience?"

"I only did it because... Azura can be a very persuasive woman. I'm not saying... I only did what I did because she asked me."

"Asked you what? Specifically. What did she want you to find out?"

"If you knew who'd killed Maddy. Or, you know, where the investigation had gone, where it was going. How far you'd got. Just, I don't know. Information."

"And you never got suspicious this woman wanted to know— sorry, to find out in an underhand way—details about a murder investigation? That didn't hit you as being some weird goddamn behavior?"

Virginia sighed again. I thought I'd slap her if she did it one more time. She said, "Azura said she was just concerned. Because Madeleine was an old student, and she cared about the well-being of her girls, and all that."

"So why the subterfuge?"

"She didn't want the school to get mixed-up in all of this. It'd be bad for its reputation. Look, she asked me and I did it. Okay? Those were her reasons."

"And did you believe her?"

"Then or now?"

"Either."

"I don't know. Probably not. But I was intimidated by her, too. She's... I mean, Azura's cool in some ways. But she's not the kind of woman you want to mess with."

I leaned over and stubbed out my cigarette. I felt tired—not a good start to the working day. My body was alright, but my eyes were tired, my mind. I felt scooped-out, woozy, heat-seared.

"Genie, I swear to God I thought was she just playing some game," Virginia said. "Some angle... For all I know she is. You don't know that Azura is guilty of anything."

"For all you know," I said. "Huh. I oughta fucking arrest you for interfering with a police investigation."

"If that's what you have to do."

Oh *stop* it, I thought. Stop being so goddamn contrite and saintly. Show me some passion, that you care. Show me your other side. Show me Cassandra the night-time wonder woman.

"And of course you won't repeat any of this officially?" I asked.

Virginia shrugged and looked at the ground regretfully. Then she said quietly, "Would you want me to? Wouldn't it look bad for you?"

"Probably. But I'd probably do it anyway."

I considered this and the realization settled: what a dangerous spot for me to be in. Investigating officer in biggest murder case for decades sleeps with dead girl's best friend who's involved on the orders of the number one suspect. Oh, Jesus. I felt sick.

"You know I could lose my job over this? You do realize that, right? I could get my ass *canned* for this. Fuck it, what am I saying? I could possibly go to *jail*."

Virginia said, "I won't let that happen. I'll deny anything took place. I'll lie if I have to. I'll say I haven't met Azura LaVey in years. Please don't worry about your job, Genie."

I stood and grabbed my coat, slipped it on over my sweater. I loved this sweater: I'd had it for years, it felt like a second skin by now. Warm and tight, nicely ragged, cozy, familiar. Virginia finally got off her knees, sliding back onto the couch.

"So long, wonder woman," I said. "It was fun, I suppose."

I began moving towards the door and she leaped up, took two giant steps and blocked my way. "Wait."

"For what? More stories? Sorry, Virginia, I don't have time for stories. Got things to do in the real world."

She placed her hands on my shoulders, pressing down quite firmly, pressure through her fingertips, through the fabric of my overcoat and my warm familiar sweater.

"Wait."

I waited. She composed herself. I waited some more.

"It *did* start...like that," she said finally. "I admit it. It's horrible, I was totally in the wrong. If I could take it back I would, a thousand times. But now... *Listen* to me. Now it's different. After dinner the other night. That conversation we had, that deep conversation. I felt something. Something changed in my heart. I got to know you. And like you. I hope you can believe me, maybe you can't, but it's true in either case. I really like you, Genie. I feel so comfortable around you—at ease. Like I can..." She smiled gently. "Like I can be myself. I mean that. There's something...special about you. About us. Yeah. This could be something special." She lifted her hands and held them in the air, looking like a hoodlum who knows the game is up. "That's it. That's all I wanted to say."

I took a step back and said, "Aw, bullshit. You were pumping me for information."

"In the beginning. Not later. Not now."

"Why did LaVey pick you, anyway? And not one of her other girls. One of the current students. You weren't there but—what, six months?"

"Nine, actually."

"Fine. Nine. So why pick you for this little charade? What is it between you and LaVey?"

"Nothing. There is *nothing* between us. I just know her. From back then, and we've sort of kept in touch. She buys from my shop sometimes. I don't know why Azura asked me. I suppose it was... I'm good-looking, right? You're always saying that. People...like me."

I said in a tone so cynical it practically came in italics, "Yeah. They *like* you. People like you a hell of a lot, I have no doubt."

She ignored my jibe and said, "I don't know. Maybe it's... I'm a chameleon. I have a gift for changing into other people. For— what's that phrase? 'Hiding in plain sight.'"

"The fucking femme fatale chameleon. Bravo for you."

"Genie, stop it. Don't make this any worse. Don't do that to yourself."

I examined her: she really *did* look totally different. The hot-red vamp from the bar, the voluptuous beauty from the restaurant—if you lined up a picture of Cassandra beside one of Virginia, the dowdy girl with her handmade linen clothes and tousled hair, you'd have to stare pretty hard before you realized they were one and the same. What a strange quality to have, indefinable but very real: the ability to change, to mutate, to blend in. The ability to be invisible or memorable or both. It felt like it was a gift and a curse at the same time.

Something hit me, a little memory-tweak: "You were the girl

with Madeleine. At the theater, three or four weeks ago. Mary-Jane Tussing met you two. She remembered you. She said you were a knockout."

"Yes. Lady Gregory. That was me."

"You were blonde that night."

"Right again."

"Tussing didn't know you. At least she said she didn't. Is that possible? Maybe you really are a chameleon."

"I don't know. Why she would say that, I mean. We know each other. Not too well, but she'd have met me a few times."

"So why did she act like that? She actually claimed she thought you were a prostitute."

Virginia laughed. "Not again? You two will have to compare notes."

I brought us back to serious: "Why, Virginia?"

"I haven't a clue, Genie. That's the truth. Maybe she really didn't recognize me—we only met for 30 seconds. Getting drinks at the interval. We didn't speak, just, you know, just nodded hello, really. Or maybe she lied to you and *did* recognize me. Why, you'll have to ask her. Besides," she said angrily, "Tussing is a fucking snob. She wouldn't want to be seen spending too much time in public with someone as 'disreputable' as Madeleine Greenhill."

At the door I stopped as another question came to mind, popping into existence like a sub-atomic particle, a flash of energy, there and gone. "Why was your hair blonde that night? The night at the theater. Is this another role, another you? The blonde, the redhead, the brunette. It's hard to keep track."

She shrugged, a tired motion—she looked beat, out of juice. I gave myself evens that she'd curl up on that settee the second I left and stare into the fireplace until afternoon. The thought didn't give me as much comfort as I'd assumed it would.

Virginia said, "Again, and forgive me for repeating myself, I don't know. It had nothing to do with you, or…this, if that's what you're thinking. I just...I like to dress up. Play a role. Inhabit another character. *Be* another person. It's as simple as that. I need to—escape from the real me for a while. Do you understand...? Sometimes I get tired of always being conscious of my own existence. You know? So I...I change. For a little while. It's nice, every now and again. Just...destroy that 'you' that's always hanging around. Be someone new."

I shrugged, partly in silent agreement and partly because now I wanted out: out of this room, this conversation, out of the clutches of this goddamn chameleon and her quicksilver personality, the attractive, elusive power of her, like beads of mercury in a magnetic field. I left without saying goodbye or resolving anything; Christ, I hadn't even asked her the thorough list of questions I'd made out for "Virginia Newman" the night before. I knew I was being unprofessional; I tried to care, but it was hard. My heart was dragging my sense of responsibility down to its level.

I'd still need to talk to her. Oh, what fun that'd be. It started to rain, spatters on the windshield, as I revved the engine and peeled away from the house, spraying gravel, spitting curses under my breath. Damn you, Virginia. Fuck you, Cassandra. I hope you're happy now, you bitch. I hope your beauty turns to rottenness and dust. I hope I never see you again.

As I pulled out into the sluggish traffic I thought of the fire in her voice when she spoke of Madeleine, and remembered Misery's words at the funeral: "She clearly cared for my daughter." To be fair, Virginia had been one of the first people in this whole sorry story to give the impression she actually missed Madeleine, and regretted her loss, and loved her. Well, that's something you've got on the credit side, honey. And it *was* something, a very big something—but not enough to keep me there.

Chapter 20

Dinah

JESUS. Barely a quarter past nine in the morning and already I felt like going home. I shuffled in the main door at Dicks Division, through a squally burst of rain and wind and street debris that cut and swirled down the street like the licking tongue of a devil's vengeance. I was glad to get inside, but I still wanted to turn tail and go straight back out again.

Then Marcella Donat came riding to the rescue. Sitting on my desk when I reached it was a light package from that heavy lady. I carefully placed my mug of coffee on the desk, pulled a letter-knife from the drawer and cut open the envelope. Attagirl, Cella: she'd run down the details of That Island in double-quick time. Full address, gas and electricity account numbers, date of construction—and the biggie, ownership. The joint was owned by a subsidiary company called Claydice Ltd, and that in turn was registered to one Elizabeth Rhonda Arendt. So: one of my five little songbirds "owned" the mysterious private club that so many people seemed to get worked up about. I noticed that That Island was listed as a "private residence." It had no official existence as a business, no phone or fax numbers. Well, now its existence was my business.

No sign of LaVey's fingerprints over this one, but that didn't mean a goddamn thing. She was clever, good at covering her tracks. And I just wasn't looking at it from the correct angle, or under the right light. Maybe I needed some kind of magnifying glass here, print-dust, UV rays, blue and penetrating. I'd have to keep looking.

No time like the present, as my teachers used to say. While I slugged back my coffee I debated internally whether or not to update the Chief. I was leaning towards "no" when a call buzzed through: Farrington with Bethany Gilbert's autopsy report.

"Hey-ho, all you good people, give it up for the gorgeous Joanne Farrington, live from the corpse house. How ya keeping, Genie?"

I said dryly, "*How* can you be so energetic this early in the morning?"

"This ain't early, my little chum. This is late. Your old pal has been up slicing and dicing all night. And you know why I do it? Because I care."

"Yeah, yeah," I laughed. "Spare me the pitch for the medal of honor. What have you got, Farr?"

"Alrighty. Our victim—sorry, *your* victim; I just work here. Bethany Daria Gilbert, aged 21, brown hair, hazel eyes, five foot four, 100 and blah blah blah pounds. Here's the important stuff: the girl died from a combination of brain injury and loss of blood. Caused by dozens of incisions to the face, head and neck. Don't ask me what kind of weapon did this, Genie—that's your department—but this was one savage fucking attack. And I mean, this is *me* saying this. She who cannot be shocked."

"Yeah, I saw the... I saw her. She was..."

"She was a mess."

"Yep."

"Like, the sheer strength that would have been needed to do that," Farrington continued. "Her skull is pierced over and over. Her *skull*. Dense bone. Hard stuff there. Your killer obviously used something thin and sharp with a high tensile strength. And a hell of a lot of muscle-power. The wounds are a strange sort of shape. Very small, I mean tiny. Maybe a needle, something like that. A steel spike, I don't know. Whatever it was, it did for poor little Beth."

"Okay," I said. "Okay, thanks again, Farr."

Erika Baton. She might as well have left a business card. The ferocity, the insanity, the sheer brute strength...and the intimate nature of the attack. Again, it was up close and personal. Just like with Madeleine. And almost with me. Most pros killed from a

distance, both spatially and emotionally. Erika clearly liked to
get her hands dirty. You horrible bitch, I thought; you vicious
brutal heartless motherfucker.

"...owe me that beer."

Farrington's voice shocked me back to reality. I said reflexively, "Sorry, what? Sorry, I'd zoned out there."

"I said you still owe me a beer. We meeting for drinks or
what?"

"I... You know, give me a few days, huh? It's crazy busy here
at the moment."

"Yeah, no problem. I got a date tonight anyways. How's next
week sound?"

"Next week. Yeah. Next week is cool, Farr. Sure."

"Alright. I'll call ya. Keep out of trouble, Genie."

She rang off, her words ringing in my ears. Keep out of
trouble. Meet for a drink next week. I smiled wryly and thought,
One depends on the other, doesn't it? A beer next week. Sounds
lovely. If I'm still around by then. I killed my coffee, grabbed my
coat and left. The Chief could wait as well as the drinks.

Bethany Gilbert had been right on the money with something she
said—maybe the last thing she ever said—Shrewsbury was a
posh, pretentious area, no doubting it. The place positively
reeked of wealth, snobbery, aspiration and a sense of entitlement.
That was the most unattractive quality anyone could possess, I'd
always felt: that inherited assumption that you're special, you
deserve special treatment, the rest of the world is somehow of
less value than you. I came from a regular working-class
background: we weren't poor but my mom held down cleaning
jobs all her life to support us. We rented a small one-bed
apartment with a pull-out couch in the sitting-room and had to
share a bathroom with the family of five girls and their belea-
guered and constantly exhausted mother who lived across the
hall. But I'm not complaining, it was a happy childhood. Frugal,

sometimes stony broke, but noisy, clamorous, cheerful, happy.

When I had saved some money I told my mom she could move out now, I'd support her, she could live somewhere else, somewhere better. She looked at me like I'd offered her a parcel of dog-shit, minus the parcel. "This is our home, Genie," she'd said. "Why would I leave my home? And Sunita needs me, she's all on her own now." I never felt like such an asshole. To make amends I bought the apartment off the senile old bat who owned it and gave my mother the deeds for her 50th birthday. I lost her less than 18 months later; a heart attack brought on by a congenital defect. But at least she died at home. I still haven't gotten around to selling the joint on; it's stupid because I rent somewhere else myself while that place sits empty. But I haven't the heart to lease it out, either. Someday I'll take care of it.

Rue de Claudel. Long, broad, elegant, a gifted architect's touch all over it. Even the trees looked designed, aesthetically correct, in just the right proportion and position. Really, what a beautiful place to live. Fit for a queen. And so quiet: the suburbs usually are in Hera. It felt disconnected from the city, or barely connected, the thinnest thread of association between them. Linked by roads and the jagged-tooth topography of urban development, but spiritually on separate planets. Not surprisingly, an area with such grandiose notions didn't lower itself to vulgarities like actual numbers on the buildings, so it took me a while to find Number 44. I slowed the car to a cruise and asked these two old dames walking a tiny dog, its tiny legs pumping like a clockwork toy even though the women were barely shuffling. They directed me back the way I'd come. I turned and returned and eventually pulled up outside That Island.

No name, naturally. No indicator that this was anything but another large house in another large garden in an area overflowing with them. I parked on the street and pushed against the huge wrought-iron gates—open. That was good: I'd been wondering about my next move should they be locked. Without a warrant I'd no legal authority to vault the gates and stroll on up there. But I probably would have done it anyway, and hang the consequences. Now I stepped through the gates as they creaked ominously, pulling them closed behind me.

The gardens were lush, verdant, rather overgrown. Not as smartly kept as at Caritas Heights, but there was an agreeable sense of disorder about the place. Like the vegetation had been let run wild, up to a point. I liked it. Coniferous trees stretching for the heavens like giant fingers, shorter deciduous ones spreading and shedding and blocking the light from the long grass on which they stood. Creepers curling up and around trellises, rose bushes that reached three feet above my head, a not unpleasant smell of soft rottenness. This garden was dense with life, super-organic, ripe and heady. The house was coming into view as I walked the winding path, crunching through the blue and white pea gravel at my feet. It looked artificially colored, giving a nice contrast to the bounding nature all around. I hadn't seen anyone else yet—not one living soul—which seemed a little weird to me. Shouldn't there be a gardening staff, maintenance, security out front? I subconsciously touched the butt of my gun as it jostled against my hip.

Now I could see That Island, the house itself. Again, not as impressive as Caritas—smaller, less striking, less shocking—but pleasing nonetheless. It was huge by any regular standard, three stories, with a steep pointed roof in the center, small turrets at either side, a stone-faced front, large windows, decorative wood beams, a widow's walk running what looked like the whole way around. Old and old-fashioned, a little mixed-up, getting shabby, but charming and picturesque. It took me half a minute to reach the building, and still no sign of life. The place was silent but for vague, distant sounds of insects, arthritic tree branches moaning, a pond babbling somewhere. No traffic noise in this far. No noises at all. Eerily quiet.

That Island was closed. Closed for business, closed to all

activity. I shook the door by its brass handle to make sure but it was obvious: nobody was home. There weren't any signs proclaiming it, the windows weren't boarded up, but this joint was emptied out, ghostly. I peeked in the window to the left of the door and saw a greeting room, a sort of small foyer, with a walnut reception desk, rich-colored carpets, two armchairs, brackets in the wall for large candles. No dust, no cobwebs, no sheets covering the furniture. But no life either. It was like the Mary Celeste on land: as though everyone had simply vanished, *poof*, in an instant. There and then gone.

Damn it. This was no good to me. I needed in. I projected ahead, envisaged calling Etienne, making up some bullshit story about chasing a perp to this place, seeing them bust in the window and following through... Yeah. That would have to do. I was going into That Island.

I stepped back, looked around for something to throw, a rock, a heavy lump of wood. A smallish red brick lay nestled under weeds and moss, drowning in it, swallowed by all that hungry life. I bent down and worked the brick out of its spongy grave, turned back to the house, took a deep breath and leaned back to throw as hard as I could.

Which meant I was off balance when a crazed fucking demon attacked me, leaping out of nowhere and clawing at my face, screaming like a banshee. Which led me to fall backwards, bringing her down too, crashing hard onto the gravel, bashing my coccyx off the brick I'd dropped behind me. A shard of pain spiked up my back and down my ass and leg, and the woman was still screeching, nails scratching at my face like a cat in an alleyway fight, and my own fighting instinct kicked in and I flapped at her hands with my hands, keep her away from the eyes, take the cuts to your flesh but keep her *out* of the goddamn eyes. My mind was shocked and dazzled, stunned numb, but my body was fighting back. She drew blood in two, three, four places on my cheeks and forehead, and I winced and took in tight little breaths and let myself go low to the ground and then *pushed* with my hips, with all my strength, ejecting her off me and springing to a standing position. I still couldn't see her face as she rose from the ground, damp tendrils of hair straggling down it, obscuring it, but fuck that, I didn't need to recognize her to hit her. I planted one foot in front of me and stepped forward with the other, my arm locked, my fist coiled and strong. I caught her good on the eye socket and she stumbled backwards but didn't fall.

My breath was coming fast and uneven, adrenaline flooding my system, making me feel high, kinetic, almost unhinged. Then she screamed again, a horrible, animalistic sound, and launched herself at me, claws out, eyes rolling wildly behind the veil of hair. The woman grabbed for my own hair and I thanked my lucky stars I decided to chop it all those years ago, pulling my head out of harm's way, smacking her with my open palm on the ear as her momentum carried her past. The sound rang out, it sounded painful, and the maniac dashed off, around the side of the house. She was out of sight before my mind rejoined the battle and told the rest of me, *Run*, you asshole, get after her.

I ran. I sped around the corner and saw her kicking heels speeding around the next corner and ran harder. I came around the back of the house, the garden different here, neater, smaller, more artifice than out front. I looked around, breathing through my nose, willing oxygen into my bloodstream, my teeth gritted, my face beginning to hurt. No sign of the crazy woman and then I heard her, wailing in pain as she struggled through a hedge at the edge of the property, maybe 15 yards away, hidden behind more of those massive trees. I ran towards the sound and through the hole she'd made in the hedge, my little frame slipping through easily. There she was, across the road, one quick glance back at me, panic and loathing on her face, and she was gone. I started running again.

We fish-knifed through three or four streets, a small public park, the yard of a private boarding school, she always that little bit ahead of me but the distance diminishing. The woman was tiring, you could tell it by the way her head was starting to wobble. I was tiring too but I couldn't let my head go, couldn't let myself go, had to keep pushing hard and harder and harder still. I rounded a corner of yet another plush garden and saw nothing for a moment and then I saw her, she was on me again, charging with something long in her hands, a garden implement maybe, a rake or a fork, raised above her head like the executioner's axe. She screamed and I yelled and charged right back at her, instinct driving me now, and as we came within each other's orbits I ducked down low, bending my left leg and skidding on my left foot along the wet pavement and kicking like a fucking mule with the right. *Bang*, I caught her on the knee as she swung the weapon uselessly and she buckled and stumbled and fell, her head cracking off the ground, hopping back up into the air with the force of the impact, smacking down a second time, hopping, smacking, finally stopping. Her eyes rolled into dull oblivion and her head didn't move again.

I stood and absently rubbed my torn trousers, touched the bloodied knee underneath. My attacker was out cold. With a knock like that, she'd be lucky if she didn't fracture her skull, but that wasn't my worry right now. My breath was coming back to normal, I was forcing it back, deeper, slower, calmer. Be calm, Genie. Breathe and be calm. It was quiet and we were alone. After all that, I still hadn't seen anyone else. That Island was an island, alright.

I found a cigarette somewhere on my person, as if by radar, lit it and took a few deep drags. I smiled and shook my head, a little hysterical underneath the overwhelming relief, ecstatic to be alive and more-or-less in one piece. Then I crouched down to my attacker and pulled her hair to the side. I was looking at the insensible form of Dinah Spaulding, actor and creative consultant, and one of the "confessors" to Madeleine's murder. I smiled again and patted her on the cheek.

"Thanks, Dinah," I muttered. "Thanks a lot, sweetheart." The crazy gal with the sharp nails had just proved to me that there was a conspiracy.

Chapter 21

Odette

EVERYTHING was speeding up, taking on its own impetus, a worrying velocity. Within two hours of my little dance with danger, That Island had been razed to the ground, Dinah Spaulding was claiming insanity and Liz Arendt had gone deep underground. I had to get a handle on all of this. I had to finish things soon.

After gathering myself I'd grabbed a passerby and told her to call the emergency number and request back-up for Detective Auf der Maur, Homicide, while I stood guard over Spaulding. The cuts on my face began to really hurt as I waited for the cavalry, pinching and piercing in the cool air. A patrol car screeched to a halt, _très_ dramatically, about ten minutes later. They bundled Spaulding into the back and I grabbed their standard-issue first aid kit, applying antiseptic cleanser with a thick cotton ball. It hurt like all hell but had to be done. The cuts were only skin-deep, I figured, no real damage caused. They'd fade in a few days. The patrol car whooshed Spaulding to lock-up and I walked back to That Island.

We must have run faster and farther than it seemed at the time, because the return journey took about 15 minutes and when I got there the house was ablaze. I could see black smoke from the distance and broke into a trot as fast as my sore ass would allow. By the time I reached Number 44 I could see huge pillars of flame, orange and red, roaring into the sky. A small crowd had gathered in shock and curiosity, all remaining at a discreet distance outside the garden walls. I guess people really didn't interfere in each other's business around here; decorum and propriety were everything. Not for me, though. I rudely shoved my way through them, hollering and waving my badge in the air like it was a fire-hose and I was here to quench the blaze, but nobody could have put this out. As I approached the building a fierce geyser of fire shot up from somewhere in the bowels of the house and ripped through the roof, which started to cave in on itself. It smelled like a professional job, literally: the sickly sweet odor of flammable oil suffused the air. And the fire appeared to be coming from within, from right in the center—*The Arsonist's Handbook*, chapter one, page one. But I couldn't get close enough to know for sure, couldn't get any closer than about 25 yards away; the heat was too much, it was searing and unbearable.

I went back to the front gate and had one of the rubberneckers call the fire brigade, though there wasn't really any fear of the inferno spreading to other houses. The garden was heavy and sodden, it wouldn't catch fire. I also had them call in two more prowlers and a forensics team on my authority. Still nobody had moved closer to the flaming building, and still I'd seen nobody inside or outside the doomed house. I made one last, wholly superfluous check that the crowd was keeping a safe distance from danger. Then I turned and watched That Island burn.

Nobody knows nothing. Nobody seen nothing. You *got* nothing, cop.

All the old clichés of police movies and paperback potboilers were starting to come true in my real life. Now I was sitting in Etienne's office, weary, befuddled, slightly soot-blackened, with a plaster over the stitched-up cut on my forehead that had proved, on inspection, to be slightly more than just a scratch— Spaulding had nails like a hellcat. The Chief and me were running through the morning's events, and I couldn't tell which of our heads was spinning the quickest. It had been a *weird* fucking day so far.

Etienne said, "No one saw anything. That's, basically that's where we stand, correct?"

"Yep. Six officers corralled and questioned everybody at the scene of the fire. None of them noticed anyone acting suspiciously."

"And do you believe that?"

"Mm…yeah. I think I do. I mean, this area, Chief. It's real spread-out, big gardens, very private gardens, you know… Sure. Someone could have snuck in there, started the fire and snuck back out before it had really caught. Easy. People up there don't pay much attention to other people's business, either. They consider it a badge of honor to walk around with your nose stuck in the air."

"Alright, Auf der Maur, save the political speeches for later. Go on."

"Okay, uh, forensics can't say yet what started the blaze. Like, the house was still burning by the time I left to come here. But one of 'em I spoke to, what was her name? Koutchner, right, the team leader. She reckons it was an incendiary device, like a small homemade bomb, maybe. Relatively simple to put together. Set off inside the house, probably in a center room, gasoline splashed around to speed up the process. Definitely wasn't the outside of the building that was torched. So we're maybe talking someone who had access. But this is all just speculation yet."

"The owner?" Etienne asked. "This Elizabeth Arendt? Could it have been her?"

"I…suppose so. Yeah. Why not? Or with some help from her friends."

"And she's disappeared?"

"Uh-huh. Soon as I left That Island—that's the name of the joint—I issued an arrest order on Arendt. Had one of our patrol cars head straight to her place of work. You know she's an accountant or something, a financial controller, like a number cruncher? Works in MacDaffy's, huge place down in the financial district. Wasn't there. Her colleagues haven't seen her all week. Which, they say, isn't like Liz. She's a real little busy bee, that one. Normally."

"And we've checked her home."

"Yep. That and her mom's home and her sister's. Of Liz, there is no trace. And none of them have had any contact with her since last week sometime. Didn't even know she'd been arrested. Figured she was just busy with work or whatever."

"Could they be covering?"

"They could... I mean, family is family, right? But I don't think so. I don't think they know anything about Lizzie's weird other life."

"I understand Spaulding is going to try for a psyche plea."

I hummed cynically. "Yeah. Claims temporary insanity. Says she's never even heard of That Island. Spaulding can't, or more likely won't, say why she was there or why she attacked me. She actually is saying all this. Just, I mean, brazen like that. Says she doesn't remember anything for weeks. Not the Madeleine confession, being questioned, Jamie Sobel, nada. Doesn't know how she ended up in the clink. I could tell her."

I pointed to the cuts on my face and smiled wryly. Etienne allowed herself a smile—just a small one, all strictly within departmental guidelines—lifted her phone and muttered into it, "Kim, bring us in two coffees, would you, please?" She looked at me: "You'll have coffee?" I nodded and Etienne repeated, "Two coffees, Kim, thank you."

She hung up and continued looking at me, that piercing gaze that made grown women feel like they were back in the infants' class. I think I actually gulped as the Chief said, "Where do we stand now, Detective? The full story, if you would."

I gave it to her: "Okay. First up, this place today, this club. I went there because it came up in... Various sources pointed me towards it. A few I don't want to name, a few I can tell you about when this is all wrapped up."

She nodded her assent. I went on, "Basically, That Island has something to do with Madeleine Greenhill's murder. Or her life, at any rate. The fact that Arendt and Spaulding are involved proves it, I think. It's all tied in somehow. Anyway, this is why I was there in the first place. Figured I'd poke around, maybe dig something up. But now, I mean, forget it. The place being torched like that—we won't find anything now."

"Until we track down Ms Arendt."

"Exactly. Next up, Bethany Gilbert's killing last night: the two are connected. Her and Madeleine, they're connected. I'm about 99 per cent sure the same woman did both murders."

"This…Erika something who tried to kill you?"

"Twice. Uh-huh. Same one. Erika Baton they call her. I'm sure it was her killed the Gilbert girl too."

"What did Joanne Farrington say?"

"Not the same weapon—the retractable steel baton thing—but Chief, it's the same MO. I can feel it in my bones. It's *her*."

Etienne dropped her head into her hand. "Jesus. And we knew this a few days ago. You and me, we knew who'd killed Madeleine Greenhill and allowed her to continue walking around. Now another girl is dead."

"There's nothing we could have done, Chief. Honest to God, putting out an APB on Erika Baton would just have driven her into hiding. You don't just trace an address and march in there and arrest someone like that. This woman is smart, she's a professional killer with a sewer rat's instinct. She knows how to hide. And we've got a leak, somewhere inside. You know this. Someone here is connected to all this. We'll have to catch Erika by the side door, you know?"

Etienne's assistant Kim, a thin girl with an electric shock of corkscrew curls, eased open the door and placed a tray on the desk: coffee, sugar, cream. She smiled at me and exited without a word. Etienne did the needful, sweetening and coloring our coffees without asking me how I took mine. I didn't correct her, I just wanted something hot inside me.

The Chief took a short sip and heaved a long sigh. "I know, Auf der Maur. In all probability you're right. But that won't stop me having regrets about this one for a long time." She smiled ruefully into space. "The responsibilities of the job, I suppose."

I said urgently, "Ma'am, I *will* get her. That psycho Baton, I've got the word out. I'll find her and nail her for the lot of them."

"You sound confident. I'm glad."

"I am confident." My voice, thankfully, held a conviction my soul had yet to fully embrace.

"Alright. What else?"

"Okay. This is the big one. I still have no solid evidence— nothing we can use in court—but Azura LaVey is involved. I'm not sure exactly how or how deeply, but she is. I'm stone sure of it. But, like I say...evidence, or lack of. Not enough for a search warrant. Probably not even enough to bring her in for questioning."

"Why so? What's stopping us?"

"LaVey is a powerful woman. She's got powerful friends, she's well-connected... I mean, we could. Just drag her in here, let her sit in a cell for a while, let her get uncomfortable... See how the gracious educator would react to that. But I don't know, Chief. It could whip up a shit-storm for us. For you. Pardon my language."

Etienne nodded, mulling it over. She drained her coffee, head leaning back, almost looking at the ceiling. She delicately replaced her cup on its saucer and said, "I am... At this point I'm almost willing to say 'fuck it' and just bring LaVey in. Yes, Auf der Maur, I said 'fuck.'"

She wasn't smiling, which just made the whole thing funnier. I laughed, spluttering coffee, and said, "You cracked a joke. To be honest, I mean, that's what's really caught me off-guard."

"Mm, well... I have been known to make jokes from time to time. Terrible ones, my daughter insists. Anyway, yes, Azura LaVey. You're right, she does know powerful people. Our own Chief of Police Ealing is in the same tennis club. And yet I'm inclined to disregard all that anyway, and bring her down here. Like you say, let her sweat in a cell for a while. See if she cracks."

"Chief, I appreciate it, but I'm not sure. She's clever too, Azura. Cunning. Like that lunatic Baton. Go for her now and it could spook the horses, you know? She'd close off all the avenues then, and we'd never know... Give me another few days. Three days, tops. If this thing isn't done and done by then, we'll haul her in. What do you think?"

"Fine. You've got three days." She paused. "I hope you're right, Auf der Maur. About how to play this. I really do."

"Yes, Ma'am. So do I."

Etienne turned to her paperwork. I was dismissed, and left.

"The dead arose and spoke to many. Finally, we get to talk."

I had tried my best to keep the sarcasm from my voice but I'm sure it leaked out somewhere, out the side maybe, dribbling past the edge of my words. But how could I *not* be sarcastic? After several days of chasing her, Odette had actually phoned me. I simultaneously felt relieved, happy, embittered...and bewildered at why I simultaneously felt relieved, happy and embittered. I'd been at my desk a bare five minutes when the call came through and her soft, unhurried tones were there on the other end, whispering in my ear: "Genie. It's Odette. How have you been?"

Which is where my sarcasm came in. She dealt with it graciously enough, saying, "I'm sorry, have you been looking for me?"

I spluttered, "Have I been...? Yeah, Odette, I've been looking for you. For *days*."

"Oh, I am sorry. I didn't... I must have missed your message."

My face reddened as I recalled my very deliberate decision *not* to leave a message: phone, note or any other kind. So what the fuck gives you the right to be annoyed with her, Genie? How was she supposed to know you wanted to talk—by telepathy or osmosis, or maybe just a hunch?

I quit chiding myself and chiding her, and said, "Uh, yeah. Yeah, those things, those machines... Look, we're talking now so let's, you know. Let's crack on with it, huh?"

"Sure. How can I help the Hera City police? This is about work, I presume?"

"It is. It is. Uh, it's about Madeleine Greenhill. I need to ask you a few things. About you and her."

A moment of flat silence, then Odette said, "Of course, yes, anything you need. Any way I can help, Genie."

"Cool. Alright."

I hesitated, unsure how to start, how to broach the subject. A possible can of worms, a Pandora's box, a hell of a mess. Did I really want to open something like that? But the question was pointless, I didn't have a choice.

I took a deep breath and said, "When did you last see Madeleine?"

"When did I last see her...? Hmm. I'd say maybe...two-and-a-half years ago."

"Two-and-a-half years. You're sure about that?"

"Mm-hm. Yes. She started taking music lessons aged 17 and she stopped coming to me after about six months. So, yes, I think that's about right. But I could check my diary if you need me to be more exact."

I said quietly, "Right. It's just that, uh, I have information that you and her remained acquaintances after that. After the music thing ended. That you saw her fairly regularly, actually. Up until quite recently."

"You... Hmm. How odd. That someone would say that. May I...? Do I know the person who told you this?"

"I don't think so. Is it true, Odette?"

"No, it certainly is not true, Genie. It's completely *untrue*. Who...? Sorry, I shouldn't ask you that."

"So you haven't seen Madeleine Greenhill recently."

"No."

"Well, maybe you've met someone she might have known. Mutual acquaintances, people like that."

"No. That is, not to my knowledge.You do believe me, don't you?"

"I'm just doing my job here, Odette. Asking questions and doing my job."

"But *you* believe me? You, the Genie I used to live with. Not Detective Auf der Maur. You believe me."

Did I believe her? I suppose so. I mean, I had no reason not to. And I suddenly realized it didn't really matter anyway. Odette had nothing to do with this, Misery's information was all screwy, someone got a hold of something all wrong and twisted it into a relationship that obviously didn't exist.

"Odette, that's fine. That's all I needed to know. You say you didn't have any connection to Madeleine, it's good enough for me. So, uh, we're done. I've no more questions."

She sighed, clearly relieved. "Thank you, Genie."

"Sure. Listen, I got a shit-load of things to do. I'm gonna have to bail on you."

"That's alright. I know you're busy with this investigation, such a big crime after all... So how is it going anyway? Your case."

"Um...okay. You know, slow and steady. We're getting there."

"And how are you? You're on top of things?"

"Yeah. I mean, I guess so, yeah. Things are—a little crazy sometimes. I, ah..." I laughed. "Ha! You wanna hear a funny story?"

"One of your grisly cop tales, no doubt," Odette said playfully. "Go ahead."

"The day I called to Datlow? After we spoke, you remember, I was telling you about Madeleine. Anyway, that day. After you'd gone back upstairs I turned back onto the street and, ah...someone tried to run me over. Swear to God. So whaddya think of them apples?"

I laughed again. Odette gasped in shock. "Oh my God! Genie! Are you alright? I mean, of course you're alright, you're talking to me now. But seriously. Someone tried to kill you? What happened?"

"Not much. She basically, this crazy bitch gunned her car for me. Big mother of a thing. Engine sounded like an articulated truck. I dived out of the way, fired off a few shots, she skedaddled. And all this right outside your door. On prosperous Datlow Street. What would the neighbors think!?"

"And did you catch her?"

"Nah, she... I know who it was, though. She broke through the traffic, I was on foot. So I didn't get her that day. But I will. I hope."

"Uh-huh... Well, me too, I hope you catch this—maniac. My God... Well, here's hoping you find her. Or her car, maybe. I'm sure there can't be that many cars with a stick shift in Hera. Most use automatic, don't they?"

It felt like my blood had suddenly chilled, like something from the cheesy vampire stories I devoured as a child. As though someone had injected below-zero dry ice into my veins. I felt a cold, pure horror descend on me as I realized: I hadn't told Odette that Erika Baton drove a car with a manual gear-stick. She *knows*.

I whispered, "What did you just say?"

"I said I hope you catch her. Because, you know, attacking a police officer... This woman is obviously a menace. A very dangerous person."

I thought hard, running it through the circuits in my head faster than the speed of light, and came back to the same conclusion again and again: she knows. Odette knows. And by extension Odette is involved—in the killing of Madeleine and the attempt on my life.

No. It couldn't be. This is madness, I told myself, not really heeding it at the same time. Odette's a goddamn music teacher. She's a well-bred princess, she likes *haute cuisine* and scouting for antique furniture and reading ostentatiously obscure novels. She does Pilates, for Christ's sake, she laughs at her horoscope in the paper and her mother is one of Hera's most renowned charity dames. This is *Odette*, dumb-ass. The woman you shared a home and a life with. The woman you loved, and maybe still love.

I must have misheard. That's it, some wicked little part of me wanted to hear her say something damning and I heard it. I thought I heard it. But she never said it. Except she did. I think she did. Oh, shit.

She was speaking again: "...you okay? *Genie*. Are you okay? You've gone awfully silent."

I replied on auto-pilot, mumbling some trite deflection, some bullshit excuse that I don't remember exactly. Then Odette was saying goodbye and hanging up the phone. The pips sounded in my ear and withdrew to nothingness as I sat there, dumbstruck, receiver in my hand, a fearful hammering in my heart.

I still didn't want to believe it but a part of me believed it. My head was in denial, my gut screaming to be heard. She knows. She's involved. This woman you loved for three years tried to have you killed.

It couldn't be true. There had to be another explanation. I hadn't a clue what that might have been, but there *had* to be one. I needed there to be another explanation, something that made sense out of all this, something that made me slap my head and smile and say, "Ah! Of course! How stupid I've been, how could I ever have doubted her?"

I needed that badly, like a drug. In fact I needed an actual drug but I didn't do drugs, so I needed a drink. I needed to get out of there and fix one. So I got out, stumbling to my car and driving home in a horrified daze.

Chapter 22

Rose

BY the time I'd skulled my second whiskey I'd decided: I would let this Odette thing lie for the moment. No telling Etienne, no telling Cella, nobody. I needed to know myself for sure, and I'd no way of doing that just yet. The thought of wrongly accusing her of something so heinous, so enormous... Our relationship was dead in the water—I finally accepted it—but that didn't mean a potential friendship had to be strangled at birth. And besides, what practical different would arresting Odette make? If she was involved, she'd clam up and say nothing, and worse, serve as a warning to the others that we were closing in. If she wasn't, well... The consequences of that particular fuck-up could reverberate for the ages. Anyway, Odette wasn't the ringmaster here; however she was connected to all this, surely it was tangential at worst. Maybe she'd become mixed-up in something, an innocent standing on the edges, just more collateral damage in this bloody war...

Nah, I didn't really believe it myself, either. And yet I didn't act on it. I couldn't. Something stopped me, some hesitancy, some bind with the past. I needed to know for sure. For her sake, and for mine.

I lit another cigarette and let a third splash of whiskey fall into the china cup. My apartment was dim, cold and depressing—perfect surroundings in which to drink myself miserable. I thought about turning on the gas heating but decided against it. I felt like I deserved to sit here, in this broken-down old armchair and this chilly, gloomy place. It felt appropriate to my mood, and that mood was black.

Too black. I was in danger of drowning in it, being swamped in regrets and conflicting impulses and booze-sodden self-indulgence. When you don't know what to do, my mom used say, just do something. The act of beginning creates its own narrative. So get back out there, Genie. Get back in the game.

I drained the last of the whiskey and cradled the empty cup in my hands. I'd purchased this china tea-set in a charity shop for next to nothing, along with a scuffed suede jacket, a book of surrealist poetry and a lamp-shade that I hadn't yet got around to buying a lamp for. The cup had a design on the side, like chinaware often does; a delicate illustration of a flower, a lovely, simple blossom, a daffodil or buttercup. *Click*: a light went on. Buttercup—that's what Poison Rose's trick had called her the night of Madeleine's murder. What Erika Baton had whispered to me as she leaned over to end my life. So, another tick in Erika's "guilty" account.

I thought about Rose then. I pictured her stumbling from that sordid encounter in a dockside alleyway, maybe taking a nip from her ever-present alcoholic crutch, looking around for more trade, hoping for more but unlikely to find it. I saw her enter Whinlatter, lurch towards the water, swaying, looking sick and destitute, then... Then she sees Madeleine's body, floating on the water, lifeless and destroyed, in stark, terrible black and white. I pictured Rose retching from the shock, putting a hand to her mouth, holding it down—that stomach would be used to anything, wouldn't it? Imagining her, shaking that wrecked old head, sad and tender, then shambling back to find a phone and report what she'd seen.

There might be something more to discover down there. Something I had missed, some detail I'd overlooked. Whinlatter Docks, where this had all begun. Fuck it, it was worth a shot. Anything was better than crashing out here, feeling sorry for myself. I rinsed out my mouth with a half-can of flat coke and spat viciously into the wash-basin. Get up, get out, get moving. Begin at the beginning and let the rest take care of itself.

It was raining when I reached Whinlatter, a weak, greasy pall of murkiness and foreboding. The day was turning dark though it wasn't late. Talk about pathetic fallacy. I felt as if the elements were mocking me, the gods of weather crying and laughing at me from their celestial balconies. I'm not sure what I was looking for: a clue, a vibe, the ghost of something. Maybe an actual ghost. I pulled my collar up around my face and strode the docks, thinking of Madeleine, calling on her, whispering: "Come on, kid. Give me something. *Talk* to me…"

The area was almost deserted—a few sailors doing whatever sailors do about 100 yards seaward, distant sounds of engines firing up, cutting out, being manhandled back to life. Isolated shouts, angry swears, an oddly bitter laughter. Christ, what a place to spend your every day. I kept walking, down further, past Piers 19, 20, 21. Then I was at Pier 22, the site of Madeleine's doom. It looked normal by daylight, bland and unremarkable, almost too normal. I felt like there should be a marker at this spot, a cenotaph, something to record that a young girl lost her life here, violently and needlessly. Something to honor that death.

"You're that cop, right?"

I turned around. Two girls were sheltering from the rain under the jutting wooden roof of a locked warehouse, huddled together for warmth. They were both youngish—maybe early twenties, though it was hard to tell with pros. They could have passed for 30 or older, they were so haggard and thin, so drained of the plump exuberance of youth. That's what prostitution does to you, I guess. It steals your best days and hurls you through life so quickly that the speed eventually kills you.

I nodded and said, "What cop is that?"

The taller of the two spoke again: "You're investigating the murder. That girl was killed down here. The rich kid."

I took a few steps towards them and they visibly flinched. I raised my hands in an "easy now" gesture and kept walking, nice and smooth, until I was within a few yards of them. The shorter girl sniffled like she had a bad cold and snuggled into her friend's flank. The other girl embraced her and pulled her to the warm comfort of her underarm.

"You want a drink?"

She pulled a bottle of vodka from a bag hung across her chest and proffered it to me.

"No thanks. But I appreciate the offer."

"Right. Working, huh? 'On duty.'"

"That's right. You want a cigarette?"

She nodded. I took a Dark Nine for myself and handed her the rest of the pack. She lit one and pocketed the box.

"Thanks. What's your name anyway?"

"Genie. Detective Auf der Maur full title, but you can call me Genie."

"Hi, Genie. I'm Chrissy. This one here's Tilda."

The little one smiled dozily and muttered, "'S short for Matilda."

She looked chemically whacked, totally fucked. She listed to the side and Chrissy righted her. I wouldn't get much out of Tilda, that was certain. But Chrissy looked fairly alert, her limpid green eyes sparkling beneath the drained, anemic pallor of her face. What an oddly lovely juxtaposition: her eyes were like gems in a puddle of dried-out mud.

I tentatively drew a 20 from my wallet and held it up at shoulder-height. "You feel like answering a few questions, Chrissy? About that girl who was murdered."

She waved a hand. "Put your money away, Genie. You don't need to bribe me. I'll tell you whatever I can. Fuck, that kid was younger than me, you know? I *want* to help."

"Alright. Thank you."

"And anyway, that vicious fuck who did it. You're gonna get her, right? Lock the bitch up for life. So it's in my own best interests anyway. Can't have someone like that prowling 'round these parts at night. And I got Tilda to think of too."

"I'm gonna get her, Chrissy. Hopefully you can help me with that."

She took a long slug of vodka, her pale throat contracting as she swallowed, like a small animal wriggling under water. Chrissy wiped her mouth and said, "Get the old gray matter revving, you know? Okay, shoot."

"Were you here the night Madeleine Greenhill died?"

"Yes and no. We were here... Huh?"

Tilda was mumbling something to her. Chrissy listened then said, "Right. She says she wasn't working that night and do I remember because she had her period. So that's correct, I do remember that. Which makes me—I was here on the night. But only for part of it. Until about 11, maybe."

"Did you see anyone suspicious-looking? Anyone unusual?"

"Well I saw a few people I'd never seen before, if that's what you mean. Sorta comes with the job, though, you know?" She laughed. "Nah, I know what you mean. I'm just kidding. Did I spot anyone shifty? Mmm...no. Not that I can think of. Just the usual perverts and scumbags come down here for a quick fix."

"You left at 11? I have that right?"

"'Bout that, yeah. I don't have a watch, so..."

"Any reason why? You don't have to be specific, I'm not interested in your activities. I'm just trying to work this out."

"That's okay, Genie. I get it. Yeah, uh, where was I? Okay, yeah, we all left at about 11."

"All? What do you mean?"

"I mean every last working gal down here split for home when that posh broad paid us to."

"What? Who? Chrissy, tell me what happened."

"This woman. Pulled up in a fancy car, fucking beautiful thing. I think could have been a Jaguar or something? Dark-green, maybe black. Hard to tell. Anyhow she rolls the window down, beckons us come towards the car. The hand up for 'stop' when we got to within, like, five yards. We were all intrigued, thought maybe she wanted some kind of weird gang-bang type scenario, but whatever, it's all work. But that wasn't it. The woman, she says, 'I'll give each of you two nights' pay to go home right now.' Uh, what? I mean, what the fuck? Genie, that's an offer you don't hear too often. We said are you serious, she said sure. Told us clear off straight away and she'd give us our money then and there. We didn't even *need* to discuss it. The dame asked me what we'd make on a good night. I told her and added on ten per cent on the top. Then she did a quick head-count, there were eight or ten of us there. Counted off a shitload of money, wrapped it in a big rubber band and threw it out the window to me. Said, 'You hand it out. Then get out of here.' I divvied up the cash between me and my pals and, yeah, we fucked off home. Easiest money I ever made."

It explained why nobody saw what happened that night, why Poison Rose was the first to see the body, all the other girls gone by the time she got to Whinlatter after her little rendezvous with Erika Baton. Madeleine's killer coming from the docks, post-murder, the sicko blowing off some of that sick sexual tension. But who paid? Who was the woman in the flash car?

I said, "Did you see her, Chrissy? This woman, did you see her face?"

"Nuh-uh. She kept in the dark. Wouldn't let us get up near to the car."

"You didn't get the plate, I presume?"

"Nah. Didn't even look at it... She had a cap on, you know one of those peaked things?"

"Why didn't you report any of this? When you heard about Madeleine Greenhill's murder, why didn't you come forward?"

"Never put the pieces together until just now. That's the truth. Genie, I've been drinking and whoring a long time. My mind doesn't work so good as it used to. I'm dumb as shit now. It didn't even occur to me. ...Shit, I'm real sorry. I mean, if I hadda known what was gonna come down... I'd still have taken her money, to be honest. But I'd have run to the nearest phone and called you guys right away."

"I know you would, Chrissy. It's alright. You didn't do anything wrong."

"Nah. But I feel like I did."

"Yeah. I know the feeling sometimes."

Not much else for us to say now. I asked her again if she wanted money, maybe needed it. Chrissy said sure, she needed it but couldn't take it under these circumstances. I shoved a 50 into Tilda's pocket and told both of them, "It's there if you need it, okay? Consider it a loan if you like. And thanks."

Chrissy nodded, Tilda nodded off. I walked back to my car, rain sneaking in the top of my collar, wetting my neck, making me shiver as I thought: Queneau. It had to have been her. She could have made it over from the thing at the museum, the exhibition dinner. She could have excused herself and slipped over and done her dirty deed in 40 minutes, an hour tops. I visualized Queneau pulling up at the docks in some expensive car, that elegant hand reaching out the window, holding her blood money; the sneer of disdain across her aristocratic features, making that handsome face ugly. It was her. LaVey wouldn't have risked coming down here herself; she'd send the attack dog. Harder, tougher, better able to handle herself among the low, crawling things in the dangerous undergrowth of Hera City.

I reached my car, mind still churning, speculating: Erika must have somehow tricked or forced Madeleine to the docks — probably the latter — she kills her with that thing, that terrible weapon, ties one leg to a concrete block and hurls her over the side. Nobody watching, no hookers as witnesses, no security guards nearby. Erika stays around for a little while, not too long because that's risky but long enough to make sure the body doesn't float back up. She leaves just a few minutes too early — it couldn't have been any more, going on the chronology — but she leaves, thinking her job is done, and about three-and-a-half minutes later the rope comes loose and Madeleine starts to float free from her murky, sodden tomb. Erika the stone cold killer is strolling home, meets Poison Rose, feels in the mood for fun. They skip into an alleyway and get down to it. Rose continues on to the docks, where poor dead Madeleine is waiting to greet her.

What an awful image, a horror show in my head. So vivid I was afraid I'd still see it when I went to bed that night, beamed onto the inside of my eyelids as though a projector was rolling inside my head. I was afraid I'd start to dream it.

Poison Rose lived in the fag-end of the east side sprawl, and if you'd ever been to the sprawl, you'd know what that signified; just how low a life had fallen. The sprawl had grown organically, if you could use such a term about a disjointed collection of buildings, streets, electric wires, sewers, people running like rats around and beneath and on top of one another. Like crazy, juiced-up rats. I hated the sprawl. It was depressing and overwhelming; it was neglect and chaos made real in chipped concrete, given shape in the sad leaning lampposts and broken asphalt. It made sense that Rose would live there. The sprawl was the end of the line in Hera, bottom of the barrel, the pathetic last stand of a failed life.

Her apartment was depression squared. A tiny, one-roomed shack on the seventh floor of a building that looked in violation of every fire and safety regulation the city possessed, and a few we hadn't signed into law — the city mothers usually waited for someone to die before acting on these matters. The walls were smeared with the creeping black marks of damp, the carpet was filthy where it wasn't worn clean through; a smell of alcohol and sewerage wafted through the place like the warning of a chemical spill. I needed to make this quick and felt bad about needing it.

I'd found Rose and her grim abode surprisingly easily: Dispatch had a last known address only two blocks away, and the current resident—a jumpy pill-popper who said she'd been bedridden for the last three months—told me where Rose had moved to. Some problem with the landlady, apparently. Everybody had a problem with somebody down here. Rose was asleep when I knocked on her door, or maybe she was passed out inside; whatever, I'd smoked half a Dark Nine by the time she dragged her bare feet across the timeworn carpet and opened up. No chain on the door; probably no lock on the inside. And besides, anyone, even a titch like me, could easily kick the door off the hinges. Rusted metal and rotting wood slowly drifting apart, saying their regretful farewells. She didn't act like she recognized me when she saw me but stood aside to let me in anyway. I didn't move; I felt she deserved the dignity of formality.

I held up my badge and said, "Detective Auf der Maur. We met at Whinlatter Docks. Do you remember? The night you found that girl's dead body. May I come in?"

She nodded and muttered, "Sure", and beckoned me to enter. I doubted if she did remember. I pocketed the shield and stepped inside. Rose set the door ajar and shuffled over to an armchair. As she sat down she started coughing: it sounded like death getting warmed up inside her chest. Jesus, she looked dreadful. Her face was alternately corpse-white and arterial-red, eyes popping out of their sockets as she hacked and heaved, a cycle of labored breath and painful expulsion. I turned away so she could gather mucus and spit it into the corner. Something for the rats, a diseased delicacy.

Eventually she spoke, so quietly I had to strain to hear: "Sorry. Bad chest."

I waved a hand, don't worry about it, and said softly, "Do you remember me, Rose? Talking to me? At the docks, and down the station next day."

She squinted at me, through the gloom, through the fog of her memories, the ruination of her drink-soaked brain-cells. I thought I saw the tiniest glint of recognition, of awareness. I caught my breath and held it, waiting.

"Yeah. I remember you," Rose said. "You were alright."

"You're sure."

"Sure I'm sure. The pretty little miss with all the big questions." She smiled slyly. "You fell. Toppled over on your heel, leaving Whinlatter. Did it hurt?"

I smiled too. "I'm surprised you remember that. Nah, it didn't hurt. Ruined a good pair of shoes, though."

"Want something to drink? I think there's gin lying around somewhere, or some Scotch... There might be coffee in that cupboard."

She wasn't pointing at a cupboard—actually I couldn't see any cupboards—so I declined the offer of coffee. Instead I sat on a wobbly kitchen chair opposite her, stubbing my cigarette out on the ashtray she'd balanced on her lap.

I said, "Rose, I think I know the woman who killed the girl that night."

"Madeleine Greenhill."

"That's right. I think I know who killed her."

"Well, good for you, little miss. Good for you."

"Is there anything you remember about that night? Anything at all that you mightn't have told us."

Her face creased into a ghastly smile, a rictus of degradation and undoing. "Shit! I can't even recall what I told you before!" She paused. "Who is she? The bitch killed that little girl."

"I can't tell you that, but I know her name. And we're closing in. I...I think you met her, Rose. On your way to Whinlatter. Your trick, do you remember? The big woman, with the cropped hair. She called you 'buttercup.'"

Rose nodded. She was pretty lucid now—horrendously hungover, it was obvious, but thinking straight enough. "Yeah. 'Buttercup.' That's what she said. So she was the one, huh? The one who done it."

"I'm almost certain."

"Hm. Ain't that weird?"

"What direction was she coming from when you met her, Rose? I'm just joining the dots here. Was the woman coming from the docks?"

She nodded once more. I said, "Listen, think, please. Think really hard. Can you remember anything else? About that night, or her. Anything. Did she tell you anything about herself, where she lived maybe, where she hung out."

Rose laughed bitterly. "Sweetheart, she said 'lift 'em and spread 'em.' That's all any of 'em say."

I lit another cigarette. The sense of despair was toxic, it dragged you down and siphoned off all your energy. I'm sorry, Rose, I can't stay for long. Just a few more quick questions: "How did you recognize her? Madeleine. Her face had been... How did you know it was her?"

She looked at me, snapping out of some torpid daydream. "Huh? I, uh—recognized the tattoo. Up here." Rose patted her chest. "I knew it right away. It's a rose, y'see? A pretty red rose, just like me."

That smile again, the demented leer that made me want to smack her face and embrace her in a bear-hug at the same time. Rose continued, "I'd seen her around the scene, you know? I knew who she was. Knew she was the daughter of Misericordiae Greenhill. So when I saw it, the tattoo I mean... Sure, I knew who she was. Fuckin' shame, ain't it?"

"Fuckin' shame is right, Rose."

"Fuckin'-A it's a shame. Ain't right to do that to some young girl. Leaving a mother bereft like that. Mothers never forget, do they? They never forget and they never let go."

I took a long drag and set myself mentally and then asked it right out: "You said 'the scene'—what do you mean by that? You mean prostitution?"

"Wha-? The Greenhill girl? Fuck, no. Leastways not that I

knew of. Nah, I mean the *scene*, little miss. You know, the drinking scene. The bad end of it. The real sleazy joints. That kid could knock 'em back with the best. And she didn't give a shit whose company she kept, neither. She was alright. She wasn't no snob like some of them."

"Did you often drink with Madeleine?"

"Coupla times. She bought me booze now and then. She'd come sit by me, tell me to eat more, get some rest, all that crap. I'd tell *her*, honey I'll rest when I'm dead or rich. Ha ha! Rich like you, Maddy. Nah, she was okay. I'm just fooling. I got on fine with her. Felt...what was it? *Comfortable* around her. Yeah. I liked her. What a godawful tragedy, huh?"

I'd reached my limit, all I could take. It was funny: I didn't really have a problem being around dead bodies or blood-spattered crime scenes or violent, surly, terrifying women, but I couldn't handle this. This place, with its sour odors and low atmosphere, filling like a blocked-up water-tank with regrets and decay. Maybe she made me think of my mother, and other elderly women I'd known, though Rose was actually much younger in calendar terms. But she seemed so old, so worn-out and used-up; the train was easing to a halt, last stop, everybody out. End of the line for Poison Rose.

I couldn't even bring myself to say goodbye. I stood and stretched out my hand—she took it and shook, surprisingly heartily.

I was walking away when she said, "I hope you get her, little miss. The one who did it."

I turned back. "Yeah. Me too."

Rose smiled, smaller this time, wistful and clear-headed. "Yeah. Get her for old Rose, huh? For that poor little girl. Just fucking get her. Get all of 'em."

Chapter 23

Virginia

BY now I'd been awake since six in the morning and I was really feeling it, my head slumping forward onto my chest as I drove home from the east side slums. I had that feeling inside my skull, the one where your brain seems to be actually tipping downwards, like it's too tired to stay awake and stay functioning. It's a horrible feeling, queasy and unsettling. I badly needed sleep. But I wasn't about to get it.

My apartment door was open a crack when I stepped onto my landing. A sliver of light peeked out into the darkness of the hallway. Aw no, I thought, not more shit. Not tonight, please. I'm exhausted. I'm done. I pulled my weapon, quietly, placed a hand on the door and then pushed it in hard, stepped into the room and swung the gun around, ready to fire. As ready as anybody can be when their brain has passed the tipping point.

Virginia Newman stood in my kitchenette, wearing a full-length wool coat with military-style belt and epaulettes, fixing a coffee. I realized how sluggish my senses were, batteries run way down low: I should have picked up the smell of it 20 feet away. I holstered the weapon, feeling vaguely foolish, and said: "You're lucky I didn't blow your beautiful head off. What the hell are you doing here?"

She turned to me, holding a cup of steaming coffee under her face, arms crossed over her chest. No glasses but her eyes were their natural brown under the contact lenses. She said, "I'm sorry, I need to talk to you."

"How did you get into my apartment, Virginia?"

"The building manager let me in. I told her we were old college pals, I hadn't seen you in ages and how awful it would be to miss you, lah-dee-dah. Standard sob story."

"How easily it comes to you."

I'd hoped she would wince—she didn't. "Alright. I probably deserved that. But we still need to talk."

"Yeah? About what? There a second cup in that?"

She nodded and poured one out for me. I walked to the kitchenette and took the cup from where she'd left it on the worktop. Virginia said, "About what do you think? Madeleine, of course."

I took a sip and said, "Mm. That's good coffee. You know how to make a brew, I'll give you that."

"Okay. Great. Now can we talk?"

"What? And no chit-chat? But we're old friends, Virginia. Surely some chit-chat is in order."

Virginia shrugged and sat on one of my armchairs. She lit a long, thin menthol cigarette, wafted the match through the air until it quenched. "Fine, Genie. Whatever you like."

I sat opposite her, leaving my coat on, placed my cup on the ground and lit a Dark Nine. I took a pull and dropped my head over the back of the chair: my standard thinking position, I was starting to believe. Without looking back at her I said, "Of course you'd know where my place is even if you hadn't spent the night here, right? I'm sure Ms LaVey would be able to point you in the right direction."

"Do you have to make me feel like this?"

I finally looked at her. Goddamn, she was beautiful. What a hideous cliché but there you have it: I couldn't make myself find her unattractive, could I? I couldn't make my eyes not see what was before them, shining, luminescent, breathtaking.

"You look amazing. There. Feel better?"

Virginia smiled—against her own wishes, I felt—and looked away. A long pause. She mumbled, "Thank you", then looked at me and frowned. "You look... What happened? You look like you were in a fight with a rabid cat. And you lost."

"You're actually not too far off. But I won the fight."

Silence again. I was almost getting used to this, our conversations more filled with the absence of words than the words themselves.

"But you do, though," I said. "You look fabulous. Let's talk about that, shall we? I'll tell you that coat really suits you, you can compliment my hair. You know, nice stuff like that."

"Genie, please. This is more important than you and I."

"I'm sure you're right, *Cassandra*. You've got that gift of foresight after all, don't you?"

"Goddamn it, will you stop! This *is* more important. Madeleine is. So put your fucking bruised ego away for ten minutes, can't you?"

Alright. That was the slap in the face I needed. My hurt, offended, childish side slinked away to some punishment cell in the darkest recesses of my mind; the adult Genie came forward again.

"You're right," I said. "You're absolutely right. I apologize. Let's talk."

Virginia sighed deeply. "Just so you know, I'm not looking for forgiveness. That's not why I came here. I mean, I *want* you to forgive me, of course. But that's not…"

I said gently, "I thought we were talking about Madeleine."

"Right. We are. Okay. Will you need a notebook for this?"

"Depends on what you have to tell me."

"A lot, I think. …Alright, let's start at the end: I was with Madeleine the day she died."

"I know you were. Her mother told me. She met you two that morning. You arrived in a Porsche to pick her up, to pick up Madeleine."

"I was with her for most of the day, Genie."

I sat up straighter, silently snapped to attention. "Go on."

"We hung out for the day. Had lunch, went to see a movie. She was acting strangely all day, very edgy. I mean even more edgy than usual. I wondered if she was using again. You know she took heroin sometimes?"

"Only sometimes?"

"She'd sworn to me that that was all over. She was never chronic, really. Just—dabbled. Which, I know, that's still a stupid thing to do. It started about four months ago. I don't know who turned her onto it or where she got the drugs. But we'd talked about it and Madeleine had promised to quit. But then, that day... She didn't *seem* high. But she was acting oddly."

"Okay. Hold on a second."

Coat or no coat, I was starting to get cold. I walked briskly to the central heating unit beside the front door, kicking that closed along the way. Virginia waited until I'd resumed my seat before resuming her story.

"We went out early for a few drinks. More than a few drinks. We'd had some food beforehand, a sandwich, but Madeleine was drunk pretty quickly. This wasn't unusual—I didn't think much about it. ...Anyway, we fought. Had a blazing row in this bar, I can't remember the name of it. One of those new ones on Pasiphaë Prospect, you know, all chrome fittings and blue strobe lights. Not my cup of tea but that's where she wanted to go. That's where we fought. Christ, we'd never argued like that before. I mean, it was vicious. I said some things..." She smiled to herself. "Things I can't take back now. But that's how it goes, I suppose."

"What did you argue about, Virginia?"

"Her. Her life, what she was doing. Where it was all going to end... I mean, I've had some wild times myself, I don't deny it, but within limits. Always within limits. But Maddy... She was out of control. Even by Madeleine standards, she was on the fast-track to oblivion. The last few weeks, she'd just gone... I was worried about her. Afraid she'd do something crazy."

"There's something you're not telling me."

She said vaguely, "Is there...?"

"Yes there is. Tell me, Virginia. I can help you."

Virginia lit another menthol, its fresh odor cutting through the room like a cool breeze. She shivered. I shivered too.

"We argued about Azura LaVey," she said. "Madeleine was in

too deep. I told her this, told her to tell her mom about it, tell somebody. That thing, it was poison, it was death for her…" A long pause. "Don't quote me on this, Genie, please. You can't protect me from this so for the love of God please don't quote me. But I'm going to tell you anyway: Azura runs a cult, this far-out weird religious thing, and Maddy was involved. Deeply. They stuck their talons into her and wouldn't let her go. That's what killed her."

I hopped to my feet. "Jesus Christ. Why didn't you say something about this before? Those times we talked. Or, or, report it to someone else. Another officer."

"Please, don't… Just listen, alright? I'm telling you now. They call it The Goddess Rising. This—movement, this cult. It's based around worship of the moon. Because that rises each month, is born and passes through its life and then dies and is born again. So it ties into a theme of spiritual rebirth. That's their mantra: you can be reborn through the Risen Goddess, like the moon itself is reborn. And all this, the monthly event, ties in to our menstrual cycles as well. The moon, for them, is the Divine Mother, and of course, LaVey is her representative on earth. Because you can't have a god without a priest, right?" She shook her head, annoyed. "But forget all that. It's bullshit, the whole thing. It's a hotch-potch of mythology, New Ageism, other, older religions… Cynical crap. I don't know if I believe in something else, you know, *out there*. But this is—rubbish. Fairy stories, invented nonsense. And yet people buy it."

"How many people?"

"More than you'd think, but less than LaVey would like. She's maniacal, she's obsessed. Wants to bring more and more women into her 'family', as she calls it. It's disgusting. She's raping the very meaning of that word. That's something else you need to know: they brainwash their recruits, try to make them reject their own families, I mean their real moms and sisters. It's all about the Divine Mother and her anointed 'mother', quote-unquote, in this realm... It works, too. I've met some of the women involved. All very conformist, fanatical, mindless. Like zombies."

Like zombies. Like my weirdo empty-headed songbirds.

I said, "Tell me if you recognize any of these names: Nora Hofton. Alejandra Villegas. Dinah Spaulding. Liz or Elizabeth Arendt. Anneka Klosterman."

"Yeah...they're Risen Women. Sorry, that's what they call themselves. Risen through the Divine, et cetera et cetera. Hofton and Spaulding, I've met them. Two idiots. Not ten brain-cells to rub together between them. Villegas, I think I've met her. Arendt I don't know personally, but I've heard LaVey talk about her. ...What was the other name?"

"Klosterman. Anneka. A terrifying blonde giant."

Virginia thought for a moment. "Mm...I'm not sure. She sounds familiar. I mean, your description. I'd probably know her if I saw her." She turned to me. "Genie, you should know now: there are some pretty important Hera women involved in this thing. Not just flakes like Dinah Spaulding. I mean *powerful*."

"Such as?"

"You want actual names?"

I nodded. She hesitated for an instant, then pressed on: "Alright. In for a penny... Do you know Professor Orianne Queneau? She teaches Metaphysics at Hera U?"

"I've had the pleasure."

"She's one. She's high up, a high-level initiate. There are others: Councillor Gurney. Councilor Hulman. Assistant City Prosecutor Walkup. Uh, who else? Colette Unser, the property developer. Nicola Goldstone, she owns a chain of expensive restaurants. Dee-Ann Lehrman, you know, the singer?"

Know her? I actually liked her. Dee-Ann, with her silk-throated voice, her atmospheric torch-songs about night and the city, the perils and pleasures of love. Dee-Ann goddamn Lehrman.

I was smiling to myself—probably to break the tension—and

when you're smiling, you tend to assume that everyone else is smiling too. Like the world shares your good vibrations; like they all park their worries and problems, just for a few seconds, so as not to spoil your mood. But Virginia wasn't smiling: she looked ashen, grief-stricken, like some spirit of ill-intent had just whispered in her beautiful ear the worst news she was ever going to hear.

Then she started crying. I subconsciously took a step back, giving her some privacy, giving her time. Fat tears rolled down her pale cheeks; her eyes reddened and became angry, scalded, as ugly as it's possible for her eyes to ever get. Virginia reached for a tissue and wiped her nose.

Finally she said, still sobbing, "I want you to find her killer, Genie. I swear to God, if nothing else ever happens in my life, I want that. It's my fault she's dead. Madeleine would still be here if it wasn't for me. Why did I let her go off alone that last night? I saw the state she was in, she was a mess... So we fought. So big deal, we'd fought before. I shouldn't have let her out of my sight. I should have... You know what my last words to her were? The very last fucking words I would ever speak to my best friend? 'Fine, Madeleine—see if I care.' Jesus. 'See if I care.' That's the last thing she heard me tell her: that I didn't care about her."

She started crying harder, deeper, her shoulders lifting and her back trembling. I said softly, "I wouldn't blame yourself, Virginia. Madeleine was on a downward slide. She had a self-destructive streak, deep inside her. You knew that, her mother knew it, everybody did...she probably knew it herself. You're not to blame."

Virginia looked up at me, anger flashing in her eyes but I knew it wasn't directed at me. "You don't understand. You don't know. *I'm* the one who brought her into it in the first place. That fucking cult. I got her involved and now she's dead because of me."

She lit another cigarette; I didn't point out that her previous one was still smoldering in the ashtray, unsmoked.

"We met in college. She was wild, I was wild, we liked each other, so…we were wild together. And that was fine, until Azura goddamn LaVey… I only got into all that wacky alternative stuff for a laugh. For kicks, you know? It amused me, to go along with their mumbo-jumbo and mysticism, their goddesses and priests and stupid cycles of the moon. And God, they were so self-important about it. It was laughable. They took it all so seriously. So, of course, I didn't take it seriously at all. I was a kid, it was all a big joke to me. LaVey 'initiated' me—her word—into the 'mysteries'—also her word—of The Goddess Rising. I didn't give a shit. I saw it as a way to make money, selling them junk and trinkets… I still do it with the shop. They'll buy anything if they think it's special or blessed, or has some mystical powers. Anyway… I brought in Madeleine too. Azura was always going on about spreading out, growing, recruiting more women, more souls needing to be risen… Whatever. The usual spiel. So I thought sure, why not? Madeleine will find this as funny as I do. Which she did—she never believed any of LaVey's crap for a second. But she didn't…Madeleine didn't…"

More space, more time. Patience and silence. I waited.

Virginia continued: "I got out in time. Madeleine didn't. She *couldn't*—she'd gone in too far. LaVey had her hooks in tight and wasn't letting go. She's a seductive sort of person, you know, she always knows exactly what to say, how to persuade people, how to make them do what she wants… And Maddy, she was weak-willed. Let's face it, she was a fuck-up. Prime target for someone as unscrupulous as LaVey." She stubbed out the half-smoked cigarette and said, "And they were using her for money. I'm sure of it. Madeleine wouldn't admit it, but I know. She was an easy mark. They leeched off her for two years. And then, when she was all used up…"

I sat back down, digesting what she'd said. This was all great information, with one not-insignificant caveat: it was unusable as evidence. Legally this meant less than nothing. It was the wild accusation of one young woman of "questionable" reputation, against a revered educator and pillar of society. Still—remember all this, Genie. What was it Etienne had said? "Store it away for future access."

"I think that's why she was killed, over the money," Virginia said. "I don't know how or why exactly, but I really believe that. I'm positive."

I had a question that I didn't want to ask but felt I had to: "Why did you seduce me, Virginia? I'm not starting a fight, I don't care anymore, I just want the truth in all this. If you hate LaVey so much. Why did you do her bidding?"

She shrugged. "I'm scared of her. There, I've admitted it. She frightens the living daylights out of me. You don't know what... Azura LaVey gets what she wants, and I was scared to turn her down. ...I also wanted to know where the investigation was going. For myself, I needed to know. Genuinely. But that was only secondary. I did it because I hadn't the nerve not to."

How weird to see this beautiful, self-possessed creature, this earth-dwelling goddess, so beset by worries and doubts. Laid low by a guilty conscience. I guess she was as much Virginia as Cassandra after all.

She stood and hugged her coat tight to her chest. The tears had stopped but the sorrow lingered on, in her face, the way her shoulders slumped. Virginia walked to the door and muttered, "I truly am sorry, Genie. For all of it."

She looked back at me. I looked at the floor. She made a slight movement towards me but checked herself, held her body back. She sighed deeply and nodded and said, "Best of luck with everything, sweetheart. You'll be in my thoughts."

Then she was gone. No grandiose exit, no movie star strut and sweep of perfume in her trail; she just slinked away, quiet and defeated. I shut the door and locked it, sitting down again in my broken armchair, trying to think, trying to drown out the conflicting voices roaring across my mind—two opposing forces, vying for supremacy. My brain was screeching "steer clear." But my heart and guts and loins: they were saying something quite different.

Chapter 24

Misericordiae

MY eyes fell on a photograph of my mother, a small print in an unpainted wooden frame that I kept on top of the TV. My only physical reminder of her. There was other stuff belonging to her still in the apartment, tons of it, but I couldn't bear to have it around me. I couldn't bear to remember her all the time. One *memento mori* was enough. I needed to forget the pain sometimes. I still missed her something fierce, almost like a physical ache during the worst moments: lying awake at night, mildly insomniac, cold and jittery, her absence a ghost coming in and filling the room, chilling the room, making me shake like a junkie doing cold turkey. But always an absence: if ghosts really did exist, my mom hadn't turned into one yet. I never felt her presence in the room, just that terrible, all-encompassing, world-destroying absence. She was gone from me forever.

My mother was a lovely woman in life—I know everyone says that about their mom, but everyone who knew her said it, too. She was small, though not as small as me, but made up for it through the enormous warmth of her personality, her boundless generosity and capacity for love. She was sweet and sincere and didn't get irony or most of the wisecracks I made. She was physically affectionate, helped her neighbors without being asked, got nervous about the economy and my future professional prospects. She disapproved of swearing and cohabitation, she told me to stop smoking and asked when I'd settle down with a nice girl. She made bad jokes that you laughed in spite of, not because of. You laughed because she had made them and you wanted to see her smile: the way her mouth curled upwards and her eyes crinkled so cutely, like a wise old crone in a child's fairy story. Someone you could trust, implicitly. Someone I would always love, wholly and unconditionally. Her name was

Vivienne Auf der Maur, she was my mother and I love her.

She did used to worry about me. I wonder what she would have thought of my current predicament? Obviously I wouldn't have told her about Erika Baton and the attempts on my life, about getting my ass kicked and my face clawed. I might have told her about Virginia: the nice parts, anyway. Some vague excuse to explain why we didn't see each other anymore. She'd probably see through the lies and obfuscation and still worry.

It had started to snow outside, fat white flakes falling softly like feathers from a torn pillow. Just moseying on down to earth, being gently buffeted by the breeze, beginning to settle in their plump layers on cars, rooftops, the roads, the pavements. I lit a Dark Nine and settled back into reflection, allowing the memories their moment in the spotlight, a warm glow heating my head, running down through my body, tingling my toes. I remembered the first time I'd arrested a serious felon, this fucking lunatic who was pimping out teenagers from a bizarrely upmarket hotel on Bolo. We hammered in there and I wrestled her to the ground, younger then, gung-ho and heedless, using my martial arts training and her narcotic incapacitation to gain the advantage. And then telling my mom about it afterwards, flushed with pride, bursting with it, my chest puffed out and a smile on my face you couldn't have removed with an industrial sanding machine.

I was so happy that evening, happy and cocky and dumb: I was a big girl now, I was tougher than the rest, I'd proved I had the stuff for this job. My mother popped my balloon pretty quickly with her queries and worries and tutting and fretting, her eyes almost shining with anxiety, and I resented her for it at the time. It felt like she was spoiling my moment, being a killjoy, just for the sake of it. I realize now that she wasn't, it was all genuine. It was her job to worry about me.

I'd brushed her off by saying flippantly, "Hey, take it easy. I know what I'm doing. I'm with a good bunch of girls, we look out for each other. There's nothing to worry about."

She had replied, "There's always something to worry about; a mother is always worried. You're a part of me, Genie. You're the deepest part of me, and you always will be. You ask me not to worry, but that's impossible. It's like asking me to sever one of my own limbs. We're connected. We're the same blood. I'll always worry about you. And I wouldn't want it any other way."

A mother is always worried—ain't that the truth? Misericordiae worried incessantly about her daughter. My mom worried about me until the day she died. Probably Virginia's mother worried about her. Even Poison Rose would have worried about her kid if she'd...

If she'd had one. Stop. Rewind. My memory reached out and back, struggling to recall, clawing into the past, straining for it... Snatches of conversation with Littlestone, that day I questioned Rose in Detectives HQ, moments and words and half-sentences, popping into consciousness and fading and reappearing and fading once more... Something she had said about Rose having a daughter, probably rumors, giving the child up for adoption and going back to her hell-bound life, no, *maybe* rumors...maybe truth... And something else was there, fighting for my attention, the image of a blood-red tattoo on a white breast, stark and beautiful... And something else again, something Misery had said and something Rose had said and something Littlestone might have said...

Intuition: there it was, the thought igniting in my brain. I couldn't think it through right now, the argument would fall apart due to lack of evidence. But it felt true. It nagged at me, a subconscious itch, a whisper from the universe. It wasn't strictly germane to the investigation but on a personal level I had to know for sure.

I had to know. I had to go. I had to talk to Misery.

I was beyond exhausted by now but ignored it and kept moving.

By the time I met Misericordiae in Golden Park it was after three in the morning. I was pushing through the tiredness, pushing through my doubts and limitations. She had agreed to meet me when I phoned Caritas, more forward in my manner than before, more urgent. Ileana had called her to the blower and Misery, presumably awake, presumably prowling the long dark hallways of her empty home, answered the call promptly. I didn't even introduce myself: "We have to meet." She told me when and where.

The place was beautiful by night, in the snow. Golden was the largest forested park in Hera, more forest than park really—thick armies of deciduous and coniferous trees, broad paths snaking between them, over hundreds of acres, thousands. Unruly and elemental, a controlled wildness. The trees looked scary and intimidating and saintly under the light of a half moon, snow on the pathways reflecting the blue light back to the heavens. It felt like being inside a snow-globe, trapped within its glass dome but unwilling to leave. The stars sounding like a music-box, the moon a mournful horn. I met Misery by the Fallen Officer monument, a giant, abstract stone shrine to all the HCPD women who'd died in the line of duty. It felt appropriate. I laughed nervously to myself when I got there and thought, Let's hope it's not a portent as well.

Then Misery appeared, crunching through the snow in fur-lined boots and a long, dramatic coat. She looked smaller than I remembered; I figured it was the moonlight casting funny shadows, distorting perspective. Ileana followed in her train, four or five steps behind. She seemed to have a slight limp, though again it was hard to be sure of any visual information in the ghostly ambience. No, it was there: that airless, hovering motion was slightly off...

They stopped ten feet from me. Misery said, "Detective Auf der Maur. An interesting place and time for a meeting. I won't deny that I am intrigued. Please."

She gestured towards me with both gloved hands. I lit a

cigarette with my own shaking hands, the smoke thick and milky in the freezing air. I flicked the match away and spotted the moon in my peripheral vision, glowing against the inky blue-black sky, diffused, velvety. The Goddess Rising. Did LaVey and her cronies really believe in all of it? That this indifferent satellite somehow possessed a supernatural element, a spiritual core secreted within the blank, lifeless rock? Something so precious and enormous that it was worth killing for?

I looked back at Misery and surprised myself by saying straight out, "I think Madeleine was Poison Rose's daughter."

She surprised me even more by coming right back with "Yes. She was."

I eased out a breath, unsure of where to go from here. Misery said, "Come. Walk with me, please," and resumed her slow stately progress, away from the monument, back into the black womb of the forest, Ileana close behind.

I walked by the old lady's side, smoking, not speaking. After half a minute she said, "My doctor recommends I walk regularly. For my joints, you understand. It need not be vigorous, she says, just regular. Do you trust doctors, Detective?"

"Do I...? Uh...yeah, sure. I suppose I do."

"What did your mother die of?"

The question took me by surprise. I regained my composure and said, "Heart attack. A hereditary condition. Nothing anyone could have done, I don't think."

"She died quite young, I believe."

You believe, my ass. You *know*. "Yes. 51. Which is young, I guess."

"I'm sorry for your loss. I know how it feels to lose your mother. How did you know about Rosemary Manning?"

"Um...I'm not sure I did, until you confirmed it just there." I chanced smiling at her; could that have been a tiny smile in reply? "I thought it, I had a hunch. I go with hunches. They've served me well in the past."

"I mean, what brought on this—hunch? I'm simply curious. I don't deny any of it."

"A few things. I'd heard cop rumors that Pois...that Ms Manning had had a child, years back. Gave it up for adoption. Also, she seemed fond of Madeleine. She told me, Rose, she said she felt comfortable around the girl. Madeleine used to take care of her some, give her money, tell her look after herself; like she had a vested interest, some emotional tie. And then there was her tattoo, a rose, a red rose... I don't know. I just, it all seemed to fit together in my head."

"I see. Well, it's true. I presume you want to know the details of the matter?"

"Not unless you want to tell me. As a cop, I don't need to know. As a woman, I'd like to know."

The moon passed behind a pillow of cloud for a brief moment, dimming the light, like a curtain being dropped and then raised again from the stage. Misery said, "I knew Rosemary Manning. Knew her before her—descent into prostitution. Her life... It's a sad story. I knew her when she was a teacher. You are aware of her distant past, I presume. Rosemary taught English Literature at my old alma mater. After my own time as a student but I was on the board of management for a spell. We worked together during that period. A fine mind. A fine *woman*. Elegant, refined, so learned and widely read... Well. Something happened to Rosemary when she was about 25 or 26. I never knew what. Some things are beyond even my reach, Detective. Something dreadful, anyway. Life-changing. It changed her. She began to drink heavily, her work suffered. There were missed days, lost papers, carelessness; one or two unpleasant incidents with parents, though the children seemed to still like her well enough. The school was impatient with her; we all subsequently regretted it, but... Ah. No point to such regrets. We were too hasty— Rosemary was let go. There is the sum of it. A generous severance package but she drank it all within months. And there was no way she was going to get another job in Hera. Not one in education, at any rate."

Misericordiae coughed a few times, saying, "Excuse me. A chest infection. They can be difficult to shake. So: thus began Rosemary Manning's decline and fall. Within a year or so she was a full-blown alcoholic, selling herself to perverts to pay for her addiction. Such an unfortunate story... I don't particularly blame myself for it, but I do feel some measure of guilt for abandoning her so readily to her fate. A few token efforts at mediation and help, in the early days; but once she slid into that morass, that moral swamp, I left her to it. I left her."

"With all due respect, I don't think you're to blame for any of it."

"No—certainly not all of it. We each of us choose our path, to a greater or lesser extent. Madeleine did. And Rosemary reacted poorly to the vicissitudes of life. So it is with certain people. Yet I still felt in some way...perhaps 'responsible' is a more appropriate word than 'guilty.' I felt compassion for that woman. I admit that I truly am a bitch, Detective; but I'm not an absolute monster. I may not want people to know about it—bad for my reputation, you see—but I too can be charitable. ...She contracted a sexually transmitted disease and gave it to dozens of—what do your colleagues in the police force call them? Johns? Clients? That, I believe, is where the nickname originated. 'Poison Rose.' They considered *her* to be poison. Such...filthy animals, how dare they cast judgment on anyone...?" She paused. "Rosemary was beaten close to death by a number of clients. Those—disgusting women. They were angry with her for giving them the disease. ...Yes, I felt compassion."

I said nothing. This story wasn't necessarily going anywhere in a hurry, but it was fascinating all the same. Misery continued, "When Rosemary awoke from her coma the doctors told her she was pregnant. She didn't want her baby to grow up as the child of a prostitute so...an arrangement was made. An accommodation that suited all parties. Through my Church, through dear Mother Torres. I took charge of the girl, the infant, and passed her off as my own. I had wanted a daughter for years, but by then was too old to have one myself. Rosemary never knew who took the child. I'm not sure that she wanted to know—it might have been too painful, seeing the fruit of her womb growing up, going to school, moving into womanhood; having a familial relationship with a woman who wasn't her mother. And then...then I brought Madeleine home to Caritas Heights and never saw Rosemary Manning again."

"You had nothing more to do with her?"

"Nothing. The last time I saw her she was asleep in a hospital bed, knocked out with painkillers. And of course, I hadn't spoken to her for a number of years prior to that."

"Was she paid? Rose, did she get paid off?"

"Not a penny. We offered, Mother Torres did. She wouldn't take anything. Once the girl was safe—that was all she wanted."

We'd reached a small clearing in the trees, a patch of grass and planted flowers, a rectangle of order cut out of the wild. Misery took a long look at it, bathed in the eerie but beautiful blue moonlight, then turned about and began walking back in the direction from which we'd come. I walked with her, Ileana as always floating in the background, watchful, ready, unnervingly soundless.

I said, "So, Madeleine: she knew? Which would explain the tattoo, the rose."

"Yes, she knew. How, I'm not sure. Maybe pure instinct, some low note of blood humming between her and Rosemary, inaudible to everyone else... We never spoke of it, but she knew."

"Did you mind her getting that tattoo? Did it annoy you? Stop me if I'm overstepping the mark here, but I feel compelled to ask."

"It's alright. You're a Detective, asking questions is part of who you are. ...No, I didn't mind. Her mother was her mother.

Madeleine had the right to express it. That was part of who *she* was. Though, having said that, *I* was her mother also. Every bit as much as if I had physically carried her and borne her. I was her mother, Madeleine was my daughter. Nothing matters but that. All the rest is—trifling detail."

I lit another cigarette and said, "Okay, well I'm going to ask another one: did finding out about Rose drive Madeleine to her destruction? What I'm saying is, was that what knocked her off the rails? The shock of it."

Misery considered the question. "No. I don't believe so. We can never be sure about such things, but... Madeleine was a smart girl. She had understanding beyond her years, for all her faults. I think she understood this—this matter. How and why it had to happen. I don't believe she would have harbored any...resentments, any anger or bitterness. She knew she was loved. Besides, the child was hell-bent on destruction anyway. Again, it was part of who she was. It was in her nature."

I realized then, fully and for the first time: Misery was a bad woman in a lot of ways—a true bitch, as she admitted herself— but she was also a proper lioness. She hadn't spelled it out but I knew she would protect or avenge her offspring at all costs, even the ultimate cost to herself, right to the end. Though Madeleine hadn't been her biological daughter, she would still die for her or kill for her. And the fact that the girl was already dead didn't change any of that. Love and yearning and the interconnect- edness of their years as a family, the way their souls had sewn together, deep and intricate patterns formed in the very depths of their being... Misericordiae was right. Madeleine was her daughter, she was the girl's mother. The rest was just details.

I figured then, might as well get the whole truth, Genie. Might as well know it all while you have the chance to ask. I said quietly, "You knew she was a drug user?"

"I did."

"From Chief Etienne?"

"Your superior officer...allowed certain information to pass to me. A confidence which I will honor. Ann Etienne is herself an honorable woman. She did what she thought was the most moral thing to do. I respect her. Don't worry, none of this will come back on her."

"I appreciate that. I respect her, too."

"I knew already. About the drug abuse, of course I knew—what mother wouldn't spot the signs? I don't just mean the physical ones; Madeleine was an expert at covering her tracks. The pun is unintentional. No, I mean something more vague, less immediately tangible; those changes to the soul and the psyche, you understand? The way that poison scoops you out, the purest part of you... It leaves nothing behind. Just a shell of the person your loved ones once knew."

"Was that very difficult for you? Was it hard to accept? I mean, uh, I mean a woman in your—position."

She answered immediately: "Yes. It was hard. Very hard. But not the way you think. I don't care, fundamentally, who else knows about this. I will endeavor to keep it secret, obviously, but that's more habit than anything. My daughter is dead, Detective: why should it matter if all of Hera City now knows she was a heroin addict as well? She will still be dead." She coughed again, deeper this time, a more ragged sound. "You know by this stage, I'm sure, what kind of woman I am. I believe in moral certainty, eternal truths handed down from distant ages. I see things in black and white, and do not apologize for that. Madeleine wasn't some teenage single mother from the slums. Such women choosing narcotic oblivion, I can understand, if not condone. But Madeleine—she was privileged and protected. She had no *need* to use that filth. It was self-indulgent and debauched. She did it for no good reason, if indeed there truly are good reasons. She took drugs because she could. Such is the folly of youth. Madeleine was a deeply flawed young woman, Detective. I loved her more because of them, but I wish she had not had those flaws."

The Fallen Officer monument was looming ahead of us, shimmering softly, appropriately spectral in the moonlight. Our feet moved quietly over the snow. It was weird talking to Misery: things were said, private, awkward things, dreadful things, and it felt okay; comfortable, almost. She had a way of expressing herself that seemed to add an invisible full-stop to the conversation. I didn't feel obliged to respond, to dole out conciliatory platitudes, well-meaning waffle to soften her anguish. She had the strongest personality of anyone I'd ever encountered. She accepted how things were; further comment was redundant. The listener stayed silent.

What I did feel was an obligation to provide some feedback — she'd opened up to me, no harm in returning the compliment. I said, "I know who killed her. Madeleine, I know her murderer."

Misery didn't reply. I went on, "A woman called Erika Baton. Hired gun. A very dangerous individual. She's already tried to take me out. More than once."

"But she's not the real killer, is she?"

"No." Perceptive as always, Misery.

"She is merely the weapon," she continued. "I want whoever ordered the murder. Somebody paid this woman to kill my daughter, is that not so?"

"Yes, Ma'am. That's almost certainly what happened. Erika Baton is a professional assassin. She kills for money. Someone paid her to do this."

We'd reached the monument and stopped walking. I shuddered in the cold, my body belatedly realizing that it wasn't moving anymore.

Misery said, "And do you know who that someone is? Again, I respect the integrity of your investigation. But you understand my compulsion to ask, regardless."

Should I tell her about LaVey? The debate raged inside my head, a slow-burn cacophony. To be honest I didn't really give a shit about La Dame Azura or what happened to her when Misery was sure she was the one. I'd try to prevent any harm coming to her, of course—it was my job—but down in the viscera, I didn't begrudge this bereaved woman her shot at vengeance. It's not like LaVey wouldn't deserve a horrible ending. That's not what stopped me from speaking. I still had doubts of my own, about Virginia and what she'd told me: it felt true, but I couldn't be definite. Could she be trusted? Maybe that was all just more lies, a whole bundle of them, dense and knotty, impossible to unravel. Maybe I should keep my trap shut for now, for just a little while longer, until I was absolutely positive that...

I felt her presence before I saw her coming. No, more than that: I felt Ileana feeling her presence before either of us saw her. I looked at the silent butler who was tensed like a guard dog at a wire fence. Then I looked beyond her and saw a woman approaching through the darkness, stepping into the light, a slow, strolling sort of shuffle, easiness in the movement, her limbs loose like swinging ropes. Something vaguely threatening about her, the way her face was half-hidden by the brim of a hat; suggestions of strength, unruliness, the possibility of sudden violence. Ileana made like a bodyguard and stepped between the newcomer and Misericordiae, flexing her fingers then balling her fists, rising ever-so-slightly on her toes.

I moved forward and said, "You can relax, Ileana. I know this chick. How's it going, Merrylegs?"

Camilla's gunsel gave a small bow—it came across as sincere, not sarcastic—and a smaller smile. "It goes well, Detective Auf der Maur. I have a message for you from Ms Castelmagno."

She glanced at Misery and Ileana, then back at me, and raised her eyebrows.

I said, "It's cool. You can speak in front of them."

Merrylegs lit a cigarette, the match-strike casting her face in wan yellow. She said, "My employer said you'd want to know this. We've located Erika Baton."

Chapter 25

Erika

I GOT the jump on her. At least, I thought I had.

Standing in the door frame of Erika Baton's apartment, my gun pointed directly at the center of her face, I thought: I have you now, you fucker. Dead bang. Then I said out loud, "Move just a half-inch and I'll paint the wall with your brains." She didn't react. She didn't seem worried. She didn't even seem surprised. Erika sneered and put down her can of beer and mumbled, "Oh, don't worry. I'm not going anywhere, buttercup."

I had bid a hasty goodbye to Misery at the Fallen Officer monument. After Merrylegs' bombshell there wasn't time for explanations or apologies. The old lady seemed to understand: she just nodded gravely, as if to say: "Go do what you have to." I said, "We'll talk again", grabbed Merrylegs by the arm and started walking briskly, almost jogging, towards the entrance to Golden Park. The skinny heavy didn't object, just ambled along beside me.

I said, breathless, "Where is she?"

"Holed up in an apartment. Above a laundromat on the corner of Fairywren and White Sands. You know it?"

I knew it. A scummy part of town, no doubt a scummy apartment...where else would a scumbag like Erika hide out, like the rat she was?

I nodded. Merrylegs said, "Number 4C. Top floor. Elevator's busted—you'll have to go up by the stairs. Our source says she's on her own all day. Nobody in or out. *She* don't go in or out. I don't know what she does in there all day. Personally I'd get kinda...bored."

She gave me that funny, crooked smile. I smiled back and let go of her arm as we passed through the black wrought-iron gates, frosted with snow around the edges like some kind of elaborate, food-as-art-statement confectionary.

"Thanks," I said. "And tell Camilla the same."

"Sure. Hey, uh… I don't know I should be saying this but: you need some back-up? This Baton broad, I heard she can be pretty saucy when she wants to be."

Jesus, that's all I needed—a racketeer's henchwoman riding shotgun on an official bust. I said, "No. But thank you. I'm okay. I'll be okay."

I patted the bulge under my jacket and grinned, momentarily feeling braver than I really did. A false courage, I guess, flooding through my system, flushed by all that adrenaline. Merrylegs said, "Alright", tipped her hat to me and withdrew into the shadows like a spirit stealing away, leaving me on my own. I checked my watch: the small hand creeping past four. I was tired and colder than I'd realized but I had to keep going.

Fairywren and White Sands: you couldn't get two bigger misnomers on the entire map of Hera City. One sounded like an enchanted glade in a children's fable, the other like a beautiful beach or an exclusive golfing resort. But these two streets, and the junction at which they met, were the complete opposite to any of that: run-down, sleazy, rubbish-strewn, dangerous. Above all, dangerous. This was a place where, like in the old cliché, life was cheap and everything was for sale. Drugs, guns, prostitutes, even kids, illegal exotic pets, body parts, assassinations…and assassins. I parked three blocks away and walked the rest of the way. A panhandler lurched towards me as I approached along Fairywren, padding through the dank pools of light cast by crooked streetlamps. She moaned, "Something for my head, come on, come on, gimme something for the *head*." I ignored her and kept padding. A piece of crumpled plastic rattled along in the quiet, blown by the wind. There was even something menacing in that sound.

Nobody hanging around outside Kleen 'n' Kleer Laundromat,

nobody walking the streets that I could see. I stopped ten yards from the junction and scoped out Fairywren both ways—still nobody—then flitted across the street on light feet. I dashed into the alcove next to the laundromat, the entrance to the apartments above, pulling back into the darkness. Deep breaths, slowing my system down, getting the measure of things. I leaned against the door; it was unlocked, as these places always are. They're supposed to have a street-side locking and alarm system—you're supposed to have to buzz through for someone inside to allow you access—but in a shithole like this, locks are a luxury and alarms are little more than a myth. I eased the door open.

Darkness. It took my eyes eight or ten seconds to adjust, to dredge whatever residual light there was from the atmosphere and process it into visuals. The joint looked slightly better inside than outside, but only just. Shabby, depressing, with cracks on the wall, peeling paint, mold and damp spreading on the ceiling like a black disease. A smell of burst pipes somewhere, that vague but always recognizable tang of human effluent. And fumes off harsh chemicals, presumably from the laundromat, which were strong enough to make your eyes water. The place came into focus: a block of mailboxes, access door to stairs and elevator, a large but sickly-looking houseplant in a pot, a chair standing in the middle of the corridor for no obvious reason. Apartment 4C, that's what Merrylegs had said. I moved towards the stairs.

Quietly, carefully—my life could depend on it. I crept up each floor, wincing at each creak of the wood, each heavy footfall, my heart hammering up high in my throat, my head filled with that irrational but overwhelming thought that everyone else can hear it. Ba-*dum*-dum, ba-*dum*-dum... Stay cool, Genie. Then I was at Erika's floor, and at Erika's door. I almost walked past it, because 4C was directly across the corridor when I opened the access door on that story. I clocked the number in imitation brass and took five or six steps towards the next door and realised what I'd seen and came back on tiptoes. 4C.

This was it. I pulled my gun, chambered a round and leaned towards the door. No sound inside. I stood like that for what seemed an age—maybe three minutes in reality, maybe more. Just listening, for any sound of movement, of life inside, with one eye always on the door to the stairs in case Erika might be getting in late herself. Still no sound. I ran through my options: kick the door down and burst in there? Pick the lock and sneak through? Either way I didn't know the layout of the place. I had surprise on my side but fumbling around for a light switch or tripping over the couch would negate that. Call for back-up? I was reluctant: there were other people in this building, regular people, and who knew what kind of bullets-flying clusterfuck Erika would unleash if she thought she was trapped?

Then the woman herself solved my conundrum—I heard bedsprings creak and footsteps from a room to the right of the door, coming left, stopping straight in front of where I stood. A heavy sigh. A light came on inside, visible through the large gap at the foot of the door. Another creak sounded, this time of a large body sitting into an armchair. A can of something being cracked open. A TV blurting into life, gabbled talkshow bullshit at a low volume. Looked like Erika Baton suffered the same sleep problems as the rest of us.

I waited another two minutes, silent, unmoving, petrified. Then I chanced a peek through the keyhole and there she sat, slumped and beefy, wearing a vest and shorts, drinking a beer, staring dully at the TV, her face bathed in the electric blue of the screen and the greenish-yellow cast of a tall lamp with a fringed shade. In that light, in that position, she didn't look like a remorseless killing machine. Erika looked like a fucking slob.

No more thinking, no more waiting. I took a few steps back, went down low on one leg and kicked hard with the other. The door-lock went straight away, crappy little thing, useless to all intents and purposes, like they always are in these dumps. The door flew inwards and I stepped in after it, standing in the doorframe with my legs set wide apart, gun in both hands, her head the target. Bang. Got you.

Which brings us back to the start. Cue cool line about using her brains as house-paint. Cue her nonplussed retort. The place was a toilet, a shitty dive. It smelled as bad as it looked, and it looked even worse than the rest of this building. I took one step forward and felt really goddamn nervous, even though I was drawing a bead with a fully loaded Beretta 950 and I knew that she knew that I knew how to use it. That's the sort of effect a woman like that has on you: edginess, panic, even terror. I knew what she was capable of. I knew she was twice my weight and had three times my strength. I knew she was a psycho who couldn't feel a fucking thing.

Erika took a slug from her beer and let it down on the ground with a surprisingly dainty movement. She reached for something on the far side of the armchair—I tensed—she sneered again and said, "Relax, little sister. Just getting my smokes."

She brought up the pack and a lighter with exaggerated slowness and care, showing them to me and raising her eyebrows sardonically. My hands trembled slightly. Putting as much bravado as I could into my voice, I said, "I wouldn't be too cute if I were you. I've got an itchy trigger finger. A nervous one."

"Yeah, so I noticed. That day, you put ten fuckin' holes in my car. Should I bill you for the repairs?"

"The more you get cute, the more it gets itchy, Erika."

"Oh, so you know my name, huh? Well, good for you, buttercup. Won't help you in the long run, but shit. Good job by the police."

She lit a cigarette and took a few long, deep drags, then flicked ash on the floor. She turned to face me full-on and said, "So—how can I help the HCPD?"

I noticed she had a large, vivid bruise on the left side of her face, running from the jawline right up to the eyebrow. It looked bad. It looked the color of an over-ripe aubergine. It looked like the tough gal had met someone tougher.

"What happened your face?"

"I was born like this. Genetics, they call it."

"You know what I mean. How does it feel to be on the receiving end for once?"

"Oh, you mean this?" She pointed to the bruise. "She wants to know how does it feel. Not so good, Detective Auf der Maur. But don't worry. I'll get mine yet."

The gun, my hands, my whole body trembled a little more. "How do you know my name?"

Erika gave me a look as if to say, Don't be so fucking stupid. And she was right in a way—the question was totally redundant, on every level. I said, "You didn't answer me. Who gave you the shiner?"

"Why? Are you gonna *investigate*? Collar someone for assault?" She laughed. "Some crazy bitch jumped me with a tire-iron. I fought her off. She's a dead woman, she just don't know it yet."

"It looks painful, Erika. I'm glad."

"Now, that ain't a very charitable thing to say."

"I'm not in a charitable mood. I saw what you did to Madeleine Greenhill."

She let the smoke drop into the can of beer—it quenched with a wet fizzle. Then she said, "What I did? And what exactly was that, buttercup?"

I took another few steps towards her, feeling ever-so-slightly emboldened. I mean, I *had* her: she wasn't getting out of this, she couldn't get to me. I said, "Come off it. What you *did*? Quit the shit, please. It's boring for both of us."

She smiled and shrugged. I said, "You ruined her face. That poor girl, you smashed it up. So what I want to know is: how does it feel, motherfucker? To get a taste of your own medicine?"

"I told you. It doesn't feel too good." She paused. "Okay. Suppose I—what's the word for it? Suppose I hypothetically agree with you. I say, sure, it's possible I may have had something to do with that little cooze dying. So what?"

"Watch how you fucking speak about her, Erika."

"Oh, so she got to you too, huh? Poor Madeleine. That little cunt is everyone's favorite victim, ain't she?"

"I said watch your fucking *mouth*!"

I realized I was shouting and angry. I realized she'd got to me. Dumb, Genie, really dumb. Erika smiled, pleased and smug. I calmed my mind, stared into space, breathed urgently and as quietly as I could. Stay *cool*, for Christ's sake. For your sake. I transferred the Beretta to my right hand and wriggled a pack of Dark Nine out of my jacket pocket with my left and wriggled a smoke out of the pack.

Putting it in my mouth I said, "I wanna know. Why did you destroy her face like that? What was it, throw the cops off the scent for a while longer? You might as well tell me now. Were you paid extra for it?"

I wriggled out my lighter and lit the Dark Nine while she said, "Fine. Fuck it. Won't make a lick of difference anyway. Sure, I killed her. I fucked her up good. But I didn't deliberately do the face. No extra money. My orders were, kill the bitch, dump the body, thank you and goodnight."

"So what happened to her face?"

"The fish happened to her face. The fucking animals in the water, buttercup. They gotta eat something, right? I killed the kid by hammering her skull with my best friend. Several times. I only aimed for the head but she probably took a few to the face as well, I don't know. I wasn't being real careful, you know what I'm saying? Anyway, what difference does it make to you? She's dead. She don't care how she looks."

"Your best friend. That's what you call it—that weapon. The, the, baton thing."

She pointed to herself and smiled again. "Hence the name. Yeah, you've met my best friend, ain't you? Got real close to it in the Zig-Zag the other night. Actually, you're real special, buttercup."

"How's that?"

"Very few people get a kiss from my best friend and live to tell the tale. ...It's a thing of beauty, you know that? Place it nice and close to the head, release the catch and boom-boom: lights out. Really is beautiful."

"You're sick. You're, you actually have a psychiatric problem."

Jesus Christ, Genie, shut *up*. Don't let her rattle you. She's trying to rattle you. And it's working.

I gulped heavily and said, "Alright, that's enough. Get up. We're going downtown."

I took a few quick drags on my smoke, tossed it to the floor and edged further into the room, creeping along by the wall, painfully slowly, so slowly I was barely moving. Past a high cupboard, rotting wood curling at the edges of the floor, grime in there, probably roaches, maybe rats. I felt dirty just being here.

Erika gave that horrible unhinged smile and said, "I got time for another beer?"

"I said get up, you bitch. *Now*."

"Ooh. She's impatient, this one. But don't worry, buttercup. Not long to wait now. Not long at all."

"Not long for what?"

"For your fucking death, whaddyou think?"

"And that's another one I've got you on: threatening a police officer. I'll just add that to all the others."

"Do what you like. I told you—won't make no difference. You're dead. You're all fucking dead."

She actually growled at this point, low and ragged, from the chest. The monster was waking up, and I didn't like it one bit. But I had to know: "So I *was* the intended target all along, then? On Datlow Street, in the rain that day? It's funny: I figured you had the wrong woman. Figured on mistaken identity. Guess I was wrong. Who put out the hit on me, Erika? And why?"

"Well, there's the thing, buttercup: you figured right. I *did* think you were someone else. Not that it woulda bothered me to ice you too, but you weren't the target. You are now, but you weren't then." She stood out of the chair and I remembered how large she was, brawny and hulking; I remembered her bulk leaning over me in the Zig-Zag, my doom in her thick muscular hands.

I waggled the gun at her and said, "Alright, that'll do. Just stay right where you are. ...So who? That day, the first day. Who was your real target? I'll get it out of you eventually, might as well 'fess up now."

I stopped at an archway which led, I figured, through to an ante-room and then onto the bedroom. I took the Beretta in my left hand and began fumbling for my cuffs with the other.

Erika took two quick steps towards me. My heart-rate shot up another notch, a new tempo, more panicky: badda-*dum*-badda-*dum*-badda-*dum*. She said, "You won't get shit from me, and we both know it." Another notch, and another, I was like a fucking mouse on a treadmill, I didn't think a person's heart could beat that fast.

She was one more step closer to me and I took my hand back around from the cuffs and placed it on the gun again and steadied both trembling hands and yelled, "I said that's *enough*. One more step and I'll fire. Last warning."

She smiled and stopped. She put up her hands in surrender. She glanced for a split-second to a spot behind my right shoulder. Before I'd even processed it, let alone had time to physically react, someone unseen had cracked me on the back of the head with something heavy and hard-edged. My mind was swamped with unconsciousness for a second and then I resurfaced but groggy, weak-kneed, on the way out. I think my gun might have fired once. I think I might have heard it fire. Then the unseen someone was pinning my arms to my sides while Erika stepped forward much quicker than I would have thought someone that big could move and knocked the Beretta to the ground. She smiled at me once more. Unconsciousness beckoned me back and Erika sent me to it with a right fist that nearly took my little fucking head off.

When I came around, it wasn't quite me that was coming around. I felt nauseous, off-kilter, my brain trying to stage-dive out of my skull. And it wasn't just concussion from the knock-out blow. She'd given me something—some wicked little chemical, sneaking into my system like molecular spies of Jericho, snooping around, doing damage, a very precise kind of sabotage.

I opened my eyes a fraction and promptly closed them again. The light was too bright, it seared my eyeballs and took a razor to my forebrain. Or maybe the light wasn't bright at all, maybe my perception was all blooey and I just thought it was too bright. I don't know; I never was all that bright. I moved my left arm to rub my eyes, soothe the ache, distract myself from how bad I felt, and it was strapped to the chair in which I sat. Same for the other one. Erika Baton had me, and good.

"Untie me. Right now."

Jesus. That didn't sound like my own voice at all. Or rather, it sounded like a tape recording of my voice, exposed to humidity and sunshine, scratched, dragged along the floor, then played back at the wrong speed in a different room.

"I said fucking untie me. *Now.*"

I squinted up and saw Erika standing at a table about 20 feet away, smiling at me over her muscular shoulder. I noticed now that it was bandaged, courtesy of that gunshot wound I'd given her in the Zig-Zag. She was fiddling with something but I couldn't say what for sure—my eyes were getting accustomed to the light, the headache receding in the slow pulse of a wave, but my vision was still blurring in and out like a camera being focused.

She said, "Oh, I'll untie you, buttercup. When we're done. Or should I say, when *you're* done. And you will be, eventually." She gave a curt laugh. "Probably wondering why I didn't just do ya back in the apartment, right? Once you were out cold, just drive my best friend right through your fucking eyeball. Like I woulda done in the Zig-Zag if that Chink bitch hadn't come along and distracted me. Well, I could have. Easy. But the women who're paying me don't want you dead until I get some information. And I'm *gonna* get that information, you can be sure. I always deliver what I've been paid for."

I looked down and to the side: my arms were pinioned by old-fashioned leather straps. I would have expected something a little more sophisticated from this professional assassin, this unfeeling killer, but these sufficed well enough, pulled tight, the leather stretching slightly, grooving into my flesh. And besides, I was half-paralyzed, physically drained and psychologically neutralized. And more besides, this didn't seem a particularly well-stocked torture chamber—more like someone's basement, or a utilities room deep in the bowels of a warehouse.

"Where the hell is this, anyway?"

Shit. Had I *said* that aloud or just thought it? My brain did another sideways parachute jump and I felt like I was going to vomit. Erika was looking back at me again, giving that same unhinged dead-soul smile.

"The old truth serum is kicking in. Excellent. Keep talking, buttercup. Just babble your pretty little head off. It'll be easier that way."

"Fuck you, you fucking animal." I heard it as "fuggyooofug-ginanneemal", and wondered how it sounded to her, and wondered why I cared how it sounded to her, and then I wondered, what was with all the swearing? Must be the fucking drug, giving me a goddamn dirty motherfucking mouth.

"What is it?" I asked. "Sodium pentathol? Scopolamine? Or

some other shit?"

"Mainly the first, but my own blend. My little twist on a classic. I have it prepared for me by a very talented pharmacologist. A bit too fond of her own product, which is a shame, but makes it easier for me to keep her in line. And *now*, I think, we're ready."

Erika turned and faced me, legs planted wide apart, holding her trademark baton in both hands. They were encased in thin gloves, leather or PVC. The baton looked different in some way.

I said, "Wass with the gloves? You going for a drive in the country?"

"My hands hurt, if you really gotta know. But you don't need to worry about that. Okay, see this black shit smeared on the top of my best friend here? It's lead, melted down and ground into a paste with oil and two kinds of poison and some other stuff I found lying around. Now, I'm gonna tell you why I went to the bother of covering my best friend with this. I did it because I want you to know *exactly* how fucked you are. To the nearest decimal point. You're gonna tell me everything you've learned about Madeleine Greenhill, and everyone else who knows the same shit, and you're gonna be quick about it. Otherwise my best friend will be shoved into your mouth and as far down your throat as it will fucking go and only then will I press the release button. And you know what that means, buttercup. Wham! 18 inches of tempered steel taking a joyride down your oesophagus. And if by some miracle that doesn't rip you in two, the lead will assuredly poison your ass. And if *that* doesn't kill you, the *actual* poison will. And if you're still breathing at the end of all that, well, hell. I might just untie you and let you go hump my sister with a two-foot dildo." She stopped smiling. "But I'm fond of my sister, so that isn't gonna happen."

I was too messed up from the chemical compound to feel scared, but I still felt scared. Erika was a bad-in-the-blood sociopathic asshole, period. She would kill me whatever I did or said.

I was dead, I realized. But how could I be dead? I was a police officer.

"You're insane," I slurred. "I'm a cop."

She shrugged indifferently.

"You can't just...torture and murder a *cop*, you crazy bitch. You'll have every goddamn..." My thoughts trailed away and my voice followed suit.

"I think what you're trying to say, buttercup, is that I can't kill you because you're a police detective and I'd have the entire HCPD after me in two seconds flat and they won't stop until they've hunted me down, correct?"

I gave her a thumbs-up and started to giggle drunkenly. "Yeah. Thassit. Thanks, Erika."

"You *stupid* fucking cow. I thought you had more smarts than that. I actually gave you some credit." She swooped down to me and grabbed my face, jerking it up to meet hers, squeezing my mouth until it flopped open like a sozzled goldfish and my teeth started to hurt. "You're just as shit-stupid as the rest of them, aren't you? Sweet little Genie. Everyone's so fucking fond of you. With your big brown eyes and your pretty little face. It won't look so pretty after I cleave the fucking thing in two."

Then Erika Baton did something wholly unexpected: she leaned in and kissed me on the lips. A hard kiss but not rough, her lips squashed against mine for four or five seconds. I could hear her breathing in through her nose, one extended breath; I could smell her surprisingly saccharine perfume.

She broke off the kiss and stood again. I was too stunned to speak. Erika said, "I can and will kill you if I want, because nobody knows you're here, nobody knows who abducted you, nobody will know the real identity of your killer, and nobody gives a shit anyway. I've already got a patsy in mind to take the fall. She's so fucked up she probably *will* think she committed the crime. I'll kill you, dismember your body and burn the remains. Not much for Genie's fat friend Farrington to work with then."

My head slumped forward, my body swayed. I think I would have fallen out of the chair if I hadn't been strapped in. I said quietly, "Well, if you're gonna…do it anyway, why should I…talk to you…?"

I was slipping in and out of consciousness now; more precisely, I was floating back and forth between altered levels of consciousness. Erika's voice boomed at me one moment, grazed my ear like an intimate whisper the next: "Because that truth serum is coursing through your veins like wildfire by now. Nobody can resist the drugs, buttercup. And nobody can resist the painful things I can do to a body, *long* before the point of death. Lemme just tell you now, the anesthetic won't last forever. When it wears off you'll be begging me for another shot."

Then I heard someone say in a trembling, angry voice, "Have a shot yourself, goddamn you", and Erika's forehead exploded outwards, spraying me with hot blood and bone smithereens and indistinguishable wet matter. She hit the floor before I had time to taste her life-force on my tongue. I spat sluggishly, more like dribbling really, mixed blood and saliva running down my chin.

I heard her speak again before I saw her but I knew who it was before I heard her speak.

"Cella!" I shrieked, laughing half-hysterically. "Cella, you big fucking lump! I am *so* happy to see you."

"Genie, hold on, sweetheart."

Cella padded forward, tensed and cautious, her gun held at hip-height, wanting to be sure. Her eyes darted from me to Erika's corpse in its black-red pool to the rest of the room, and back to me. She said, "Are you okay?" I nodded like a toy dog in the backseat of a car.

She completed her recon of the room and then crouched down in front of me, putting both hands on the sides of my head. "You're okay? You're sure you're okay?"

I giggled again. "Cella. I've *missed* you, Cella. I feel all…woozy. I think you killed her."

Cella nodded and pulled down my bottom eyelashes, examining the eyeball for signs of intoxication. She nodded again and briskly untied the leather straps binding my arms. I slumped into her embrace like a marionette with cut strings.

"Thanks, Cella. You're one hell of a lady."

I dissolved into drowsy laughter as adrenaline and sodium pentathol danced a chemical tango around my bloodstream and Cella patted my back softly, rocking me like a mother soothing her child to sleep.

"Oh, Genie," she said. "You poor thing. Shhhh. I've got you now, Genie. You're safe now."

Chapter 26

Cella

I DIDN'T wake up until it was almost noon. But I woke up. Strike three for Erika Baton, and Genie Auf der Maur was still standing. Three times she'd tried to kill me; three times she'd had me in her sights. Each time I'd escaped. I didn't know if I believed in God but somebody was looking out for me. My mom, maybe. Yeah, I could imagine her up in heaven—sitting on a small cloud even though there was a bigger one available across the way but this was *her* cloud, she was used to it and why would she move now?—and looking down on me, following my progress through this vale of tears, gently nudging fate here and cajoling chance there, doing her best to make the journey less painful, less tearful. Still worrying about me. Still being a mother.

Cella had been watching over me all night—I say all night, though the dark hours were almost done by the time she got there, got to Erika's lair, just in time. By my calculation it must have been about six in the morning when she burst through that door and plugged the assassin in the head, but I couldn't know for sure. Then she held me in those big beefy arms and soothed me and stroked my hair and rocked me to sleep. I slept like a dead woman but I was not yet dead. So fuck you and take *that* to the bank, Erika goddamn Baton.

When I woke the first thing I noticed was the fact that I felt pretty good physically. Somehow, subconsciously I'd sort of expected to feel like hammered shit; I think my mind had been giving my body a forewarning as I stumbled slowly towards waking. Ever pessimistic, my mind; always expecting the worst. It needn't have worried: I was fine, or close enough to it. The worst of Erika's drugs cocktail seemed to have been worked through my system; six hours' solid sleep and the sheer zesty thrill of remembering how beautiful it is to be alive took care of the rest. I felt good, tingling slightly, revitalized, resurrected.

I was lying on a flea-ridden old couch near the door: lumpy and scuzzy but surprisingly comfortable. The place was brightly lit but still no sunlight—we were obviously in a basement somewhere. Cella sat about ten feet away on a hard-backed chair. I squinted at her and smiled, saying sleepily, "Hey. The woman who saved my life."

She looked awful: dog-tired, an emotional wreck, her skin wan and sickly. She said, "I let you sleep. You had to sleep. Let all that crap wash outta you."

"Time izzit?"

"Ten past 12."

"What day?"

She smiled. "The next day. You've been out for five or six hours."

"And you've been here the whole time."

"Yeah, well... Somebody had to. She couldn't do it."

She pointed at the far side of the room, towards Erika's body, and laughed nervously. From where I was lying I could only see her shoes, the bottom foot-and-a-half of her legs, a hand trailing away from the body, the grease-smeared baton still clutched tightly. I didn't want to see the rest of it: that ugly, hateful face blown out into space.

Cella lit a cigarette and coughed wheezily. I would have told her to quit smoking only I wanted to bum one myself. I waggled my fingers at her and said, "Can I've one of those?"

She lit one for me and stuck it in my mouth. I gagged on the first pull and coughed painfully, then got the measure of it and enjoyed the next three or four.

"Nothing else I could do, Genie," she said. "Nothing but let you sleep it off. I haven't called anyone yet. I mean, uh, like your colleagues or anybody. I've just—sat here. I wanted to wait until you woke. I mean, shit. I'm not a cop anymore, you know? I don't know that I'm even supposed to be here. And then *this*..."

She gestured vaguely in the direction of the body once more. Cella really looked shook-up. I wondered if she'd ever killed somebody before. I was afraid to ask. She looked like she might burst into tears, or have some kind of nervous breakdown. I think the prospect of tears freaked me out more.

I said quietly, "Okay, Cella. Thanks. You did the right thing. You didn't call it in?"

She shook her head. I continued, "I think maybe that's better. Yeah. I'll tell Etienne myself. On the hush-hush. Listen, I don't want anyone else knowing about any of this, okay? Can you do that for me, Cella?"

This time she nodded. She seemed relieved that someone else was taking the responsibility now; the forces of official authority were on the scene, tan-ta-ta-*raah*, bugles blowing, horses thundering, it's all okay now Ma'am, we'll handle it from here.

I sat up and the blood plummeted from my head like an elevator with two broken cables. I moaned and put a hand to my temple, then realized it was the hand holding my cigarette and I didn't want to sizzle my hair off to the root.

Cella said, "You okay? Gimme that, Genie. You shouldn't be smoking in your condition."

I said, mock-contritely, "Yes, Mommy" and handed her the cancer stick. Then I said, "Listen: we have a leak. I can't remember if I told you this already but anyway I'm telling you now. We have a leak, inside the HCPD. Someone's giving out information, about this case, my investigation, the whole thing. I'm trusting you with this knowledge, Cella. *Nobody* is to know about what happened here. I'll tell Etienne right now, I'll go straight to her office. But nobody else knows, got it? Just the Chief and you and me. And nobody's to find out about the leak, either. I don't want the bastards to know I'm onto them."

She looked even more relieved—I figured the threat of breakdown or a tsunami of tears had passed. She said, "Cool. That's cool, Genie. Whatever you say."

I smiled wryly. "Besides…I don't want Erika's paymistress to know she's dead. I want her to get nice and comfy, figuring her attack dog there is on the job."

"Well, you're safe now, that's for sure. That animal isn't going to hurt anyone again. Here." She handed me my gun, my Beretta, saying, "Found it on the desk there. I knew it was yours, straight away. Recognized the scratch along the barrel. Would you believe I actually remember where that happened? You've had that old thing as long as I've known you."

"That's me, sweetheart: sentimental to the last. Just can't give the old girl up."

Cella threw me the holster as well, and I fixed the weapon into that and that onto me. "I'll tell Etienne I did it. The kill, I mean. I'll take the responsibility. She doesn't even have to know you were here."

"Nah, don't do that. 'Cause it could come back on you down the road, I mean, other people know where I was headed last night… No. No, forget it, don't. It's fine, Genie. I fired in self-defense or, like, to protect you. It's fine, I'll stand over it."

I looked around. There was something eerily normal about the place. Feverish flights of fancy would have prompted me to visualize Erika Baton's torture lair as, well, a torture lair: dark, dank, cobwebbed, like a medieval prison, with slime and blood on the walls, hand manacles hanging from the stone, a rack in one corner and an Iron Maiden in the other, the howls of the doomed reverberating through its corridors like the sound of ghosts before their time. But this was so…bland. So unthreat-ening, if you were to just walk in here and check it out. It was a basement. Tools, furniture, bare light fittings, various bits and pieces of rubbish and junk lying around. No more menacing than the average suburban garage. The truth of this awful place wasn't obvious unless you already knew it.

I turned to Cella and said, "Where *were* you headed last night, anyway? Where is this?"

"We're in a disused basement in an empty warehouse. About five blocks from the docks. Do you remember anything?"

"No, I... The last thing I remember is being in her apartment. Someone slugged me on the back of the head. It was some dump off Fairywren. Yeah, I had my gun drawn on her and then whack, someone hit me from behind and Erika finished the job. Jesus. I think she might have loosened a tooth. That woman knew how to *hit*."

"She must have—*they* must have brought you here."

"How did you find me?"

"I got a tip-off last night, about two-ish. One of my regular snitches, this fucking idiot called Lalou. Wouldn't trust her as far as I could throw her but she's not the worst. Anyway she put me onto another broad who'd heard about 'that crazy bitch', meaning the assassin there, gunning for 'the titchy detective.' That means you. Seems like Erika was hated and feared by most of the other crims. She was fucking crazy, she was out of control. They were only too happy to turn her in."

"Well, hell... I'm glad they did."

"I'd been looking for you for ages, all night. I tried your home, your office, loads of places... I even went to Odette Crawford's house. I don't know if you two still..."

She left that hanging. I said wearily, "Yeah, well. I don't think you have to worry about that anymore. Odette and me, we, uh...we're not so close these days."

Cella said, "Finally I went back and, uh, I beat the location out of the snitch. The other chick, not Lalou. Where does Erika Baton—*bring* people? That's what I wanted to know. Took a while, but..." She winced and stared at her knuckles, curling and uncurling her fingers. "Fuck it. It had to be done. I'm not a violent woman but I had to do it, right, Genie? I had to know or you'd be dead now."

She looked at me, wide-eyed, seeking absolution. I would have lied in any case, but in this case I didn't need to. I said gently, "Thank you, Cella. I know that can't have been easy for you. I'll always appreciate what you did for me last night. I mean that."

"Ah, stop it. Shut up, for God's sake."

We smiled at each other for a moment. Then Cella said, so quietly I barely heard it, "It's an empty warehouse. All of these rooms. *Empty*. There's nobody around. That fucking psycho could have done whatever she wanted and no one would have found you. I had to come."

I felt a whispered shiver of own mortality. Jesus. How close I'd come to the end...

Alright, enough of that. Get back on the horse, Genie. Forget about that and get back to work. Forget it or you might go crazy thinking about it. I stood and stretched my back out, then got that blood-rush again. I staggered like a newborn animal and had to put my hand on the sofa to steady myself.

Cella said, "Genie, you're a mess. Sit down, for Christ's sake. Do you need a doctor? Will I call a doctor?"

I shook my head. "No. Just...gimme a minute. I'm okay." I let the moment pass, waited until I could feel some strength returning to my legs. "I'm okay. I don't need a doctor."

"You're far from okay. You're a mess."

I laughed and said, "Hey, didn't you know? I'm the hero of this *noir* detective story, goddamn it. Genie the gunslinger, righter of wrongs, scourge of the underworld. And you know all the great *noir* heroes are always willing to take an ass-kicking. At least once in every story. It's the rule."

"Now I really *do* think you need a medic. What the hell are you talking about?"

"Come on—let's scope this place out. See what we can see."

We scoped: still nothing much to see. Again, the joint was weirdly *normal*. Except, of course, for the dead body, almost headless, lying cold on the cold floor. We inched closer to it, trying not to look at the top end, the part that was missing a part.

She still wore the thin gloves, of course; in death they looked ridiculous, almost obscene. What had she said, something about a pain in her hands...? I tried to remember and failed. But I was intrigued all the same. I looked around and found a small pair of pliers, coated with rust but useable. I knelt down and eased off Erika's gloves with the pliers, tossing them aside. Both hands were scarred in an odd kind of way, punctured with tiny holes — not many, maybe a dozen on each palm, a few more on random fingers.

I pointed at the wounds. "Weird, isn't it? What do you think did that?"

Cella gingerly leaned in, a look of unease and disgust on her face. "I...dunno, Genie. I haven't got a clue. Look, can we get out of here? This place gives me the creeps. *That* gives me the creeps."

She pointed at the body, looking away. I said, "Sure, Cella. We'll go in two seconds. Whyn't you wait by the door there?"

She nodded gratefully. I stood and wandered around the basement for another few minutes, gazing dully at the work-benches, the floor, the walls. I finished my recce at the table where Erika had customized the baton. It was a greasy, filthy mess. She hadn't taken too much care in prepping for the job on me: there was a pool of oil under the table, small and viscous, almost gleaming, like blood mixed with rich chocolate syrup. And there on the top, brightly colored against the impenetrable darkness...I saw something. I bent down slowly: a sort of needle, resting on the oil, held buoyant by surface tension. I picked it out and stood. Hardly any oil on it; just a few molecules touching. It was some kind of spike from a plant, a cactus maybe: pale yellow-green in color, thin, extremely hard, a pointed tip. I absentmindedly put it into my pocket and went towards the door. Cella already had it open, she was standing halfway into the corridor.

She looked back at Erika's body and didn't speak for a long while. Then she said quietly, "I feel bad. For killing her, you know? I, ah…I never killed anybody, Genie. I mean, she was a fucking asshole but still. …I didn't have a choice. I mean, I mean, it was her or us, right? She wouldn't have come quietly. It was her or us, and I fucking chose us."

Silence. I nodded supportively. More silence. Then Cella said, "I was, uh…I was scared, Genie. When I came in here last night and saw the two of you… Yeah. That's the truth of it. I was scared. I didn't… I was so fucking terrified. Of what she might do to you—or me. I couldn't take the, you know, take the *risk*. Could I? I had to… It was her or me."

And yet more silence. I remained that way myself. Finally Cella smiled ruefully and said, "I think I always was, you know that? Scared, I mean. Of cop work, of the people we had to deal with. I was… I'm not like you. I can't just, like, gather up my courage and say fuck it and do it anyway. The fear is stronger than me. …I think maybe that's why I quit the force. I had a bad back, sure, but did I? Maybe it was psychosomatic. All in my head, you know. I think, uh… Hell. I *know*. The bad back was an excuse. I was scared."

She smiled again and shrugged those big strong shoulders. I smiled back.

"Cella, don't fret it. For God's sake, you've been through a traumatic experience. Don't, you know, don't worry about it too much. You *did* come here, that's the important thing. You saved my life, girl. And we all get scared. More often than you'd think."

Cella thought about this for a moment and seemed to accept it, or at least was able to lie to herself just enough to believe she did. She said, "It was my birthday yesterday. Can you believe that? 34 years young. Jesus. What a celebration, huh?"

"Yeah? Well, I hope you got something nice."

"Mm. Like a bottle of whiskey and just one glass."

"Come on. Let's have a drink now. I know a place. 'Sgot one of those early opening licenses. Full of dockers and other rough sorts. You'll fit right in." I slapped her on the back. "'Mon. Let's blow this joint."

She started walking away. I stopped at the door and looked back. Another shudder of realization slithered through my body. I'd had a bad feeling about this whole thing almost from the get-go, and it had been proven right. Cella talked about feeling scared; I was starting to get that way myself. There was something about this case, something awfully hinky, askew, out-of-whack. I always reckoned I was born under a lucky star but this… It felt like my luck had to run out sometime. I'd never come so close to dying so many times.

I had to close it off, fast. And fast is how it all played out from that moment on. So fast it made my heart leap and my head spin.

Chapter 27

Madeleine

CAMILLA Castelmagno rang me at my desk in Detectives HQ about four hours later and told me she had more information. I asked what kind, she clammed up, insisting that she'd only talk to me in person. We arranged for me to swing by Coochie Coo's some time that evening. Cella had driven straight to my docker bar from Erika's basement and straight to where my car was parked after we'd both had a quick shot of vodka.

Then I drove straight to HQ and marched straight to the Chief's office once I stepped inside, discreetly notifying Etienne about all that had happened. She agreed to keep schtum on everything until the following morning. After that it was: resolve the case or lose the case. I agreed back. We arranged for the assassin's body to be collected and the whole place to be swept by a tech team of people she could trust. I suggested Leigh Knowles: she was good at the job and she was 100 per cent honest. Etienne was fine with that.

I crashed out on a hammock they'd set up in one of the store-rooms—not too comfortable for a normal-sized cop but not bad for a little gal like me. I slept poorly for a few hours. Then I woke, drained a gallon of coffee and stared at the not-very-humorous humorous calendar on my desk for about an hour, trying to think about things. Failing to think about anything. Finally Camilla's phone-call rescued me from the pretence. I signed out, went home and clocked up a higher quality 90 minutes of sack-time. I woke after six, showered and changed my clothes, made some toast and grilled two sausages. Several more quick cups of coffee, though by that stage I didn't know if they were having any effect, and one or two slow cigarettes.

Then I hit for Coochie Coo's. The place was fairly busy for that early in the evening: two or three couples enjoying a quiet one, a few old soaks looking horribly out of place drinking hard and on their own, a raucous but good-natured group of girls on a work night out. Camilla was sitting at the bar, nursing some sort of concoction that looked more like a drowned salad than an alcoholic drink. Stringy bits of green vegetation floated in a slightly opaque liquid, held under the surface by ice-cubes, a slice of lime and a cocktail umbrella. She didn't look up as I hopped onto the stool next to her and said cheerily, "I like the brolly, Camilla. It's, you know, it's cute. Very *you*."

"My little genius. Prompt as always."

"Thanks for the tip. About the lady with the baton."

"You're welcome for the tip. How'd that work out for you?"

"Fine, yeah. Everything's cool."

She gave me a sideways look as if to say, I know for a fucking fact that everything is very far from being cool, but I'm not going to push it. She muttered, "Work crowds. Christ. They're always the worst."

I glanced over at the group of girls, who were shrieking and laughing as they handed around pieces of chocolate underwear. "Who, them? They don't seem like any trouble."

"Yeah, but they're so goddamn *loud*. My head is exploding here. Just *one* of 'em screams, just once more…"

"You're getting old, Camilla."

"Ain't that the truth."

"Where's Merrylegs? I wanted to buy her a drink. Say thanks."

"I gave her the night off. She's gone to a modern art exhibition, if you can believe it. Merrylegs. Modern fucking art." She shook her head. "You want a drink?"

"Sure. Uh, whiskey sour."

Camilla gestured to the bartender. "What she said."

I lit a Dark Nine and settled into the stool. "You had something else for me."

"Yeah," she drawled. "Yeah, I do. Okay, first thing: I lied to you—sort of—the last time you were here. About when I'd last seen the girl, the Greenhill kid. I didn't want all that heat around me, understand what I'm saying?"

I nodded. She went on, "But believe it or not I actually wanna help you. *Me*. I wanna help the HCPD. That girl was an alright kid, you know? And I didn't like to hear about what happened to her, being dumped in the water like that, like a goddamn refuse sack... Besides, she was a good customer, and you know me, Genie: I hate to lose a good customer."

I allowed myself a small smile. "Alright. It's done and done. What say we forget the past and start again? What can you tell me?"

The girl returned with my drink and I killed half of it in one swallow. Damn, that tasted good and felt better. I could already sense the whiskey's warming sensation, physically and psychologically.

Camilla said, "I've had the word out with my people, and my people have reported back with some info—on Madeleine Greenhill's movements on her last night on this earth."

"Right."

"Someone saw her earlier that day, drinking with a second girl. Some fancy-pants joint on Pasiphaë, one of the newer ones. Then she was spotted on her own, in another and another and another, really slugging them back. You know, drinking 'til it hurts. Finally she fetched up in one of mine—not this one, a different place I got, a real dive on the east side. Boozing with one of my girls for a few hours."

"Hold up. This other girl, in the first bar: tall, beautiful, am I right? I mean, really striking. The kind of girl you'd remember seeing."

"Think so, yeah. My source said she'd have screwed this broad six ways from Sunday. That's just the way these hoodlums talk."

Virginia, obviously. Before she fought with Madeleine and walked out on her forever. I said, "Go on."

"The kid, Madeleine, she seemed real anxious, jittery, maybe even scared. More so than usual, even. I mean, let's face it, the girl was a fucking flake. She was *born* jittery. But this…this was different. My girl said Madeleine was talking about 'putting an end' to something, quote-unquote. Your guess is as good as mine. Said she felt like she was shaming her mother and it was all getting out of control, whatever any of that means. So about 11 o'clock she gets a phone-call from some other chick: 'Ovidie' or 'Odette' or something. She throws down a 50 and splits, saying she has to meet someone across town. And that's all I got for you, my detective pal. Hope it helps."

My heart just about stopped beating. A meeting across town, which would bring her towards the docks. Towards Odette. Now I knew for sure, now it was definite—she was dirty. The woman I had once trusted more than anyone in my life was centrally involved in murder. I swallowed the rest of my whiskey to wash out the bitter taste of shock and nausea. It didn't work. Then I realized: I'd known all along. From the moment she mentioned Erika's car, I'd known. I just didn't admit it to myself. How could I? It was almost a mental impossibility.

Well, the impossible had just been made real. I thanked Camilla, stubbed out my cigarette and moved.

Back to the station and a message from Detective Littlestone, asking me to find her or call her. I mentally filed it away for later, went downstairs to the Weapons lock-up and grabbed two fresh clips for the Beretta, shoving them into my jacket pocket, and a third into the gun itself. Then I fit on a Kevlar vest under my shirt. It was uncomfortable, chafing against my skin like that; it felt like I stomped rather than walked back to my floor. Etienne had left for the evening but what difference did that make? I was set on a course now, trammeled, locked in; the whole thing would play itself out the way it played itself out. By that stage it was all or nothing.

Odette Ségolène de Courcy Crawford. Odette, with her goddamn tongue-twisting aristocratic name and pretensions of grandeur. Odette, with the blood of a 20-year-old girl, virtually a child, on her hands. Genie is coming for you, sweetheart. I stomped downstairs, hard-faced, resolute. All or fucking nothing.

I had reached the street exit when Littlestone cornered me. She looked like she'd been waiting around for me, and said, "Hey, Auf der Maur, I've been looking for you. Poison Rose is dead. You're still working that case, right? Anyway, figured you should know this."

"What? What are you..." My head was reeling.

"She's dead. Stabbed to death in the Zig-Zag earlier today. That's all we know so far. One of the other Homicide chicks mentioned it over coffee this afternoon. Uh, Prentiss, I think. She took the squeal. Anyway, like I say. Figured you'd want to know."

"Right... I do, yeah. I mean, thanks."

"Sure. There's a bunch of us heading to The Pipes tonight for drinks if you're interested. Someone's birthday or some shit. Might see you there?"

I muttered some noncommittal reply. She left. I stood inside the entrance, trying to work this out: it could have just been a trick gone wrong. Perils of the profession, right? Or maybe not— maybe it was someone closing off all the avenues, tying off loose ends...

I gunned it for Datlow Street, slid the car to a halt outside Odette's building. I rang the bell several times, hammered it with my palm, punched it once or twice; I stood back and shouted up at her window even though I knew my voice couldn't carry that far. Then a thought: my key. Did I have my old key? In the car, maybe, or secreted inside one of the many pockets of this jacket along with all the other junk I tended to accumulate and never get around to jettisoning... I had turned back to the vehicle, absentmindedly feeling around inside my pockets, pondering whether to just shoot the lock out and be done with it, when I felt a prick. I yelped, pulled out my finger and sucked on the tiny bead of blood forming at its tip. What was that? I gingerly reached in again. The needle, the hard spike from some plant or other that I'd picked up in Erika Baton's basement. I continued sucking on the blood as it trickled out, thick and ferrous-tasting. What sort of plant, anyway…?

Wait. LaVey's office. She'd had a lot of weird-looking vegetation in there. I remembered now, how her plants had creeped me out, like something out of a horror movie. LaVey and her cactus plants and Erika the killer and the odd little puncture marks on her hands…

Bethany Gilbert. Her face and head ruined with dozens of holes, dead from brain injuries and blood-loss. Jesus, Erika had killed her with one of those cactuses, right there on LaVey's campus. A bizarre way to do it but most everything about this case was off-the-wall anyway. So there was my proof: tie the dead girl to the plant to the plant's owner. The forensics could be enough to nail the bitch. Definitely enough for full search and arrest warrants.

Back in the car, wrenching the gearstick, putting the old girl through hell. The vehicle squealed in protest but I didn't have time for sympathy as I slalomed through the streets, a character in a videogame, left right dead ahead quick turn brake speed up drive drive drive, my heart hammering, blood pulsing in my ears like it was marking off time, the deadening loudness of the countdown clock. Across town in record speed to the campus of the LaVey Institute…except the LaVey Institute no longer existed. The main building complex, at any rate: it had been burned to a ruin. Lecture theaters, faculty offices, the gymnasium, the concert hall, and worst of all, LaVey's private chambers—all gone. Jagged spikes of masonry and glass rose from the ashes like giant's teeth. Smoke so thick and black it appeared almost artificial, like a trick effect in a movie, belching into the dusk sky. The pervasive smell of gasoline, sweet and greasy, made me want to retch. Two fire trucks, two patrol cars, a handful of press reporters and photographers; hundreds of disorientated or shivering or tearful students clustered around like the naïve kids they were, waiting for someone to tell them what was going on and what they should now do. Well, don't look at me, girls. I don't have any answers for you.

Then I spotted Cella and she spotted me and we barreled our way through the crowds and towards each other, breathless, taking a moment to get our bearings.

I said, "Tell me you know what the fuck is going on."

"I heard about the fire on the emergency services radio band. You know, I got one of those scanners—it's useful for my job. Reports of a fire about an hour ago. Once I heard the address, I was rolling. Got here about 30 minutes after that. Place was already almost gone. Someone did a real professional job."

"Yeah. I wonder who."

"I figured you'd get here eventually. Listen, forget all of this shit here. I've been doing some research. So get this: all those women who confessed last week—you know, the five strange-os you had in lock-up until they changed their tune—they *all* are past students of the LaVey Institute. Every one. I checked and double-checked. Genie, this is *big*."

"Jesus. Well, it makes sense."

"Shit yeah, it makes sense," Cella said. "I checked 'em all out: ran backgrounds, blah blah, the whole nine yards. Spoke to some people who knew them, workmates, buddies, even family members. They're fucked up, totally fanatical. Involved with some kind of cult or something, but they didn't have many details. Just, like, total withdrawal from normal life. No contact with their folks anymore. Most haven't been to work in weeks. I mean, we are dealing with some serious fucking weirdoes here."

"And all willing to go to jail for obstruction of justice. But who would choose to do that? I mean, how do you persuade someone to sacrifice themselves like that?"

"I dunno. But listen, here's the best part. All of this got me onto a few more leads, and another name came up: Aaliyah Addison."

I looked at her blankly—the name meant nothing to me.

"Sorry," Cella said. "She's a cop, does desk-work, admin mainly. At the Detectives Division of the Hera City PD. Genie, she's your leak."

"Right. Feeding them information from the inside. She's another LaVey alumnus?"

"Uh-huh. Actually graduated with Spaulding, the actor."

"Why didn't this show up anywhere?"

"Why would it? There's nothing illegal about having gone to this dump. Well, there isn't *yet*."

She gave a smile that was simultaneously vindictive but totally justified. This was it, this was all we needed. More than enough to tie LaVey to Madeleine, the conspiracy...even without the records and other incriminating documents she'd just torched. We had her. We had them all.

I smiled myself and lit a cigarette. "Thanks, Cell. You've done it. We've got 'em."

"Fuck, yeah, my little friend. Bang. To. Rights."

I turned and started walking back towards my car, Cella five yards behind, back to find a phone and call Etienne and tell her I beat the deadline and then call Dispatch and issue APBs on Odette, LaVey, Queneau, the whole rotten bunch of plotters and traitors and murderers and devils. My head was in the clouds, floating high at a dizzy altitude, so I didn't notice Alejandra Villegas as she stepped in front of me, and almost bumped into her. I stopped. She smiled: blank-eyed, innocent-seeming. Then she held up her hands to show she wasn't armed.

I muttered, "What the fuck...?" and reached back for my gun.

Villegas said quietly and calmly, "Virginia Newman is dead if you do anything or contact anyone."

My hand stalled. I looked left and right, then back at the girl. "What did you say?"

"Virginia Newman is dead if you do anything or contact anyone. Take your hand from the gun."

I did. Then I caught onto myself and leaned in close to the girl: "What is this shit? Why am I taking orders from you?"

She said, "I told you: Virginia Newman will be killed if you don't do exactly as I say. You're to come with me. Now."

I could sense rather than see Cella about seven or eight yards away, bent down, pretending to tie her shoe-lace, listening in as best she could over the ambient noise, the ruckus of crowds and sirens, water gushing from fire-hoses.

"Come with you?" I said, louder than normal, as loud as I dared. "Come with you where?"

"We're wasting time. Start walking in front of me and don't try to call for help. I'll be watching."

"How do I know she's still alive?"

"You don't. Move."

"Where are we going?"

"You'll see when we get there."

"I mean what direction am I walking, genius."

"The direction of your car, Detective. Now move."

I shrugged and sloped off, making sure to pass by Cella's line of sight. She was still fumbling with the lace, staring at the ground. I risked a glance towards her. She glanced up and nodded imperceptibly. Then Cella was swallowed up by a group of anxious parents swarming towards where the students were clustered, and I was on my own.

It was almost like someone had stage-managed the entire scene. As though one of our top movie directors was producing her masterpiece, and here was the denouement, and it was going to be spectacular. Night had fallen by the time we reached Hecate Point, way out at the edge of Hera, past the urban and suburban and exurban, a place where countryside and cityscape met, nervously advancing on one another, advancing and withdrawing, pushing and pulling, though the result of this tug-of-war was never in doubt: nothing halts progress, and certainly not the timid, guileless beauty of nature. Someday all of the fields we passed and small lanes we drove down would be covered over with concrete and asphalt. But not this night: this night the world was green as well as gray. And it was blue, too, under the moonlight as I pulled up in front of Hecate Point lighthouse, standing on a single enormous slab of rock that jutted out into the sea: an iron-clad fist, a hard challenge yelled at the ever-changing sea. A cloudy night, the waning moon like half an antacid tablet softly dissolving in water.

The Point was a thin, irregularly shaped and extremely dangerous spit of land, surrounded by razor-teeth rocks and ravaged by treacherous, unpredictable currents. That's why the city authorities had built the lighthouse about a century before, to warn off approaching ships. About three decades ago the place was closed, supplanted by a complicated system of buoys and automated lights and navigational guides. Romance killed by technology. The lighthouse had stood empty since then, not even a tourist attraction; too far out from the heart of the action. I knew it had been sold by the city, years back, but didn't know who the buyer was. It didn't seem important. Nobody ever came here, nobody used this place.

The lighthouse was dark, the outside lights off, no life showing within. My car headlamps lit up the stone steps leading to the tower. I killed the engine and said, "Now what?"

Alejandra Villegas touched my gun to the back of my head and said, "Out."

She had taken the Beretta as soon as we reached my car back at the LaVey Institute, sat in the back and instructed me to drive. I'd given it to her, breaking one of the cardinal rules of police work: never lose your weapon. But what choice did I have? I knew they had Virginia, I didn't need proof. We stepped out of the car and were hit by a wall of sound, waves crashing against the point. Goddamn, what an image: the director was pulling out all the stops with this one. Giant horses of sea-spray rearing up from the deep, leaping over the rocks, landing almost at our feet. All I needed now was a stirring orchestral soundtrack in my ears.

Villegas prodded me towards the entrance. The front door was open a few inches. I looked back at her: still that blank expression, like a machine in human form. That stupid, seemingly benign smile. I wanted to punch her, knock her flat on her cute little ass, grab the gun and charge in, all barrels blazing. Obviously I was never going to do that. I noticed a light blink on near the top of the lighthouse, the living quarters, maybe 150 feet off the ground. A soft light, weak, orange, almost welcoming. Villegas nodded at the dark doorway. I did the only thing I could: I gathered my courage and walked into that darkness, fearless and determined, no matter the circumstances.

We walked together, me in front, her following four or five steps behind like an automaton, slowly climbing, step by step. Our feet rang out as they hit the metal. The building was colder inside than out, a chill seeped through to the bones of the place, a cold of age and isolation. And then we were at the top of the circular stairs and Villegas was pushing me through into the living quarters. A large, slightly elliptical room with fitted cupboards, curved to meet the shape of the walls, which were the only remaining vestige of its previous life. It had been totally transformed, set up like a real kinky scene, as if the director had now decided to shift focus from serious drama to lurid melodrama: torches burning in wall brackets, two large sofas, cushions and rugs strewn around the floor, candelabras, incense burners, drapes, low tables with glasses of wine and bowls of fruit, bizarre statuettes and other cultural paraphernalia standing guard in a distant circle.

And there to welcome me: Azura LaVey, Mary-Jane Tussing

and Odette Crawford. LaVey was sitting on one of the couches, smiling and cradling a glass of sparkling vino; the other two stood behind her and pointed handguns at me, old-style revolvers. Odette looked past my head—I'd like to think she at least felt some embarrassment—but Tussing stared straight at me, almost daring me to do something, to provoke her. All three women were wearing white robes, sort of classical garb, like something you'd see in a bad, historically confused TV show about the Greek pantheon or Ancient Egypt: pinned at the collarbone with gold brooches, their hair swept high and elegant, thin brass bracelets snaking around their wrists and arms. Cleopatra's den meets the waxwork house of horrors.

"Detective Auf der Maur. Please, come in."

LaVey swept a hand before her in a way which left me in no doubt: that wasn't an invitation but a command. I stepped in, stopped, looked around. I could see the balcony outside, metal and chipped white paint, which circled the lighthouse, and the exit door leading to that; the actual control room and now-defunct light were off to the left, through a small closed door.

Villegas dug the gun into my back. I said without turning around, "Do that again and I'll take it and cram it up your ass, you fucking zombie."

She didn't respond. LaVey chuckled and said, "Come now. Let's not have any...unnecessary unpleasantness, shall we?"

"Yeah. Just the necessary kind, right?"

I took another few steps forward. There was something about this room; I thought I remembered it from somewhere. It reminded me of the place in my dream, the one where Virginia— Cassandra as I knew her then—was naked on a fur rug in a round room...

Lightning crackled outside with a ferocious, scarcely believable volume, lighting up the room in epileptic flashes, making me jump nearly out of my skin. Jesus, an electrical storm? My fictitious director was really going nutso now, throwing everything at the audience. To hell with subtlety, just sit back and enjoy the ride. Rain started falling, a deluge, almost Biblical, as more lightning cracked and thunder bellowed across the sky like a godlike drum-roll.

I said, "Where is Virginia?"

"Strip to your bra and underpants," LaVey commanded. "Alejandra, take the detective's clothes."

I did as I was told. Her slave gathered my clothes, and the Kevlar vest, from the floor and folded them neatly in a pile by the wall. My feet were cold on the floor and I started to shiver a little.

"Come on, LaVey—I did what you said, now where is she?"

She nodded at Tussing, who moved to the small side door, yanking it open. Anneka Klosterman took two giant steps into the main room, dragging someone behind her. Klosterman wasn't wearing a robe, but black combat pants, boots and sweater, like she was just about to climb a mountain using those big fingers as hooks. Virginia stumbled out in her underwear, half-covering her chest and tummy with her arms. She looked bewildered, frightened, disorientated. Then she saw me and skipped over, her feet arched up off the cold floor. Virginia turned to me and whispered, "*Now* do you believe me?"

I looked at her and smiled. Despite everything, I smiled.

"You approve of what I've done with the place?" LaVey had stood and was casting her arm around the room, smug and proud, acting the role of tasteful homeowner. "You know, of course, that the LaVey Institute bought this facility some years ago? Now fully owned by us. Or rather, by me."

"I didn't know that," I said. "But there's a lot of things I don't know, it seems."

LaVey smirked and fitted a cigarette into her gold-plated holder. Klosterman strode over, leaned in and lit it without being asked. LaVey said, "Things? Really. Such as?"

"Such as why you had Madeleine Greenhill murdered."

I flashed a look at Odette; she quickly looked away, then took a few steps back towards the exterior balcony.

LaVey sighed, like she was a patient teacher explaining something to a particularly dumb-headed child. Maybe I was one. She said, "The thing is, Detective, I didn't. Oh, I was *going* to have the little wretch killed. She was… Well. Let's just say she was becoming the proverbial thorn in my side. An inconvenience to me."

"An inconvenience?" I spluttered. "A fucking *inconvenience*?!"

Virginia yelled, "Madeleine was a human being, you motherfucker! She was my friend!"

Good to see the old fire hadn't died completely. Good to see the return of Cassandra my wonder woman.

LaVey flapped a hand dismissively. "Please, Virginia. No childish melodramatics. It embarrasses us both." She turned to me. "I'm sorry. Where were we?"

"You were lying about not being involved in Madeleine's death."

"No lie, Detective. As I said, I was going to do it; I certainly had reason to. But then—someone beat me to it. Put your hands on your head. Both of you."

Virginia and me did as instructed. I said, "Bullshit."

LaVey said, "Why would I lie? I mean, really. Why on earth would I lie at this stage? Perhaps you haven't noticed it, but *I* have the upper hand here. I could have you shot dead…" She snapped her fingers. "…like that. So again: why would I lie? Why should I *bother*?"

"You're telling me Erika Baton didn't bludgeon that girl to death, and you know nothing about it if she did?"

"Oh, no. Not at all. Erika certainly *did* kill her—we all know that. But I had nothing to do with it. I won't deny that I was happy it had happened; I played along as circumstances dictated. I took advantage. That's what visionaries do: they see the flows and currents of fate and use them to their advantage."

I laughed bitterly. "A visionary? That's how you see yourself?"

"That's how everybody sees me."

I tutted with contempt. LaVey went on, "No, the Greenhill girl's death was not due to me. However, I did subsequently pay Ms Baton for her…services."

"Bethany Gilbert."

"Correct. I can see now why you've flown through the ranks of the Hera City Police Department. And, of course, she was also paid to do you." An angry look passed over her face. "Stupid bitch couldn't manage that one. But it's my own fault. I should have known better than to employ a sexual psychotic like Erika. And where the hell is she, anyway? Anneka?"

Klosterman gestured that she didn't know. LaVey stubbed out her cigarette and said, "That moron could have just shot you but she had to be clever; she couldn't do it the easy way. Jesus Christ, she even took care of Bethany Gilbert *on campus*! Soiling my beautiful institution like that. Dirtying my place of love and splendor with the sticky grime of death… She's lucky I haven't taken out a hit on *her*."

"There's no need. She's dead already."

LaVey frowned. "How?"

"I blew her fucking brains all over the floor. It was, ah, it was sticky *and* grimy. Oh yeah."

More lightning outside, flashing incredibly brightly; the latticed window of the lighthouse looked like a chessboard on fire. I felt momentarily overwhelmed, almost afraid to move, to attract its attention. I sensed Virginia moving closer to me, her body still giving off warmth despite her lack of clothing.

LaVey was pondering what I'd said. Eventually she shrugged and said lightly, "Oh well. Comes with the territory, I suppose. The world is a better place without Erika Baton, I think you'll agree, Detective."

I forced some bravado into my voice: "And it'll be better yet when you join her."

She smiled and clapped her hands. "How charming. The feisty little cop, defiant to the last. ...You know, I like you, Det—may I call you Eugenie? I like you, Eugenie. I really do. You've got fire in you. You remind me of myself as a younger woman."

"We are nothing alike, LaVey. I'm a normal human being, you're a fucking crackpot."

"You see? *Fire*. I like that." She paused. "Go ahead. Ask me some questions. Anything you want to know. Anneka, give her a cigarette."

Klosterman stomped over and jammed a smoke in my mouth without asking. I didn't object. Instead I nodded towards Virginia and said, "Her too." Klosterman looked back at LaVey. I said mockingly, "Come on, Superwoman. You don't need permission to give someone a cigarette, do you?" The monster looked back at LaVey again, then at me, then gazed into space like she was working something out in her head. Finally she shoved a smoke into Virginia's mouth also, and lit up both of us.

I took a few puffs and said, "Bethany Gilbert. Why? What possible threat was she to you?"

"The silly girl had been drunkenly shooting her mouth off about Madeleine Greenhill, how her death was connected to The Goddess Rising," LaVey said. "All over the town. She had no proof, of course, but I couldn't allow her to attract—the wrong kind of attention, shall we say. The likes of you, Eugenie. Clever little police officers with a keen nose. Snooping around, looking into my business..."

"She could have blown the whole thing wide open. Your sordid little empire, blown to smithereens."

She ignored that and said, "By that stage, anyway, we reckoned you were on the scent. That's why Erika used a different weapon to her usual one: to throw you off, make you think it was a different killer. Why she used that cactus, I don't know. I didn't care. I was more concerned about why she did it on my campus."

"Is that why she tried to kill me? Baton. Is that why? You thought I was closing in."

"She followed you from my Institute to the Zig-Zag. Yes, for the purpose of ending your life."

"And what about before that? On Datlow Street? I didn't know a goddamn thing by then, I'd only just begun my investigation."

"That wasn't meant to be you, Genie."

Banks of air and electricity collided like the end of the world—a roaring rumble, then a flash, pause, a flash again—as Odette joined the conversation. But then, she always knew how to make an entrance. I turned to her and said, "Really? Do tell me more, Odette. I really, you know, I wanna know."

She swallowed hard. "That day—the day Erika Baton almost ran you over—it wasn't meant to be you. She thought you were Bethany Gilbert exiting my building. She obviously didn't know what either of you looked like, you're both such different sizes, frames…"

"Were."

"What?"

"We *were* such different sizes. Bethany is dead now, remember?"

"Right. Right," Odette stammered. "Yes, she, ah… Bethany was at my apartment. That day you called, I said I had a music student with me. It was her."

"What's another fucking lie between friends, eh?"

"I, I knew her. From before, I knew her. She was worried, sort of crazy… I talked to her, calmed her down. Told her not to worry, that everything would be okay. That Madam LaVey would take care of everything."

"Oh, yeah," I snorted. "She took *care* of it, alright. She sure took good care of poor old Bethany."

Odette took a deep breath. "Bethany…needed to die. But we had to make it look like an accident—in this case, a road accident. When that didn't work..."

"You went onto Plan B. Right, I get it. 'Plan Baton.'"

I spat my cigarette onto the floor and thought about what Odette had just said. By her own admission she *knew* about the murder of Madeleine Greenhill, the attempt on Bethany Gilbert's life, LaVey's plans, everything. She knew that they'd tried to kill me. Finally, at that point, I was shocked: that someone I thought I knew so well could be involved with people and deeds like this. And then more shock: this had been going on all the time we lived together. Holy fuck. If I wasn't a cynical and embittered woman before, I certainly was now.

But Odette could wait—I needed to know more. The surrounding details, the scenery, then delving in, burrowing through to the main matter of business. I turned back to LaVey: "Dinah Spaulding. Why did she try to kill me? At that place, the private club."

LaVey stood and began pacing the floor, her robes dragging along it, creating an eerie effect in the candlelight; it looked like melted marble was flowing down her back. She said, "She was only supposed to burn That Island, but Dinah took it on herself to attack you. Ah, such devotion, *true* devotion to a cause, a higher calling..."

"Burn it to destroy any evidence of your little—parties there." She nodded.

"So who did it, anyway? Who burned That Island? It wasn't Spaulding, she couldn't have. She was out cold."

LaVey smirked and nodded at Villegas. She didn't react.

I said, "And what's with that, anyway, LaVey? All your little slaves. What's with the blank eyes? Like a bunch of zombies. Dear old Dinah, she was a maniac that day but not a normal one. And believe me, I've dealt with enough of those to know 'em when I see 'em. Spaulding was like—like she was programmed." I turned back to Villegas, standing near the door and staring straight ahead, not moving, hardly blinking. I said, "I mean, look at this one. She's like a robot."

I took one hand off my head and waved it in front of Villegas' eyes, clicked my fingers. No reaction. Klosterman barked, "Both hands on your head! Do it."

I did it and said, "All the women, the confessors. All the same. 'Cept for the blonde giant here, of course. So what's with that?"

"Orianne Queneau," LaVey said, "is a master hypnotist. She has studied it for years. Decades. Her powers are remarkable. She can persuade any woman—*any* woman, Eugenie—to do anything she asks of them. Or anything I ask of her. Oh, of course all those women were believers anyway, but a little helping hand never hurts."

"Hypnosis. You're kidding me. You have *got* to be joking."

She stopped pacing and looked at me. "I assure you I am not. Alejandra here is...how do I put this? Unaware: of her actions, of where she is; of who she is. She is a mere tool, to do my bidding."

"Did she burn the Institute too?"

"It doesn't really matter who, does it?"

"No. I suppose not."

More lightning outside, and more and more, violent and lovely, brighter than anything womankind could ever create. And the rain was falling heavier and harder, thrashing onto the roof, flinging itself at the windows, pounding the sea, churning it, whipping it into a liquid frenzy.

"But it was all so lame," I said. "You do realize that, right? All that messing around with fake confessions. It was lame, LaVey. Amateurish. I'd've expected better from you. You should have known we'd figure out that none of those space-cadets had killed Madeleine."

"I did know. It was merely a means of slowing you down."

"Slowing me down until what?"

"Until I worked out the best way of squaring off this whole thing." She took a good long look at me, then a briefer look at Virginia, and nodded to herself, as if satisfied with what she saw.

"I wanted to get you involved more deeply in this matter before making my final move—my *coup de grace*, if you will." She leaned in and touched Virginia's hair, caressing the ends of it as it hung over her bare shoulder. "You see, you'd already been seen leaving a few late-night bars with this slut…"

I shouted "Don't call her that, asshole!" Virginia slapped LaVey's hand away and linked her arms through the crook of my elbow. Then she raised an eyebrow to me and gave an amused little smile.

LaVey continued, "You'd got in too deep, Eugenie, lost your way… You were harassing me, threatening to frame me for the murder. Crazy. Gone off the deep end. The pressures of work, of trying to resolve this distressing case, why, it could affect anyone… That's the story I shall be telling your superiors, and I have several highly respected women who will corroborate it. And here's the closing chapter: you finally killed yourself, and them, in a bizarre love-triangle with your lover and little Miss Villegas here."

Jesus. Villegas didn't even react. She was still totally blank-eyed.

"One of those dreadful, tragic murder-suicide cases. The three of you will be found here, tomorrow morning, naked, with traces of narcotics in your blood—and dead. It will be easy enough then for your HCPD colleagues to link you back to Madeleine through Ms Newman. I shall—guide them in the right direction. Discreetly, of course. …I'm still not sure exactly *why* you and your beautiful friend killed Madeleine Greenhill; I haven't quite decided yet. For money, perhaps. Or simple jealous rage. By that stage it won't matter."

"Why," I said. "That's the fucking question, isn't it: *why*, LaVey? Why did you kill Madeleine?"

"I told you, I did not have her killed."

"Fine. Whatever. Why were you glad that she was dead?"

"To protect me. From her mother's retribution."

Another stormy explosion. It was simultaneously thrilling and terrifying—Nature voiding its lungs, howling at us: "I am still here."

Tussing moved to one of the tables, still drawing a bead on me, and dexterously poured two glasses of wine. She handed one to Klosterman as LaVey said, "As simple as that. Misericordiae Greenhill is a fearsome woman, Eugenie. You do not know what she's capable of—what she would have done to me had she found out what I was doing to her daughter."

"Well, hope springs eternal," I said. "What were you doing, exactly?"

"Misericordiae would have thought—I'm sure of this—she would have considered that I had ruined the girl. When nothing could be further from the truth. I showed Madeleine a new world, I gifted it to her: a world of beauty and possibility, of everlasting life..."

"Oh, cut the shit. Please, just... Cut it out. You might as well tell me the truth. Like you said, you've no reason to lie now."

LaVey smiled and put a finger to her lips. "Sharp as a tack... Very well. The truth: I initiated her into something she couldn't handle, and it drove her into the arms of drugs and promiscuity. It unhinged her. She simply couldn't handle it. Some women are weak like that. No fault on any side, that's just how it goes sometimes, but Madam Greenhill almost certainly wouldn't see it like that. And more importantly: I used the girl. She was stealing from her mother—for me. Of course, my Institute charges fees but... Well. Spiritual journeys aren't cheap. The quest for truth isn't cheap. And all of us, even the well-off, can always do with a little more."

Money. Of course. It's always money. The basest instinct, the most common motive.

"So yes—I was using her for money," LaVey said. "And I kept using her. Why not? Why not squeeze every last drop out of that pampered brat? She would have only shoved it into her arm or down some floozy's underwear anyway."

"You said she only took to drugs and sleeping around because of what you'd done to her. You admitted it yourself."

"I did—but the debauchery was only partly to blank out the reality of her life. Her unhappiness. Madeleine Greenhill had an inherent self-destructive streak anyway. I can tell these things. I have a gift for it. And eventually it would have killed her. That girl would have killed herself, one way or the other."

Virginia said quietly, her voice trembling, "You don't know that. People change. Turn their lives around."

"I do know it, Virginia. And you do, too. Your loyalty to a friend is admirable, and touching. But you're wrong."

I cut in: "It always comes back to why, though, doesn't it? Why would Madeleine steal from Misericordiae? Just on your say-so? I can see people are easily impressed by you, with all your bullshit. But Madeleine saw through all that. She saw you for the charlatan you really are."

LaVey looked back at me. After a long pause she said, "You're correct. Madeleine needed a little more persuasion than is usual."

"Did you hypnotize her, too?"

"Oh, no. Hypnosis only lasts for a relatively short period, and its effects can be slightly…unpredictable. No, nothing so fancy as all that. For her we used good old-fashioned blackmail."

She gestured to Odette to give her the gun. My former lover handed it over with evident relief. She glanced at me like a puppy-dog that's puked on the shag carpet. Sorry, sweetheart, there's gonna be no forgiveness coming from this end. You're on your own now. You've been on your own for a long, long time.

LaVey trained the gun on me and said, "I came across some information about Madeleine. Specifically, the fact that she was actually the daughter of a VD-riddled whore. A woman called Rosemary Manning, a lush who sold herself for change and whiskey. Disgusting, really."

"The *late* Rosemary Manning. Stabbed to death this morning.

But of course you wouldn't know anything about that, would you?"

She didn't answer. Instead she said, "I put it to the girl: how would the great and wonderful Misericordiae Greenhill feel if all of Hera City knew her precious daughter wasn't really hers—but was adopted from a common prostitute? Her reputation, everything: ruined. Madeleine saw the sense in what I was saying. She agreed to...fund my ongoing investigations into the realms of enlightenment."

So Madeleine was also protecting her mother, even as Misery strove to protect her. So Madeleine wasn't such a brat. So she was a loving and self-sacrificing daughter after all.

"Eventually that gravy train ground to a halt," La Vey said. "Madeleine was completely out of control near the end, and I didn't know what she'd do. All that shame and regret, narcotics messing with her mind, fear of Mommy and guilt about what she was doing to her... I had to end it; with great regret, I might add. I couldn't have her crack and tell her mother all about our little arrangement. I had even begun setting the wheels in motion—I had a woman earmarked for the job, a professional killer called Slaymaker. A name, I must say, which I find immensely amusing."

"She's dead now, too," I said. "Case you're looking for someone in the future. You can knock her out of the Rolodex."

"Oh? Anyway, then, as I say, someone else took care of the problem for me. We arranged a meeting—my associate Odette here arranged it—I assured Madeleine this would be her final payment, there would be no more, her secret was safe with me. She set off for Whinlatter Docks to meet Odette, to hand over that one last pay-off."

"But instead you had Baton waiting."

"No!" LaVey looked like she was about to lose her temper. I think she would have struck me with her hand if the gun hadn't been in it. Then she corralled her atypical loss of self-control and said smoothly, "Once more, Eugenie, and for the last time: I had nothing to do with that. No, the girl was not to be touched that night. Odette was to collect the money and leave. We would take care of the Madeleine problem soon afterwards; within a few days. I was putting the arrangements in place when I got the news. So, I cut Ms Slaymaker loose—a little gift to keep her quiet—then found out who had killed Madeleine and figured, well, she did such a good job for someone else...now she can do one for me."

"Supposing I believe this fucking fairytale: did Erika tell you who paid her to murder Madeleine?"

"No. I didn't ask. As I say, it suited me, so... Let sleeping dogs lie and all that."

"And you never got the money, correct?"

"No. I assumed the woman had taken it, the assassin. But what was I supposed to do: lodge a complaint? I wrote is off as a price worth paying."

Madeleine knew she was going to her death that night. Not that it mattered, but she knew what was about to happen. Whether it was LaVey or someone else, whether she had the money or not, she knew.

LaVey said, "Now, the two of you: kneel on the floor."

She waggled the gun at Virginia and me. We slowly got down onto our knees, the floor hard and uncomfortable beneath us. Then she said to Klosterman, "Anneka, go downstairs and keep watch. Make sure nobody comes near us. I don't think we need you here anymore."

The giant trotted down the metal steps and Tussing moved forward to cover us. I caught her eye: "And you? What's your story?"

The girl shrugged. "Simple, really—money. My mom lost almost her entire fortune. *My* fucking fortune, actually. My inheritance. I found out about two weeks before entering the LaVey Institute. That goddamn stupid bitch. The fucking dog would have made better investment choices." The composed, overly polite façade had slipped, revealing the tough, manipulative little asshole underneath. She went on, "I was used to living well, and obviously I couldn't admit these new circumstances to anyone. So I sponged off dear, sweet little Madeleine for a while, as long as I could. And then when Madam LaVey introduced me to The Goddess Rising, well..."

I said drily, "I can almost *see* your eyes twirling like a one-armed bandit."

Tussing stepped forward, swapped the gun from right hand to left and smacked me, good and proper, on the cheek. Blood ran into my mouth and I heard Virginia distantly screaming, "Leave her alone!"

Tussing smiled viciously. "Quiet, you whore. Or you'll get a taste of the same." She turned back to me: "I don't really believe in any of it; all that mystical bullshit. But hey—I believe in the material benefits. Seems manna and God *can* co-exist." Tussing smiled smugly.

"Right," I said. "Comparative Religion, isn't it?"

"That's right."

"How'd that exam go for you?"

She looked at me with some confusion, a little nervousness coming into the smile. "That...? Oh, the exam. Oh yes, I mentioned it to you. Yes, it went fine."

"Good. I'm glad to hear that." I spat blood and saliva onto the floor at her feet. "Because that's the last fucking exam you're ever gonna take, May-Jay."

Tussing stepped back, disgusted, then kicked out at me, but there was no conviction in the kick. She was getting worried now. She turned to LaVey and said, "Can't we just do it already? I mean, what the fuck...? Why are we waiting?"

LaVey nodded reassuringly. "Alright, Mary-Jane. Yes, I think you're right. I think it's time."

Shit. Time—I needed time, needed to buy some time while I

wracked my brains and tried to work out an escape plan. I'd been stalling pretty successfully but all to no avail: I still couldn't see a way out. I didn't know what to do but keep stalling.

I said urgently, "Why didn't you tell me you recognized Virginia at the theater that time? With Madeleine, the Lady Gregory thing. You knew who she was."

Tussing shrugged. "I did. I felt I had to say something about who Madeleine was with; you know, during that interview you did with me. Otherwise it might seem suspicious, like I was holding out on you for some reason. And I figured, hey, by mentioning the other girl was a blonde—you wouldn't put two and two together. Might throw you off track or something." She smirked. "Sure, I knew Virginia Newman. I don't think there's a girl on campus who doesn't know her. *Intimately.*"

Virginia snarled, "Fuck you, you skinny shit-bird. I wouldn't sleep with you if you were the last woman left alive."

"Well, I may yet be, Virginia. But you won't."

She cocked the hammer of her revolver and pressed it to the crown of my head. Virginia gasped in horror, I winced and grit my teeth. Then LaVey commanded, "Stop! Not like that. It has to be *her* gun, you idiot. They can tell these things. Where is it, Alejandra?"

Villegas patted herself down, still staring like an imbecile. She pulled my Beretta from her back pocket and handed it to LaVey. Come on, Genie, *do* something, anything.

"Hold up," I said. "Wait. I want Odette to do it. Whaddya think, lover? For old times' sake?"

She smiled, embarrassed, anxious; she looked to LaVey for guidance. The guru smiled herself, much more at ease. "Yes. Why not? I rather like that notion. A certain...poetry to it. A certain symmetry. Yes, come forward, Odette."

My ex-partner began walking extremely slowly towards us. Odette had no stomach for something like this, I knew. At least it might buy us a few seconds. I looked up at her and said, "Now I guess it's your turn, babes. Time for your story. How did a nice girl like you et cetera et cetera blah-dee-fuckin'-blah. Don't tell me 'cause I know already: you met that idiot Queneau in Hera U, she 'initiated' you. You took to it like a duck to water and kept it from me the whole time. I think I've got that right?"

She stopped at the far side of a table. "I... How do I explain something like this, Genie? It's...sort of beyond words in some ways."

"Tut tut. You're just not *trying*."

She had that vacant look in her eyes—that look which used to be so familiar to me, an endearing look of contemplation. Now it was the hollow-eyed stare of a statue, a lifeless thing, cold, inert, distant. Odette said, "You know, you think you know someone. But it's not always like that. No matter how well you know them, there's always another...a secret, other life, another *self*..."

I muttered to Virginia, "Christ. She sounds like you," then said to Odette, "Stop. I actually don't care anyway. I don't give a shit about your stupid cult. Just confirm one thing for me: you phoned Madeleine that night because you knew—you all knew—she'd trust you. She'd trust good old Odette. Civilized, cultured fucking Odette. You offered her help, a way out; you knew she'd come to meet you. Do I have that right!?"

I'd started to shout. Odette nodded and didn't reply. The room was quiet—much quieter than before. Silence and electricity hung in the air like molecules in a laboratory jar, drifting slowly, bouncing gently off each other. Then I realized that the storm had stopped...and time was up. *Fuck.*

I turned to Virginia, whispered: "I'm sorry, honey. I truly am sorry."

By now Odette had reached us. I looked at the ground and sensed LaVey handing her my gun, Odette taking it hesitantly. LaVey said, "Go on, dear. One squeeze, two squeezes, and it's done. The Goddess will reward you."

I could feel a tear trickle out, hot and bitter, as I thought: You beat me, LaVey. You win, you bitch. And Nana is going to spend eternity telling me, I told you so—I took a set against her from the very first minute.

I looked up at LaVey, that hag, in all her finery, her jewels and sculpted hair, and said wearily, "For what it's worth, and that's not a lot, I still don't believe you. I think *you* had Madeleine murdered."

She shrugged. "So be it."

"So you, you, have no moral regrets over any of this? You just…it is how it is."

"None. Exactly. It is how it is."

"I need to know one last thing: do you even believe in it? The Goddess Rising, all that crap. Genuinely—do you believe?"

LaVey gestured to Odette to pause; she considered my question. After a long moment she said, "Do I believe…? I do. I do not. Sometimes yes, sometimes no. Does it matter? …I believe in power and money; in knowing how to use them and enjoying their benefits. I believe some women were put here to serve others. I am not one of those women. I am here to be served. …I believe in the goddess within, Eugenie. I believe in me."

Even now, at the very point of death, I was disgusted by her cynicism. I spat, "God. It almost would have been better if you were some kind of religious nut—a real one, and not the fake you are. At least, I mean at least that would have given *some* sort of meaning to Madeleine's death, however fucked-up it was."

"Yes, well… Death has no meaning, my brave little detective."

"No resurrection, then? No eternal life with your fucking Goddess Rising?"

"Psh. One minute you're here, the next you're not. As you are about to find out. Odette."

She nodded. Odette raised the gun to my head. I screwed my eyes shut and soundlessly cursed them all to hell. I could hear the bullet being chambered, that dull clunk of metal moving on metal. Then I heard Virginia say wryly, and so sadly, "We need a miracle now, Genie."

I opened my eyes and looked at her. We smiled at each other through our blurred vision and I thought, This ain't so bad. Not such a bad way to go at all.

And then the miracle happened: it materialized in that room like a whirlwind, a spinning dervish of pastel-colored fabrics and flying hair and clawing hands.

"Liar! Fraud! Imposter!"

Orianne Queneau had launched herself at LaVey, who stepped back, stumbling, laughing, half-concerned and half-amused. Her sidekick had evidently entered from the circular stairs without anyone noticing; now she was attacking LaVey, who pushed her off and took another step away. Odette and Tussing tensed and drew the guns on Queneau. They looked at LaVey for guidance. She breathed rapidly, brushed away an errant lock of hair and said, "My God, Orianne. What's the meaning of all this?"

"You devil! You faithless *whore!*" Queneau was screaming, spittle flying, her hair tangled around her face. "I heard, Azura. I heard it *all*! I heard you admit you were without faith. By your own words are you damned!"

LaVey laughed again, almost enjoying the situation in all its strangeness. She said, "What on earth are you babbling about, sweetie?"

"I heard you! You told this woman you didn't believe in The Goddess, but only in yourself. I always suspected it, I knew it in my deepest heart. But not until I heard you utter those words did I *know*! ...Everything, Azura. Everything we have worked for, for so many years. Everything... All the best parts of me, all that I am..." Queneau's shoulders slumped; she breathed slowly and heavily. She said quietly, "*I* believe, you bitch. For me it is real and true; it is everything. Now I know I have been foolish. I put my trust in a manipulative witch, heartless and cruel. We built The Goddess Rising from nothing in order to create *something*, a very great something, the only something that matters. And now, and now... Money and power—you said it yourself. Those are your gods, Azura. Those were always your gods. I see that now... Witch! Liar! *Demon!*"

She went for LaVey again, nails like talons, an unearthly scream coming from deep within her. LaVey stumbled again, not so amused now, genuinely frightened. She tried to slap Queneau's hands away but the other woman was too strong, she was on her, raking those nails down LaVey's cheek, drawing blood, drawing an anguished yell from the other woman.

LaVey shouted, "Get this demented bitch off me!"

Tussing and Odette hesitantly moved towards her. And that's when the second part of the miracle happened.

I heard a holler, a rough bellow: "Freeze! Hera City Police!" I knew that voice. Cella, you big fat fucking beautiful ball of a woman. She peeked her head into the room, from the stairs below, gun stretched in her two arms. Odette and Tussing looked at each other, looked at Cella, looked at me and chose the most sensible course of action: they each fired off a shot that went a mile wide and dashed for cover, at opposite sides of the room, crouching low behind the furniture. LaVey and Queneau were still entangled in their wrestle. I sprang to my feet and said urgently to Virginia, "Run. Hide somewhere." She didn't move. "*Go,*" I whispered and pushed her towards the back, away from the others. Virginia hunkered down into a squat, pulling her knees up and hiding her face.

I ran over and reached down and pulled Cella into the room. She took one look at me and said, "Why aren't you wearing any clothes?"

"Later, sweetheart. You got a second gun?"

She pulled one from her inside jacket pocket, flipped it around and handed it to me by the butt. I chambered a round and stood in the shooting stance, feeling more than a bit ridiculous given I was only wearing my underwear but willing to get over it for the moment, and shouted: "Everybody hold it! You're all under arrest, you motherfuckers." Then I took a deep breath and fired one into the ceiling. The shot sounded like the loudest echo you ever heard in your life.

Then LaVey and Queneau sprawled across our sightline, locked together, a bizarre hydra of flailing hands and screeching mouths and hair torn out in clumps. They tripped and fell against one of the tall candelabras, knocking it onto the rug, wax spilling like thick yellow blood. The rug caught fire, burning its own fabric and more wax and then Queneau's garment trailed into it and that too was set ablaze. She didn't even notice, still clawing at LaVey's eyes and throwing every damnation she knew onto her newfound enemy's head.

LaVey noticed, though: she looked down in shock at the flames licking up Queneau's robes and said, "Orianne—stop— your clothes. Stop, you'll burn…"

Queneau didn't care; let the whole world burn, she was a fanatic on a mission. Death was of no importance. By now the fire was spreading, devouring a second rug and one of the couches, licking hungrily at the curtains, splintering wine glasses. I turned to Cella, shouting, "Fuck! This whole place could go up. We've gotta get out of here."

She nodded in agreement just as Odette made a dash for the light-room off the main area and moments before Mary-Jane Tussing emitted a fearful shriek and ran towards us, throwing her gun aside, seeking freedom, driving for it. Cella raised that meaty fist and cold-cocked her, *bang*, right under the chin. Tussing dropped like a sack of cement.

I jerked my thumb back at Virginia and said, "Take care of her, and get this other shithead out. I'll try to break these two up."

Cella nodded again, beckoned Virginia towards her, bent and lifted Tussing's prone figure onto her shoulder. They clanged away down the stairs as I turned back to LaVey and Queneau, almost indistinguishable now in their tangle of clothing and limbs and frantic violence. I dashed to them, tried to shove my little arms between their bodies, but it was pointless. Queneau was totally manic now, crazed; she didn't care if she lived or died. She knocked me aside with her elbow, I think without even noticing I was there. LaVey looked terrified—she glanced at me, sprawled on the floor, a look of supplication, an appeal for help. And I hated her at that moment. So callous in snuffing out the lives of Madeleine and Bethany Gilbert, and probably Poison Rose too, she now had the gall to ask for aid, to save her own goddamn worthless life. I hated her right then. I *wanted* her dead.

Would I have given aid if I could have? I don't know. I didn't get to make that choice. Suddenly Queneau was all aflame, her robes erupting in strangely beautiful colors, her screams of pain almost muted within the hellish roar. She fell forward, trapping LaVey, and I knew her goose was cooked as well. The two of them burned together, locked in one another's arms, an infernal embrace. Sweet fucking dreams, ladies.

I scrambled to my feet and turned and my exit route was blocked: flames dancing and leaping across the room, over the stairway entrance, fiercely hot, almost enough to singe the skin. Alejandra Villegas was still standing at that side of the room, dumbstruck, incapable of action. I shouted and beckoned her to me: "Hey! Come on! You're dead if you stay there!"

She smiled vacantly and didn't move. I realized: the girl was dead already. There was nothing I could do for her. I turned back, spotted Tussing's gun and grabbed it from the ground, then sprinted to where I'd seen Odette go: the small anteroom, from where the light used to shine. The door was jammed—I shoved at it, once, twice, black smoke starting to cloud my sight, breathing that toxic, deadly miasma, clouding my head too, I had to get out *now*. I shoved again and thank God, it gave, just a little. Another shove and I was through, stumbling into the small room. A jolt of cold air gusted in the window and cleared my mind. Vision readjusting, lungs filling with fresh air...

Then I saw her: Odette crumpled in a lifeless heap by the round window, a large shard of glass in her neck, actually running her through. Blood gurgled down her chest and robes. Her eyes were closed, thankfully. She must have tried to smash her way out, broke the glass with something and attempted to crawl clear. It hadn't worked; some of it obviously fell on her, slicing her fatally. Odette had fallen back into the room and now half-sat, half-lay under the window, contorted, pale, dead. Sweet fucking dreams to you too, O.

The fire roared again outside and I could feel it heating up the door, preparing to launch its assault on this final room. I ran towards the window, looked outside and smiled; for the first time in my life I was completely happy to be such a little woman. I bashed the rest of the glass out with the gun barrel then looked around for something to wrap myself in, something to protect me. A few threadbare blankets, some old Styrofoam padding, sheets of cardboard...it would have to do. I tossed the gun, swiftly bound myself in the blankets and pulled the polystyrene over my head, and as the conflagration roared into the room like a dragon's tongue I took a run at the window and bounced up and through and out...

Chapter 28

Misericordiae

WHEN Cella and Virginia pulled me from the water I was soaked to the bone, very cold and a bit bloodied but I didn't mind: I felt lucky. I was lucky. I was still alive. I'd looked out the window of that lighthouse room and seen life: a pool, directly beneath me, big enough and deep enough to jump into and come up breathing. No jagged rocks, no stony death awaiting, greedy mouth wide open. That pool of water—small, choppy, freezing, murky—it really was life for me.

I jumped and plunged down deep and kicked like a mother-fucker and pushed myself back to the surface. I broke the water and gasped in air. I gasped from the cold. I saw car headlights and managed to wail for help and heard Cella calling to me and coming towards me. And I knew I was saved.

She was great: she hugged me and briskly rubbed my goose-bump arms, found an old rug in her car and wrapped me in it. Tussing was fixed to the steering-wheel by a plastic cable tie, waking painfully out of unconsciousness. Virginia stood next to the vehicle, smoking a cigarette and shivering. Looking like a goddess.

I smiled and said, "You look good in your underwear. I'd forgotten how good."

She smiled too, then sniffed back a tear. She looked shattered, overwhelmed by relief and adrenaline and happiness. Too much to take in. She didn't say anything.

"It's all okay, Virginia," I said softly. "It's over now. They're all dead." Then I turned to Cella and said, "Thanks, big mama. You've got some sense of timing."

She slapped me on the back. "You're welcome, little mama. Sorry I was, uh, so late getting here. Caught in traffic, you know."

"Cella—was that a joke? An actual joke?"

Cella handed me a cigarette and I sucked on that death-stick like it was the most beautiful thing I'd ever tasted. "Did you see Klosterman?" I said. "She left a few minutes ago. Came downstairs."

She lifted a fist and grinned wickedly. "This did. Met her coming out of the building. I punched that blonde asshole right in the puss. Knocked her clean out, cuffed her and stuck her in the boot. Still got my old set from the old days, the HCPD days. ...Two for two, that's my record for today. Two punches, two KOs. Pretty good going, huh?"

"Yeah, pretty good, Cella. You sure you don't wanna come back to real detective work? I can get you an in with the Chief."

I returned the back-slap—more on her waist than her back, really—then we turned and looked at Hecate Point lighthouse burning. A white tube glowing red and orange and blue-white on the inside, like some kind of giant child's toy, something expensive, with batteries and intoxicating lights. The top roof hadn't gone yet; it mightn't, the building being made of stone. Maybe just the inside would be gutted, burned away, ruined, reduced to ash and blackness. I pictured the four bodies in there: Queneau, LaVey, Villegas and Odette. There'd be nothing left by the time the fire had run its course. Good job I wouldn't need dental records, but I had witnesses; others who could retell the narrative of Madeleine Greenhill's death at the hands of The Goddess Rising.

I turned to them and said, "I still don't believe her, you know. LaVey. I don't believe her denials. And Orianne Queneau said nothing to confirm or deny her partner's story. I think she was the one."

Virginia muttered, "Who killed Maddy. That evil bitch. I'm glad she's dead."

I shrugged. "Yeah. Guess I am, too. But don't quote me on that to Chief Etienne."

The lighthouse continued to crackle and burn, incredibly

thick smoke wafting into the night air. It smelled like paint and hair and old dust. I went to my car—still open—and rummaged around for a spare pair of track pants and a stinking old sweater that I'd forgotten was shoved underneath the passenger seat. Then I called it in: summoned two patrol cars, a crime scene unit and paramedics. Chief Etienne could wait until the morning, I figured; fuck it, by that stage she'd know the whole story herself anyway.

Finally, we sat and waited. Smoking, resting, watching a bad part of this world burn away.

I woke earlier than I wanted to—about five in the morning. It was after midnight by the time I got home, after giving all the details to the patrol cops, filling in a report, ushering Virginia into the ambulance, getting some on-the-spot repairs myself from the medics. I'd wanted to sleep for longer but I woke early; I don't know why that was, I felt exhausted, but what can you do? Your body decides what it decides. I fixed some coffee and dug into a fresh pack of Dark Nines: my emergency 20, secreted away in the top drawer of my bedside locker.

I'd come home on my own; I wanted quiet time to think it all over, get it straight in my head. Virginia and me, well…that could wait. If there even was something to wait for. It was still dark so I flicked on a lamp, its warm light gently filling the room. I crushed out my smoke and lit another, poured more coffee and sort of let my mind go free: let it float like a breeze over the events of the last several days, gazing down upon them like a bird in flight.

It really was all over. I almost couldn't believe it. I'd made it through, I was still breathing and we had won. I pictured Nana and my mom smiling down on me and smiled myself. All over. I thought of LaVey and Erika Baton, Misericordiae and Ileana, poor old Poison Rose and Bethany Gilbert, Merrylegs, Officer Kildare, Anneka Klosterman and the other four songbirds,

Camilla and Queneau, That Island, Mother Torres, Cella and Tussing, Mulqueen and Browne and Chief Etienne, Young Ma saving my life, Chrissy and Tilda, the docks, the Institute, the Zig-Zag and Golden Park, Erika's basement, Caritas Heights, my old place on Datlow Street. I didn't think of Odette; I couldn't quite do it yet. It hurt my heart too much.

I stood up and started walking around the room, very slowly, shuffling really. Images of lurid newspaper headlines and cheap pulp novels came into my head, unbidden, drifting there as if they were radio-waves crossing the cosmic ether: Murder and Madness. Their Goddess was Death!! Justice for Madeleine. Killers Burn for Their Sins. The Astounding Case of the Polka Dot Girl.

Madeleine and her polka dot dress. Madeleine going to her doom. Madeleine the unsung hero who courageously tried to protect her mother's reputation. Madeleine who brought disgrace on her family and redeemed herself in death…

Then I bumped against a piece of furniture, the arm of the couch; it jolted me out of my strolling reverie, my mental trance. And it seemed to knock something into place: the final jigsaw piece inside my mind.

I held my breath. I whispered, "Jesus Christ."

LaVey was guilty, for sure—but she wasn't the only one.

Still dark by the time I pulled up in front of Caritas, though dawn was beginning to peek over the horizon. The old place looked lovely and gloomy and exuberant and terrifying all at once: the fabulous confusion of a unique building. The electric gates out front had been open; I sort of knew they would be. It seemed right. No lights on inside the house, but the tall outside lamp illuminated the gravel drive, the surrounding plants—and the dark-green Jaguar parked to the side of the house. I walked to the front door and knocked hard, three or four times, with my full fist. Instinctively reached back to check my gun, and of course…I didn't have it. Stupid, Genie, stupid. Too tired, getting sloppy. But too late to turn back now.

I heard her footsteps approaching the door and tensed reflexively. It opened, a dim light streaming out. She gave a tiny bow and said, "I'm sorry, Detective, Madam Greenhill is sleeping. Could you call back later this morning?"

"Actually, Ileana, it's you I want to talk to."

She nodded and stepped aside to allow me in, her face like stone, impossible to read. We were in the gigantic entrance hallway—every bit as opulent and ridiculous and beautiful as I remembered. The butler pointed towards the sitting-room I'd visited the last time I was here.

"Please," she said. "Make yourself comfortable. I'll just be a moment. All the other staff are off so we'll be able to talk in private."

Oh, I'm sure we will, Ileana. Private as the grave. I walked in and stood about five feet inside the room. Gazed around at the rare artwork, the Kahlo and Anguissola, the luxurious furniture, the fireplace where I had sat with Misery and told her that her little girl was dead. The sound of the gun being cocked was louder than a click.

Ileana held it in one hand, a beam to my heart; with the other she gently closed the door behind her. She didn't speak, so I got right to it: "Don't be stupid, Ileana. It's over. I know it was you."

No reply. I laughed and lit a cigarette. "'The butler did it.' Jesus Christ. What a godawful cliché."

Still no answer, no reaction. I continued, "You were protecting your mistress; her family name. Right? You've served her all your life. Now you saw that Madeleine had gotten out of control and you couldn't bear it. You couldn't bear seeing Misericordiae in such pain. Being embarrassed like that, by this brat, this reckless girl. Bringing scandal on the Greenhill name. You couldn't stand it. I get that, Ileana. Really. I can see why you did it. Now give me the gun."

And still no reaction. I was running out of things to say here. Finally, finally: she dropped the weapon a fraction and spoke. "We argued that night. Miss Greenhill, when she came home that—the last night. We argued. I'm not proud of it. I have never raised my voice to the girl before. I loved her. But I couldn't watch her destroy herself and my mistress. I couldn't allow that to continue, Detective. She would have ruined everything."

A long, eerie pause, weighted, pregnant with dread possibility. She sighed and said, "I...I wanted it to be painless. I felt bad about the suffering that woman caused Madeleine; that Baton woman. I even tried to kill *her*—later, when it didn't matter anyway. I tried to kill the woman, for hurting her. It was meant to be quick and painless, not...not like that."

Erika's "crazy bitch" with the tire-iron. I said, "You always knew the girl was adopted?"

"Of course. But I loved her all the same. That didn't matter. My mistress chose Madeleine as her daughter so she *was* her daughter."

"And it was you who paid off the prostitutes that night? To vacate Whinlatter Docks so there'd be no witnesses?"

Ileana hesitated, then nodded.

"Come on, Ileana," I said, reaching out my hand. "Hand it over. Don't be foolish. It's *over*. You did what you did, now give it up and face the consequences."

She didn't hand it over—she raised it again. Way to play someone, Genie. She said, "I...won't allow more shame to be brought on the Greenhill family."

"And what? By killing a cop, you think killing a member of the HCPD will avert that? It'll make things worse. For everyone."

She frowned, a look of confusion on her thin face; I could almost see her mind working it through, thinking ahead, trying to solve the puzzle. She said, "I... Nobody will know. I will...I'll hide your body somewhere, or... I'm sorry, Detective, I don't want to kill you. You seem like a good woman. But I have to. I won't make the situation any worse for my mistress."

"You're too late. I've already told others. Colleagues, other people."

"You're lying. You haven't told anyone."

How did she know that? As if reading my thoughts, the woman said, "Because I don't believe that you want to hurt or shame her anymore either."

Maybe she was right. Maybe I actually gave a shit about the reputation and feelings of Misericordiae goddamn Greenhill. Maybe none of it mattered anyway because Ileana seemed dead set on ending my life in two seconds flat.

None of it did matter: at that moment Misery strode into the room and declared, "Ileana, lower that gun and hand it to me."

The butler did as she was ordered, unquestioningly. Then she stood with her hands by her side and her head hanging low like a chastened dog. Misery came towards me, her dressing-gown scraping the floor, a pair of incongruously cutesy slippers on her feet.

"Detective Auf der Maur," she said. "I must apologize for my servant's behavior. She... A part of me understands why she acted as she did. I even—appreciate it on some level. But she must be punished for it. She will atone for her sins."

I wasn't sure I liked the sound of that. I definitely didn't like the fact that Misery now had a loaded gun in her hand. I opened my mouth to ask for it; before I could speak she said, "That woman is dead. The teacher, LaVey. She died last night, isn't that right?"

Surprise knocked on my mental door for just an instant. Then realization slammed it shut. "You have someone. Inside the HCPD, or the medical team. You have inside knowledge."

"I do."

"Alright. Well, your information is good: Azura LaVey was killed last night. This morning, to be more precise."

"Did you kill her? You don't have to answer that if you feel it compromises your professional integrity."

"I'll answer. No, I didn't kill her. Least, not directly. I was there but I didn't do it. She burned to death inside Hecate Point lighthouse. Along with her co-conspirators Orianna Queneau, Alejandra Villegas and Odette Crawford."

"I am...happy. Can one use that word in such awful circumstances?"

"I think you're allowed, considering everything. Madam Greenhill, pass me the gun."

She seemed to ignore my request, or else she hadn't heard it. "I would have killed her. With my own hands, for what she did."

"Azura LaVey did not murder Madeleine. You just heard this woman confess to it."

A bitter smile crossed Misery's lips. "She was just as guilty, and I am glad she's dead. She used my daughter up and threw her out like a piece of trash. I would have killed her, do not doubt it: both for Madeleine's sake and that other girl who died, and *her* poor mother too..."

She must have been referring to Bethany Gilbert. Misery continued, "You'll know this soon enough: a woman will be pulled from the lake in Golden Park sometime today. Shot three times in the head. With this gun."

"Who is she?"

"A drug dealer. I won't moralize or pontificate about her character or her misdeeds. All I know is her name, and the fact that she sold heroin to Madeleine. For that, she forfeits her own life."

Holy shit. It gets worse and worse. Now I was really starting to get nervous. I edged closer to Misericordiae and held out my hand.

She turned to Ileana and said, "Bring Detective Auf der Maur an ashtray for her cigarette."

The servant scurried over to the side of the room, returning to me with the turtle-shaped ashtray I remembered, then scurrying back to her penitential corner. I stubbed out the Dark Nine and waited, just standing there, holding that piece of metal, dull and heavy in my hand, the weight of it pressing down, recognized by my flesh. Heavy, for such a small thing.

Misery began speaking quietly, little more than a whisper: "I have...regrets now. I should have taken charge of her life, I think. I should have imprisoned her, more-or-less, until she was older. Until she got sense. Perhaps I was...too soft. Because my child came to me late in life. I was too soft on Madeleine. But that's forgivable, I think, in a woman of more mature years. This blessing, late in one's life... I petted her. Allowed her too much freedom... Yes, I regret a lot of things, Detective. I don't blame myself for what happened—that would be irrational. And yet: I regret what I did. Or rather, what I didn't do."

I said, "Madeleine loved you. She may not have always shown it but she did. She loved you and tried to protect you."

She looked at me, a gleam in her eye. "Oh, yes: I knew that. I never doubted it. Never. She told me—you know this already— she told me she loved me that last day. Perhaps... I wonder did she know? That she was going to her death?"

"I think she did. I think she went there for you. Madeleine died to save both of you. That's why she wore the polka dot dress that night: it was a symbol for her, a symbol of something good and positive and hopeful...like she was wearing it as a talisman, even though she knew it wouldn't do any good."

"Yes. She was a good girl."

Misery had a faraway expression, a sort of melancholy rapture; for a moment I debated jumping forward and trying to wrestle the gun from her but she had it fixed in her hand, those strong, bony fingers curled around it like steel grips. Too risky. Instead I mustered as much calmness into my voice as I could and said, "Madam Greenhill. Give me the gun."

Finally she heard my words; she smiled at me, genuine warmth in it, and said, "No. I will do what I must do. Nobody is going to stop me—not even a courageous, determined young woman like you. Understand, Detective: a mother doesn't have a choice. To stand idly by and allow something so dreadful to happen to your child... You may as well not exist. Madeleine was not my biological child but she became like flesh and blood to me. Perhaps I... I think sometimes I saw that girl as being my redemption, in some way; redemption for my amoral life. Motherhood, caring for another person, and love, such simple, profound, ineffable *love*... I will never change my behavior—it is hardwired into me, to use that modern phraseology. I have a fatalistic view of life, as I'm sure you know by now. I accept the way things fundamentally are; the way I am. But Madeleine... Through her, I felt I achieved some kind of redemption, a state of grace..."

I needed something drastic now, needed to appeal to her better side. I said, "Right. You're a religious woman, aren't you?"

"I am. My Catholic faith has always been of paramount importance to me."

"So how would your faith square with shooting Ileana? 'Thou shalt not kill', remember?"

Misery nodded. "I remember. The simple answer is, it doesn't. I can't reconcile them, and yet I will shoot her anyway. Judgment will be reserved for the afterlife. And it will be severe, I have no doubt." She paused. "I have always had difficulty reconciling my faith and my actions. The moral tenets at the core of my belief. I truly feel them, in my heart. And yet I have behaved abominably at times. I have plundered and exploited and dominated, misused my power, condemned others... Well. Now *I* am condemned. Never a moment's pause; no regrets or hesitation. I did not lose one moment's sleep in my long life over hurting another. Not one lost night. But for all that I *do* believe; I *am* faithful. And this woman, this LaVey, attempting to create her own religion, to be her own god... The arrogance of it disgusts me. I belong to a more traditional faith. More humble. I strode through life blind and arrogant, yes, but my faith... There were moments when even I was humble. When I was good."

The end came quickly: Ileana took three steps forward and kneeled at Misery's feet, faithful servant to the last. She lowered her head and raised her hands and implored, "Let me kill myself, mistress. Don't stain your hands with my blood."

Misery smiled wryly. "My hands are already soaked in blood."

I said desperately, "Please. Don't. Don't make it all worse. You can still have your redemption."

She smiled again, broader this time, happier. "*She* was redemption enough."

I threw the ashtray aside and leaped forward, nothing to do now but anything at all. I was too late. Misery fired once, a ferocious bang, straight through the top of Ileana's head, bullet and brain matter exiting at the back of her neck, a thin, weirdly neat squirt of dark blood along the floor. The dead woman flopped down beside it. I gasped in shock and stopped, my heart pounding. Smoke rising from the barrel, the smell of cordite bitter and lucid, a look of stoical acceptance on Misery's face. No fear in me: I knew I was safe. And I knew there was no point arresting her for murder. It was all over for Misericordiae and the Family Greenhill. Death would have its dominion.

She turned to me and said, "Thank you for all your efforts, Detective Auf der Maur. I appreciated everything you did for us, and wish you a happy life. Goodbye."

I walked away. As I closed the sitting-room door behind me I heard her declaring, in a voice that rang out with song, "I am coming to you now, Madeleine." I stepped through those massive doors into the outside world, the normal world, where people lived their regular humdrum lives and were all the happier for it. As I opened the car-door a single shot rang out from within Caritas Heights. I gunned the engine and started for home. The dawn had arrived and I was going to sleep for a long time.

Chapter 29

Genie

I TOOK several days off work after that. Etienne insisted. She said I looked "like shit" — the second time I'd ever heard her swear. Must be my bad influence. Before the leave of absence I filled in the blanks for the Chief, told her how it had all panned out to the best of my knowledge. I chose to bury a lot of Madeleine's past — let it lie with her in the dreaming forever — because she deserved that much charity, and besides, what good would it do now? But Etienne got the gist of it alright. I also considered dissembling about the events at Caritas Heights; maybe say Ileana killed Misery and then herself. In the end I decided against it: forensics would expose the lie. The sharp spike of fact tends to unravel our fictions.

Then Etienne filled me in some. A few of LaVey's disciples had taken their own lives in grief, including Nora Hofton: hanged herself in her own kitchen. Her kids had found the body in the morning. More had been arrested and were about to be charged with conspiracy to a whole shit-storm of crimes. Some, of course, would get away with it — with LaVey and Queneau both dead, we had no way of knowing for sure who was who or who did what. Besides, the brass and city authorities were keen — though this was never stated out loud — to just sort of forget about the whole thing, as much as was possible. Too many of the city's shining lights involved; too much potential for embarrassment to the wrong women. That's how it is here. Justice and truth are fine so long as they don't cost too much.

But at least Aaliyah Addison was under investigation by the HCPD Internal Affairs division, while Klosterman, Tussing and Spaulding were in lock-up; they were all fucked, looking at life. Assistant City Prosecutor Walkup was at that moment clearing her desk and vacating the premises. Other star performers in this little drama—Councilors Gurney and Hulman, Nicola Goldstone—they'd probably do some jail-time. Colette Unser was too well-connected to go down, Dee-Ann Lehrman was too famous. Liz Arendt was still on the lam, out there somewhere, presumed alive, though nobody seemed to care much one way or the other. There were others; Etienne didn't give me names. We shook hands and I left the Dicks building with a light heart.

Two days of chilling out, slow and steady drinking, long baths, bad TV. Two days of recuperation and realignment. Two days at the end of which a letter arrived: notification from my bank that the sum of 200 grand had been deposited to my account by an unknown person four days previously, with instructions not to transfer the money until today. It had to have been Misericordiae. I left my home for the first time in 48 hours to present myself in person at the bank, and arrange for the purchase of my apartment. That left half the money, which I divvied up between a few different charities: ones helping homeless women, prostitutes and substance abusers, mostly, with a few bucks left over to go towards the steeple renovation fund at the Church of the Redemption.

And two days after *that*, Virginia showed up. I was on the street outside in the early evening, sitting on the dirty old stoop in dirty old jeans, enjoying a smoke, watching kids play jump-rope, listening to the low rumble of car engines. Then there she was, standing in front of me, wearing a woolen coat buttoned up to the neck, a brightly colored scarf, thick-cut corduroys, high boots. Her head was tilted to one side, an enigmatic smile on that heartbreakingly lovely face.

I smiled back.

She said, "You still got that nice coffee?"

"Uh-huh."

"Want to make me a cup?"

"Maybe."

She smiled, more direct this time, and sat next to me on the stoop. "Okay. I'll wait. It's good coffee."

We sat in silence for a long moment. Then Virginia said, "Did you know I'd come here?"

"I kind of figured you might."

"Did you hope I would, though?"

"Maybe."

I passed her a cigarette and lit it without a word. We sat there and smoked, watching the children together. A chill wind blew across us, down the street and around our heads. Virginia shivered and pulled her coat up higher.

She said, "I always feel the cold more than everyone else. Genie, I have something to say."

I looked at her. "Okay. No more fooling around. Shoot."

"I want us to try and make a go of it—of us. I want us to try again. What do you say? ...That's it, that's all I have to say. Your turn."

I sighed heavily. "I don't know, Virginia. I honestly don't."

"Why? I'm going to cut straight to the chase. Why? What's stopping you?"

"I don't know. I guess—I guess I'm fearful, you know? I got...burned."

"I told you. I explained all that."

"No, not...you. I understand why that happened. It's forgotten already. I mean by Odette. Shit, I know we were broken up, but... It's hard to have—optimism, or idealism, after something like that. You know? It's hard to have faith."

"I know," she said softly. "But listen. Sometimes faith... Sometimes you have to create it by having it. Do you understand? By believing in something. That's a good start."

I smiled at her. "I *want* to believe you, Virginia. I swear, I really do. I want to believe."

She stood and dragged me into a standing position too, then clapped her hands to ward off the cold and nodded her head in the direction of the apartment building. "What say we start with that coffee? See how it goes. One cup of coffee. Yeah?"

A long pause. I looked at her and for a moment I didn't see this woman I had known and caressed and connected with. Rather, I saw Madeleine's friend: devoted, non-judgmental, loyal. Her most caring friend, the best friend of all. I pictured Madeleine then, wherever she was, happy, at peace, maybe heading out somewhere nice for the night, in her prettiest polka dot dress, with someone who loved her. Maybe with Virginia and me.

I nodded. "Yeah. One cup of coffee. Come on." We turned to go inside and I said, "Hey, what *do* I call you now? It's not Cassandra anymore. So do I use the full 'Virginia' or what?"

She shrugged. "Madeleine used to call me Ginny. I always liked it. How does that sound?"

I scrunched up my nose and said doubtfully, "I dunno… Ginny, Genie…it'd never work. Too confusing."

Virginia laughed, brilliant and heavenly and breathtaking. Just like my heart remembered. She said, "It'll work", then caught my hand, lacing her fingers around mine. "It'll work."

We jogged up the steps together, our fingers entwined once more, the setting sun crowning our heads in soft gold.

THE END

Roundfire Books put simply, publish great stories. Whether it's literary or popular, a gentle tale or a pulsating thriller, the connecting theme in all Roundfire fiction titles is that once you pick them up you won't want to put them down.